Counterfeit Politics

Bucknell Studies in Latin American Literature and Theory
Series Editor: Aníbal González, Yale University

Dealing with far-reaching questions of history and modernity, language and selfhood, and power and ethics, Latin American literature sheds light on the many-faceted nature of Latin American life, as well as on the human condition as a whole. This series of books provides a forum for some of the best criticism on Latin American literature in a wide range of critical approaches, with an emphasis on works that productively combine scholarship with theory. Acknowledging the historical links and cultural affinities between Latin American and Iberian literatures, the series welcomes a consideration of Spanish and Portuguese texts and topics, while also providing a space of convergence for scholars working in Romance studies, comparative literature, cultural studies, and literary theory.

Titles in the Series

Counterfeit Politics

Secret Plots and Conspiracy Narratives in the Americas

David Kelman

Lewisburg
BUCKNELL UNIVERSITY PRESS

Published by Bucknell University Press
Co-published with The Rowman & Littlefield Publishing Group, Inc.
4501 Forbes Boulevard, Suite 200, Lanham, Maryland 20706
www.rowman.com

10 Thornbury Road, Plymouth PL6 7PP, United Kingdom

British Library Cataloguing in Publication Information Available

Library of Congress Cataloging-in-Publication Data
Kelman, David, 1973–
Counterfeit politics : secret plots and conspiracy narratives in the Americas / David Kelman.
p. cm. — (The Bucknell studies in Latin American literature and theory)
Includes bibliographical references and index.
ISBN 978-1-61148-414-4 (cloth) — ISBN 978-1-61148-415-1 (electronic)
American literature—History and criticism. 2. Politics and literature—Latin America. 3. Conspiracy
in literature. I. Title.
PQ7081.K45 2012
860.9'98—23
2012033602
ISBN 978-1-6114-8587-5 (pbk)

Contents

Acknowledgments

It is no secret that this book would not have been possible without the help of friends, family, professors, and colleagues. I would like to thank Elissa Marder for being a kind mentor and a rigorous reader of earlier versions of my work. More generally, the faculty at Emory University—especially Geoffrey Bennington, Cathy Caruth, John Johnston, Claire Nouvet, José Quiroga, Karen Stolley, Donald Tuten, and Deborah White—have shown me what it might mean to be both a rigorous thinker and a professor. I would also like to thank Thomas Cerbu for helping me when I was first starting graduate studies at the University of Georgia. More than anyone else, his example taught me how to read for the unexpected event. Carl Good has supported my work and career in countless ways, and I continue to learn from his example. I would also like to thank Ricardo Piglia for giving me a kind word of support when he didn't have to.

I have always been stunned by my brilliant peers from Emory University, whose conversations continue to help me today. I would like to thank especially Brian McGrath, Ben Miller, Jeremy Paden, and Petra Schweitzer. Jennifer Ballengee has been a true friend, even and especially when she tells me "where it all falls apart."

I was given the opportunity to present parts of this book at a number of conferences, lectures, and brown bags at Emory University, Wake Forest University, Indiana University, the American Comparative Literature Association, the South Atlantic Modern Language Association, the Modern Language Association, Illinois State University, Cal State Fullerton, and the Cambridge Hispanic Research Seminar at the University of Cambridge. This book has been enriched by the thoughtful comments I received in those contexts.

I would like to thank my colleagues at Cal State Fullerton for the community I was not expecting to find in the heart of Orange County. I would also like to thank the graduate students in "Literature of the Americas" (Spring 2009) and the undergraduate students in "Modern Critical Theory" (Spring 2009). Their questions and comments forced me to rethink major parts of this book. I also thank Matthew Berger for his assistance with the index.

I have been very lucky to have parents who have always supported and encouraged my strange pursuits. There is no end to the thanks that I owe them. Finally, I would like to thank my wife Sarah (for everything) and my daughter Zoe (because she's awesome).

Earlier versions of chapters 1 and 3 were published as "The Form of the Conspiracy: Ricardo Piglia's Reading of Thomas Pynchon's *The Crying of Lot 49*" (*Pynchon Notes* 56–57 [Spring–Fall 2009]: 57–73).

The author gratefully acknowledges the use of excerpts from the following:

The Absent City by Ricardo Piglia, trans. by Sergio Waisman. Copyright © 2000 by Duke University Press. All rights reserved. Reprinted by permission of the publisher.

Formas breves by Ricardo Piglia. Copyright © by Ricardo Piglia. c/o Guillermo Schavelzon & Associates, Agencia Leteraria. www.schavelzon.com

Of Grammatology by Jacques Derrida, trans. by Gayatri Chakravorty Spivak, p. 40 quote. Copyright © 1998 by The Johns Hopkins University Press. Reprinted with permission of The Johns Hopkins University Press.

Conspiracy Theories: Secrecy and Power in American Culture by Mark Fenster. Copyright © 1999 by University of Minnesota Press.

Mumbo Jumbo by Ishmael Reed. Copyright ©1972 by Ishmael Reed. All rights reserved. Reprinted with the permission of Scribner, a Division of Simon & Schuster, Inc.

Libra by Don Dillio. Copyright © 1988 by Don DeLillo. Used by permission of Viking Penguin, a division of Penguin Group (USA) Inc.

"La segunda conspiración," by Jorge Volpi, in *Letras libres* (March 1999): 44–51.

I, Rigoberta Menchú: An Indian Women in Guatemala by Elisabeth Burgos-Debray, trans. by Ann Wright. Copyright © 1984 by Verso.

The Crying of Lot 49 by Thomas Pynchon. Copyright © 1965, 1966 by Thomas Pynchon. Copyright Renewed 1993, 1994 by Thomas Pynchon. Reprinted by permission of HarperCollins Publishers.

Gravity's Rainbow by Thomas Pynchon. Copyright © 1973 by Thomas Pynchon. Used by permission of Viking Penguin, a division of Penguin Group (USA) Inc.

Ficciones by Jorge Luis Borges. Copyright © 1962 by Grove Press, Inc. Used by permission of Grove/Atlantic, Inc.

Introduction

Usurpations, or the End of Politics

> Such a reversal of power cannot be an accidental aberration.
> —Jacques Derrida, *Of Grammatology*

In 1927 the Argentine avant-garde writer Macedonio Fernández decided to run for president of Argentina. In itself, this plan does not seem too far-fetched; after all, many literary authors have tried their luck in politics (Mario Vargas Llosa in Peru, Norman Mailer in New York City, etc.). However, Jorge Luis Borges explains that his mentor's campaign was indeed strange. In the introduction to an anthology of texts by Macedonio, Borges relates a number of anecdotes about this eccentric figure who inspired not only Borges, but also later Argentine writers like Julio Cortázar and Ricardo Piglia.[1] In one such anecdote, Borges confirms the rumor that this reclusive writer once campaigned for president for the simple reason that it was a statistically sound idea: it seemed like a good bet to run for office. Borges summarizes Macedonio's reasoning: "Muchas personas se proponen abrir una cigarrería y casi nadie ser presidente; de ese rasgo estadístico deducía que es más fácil llegar a presidente que a dueño de una cigarrería" (Many people think about opening a cigarette shop and almost no one thinks about being president; from this statistical feature he deduced that it is easier to become president than to become the owner of a cigarette shop).[2] Macedonio's campaign for the presidency consisted mainly in trying to disseminate his name around town in the most literal manner: he had Borges and some friends write down Macedonio's name on little slips of paper that they would then scatter in odd places throughout the city. The idea was that Macedonio should never show himself; these slips of paper would substitute for the bodily presence of the candidate. This clandestine manner of disseminating his name—what Todd S. Garth has called a "campaign in absence"—was Macedonio's way of doing politics.[3]

However, Macedonio quickly grew tired of this procedure. After all, the Argentine writer was someone who liked to hatch projects but did not particularly relish the idea of finishing them. His most famous novel—*El museo de la novela de la Eterna*—was written over a period of more than forty years and was only published posthumously. Macedonio enjoyed *beginning* projects (*El museo* contains about fifty prologues); he liter-

1

ally threw his plots forward (from the etymology of *pro-ject*, a "throwing-forward"), without worrying about how his projects might end up. It should be no surprise, then, that Macedonio never carried out his clandestine campaign and instead devised a new project in consultation with his co-conspirators (Borges and a few other friends). Borges writes: "De estas maniobras más o menos imaginarias . . . surgió el proyecto de una gran novela fantástica, situada en Buenos Aires, y que empezamos a escribir entre todos" (From these more or less imaginary machinations . . . emerged the project of a great fantastic novel, situated in Buenos Aires, and which all of us would write together).[4] Borges admits that the project of constructing a conspiracy novel emerged precisely from the secret maneuvers or machinations that already took place within a realm that is as much a part of the imagination as it is the "real" world of politics. From his imaginary maneuvers on the campaign trail emerged the idea for this future-oriented project, a novel that is said to bear the name *The Man Who Will Be President*.

Macedonio's projected novel would be structured as a double plot. Borges explains: "En la obra se entretejían dos argumentos: uno, visible, las curiosas gestiones de Macedonio para ser presidente de la República; otro, secreto, la conspiración urdida por una secta de millonarios neurasténicos y tal vez locos, para lograr el mismo fin" (In the work, two plots were woven together: one, visible, Macedonio's curious efforts to become president of the Republic; and another, secret, the conspiracy plotted by a sect of neurasthenic and perhaps insane millionaires, in order to achieve the same goal).[5] Macedonio's conspiracy narrative therefore has a complex structure, since it is created by weaving together two plots: a visible plot and a secret plot. Borges then goes on to explain that the second story about the sect of millionaires is never fully revealed, but rather only appears as the invasion of counterfeit objects. Although the obscure force behind the conspiracy would never appear as such, it becomes clear that these hidden agents seek to undermine the resistance of the Argentine people by introducing little inventions that will make life uncomfortable, such as a sweetener that fails to sweeten your coffee, or a comb that cuts your fingers while you comb your hair, or a double-sided pen that threatens to poke your eye out while you write, or stairs in which each step is unequal to all the others.[6] The inventions would proliferate with each chapter until, at the end of the novel, the sheer accumulation of these inventions would suggest the existence of the second, secret plot. Although both plots are told simultaneously and even move toward the same goal (the election of Macedonio as president), these two plots are told according to antagonistic logics. After all, Macedonio's campaign strategy, although a little subtle, is still a strategy for gaining political power. However, the novel's second story stands not as a presence that can be told, but rather as a withdrawal from the scene: the secret society only appears as the proliferation of counterfeit objects. These objects tend to undermine the resistance of the populace and ultimately intervene in the very sense of the political. As Borges relates in his description of the unwritten novel, by the time Macedonio gets elected, the sect of neurasthenic millionaires has already produced an interregnum, an interruption in the reigning power. Borges writes: "Al final el gobierno se viene abajo; Macedonio y Fernández Latour entran en la Casa Rosada, pero ya nada significa nada en ese mundo anárquico" (In the end the government goes under; Macedonio and Fernández Latour enter the Casa Rosada, but by that point nothing means anything in this anarchic world).[7] Thus, even though the two agents (Macedonio and the secret society) tend toward the same goal, nevertheless the second story is figured as the continuous undermining of the first story. The official institutions of political power have been invaded and undermined by an anarchic disruption.

Of course, this unwritten novel might suggest that Macedonio's conspiracy narrative is merely a substitute politics.[8] After all, instead of running for office and actively participating in politics, Macedonio and friends channel their energy into a novel that is never completed. Rather than the active life, they retreat into an imaginary world of intrigue, into mere literature. This kind of argument is common among critics of the conspiracy narrative, especially among those who prefer to read the conspiracy narrative as a symptom of a cultural phenomenon. For instance, at the end of *Conspiracy Theories*, one of the most insightful studies on the persistence of conspiracy theory in twentieth-century American culture, Mark Fenster writes:

> Nascent in [conspiracy theory] is a critique of the contemporary social order and a longing for a better one. Beyond its shortcomings as a universal theory of power and an approach to historical and political research, however, conspiracy theory ultimately fails as a political and cultural practice. It not only fails to inform us how to move from the end of the uncovered plot to the beginning of a political movement; it is also unable to locate a material position at which we can begin to organize people in a world divided by complex divisions based on class, race, gender, sexuality, and other social antagonisms.[9]

If Fenster were to read Macedonio's transition from political campaigning to the writing of a conspiracy narrative, he might view this transition as a subtle critique of politics as usual. However, for Fenster it would seem that Macedonio's decision to leave political campaigning behind would be a sign that Macedonio's critique has failed to find a *material position* that would be stable enough to organize the people. Macedonio's conspiracy narrative clearly works against this material position, in that it produces a specific effect that undermines the "normal" give-and-take of the campaign trail. Far from reducing social antagonisms, Macedonio's unwritten novel is in fact constituted by the antagonistic relationship between two stories: the visible story of "normal" politics and the invisible story that undermines the first story. From the theoretical point of view that Fenster puts forward, Macedonio's narrative might be an interesting symptom of a populism that cannot otherwise find its voice, but this failure to find its voice would ultimately mean that it also fails as a fully political narrative. In this way, as much as Fenster points to the political promise of conspiracy theories, he nevertheless insists that conspiracy narratives necessarily *fail*, especially insofar as they are not able to erase the various antagonisms that punctuate the social field. Conspiracy theories fail to move (and move us) from mere plots to true political action, from literature to politics. A similar complaint could be leveled at Macedonio's shift from campaign politics to his projected novel: Macedonio's conspiracy narrative appears to be a kind of counterfeit or substitute politics.

Implicit in this dismissal of the political significance of conspiracy theories is the idea that narrative plots are not, in themselves, political, and that they do not produce political effects. A conspiracy theory might tell a story about a political problem, but it does not posit a *material* position upon which to build a stable political platform. However, my argument is that the narrative structure suggested by Macedonio's unfinished conspiracy novel is in fact the necessary structure of any political articulation. Far from reading conspiracy theory from the perspective of pathology ("paranoia"), I begin with the fact that these "theories" are first and foremost narratives and that, as stories, they produce specific narrative effects. My claim is that an attention to the specific narrative form of conspiracy theories will show that these stories are in fact a positive condition of any *political* statement. This means that the structure of politics—especially a democratic politics—must always include the kind of conspiratorial structure that Macedonio outlines in his unfinished novel. This also means that it is necessary to begin with "literature"—or more generally "the rhetorical, figural potentiality of language"—in order to theorize the narrative form of politics.[10]

For the most part, conspiracy theory has been studied solely within the context of postmodern literature from the United States.[11] My argument will build on those studies in order to theorize conspiracy narratives within a more comparative framework. What happens when we include those literatures that do not fit so neatly into the paradigm of United States culture? How would a comparative study of conspiracy theory narratives change the way we think about this oftentimes maligned way of telling a story? In fact, Latin American novelists have recently brought up this relation between conspiracy theory and storytelling as a literary and political concern. For instance, in the "Afterword" to his 1992 novel *La ciudad ausente* (*The Absent City*), the Argentine novelist Ricardo Piglia explicitly inscribes his own fiction within the tradition of conspiracy narratives that includes writers such as William Burroughs, Don DeLillo, Thomas Pynchon, and Philip K. Dick.[12] By asking us to read his fiction outside a strict definition of Argentina's national literary traditions, Piglia opens up the possibility of reading conspiracy narratives within a transnational frame that would place fiction from the United States in relation to the very rich body of work that has been produced in Latin American countries. This kind of comparative literature of the Americas necessarily changes the way we think not only about conspiracy theory, but also about what makes a narrative "political." For that reason, *Counterfeit Politics* brings together texts that have rarely been read together, even though these authors are often explicitly responding to each other's work. On the one hand, I focus on some now-canonical conspiracy narratives by Thomas Pynchon, Ishmael Reed, and Don De-Lillo. On the other hand, I will place these texts in relation to Latin American texts by Jorge Luis Borges, Ricardo Piglia, Rigoberta Menchú, and Jorge Volpi. This list does not pretend to be exhaustive or even representative of American and Latin American literature and culture. Rather, my purpose is to focus only on those texts that especially emphasize a conspiratorial mode of telling a story that produces political effects, whether or not these texts have been traditionally labeled as "conspiracy theory" or even "political."

By placing conspiracy theory within a comparative context, it will be more difficult to follow previous critics in their assertions that these narratives are necessarily symptomatic of particular problems in U.S. culture. Rather than emphasize the way conspiracy theories may be symptoms of larger, unvoiced concerns in American culture, I will argue that the narrative form of conspiracy theory always carries within it a destabilizing secret. At first glance, this distinction might not seem very clear. After all, to say that a conspiracy theory is a symptom of a cultural problem is to say that there is always another story—an invisible story— hidden within every conspiracy theory. The task of the critic, in this scenario, is to make visible the other story that the conspiracy theory supposedly occludes. As Eva Horn and Anson Rabinbach ask in a recent issue of *New German Critique* dedicated to the subject of conspiracy narratives: "What is behind a conspiracy theory?"[13] This way of posing the question suggests that conspiracy theories are only important insofar as they refer to a symptom that the critic needs to reveal.

This symptomatic interpretation of conspiracy theory is not only common in academic treatments but also has had a strong impact on the way these narratives are viewed outside of academe. For instance, in a widely reprinted 2007 article on the so-called Amero Conspiracy (the idea that there is a conspiracy within the governments of the United States, Mexico, and Canada to create a North American Union [NAU] that would trump the sovereignty of each of the member states), the *Boston Globe* reporter Drake Bennett alludes to Mark Fenster's work in order to explain the significance of this contemporary conspiracy theory:

In a deeper sense, the apprehension and anger that sustain the NAU rumors are quite real. For all their talk about national threats, national sovereignty, and national strength, conspiracy theories are usually more about individual powerlessness, says the University of Florida's Fenster. They are a form of political populism, with its suspicion of concentrations of control and its sense that ordinary people are being shut out of the decision-making process. And the issues around which those theories grow up are as good a Rorschach as any, not so much of people's concern about their country overall, but about their own place in it.[14]

Bennett summarizes Fenster's argument in *Conspiracy Theories*, namely that conspiracy theories are significant only insofar as they voice unspoken fears in American culture. The *Boston Globe* reporter, quoting Fenster, notes that the Amero conspiracy "reflects the particular ways in which Americans feel besieged economically, powerless politically, and alienated socially."[15] The point here is not to argue against this reading of the cultural significance of the Amero conspiracy, but rather to note that this symptomatic way of reading conspiracy theories has become a more or less dominant mode of responding to what Peter Knight has called "conspiracy culture."[16]

However, the very strength of this reading forces the reader to dismiss conspiracy narratives as accidental or unnecessary. The important point of the analysis, in this mode of reading, would be to understand the cultural pathology behind the narrative. After this hidden meaning or symptomatic referent has been found, the critic can ignore the conspiracy narrative as a useful but ultimately fanciful way of referring to a meaning that would be better expressed through more direct means. Fenster, for instance, views conspiracy theories precisely as a kind of substitute politics: "Conspiracy theory displaces the citizen's desire for political significance onto a signifying regime in which interpretation and a narrative of conspiracy replace meaningful political engagement."[17] In this way, the symptomatic reading sets up conspiracy theories as disposable, unnecessary, accidental; they are secondary in relation to the cultural pathology to which they darkly allude.

Rather than turn away from the conspiracy narrative in order to talk about its allegorical referent in contemporary culture, my argument focuses attention on the strange narrative structure of conspiracy theories. By emphasizing the fact that conspiracy theory is a particular way of telling a story, one immediately notices that the symptomatic reading is actually repeating the narrative structure that defines all conspiracy theories. After all, every conspiracy theory tells the story of a secret history that the official history is not telling us, a secret story that is covered over by a visible story. To talk about conspiracy theory as if this kind of narrative were itself a symptom of a cultural malady is therefore to talk like a conspiracy theorist (there is a hidden story that the official story is not telling us explicitly). Thus, rather than dismiss conspiracy theory as a symptom that points to larger concerns in society, I argue that it is necessary to focus attention on the narrative effects of conspiracy theories.

This attention to the narrative form of conspiracy theories has already been emphasized by Ricardo Piglia in the "Afterword" to *The Absent City*. Earlier I noted that Piglia inscribed his own fiction within a tradition that included Pynchon, DeLillo, and other American writers of conspiracy narratives. However, although the notion of "conspiracy" ties these disparate authors together, Piglia suggests that "conspiracy" is not so much a theme in fiction as it is a particular formal element that produces political effects. He writes:

> [P]olitics enters the contemporary novel through the model of a conspiracy, through the narration of an intrigue—even if this conspiracy is devoid of any explicitly political characteristics. The form itself constitutes the politicizing of the novel. The conspiracy does not necessarily have to contain elements of a political intrigue (although it may, as is the case with Norman Mailer) for the mechanism of utilizing a conspiracy to be political.[18]

On the one hand, Piglia seems unique among contemporary writers in his insistence that conspiracy narratives should be read for a particular formal mechanism that produces political effects. On the other hand, the Argentine novelist is also reinscribing Richard Hofstadter's emphasis on the "paranoid style." In his 1964 essay "The Paranoid Style in American Politics," the American historian insisted that the style of conspiracy theory bears witness to a pathological politics that should be suppressed, just as an ugly style in art "is a cue to fundamental defects of taste."[19] These "defects," as I will show in later chapters, have to do with the particular style through which conspiracy theorists tell a story. Hofstadter distinguishes this style from the apparent content of an argument, and he recognizes that this style can take place on the right or the left: "It is a common ingredient of fascism, and of frustrated nationalisms, though it appeals to many who are hardly fascists and it can frequently be seen in the left-wing press."[20] Hofstadter therefore offers a useful way to theorize the relation between storytelling and politics, since his analysis goes beyond the traditional poles of left-wing or right-wing ideology. Piglia likewise emphasizes the "emptiness" of this form. However, while he retains Hofstadter's emphasis on the stylistic or formal qualities of conspiracy theories, he nevertheless eliminates Hofstadter's negative judgment that conspiracy theories are pathologically "paranoid." My argument develops Piglia's emphasis on the form of conspiracy theory, in order to ask why this seemingly illegitimate "style," in Hofstadter's own words, "appears to be all but ineradicable."[21]

At the same time, I will follow Hofstadter's admission that conspiracy theory is a way of reciting events that does not depend on a prior ideological content.[22] This refusal to distinguish between right-wing and left-wing conspiracy theories will no doubt lead some readers to believe that I am merely repeating conspiracy theory's confusion of ideological positions. However, the texts that I analyze in this study suggest that politics is not based on an ideology decided in advance, but is rather constituted through a specific type of narrative that is often called "conspiracy theory." This type of story is always a "machination," that is, a narrative mechanism that secretes, as it were, ideological labels such as the "right" or the "left." The point, then, is not that the notions of "right" and "left" have no meaning, but rather that these poles cannot be fixed in any permanent way. After all, a leftist ideology only has meaning if it is continually besieged by a rightist ideology, and vice versa. Ideological struggles, in other words, depend on this *relative* fluidity of poles. In this way, the confusion between rightist and leftist movements that one finds in conspiracy theory is in fact the condition of any ideological struggle.

In a way, then, I am indeed repeating—or reinscribing—the problems that critics have identified in the stories characteristic of conspiracy theory. Although my argument is positioned against those critics who view conspiracy theories as either unnecessary or simply illegitimate, I want to emphasize that many of the accusations against these stories are in fact quite precise. For instance, my study insists that it is indeed true that conspiracy theories are unbelievable or unconvincing, since they often fall apart precisely in the moment when these narratives make their conspiratorial connections. I also agree that conspiracy theories tend to produce fantasies of the other as a threatening force, and that this figuration ends up creating an antagonistic relation between a "we" and a "they." My argument is that these accusations are precise definitions of the destabilizing form of conspiracy narratives. However, I argue that these same accusations must also be leveled at the operations of *any* political narrative. My claim is that it is precisely the element that seems most unbelievable, most "counterfeit," that is responsible for producing the political effect of conspiracy theories. This effect—what I will call "the complot effect"—is the result of the form's double structure: every conspiracy narrative tells the story of an official or visible story that is continually undermined by a secret story. It is precisely the secret nature of this unauthorized story that leads many critics to argue that conspiracy theories fail to find a material position from which to engage in politics.[23] As I suggested above, my goal is not to argue that conspiracy theories do not contain this delegitimizing moment. On the contrary, I will suggest that conspiracy narratives *necessarily* include a "counterfeit" story and for that reason can never stand as fully legitimate or authorized statements. Therefore, to say that conspiracy narratives are always political is not to say that conspiracy narratives should simply be given legitimacy. Rather, the idea is to read the illegitimate structure of conspiracy narratives, precisely in order to show that all political statements have the form of conspiracy theory, even if they do not obviously tell a "paranoid" story. This form necessarily includes an illegitimate element, a secret or counterfeit story that produces a complot effect. *Counterfeit Politics* argues that politics, if it takes place at all, only takes place in the counterfeit form of the conspiracy narrative.

Conspiracy theory is therefore not simply a symptom of a crisis that is not being expressed (a kind of "substitute" politics), but is rather the essential narrative structure of any political articulation. In short, an attention to the narrative structure of conspiracy theories shows that every political narrative must tell the story of an illegitimate force that is undermining the legitimacy of an official or hegemonic discourse. Detractors of conspiracy theories thus repeat the very form of conspiracy theories by telling the story of an illegitimate way of doing politics that is undermining the very legitimacy of politics. These critics are therefore engaging in politics precisely in the moment that they try to exclude conspiracy theory from the *polis*. In the chapters that follow, I use various names to refer to this illegitimate force, each name as illegitimate as the next: the secret, coincidence, complot, counterfeit, or even death. Each one of these terms names an inaccessible event that cannot be fully known, what Ricardo Piglia calls "a strange manipulative movement."[24] This movement is not an accidental effect that needs to be eliminated, but rather stands as the very condition of a democratic politics. After all, one could say that democracy can only take place when an authorized discourse is continually interrupted by an illegitimate other, a voice that is never fully voiced. As Ernesto Laclau has remarked in a recent essay on populism: "We only have politics through the gesture which embraces the existing state of affairs as a system and presents an alternative to it (or, conversely, when we defend that system against existing potential alternatives). . . . We have an end of politics when the community conceived as a totality and the will representing that totality become indistinguishable from each other."[25] Laclau argues that populism is not an aberrant politics, if only because populism and consensus politics "both presuppose social division; in both we find an ambiguous *demos* which is, on the one hand, a section within the community (an underdog) and, on the other hand, an agent presenting itself, in an antagonistic way, as *the whole* community."[26] The *demos* is therefore not only an outside agent (an underdog), but is also an agent that *claims* a right to represent the entire *polis* or political community. Conspiracy narratives, in turn, figure this ambiguous *demos* as a threat, not simply because this "underdog" only represents a portion of the populace, but more precisely because this usurper is claiming a position that promises to upend the status quo. However, this moment of usurpation, which seems to spell the end of the political community, is in fact a necessary moment for democracy: a democratic politics only takes place when an illegitimate element (an "underdog") undermines the authority of the institutions of power, when an outside element is threatening the community from the inside. For this reason I will argue that the narrative structure of conspiracy theory defines any political narrative: there must always be an underdog discourse that is continually undermining the authority of the main narrative line.

The first chapter, "Reading for the Complot," develops the narrative structure of conspiracy theories. By focusing on the way these stories present the paradoxical narration of a secret that is never fully revealed, I argue that this narrative form can take place even in stories that do not contain any explicit reference to conspiracies or secret societies. At the same time, my reading of Ricardo Piglia's narrative theory and Ishmael Reed's novel *Mumbo Jumbo* suggests that conspiracy theories demand a mode of reading that bears witness to this irreducible secret, a mode of reading I call "reading for the complot." Piglia and Reed suggest that the "complot" (or "conspiracy") is not a knowable agent, but rather takes place only as the interruption of the agency of the main narrative line. This emphasis on interruption signals the fact that secrecy itself is getting redefined in these narratives. Conspiracy theories do not simply reveal a secret, as in detective fiction; rather, they present the demand that we read for the complot, that we bear witness to an incomprehensible event that never fully happens.

If the first chapter insists on the importance of secrecy in narrative, chapter 2 asks why this notion of narrative secrecy is necessarily "political." "Politics in the Age of the Imaginative Leap" focuses on the way conspiracy theories always present this secret as a gap in the narration of events. For the historian Richard Hofstadter, conspiracy theories exceed the norms of rational politics precisely at the moment when the conspiracy theorist *introduces* a gap, or "leap in imagination," in the narration of events. However, two texts about major political assassinations—Don DeLillo's *Libra*, on the assassination of John F. Kennedy, and Jorge Volpi's "The Second Conspiracy," on the assassination of Luis Donaldo Colosio—suggest that the imaginative leap is not *introduced* by the conspiracy theorist; rather, the event only takes place as a gap in knowledge. Conspiracy theories therefore bear witness to what DeLillo calls the "shattering randomness" of events through the narration of a catachresis, that is, by naming something that has no proper name. Precisely because conspiracy theories only contingently name the event, they cannot fully cover over the gap that constitutes the event in the first place. In fact, politics depends on this contingent act of naming. After all, if the event could be conclusively named and narrated, then there would be no need for political discussion: the event could be put to rest and forgotten. For that reason, a political narrative must contain a gap that is continuously named and renamed, one catachresis after another, without ever filling up the gap in a finalized way. If a narrative is to remain political, it must therefore have the "defective" form of a conspiracy theory.

The third chapter, "Why Hidden Figures Matter for Politics," develops the political significance of "reading for the complot" by focusing on the way the secret story in conspiracy narratives is often personified as a parasite that saps the strength of an institutional discourse. I compare two texts that are usually not read together—Thomas Pynchon's *The Crying of Lot 49* and Rigoberta Menchú's *I, Rigoberta Menchú*—in order to suggest that politics takes place when there is a hidden figure that continuously withdraws from the scene. In Pynchon's conspiracy novel, this hidden figure—the "Trystero" or secret society of mail carriers—appears only in the form of counterfeit objects that produce a total loss that cannot be recuperated in an economy of loss and gain. Secrecy is therefore defined not as "invisibility" (it is not something that can appear and disappear), but rather as something that cannot be recognized and therefore understood. And yet it is precisely the unknowability of the secret that gives it force. This notion of the secret is clearest in Menchú's *testimonio*, in that the hidden figure in her text is literally a hidden trap that captures the soldiers sent to drive her people from their land. This hidden figure undercuts any notion of "stable ground," since the resulting fall into the trap produces what Menchú calls a *desgaste*, a fall from power, a draining or weakening of the system. This *desgaste* is not only a negative moment, but also provides the opportunity for a political conversion. Menchú demonstrates that politics, if it happens at all, happens in the event of a fall; for political speech to take place, one must first *fall into the trap of politics*. This moment of interruption is crucial for politics; for politics to take place, there must always be a hidden figure that interrupts an authorized discourse and suggests an otherness to the way things stand.

Chapter 4, "The Discovery of Politics," returns to the accusation, articulated best by Richard Hofstadter, that conspiracy theories threaten the very existence of "normal" political discourse. This chapter agrees with Hofstadter, but only if we also say that any political narrative necessarily threatens the possibility of politics. Through a close reading of Jorge Luis Borges's short story "Tlön, Uqbar, Orbis Tertius" and Thomas Pynchon's novel *Gravity's Rainbow*, I suggest that politics only takes place when the story of a community (a "we") is invaded by the story of an enemy (a "they") that threatens the future of politics. In other words, the "invasion narrative" that is so common in conspiracy theories is not simply an element of the fantastic that has been wrongfully grafted onto political narratives. On the contrary, I argue that all political narratives necessarily contain this moment of invasion, that is, the moment when the *polis* is truly threatened by a shadowy figuration that seems to come from the outside. I go on to suggest that even consensus politics rests on the very threat to its possibility; without a complot that threatens the stability of politics, even "the usual methods of political give-and-take" (in Hofstadter's words) would not be possible. After all, there could be no political negotiation in the first place if the antagonistic other were not threatening the community. Conspiracy theory is therefore the paradoxical narrative that produces politics at the very same moment that it narrates an imminent threat to the political community.

In short, *Counterfeit Politics* argues that conspiracy theory opens up the *question* of the political, even in those moments when conspiracy theories narrate the end of politics. Conspiracy theories remind us that politics is not a safe operation, since political discourse always involves a destabilizing threat that then produces an antagonistic relation between a "we" and a "they." Conspiracy theories not only exaggerate that antagonism, but also ensure that the antagonism never disappears by narrating the threat of a menacing other that can never be fully revealed or conjured away. However, my argument is that conspiracy theories take place to some degree in any political narrative; there must always be this attempt to conjure up a usurper that is claiming something it has no right to claim and that therefore threatens the very existence of the *polis*. Thus, even though the usurper certainly disturbs the system, this disruptive event is also necessary for politics to take place at all.

Ultimately I argue that a conspiracy theory is in fact a pedagogical exercise that models the way all political narratives are formed. Specifically, conspiracy theories teach the art of reading for the complot, a practice that bears witness to the moment when a narrative tells the story of an illegitimate usurpation or an unjust claim. In the epilogue I return to Piglia and the figure of Macedonio Fernández in order to show how Piglia's *The Absent City* not only summarizes the major motifs in conspiracy theory—the secret story, the leap in imagination, the counterfeit or hidden figure, the specter of the end of politics—but also exemplifies what it would mean to teach the art of reading for the complot. In Piglia's conspiracy novel the secret story is a counterfeit narrative that antagonistically repeats the official stories of the state. This counterfeit or illegitimate story—the complot—is not an aberration or even a "revolution," but is rather a necessary condition for there to be politics in the first place. Whereas earlier critics have often insisted that this narratological problem—the narration of a secret that never fully appears—is what prevents conspiracy theory from entering into the realm of the political, my argument is that politics only takes place when one reads for this narrative moment that cannot be fully assimilated.

If conspiracy theory "teaches" something (if it is indeed a pedagogical exercise in reading), then the "lesson" is that politics must bear witness to the irreducible secret. However, this conclusion should seem disturbing, since the dominant tradition of political theory has defined politics precisely as full appearance. As Derrida observes, political theory has often insisted that "any secret is in principle a threat to the *res publica*, indeed to democratic space. This is understandable and in overall conformity with a certain essence of *politeia* as absolute phenomenality. Everything must be made to appear in the transparency of the public space and its illumination."[27] Derrida goes on to emphasize what he calls a "modern crypto-politology" or a "political cryptology" that would counter this notion of politics as absolute appearance and transparency: "By refusing any right to secrecy, the political agency, most often in the figure of state sovereignty or even of reason of state, summons everyone to behave first of all and in every regard as a responsible citizen before the law of the *polis*. Is there not here, in the name of a certain type of objective and phenomenal truth, another germ of totalitarianism with a democratic face?"[28] My argument therefore follows Derrida's "political cryptology" by emphasizing "the right to secrecy," not "beyond the order of the political," as Derrida seems to suggest, but rather against a *certain* tradition in political theory.[29] I argue against the notion of politics as full appearance; instead, I emphasize the way conspiracy theory teaches us that politics must always take place as "disappearance," but only if this "disappearance" or "invisibility" is moving toward a notion of non-phenomenality, a *resistance* to coming to light.

Politics therefore calls for a particular mode of reading narrative, which I am calling "reading for the complot." To read for the complot is to read for a delegitimizing moment that undermines the authority of any "visible" or official statement. Politics happens whenever there is this contest of stories, whenever one story is challenging another story for hegemony.[30] To say that all political narratives have the form of conspiracy theories is not to say that one must debunk the stories of politicians or other public figures in order to show that their narratives are "merely" conspiracy theories and therefore "illegitimate." Rather, to read for the complot means simply to register the way politics takes place in the narration of a destabilizing secret that never fully appears as such. This secret is paradoxical, since by remaining inaccessible it *thereby* makes possible the articulation of political demands. In this way, political narratives necessarily involve fantasies of the other, since without that moment of imagination—without that *literary* or rhetorical moment—there can be no political discourse.[31] *Counterfeit Politics* therefore argues that to read for the complot is to bear witness to the event of the political.

NOTES

1. Gonzalo Aguilar notes that the literary anecdote is strangely not external to Macedonio's corpus: "Uno de los modos de aparición de Macedonio Fernández en la literatura argentina se produce a través de las anécdotas. . . . Y aunque la crítica ha considerado las anécdotas con desdén, ya que desplazan a un segundo plano a la escritura, lo cierto es que las anécdotas de Macedonio son siempre conceptuales, . . . [L]a anécdota es la versión sintética de la Idea en el transcurso del tiempo" (Gonzalo Aguilar, "Macedonio Fernández: Modos de aparición y ausencia," in *Historia crítica de la literatura argentina: Macedonio 8*, ed. Roberto Ferro [Buenos Aires: Emecé Editores, 2007], 125). Not only do these stories about Macedonio connect fundamentally to his

thought, but they often develop out of Macedonio's various "projects," a word that cannot be rigorously separated from the texts that have been published in his name.

2. Jorge Luis Borges, *Prólogos con un prólogo de prólogos* (Madrid: Alianza Editorial, 1975), 85. All translations from Borges's essay on Macedonio Fernández are mine. It should be noted that it is common practice to refer to Macedonio Fernández by his first name.

3. Todd S. Garth, "Confused Oratory: Borges, Macedonio and the Creation of the Mythological Author," *MLN* 116 (March 2001): 356.

4. Borges, *Prólogos*, 85–86.

5. Ibid., 86.

6. Ibid., 86–87.

7. Ibid., 87.

8. It should be noted that, before Ricardo Piglia began to intervene in Macedonio criticism in the 1980s, this eccentric figure was often viewed as merely a self-referential writer, without any relevance for political thought. Jorge Fornet notes that, before Piglia's intervention, Macedonio "parecía ser el ejemplo más claro de autorreferencialidad, ajeno a cualquier 'compromiso,' desvinculado de ese carácter político que Piglia le atribuye" (Jorge Fornet, *El escritor y la tradición: En torno a la poética de Ricardo Piglia* [Havana: Letras Cubanas, 2005], 147). In fact, Piglia's various readings of Macedonio, which I will return to in the Epilogue, end up intervening in this notion of politics as "commitment" ("compromiso"), suggesting instead that politics must always be infected by "bad faith" or must take place as a "counterfeit" commitment (if this were possible).

9. Mark Fenster, *Conspiracy Theories: Secrecy and Power in American Culture* (Minneapolis: University of Minnesota Press, 1999), 225–26.

10. Paul de Man, *Allegories of Reading: Figural Language in Rousseau, Nietzsche, Rilke, and Proust* (New Haven, CT, and London: Yale University Press, 1979), 10. De Man notes the way that language is "rhetorical" when we cannot decide between literal and figural meaning. He goes on to explain that "[r]hetoric radically suspends logic and opens up vertiginous possibilities of referential aberration. And although it would perhaps be somewhat more remote from common usage, I would not hesitate to equate the rhetorical, figural potentiality of language with literature itself" (10).

11. Conspiracy theory has received most attention in those studies that focus on American literature and culture since World War II. For instance, both Peter Knight's *Conspiracy Culture* and Patrick O'Donnell's *Latent Destinies* have chapters that deal with Don DeLillo's *Libra* and Thomas Pynchon's *The Crying of Lot 49*, among other texts by contemporary American writers. However, over the last ten years there has been a steady interest in the way conspiracy narratives also appear in Victorian fiction (Adrian S. Wisnicki's *Conspiracy, Revolution, and Terrorism from Victorian Fiction to the Modern Novel* and Albert D. Pionke's *Plots of Opportunity*), nineteenth-century American fiction (Mike Lee Davis's *Reading the Text That Isn't There*), English Romanticism (Thomas Pfau's *Romantic Moods*), and even ancient Greece (Joseph Roisman's *The Rhetoric of Conspiracy in Ancient Athens*). There are relatively few comparative studies of conspiracy theory (John Farrell's *Paranoia and Modernity: Cervantes to Rousseau* is an exception). The topic has also received very little attention in Hispanic studies. Glen S. Close treats the topic of anarchism and conspiracy in the Argentine novelist Roberto Arlt and the Spanish novelist Pío Baroja in his *La imprenta enterrada: Baroja, Arlt y el imaginario anarquista*. Horacio González's essayistic *Filosofía de la conspiración: Marxistas, peronistas y carbonarios* focuses exclusively on Argentine politics and culture. However, critics have recently begun to address the theme of conspiracy in Ricardo Piglia's work (for instance, in the essays collected in *Ricardo Piglia: La escritura y el arte nuevo de la sospecha*, edited by Daniel Mesa Gancedo).

12. Ricardo Piglia, "Afterword," in *The Absent City*, trans. Sergio Waisman (Durham, NC: Duke University Press, 2000), 145. It should be noted that Piglia inscribes his own work within a *certain* national tradition, an Argentine tradition that attempts to use literature to articulate political theory. For example, in response to an interview-

er's question about the relation between politics and literature, Piglia responds: "Hay una manera de ver la política en la literatura argentina que me parece más interesante y más instructiva que los trabajos de los llamados analistas políticos, sociólogos, investigadores" (There's a way of viewing politics in Argentine literature that I find more interesting and instructive than the works of so-called political analysts, sociologists, and other researchers) (Ricardo Piglia, *Crítica y ficción* [Barcelona: Editorial Anagrama, 2001], 73). This Argentine tradition does not demand this or that political commitment from fiction, but rather reads the way that fiction defines politics, and especially the way fiction theorizes what it means to tell a political narrative. Piglia later defines this particular Argentine tradition as a kind of conspiracy narrative. While Piglia is clearly emphasizing what seems to be a tradition specific to Argentina, he tends to define this "Argentine tradition" in surprising ways. For instance, in his essay "La novela polaca," Piglia takes the translation of Witold Gombrowicz's novel *Ferdydurke* as the exemplary Argentine novel: "La novela argentina sería una novela polaca: quiero decir una novela polaca traducida a un español futuro, en un café de Buenos Aires, por una banda de conspiradores liderados por un conde apócrifo. Toda verdadera tradición es clandestina y se construye retrospectivamente y tiene la forma de un complot" (The Argentine novel would be a Polish novel: I mean a Polish novel translated into a future Spanish, in a Buenos Aires café, by a band of conspirators headed by an apocryphal count. Every true tradition is clandestine and is constructed retrospectively and has the form of a complot [Ricardo Piglia, *Formas breves* (Barcelona: Editorial Anagrama, 2000), 80]).

13. Eva Horn and Anson Rabinbach, Introduction to *Dark Powers: Conspiracies and Conspiracy Theory in History and Literature*, special issue of *New German Critique* 35 (Spring 2008): 4.

14. Drake Bennett, "The Amero Conspiracy." *New York Times*, November 25, 2007. Accessed August 19, 2009. http://www.nytimes.com/2007/11/25/world/americas/25iht25Amero.8473833.html.

15. Quoted in Bennett.

16. "A presumption towards conspiracy as both a mode of explanation and a mode of political operation have together formed what might be termed 'conspiracy culture'" (Peter Knight, *Conspiracy Culture: From Kennedy to the* X Files [London: Routledge, 2000], 3). Knight goes on to argue that this culture of conspiracy is not something internal to political action, but rather infects politics from the outside, specifically from national security policy since the Cold War: "a culture *of* conspiracy has become an implicit mode of operation in American politics, with the rise of the national security state over the last half-century. The pursuit of policy objectives through clandestine means has at various times over the last fifty years or so come to be taken for granted by the political establishment" (3). In this way, Knight suggests that the origin of politics' fall into conspiracy theory can be located, isolated, and (perhaps) contested.

17. Fenster, 80.

18. Piglia, "Afterword," 145.

19. Richard Hofstadter, *The Paranoid Style in American Politics and Other Essays* (New York: Vintage Books, 1967), 6.

20. Ibid., 7.

21. Ibid., 6.

22. See also Ernesto Laclau's attempt to understand how populist movements can migrate from the left to the right and vice versa. Laclau argues that "[t]his migration of signifiers can be described if populism is conceived as a formal principle of articulation; not if that principle is concealed behind the particular contents that incarnate it in different political conjunctures" (Ernesto Laclau, "Populism: What's in a Name?" in *Populism and the Mirror of Democracy*, ed. F. Panizza [London: Verso, 2005], 45). For that reason, he argues that it is "an idle exercise to ask oneself what social group expresses itself through [particular] populist symbols: the chains of equivalence that they formed cut across many social sectors and the radicalism that they signified could be

articulated by movements of entirely opposite political signs" (Laclau, "Populism," 45).

23. Fenster again offers a useful example of this tendency to view the non-resolution of conspiracy narrative as a political failure: "My assertion is that conspiracy must be recognized as a cultural practice that attempts to map, in narrative form, the trajectories and effects of power; yet, it not only does so in a simplistic, limited way, but also continually threatens to unravel and leave unsettled the resolution to the question of power that it attempts to address" (Fenster, 108). For Fenster, then, the unresolved nature of the plot—its secrecy—remains a stumbling block for political engagement. It should be noted that Hofstadter, in his essay on the "Paranoid Style," admits that secrecy in itself is not foreign to political strategy. He writes: "All political behavior requires strategy, many strategic acts depend for their effect upon a period of secrecy, and anything that is secret may be described, often with but little exaggeration, as conspiratorial" (Hofstadter, 29). For Hofstadter, this kind of secrecy is a momentary affair: information is temporarily withheld in order to achieve a political strategy. Unlike this normal give-and-take of politics, the paranoid views secrecy on the contrary as the very grounds of history: "The distinguishing thing about the paranoid style is not that its exponents see conspiracies or plots here and there in history, but that they regard a 'vast' or 'gigantic' conspiracy as *the motive force* in historical events" (29). As I will go on to suggest, I agree with Hofstadter's description of the paranoid style, but only if it is added that all political acts, including those based on consensus, tell the story of a hidden figure that threatens to overturn the status quo.

24. Piglia, "Afterword," 145.

25. Laclau, "Populism," 47–48.

26. Ibid., 48.

27. Jacques Derrida, "History of the Lie: Prolegomena," in *Without Alibi*, ed. and trans. Peggy Kamuf (Stanford, CA: Stanford University Press, 2002), 63.

28. Ibid.

29. Ibid., 64.

30. Or to put it in the language of Jean-Francois Lyotard's *The Differend*, politics is the threat that a conflict between two "phrases" may not be resolved. Lyotard states: "Politics, however, is the threat of the differend. It is not a genre, it is the multiplicity of genres, the diversity of ends, and par excellence the question of linkage" (Jean-Francois Lyotard, *The Differend: Phrases in Dispute*, trans. Georges Van Den Abbeele [Minneapolis: University of Minnesota Press, 1988], 138). Lyotard goes on to note: "Everything is political if politics is the possibility of the differend on the occasion of the slightest linkage. Politics is not everything, though, if by that one believes it to be the genre that contains all the genres. It is not *a* genre" (139). Politics is not a genre in itself, Lyotard explains, because politics entails precisely the conflict between heterogeneous genres, a conflict of legitimacy that cannot be adequately resolved. If the conflict is forcibly resolved using the norms of one genre, a "differend" occurs: "A case of differend between two parties takes place when the 'regulation' of the conflict that opposes them is done in the idiom of one of the parties while the wrong suffered by the other is not signified in that idiom" (9).

31. In *On Populist Reason*, Laclau addresses a similar complaint that populism is often vague or imprecise. Rather than argue against those charges, however, Laclau states: "we should start asking ourselves a different and more basic set of questions: 'is not the "vagueness" of populist discourses the consequence of social reality itself being, in some situations, vague and undetermined?' And in that case, 'wouldn't populism be, rather than a clumsy political and ideological operation, a performative act endowed with a rationality of its own—that is to say, in some situations, vagueness is a precondition to constructing relevant political meanings?'" (Ernesto Laclau, *On Populist Reason* [London: Verso, 2005], 17–18). Laclau argues that a "simplification" of the social space is a condition of politics, since only in an impossible world could one posit a kind of "piecemeal engineering" that would deal with particular differences without simplifying the social space in some way (18).

ONE

Reading for the Complot

In the 1964 bestseller *The Invisible Government*, David Wise and Thomas B. Ross present an exemplary conspiracy theory in its opening salvo about the threat posed by the U.S. intelligence communities:

> There are two governments in the United States today. One is visible. The other is invisible. The first is the government that citizens read about in their newspapers and children study about in their civics books. The second is the interlocking, hidden machinery that carries out the policies of the United States in the Cold War. [1]

The narrative presented in *The Invisible Government* contains two stories. On the one hand, there is the naïve story found in newspapers and civics books for children, which narrates the story of a government that is accountable to the people governed. The second story, which is about both an interlocking machinery and "a loose, amorphous grouping of individuals and agencies drawn from many parts of the visible government," narrates the inability of the people to know who is in control of the government. [2] In effect, the two stories contain the same information: both stories are about the same actors, the same agencies, even the same events. However, the two stories differ in the way that these actors, agencies, and events are organized. For Wise and Ross, the second story—the story of the invisible government—threatens the very notion of the American people: "there can be no meaningful consent [of the governed] where those who are governed do not know to what they are consenting." [3] Wise and Ross go on to say that it is secrecy itself that undermines the founding principles of the United States: "[B]ecause [the invisible government] was hidden, because it operated outside of the normal Constitutional checks and balances, it posed a potential threat to the very system it was designed to protect." [4] In this way, the plotting of the invisible government, which is "unseen, but there," not only threatens the official government but also threatens the invisible government itself, since it undermines the presumed basis of any governing body: the consent of the governed.[5] *The Invisible Government* therefore tells two stories—one official, the other "invisible"—but the second story ends up undermining both stories: the invisible government's presence threatens to overturn the very notion of government or the ability to govern in general.

In what follows I would like to focus on the narrative form of conspiracy theory, exemplified here by Wise and Ross's articulation of a double plot at the heart of American democracy. *The Invisible Government* is hardly unique in the way it presents a split between two stories: a visible story and an invisible story that is "unseen, but there." As I suggested in the introduction, the most significant trait of conspiracy theory is not, according to Hofstadter, its content, but rather its "style": the way this narrative always presents a "defect" in the narration of events. Strangely, this conclusion would suggest that conspiracy theories must take place even when stories do not contain any explicit reference to a secret society or a conspiracy of criminals. Rather, conspiracy theory must be read as a narrative form that takes place whenever a plot reveals a "defect," that is, when it goes awry. Conspiracy theories take place when a single plot is revealed to contain *two plots*: a "visible" plot and an "invisible" or secret plot. Nevertheless, I will argue that this "defect" is not an accidental aberration, but rather points to a condition of possibility of any kind of plot, even and especially the most rigorously constructed one. Conspiracy theory—defined, as I will show, as a particular "defect" in narration—is a possibility that disrupts any narrative form. The task ahead is to theorize what it would mean to read for this kind of secret plot.

A SECRET HISTORY OF THE WORD "PLOT"

Peter Brooks, in *Reading for the Plot*, has already suggested that all narrative plots contain some notion of a conspiratorial or secret plot. In fact, Brooks offers a curious etymological history of the very word "plot." At a specific moment in this word's history, Brooks notes, the French word "complot" (or "conspiracy") began to influence the word "plot":

> The fourth sense of the word [plot], the scheme or conspiracy, seems to have come into English through the contaminating influence of the French *complot*, and became widely known at the time of the Gunpowder Plot. I would suggest that in modern literature this sense of plot nearly always attaches itself to the others: the organizing line of plot is more often than not some scheme or machination, a concerted plan for the accomplishment of some purpose which goes against the ostensible and dominant legalities of the fictional world, the realization of a blocked and resisted desire.[6]

As the *OED* confirms, the sense of plot as "conspiracy" was popularized during the Gunpowder Plot of November 5, 1605. Brooks emphasizes that there is a strong sense of a usurpation going on in the history of this word. "Plot," he notes, was not just influenced by the French word "*complot*," but was rather *contaminated* by this foreign word: he speaks of "the contaminating influence of the French *complot*." Thereafter, the word "plot" is continually infected by a secret sense, "conspiracy." This secret sense of plot now, according to Brooks, "nearly always attaches itself to the others," as if the sense of conspiracy were a parasite that continually contaminated the host ("plot") with its meaning. The meaning of "plot" therefore contains within itself a miniature conspiratorial history: there has been an almost four-hundred-year-old conspiracy against the word "plot." It turns out this is a conspiracy about conspiracy, since this etymological history narrates the way "complot" has conspired against "plot," thereby systematically infecting the definition of "plot" with the sense of a scheme or machination. The word "plot" therefore always tells two stories. On the one hand, "plot" would be a plan of the actual or proposed arrangement of a narrative or drama; on the other hand, "plot" would be a secret plan to accomplish an illegitimate purpose (a "plan" that "goes against the ostensible and dominant legalities of the fictional world"). In other words, a visible plan is always contaminated or invaded by a secret plan. At the same time, there is a hidden agent behind this conspiracy, here figured by the French, or at least by the French word "complot."

At the same time, Brooks insists that all of the senses of plot are affected by the notion of a conspiracy ("this sense of plot nearly always attaches itself to the others"). This means that "complot" not only affects the sense of "plot" as the arrangement of a narrative, but also affects the first two senses of "plot": a measured area of land and a ground plan. Both meanings suggest the spatial demarcation of borders and the organization or arrangement of what lies within those borders. The first three senses of "plot" all suggest the creation or positing of an interiority that remains separate and closed off from whatever lies outside of it; they all suggest a clear demarcation between an inside and an outside. It would therefore seem impossible that the French word "complot" could have come along and infected the word "plot," since this is the very word that signifies the resistance to invasion; it is the word that expresses precisely the notion of demarcated interiority. Nevertheless, this invasion happened and continues to happen. "Plot" signifies the idea of interiority at the same time that it finds itself continually besieged and infected by the notion of something invisible and secret, something that seems to come from the outside, something that cannot be contained within legitimate limits, and therefore something with illegitimate or illegal purposes. In this way, the word "plot" contains a paradoxical idea: it is an impregnable inside that is continually besieged by a secret or hidden outside.

The word "plot" is then generated from this incommensurable relation between an interiority separated from what lies outside of it, and a secret that seems to infect it from the outside (from "France"). As Brooks notes, this incommensurable relation is a continual condition of all plots. To quote Brooks again: "I would suggest that in modern literature this sense of plot nearly always attaches itself to the others: the organizing line of plot is more often than not some scheme or machination, a concerted plan for the accomplishment of some purpose which goes against the ostensible and dominant legalities of the fictional world, the realization of a blocked and resisted desire."[7] In every visible story there is the continual possibility that a secret story is lying in wait; this always-possible secret threatens to interrupt the authority or "legality" of a believable world. Therefore, to read for the plot would always also mean to read for the complot, that is, to wait for the sense of "complot" to emerge from the word "plot." To read for the complot would be to wait for the uncertain emergence of a secret story.

In what follows I will develop what it means to "read for the complot" by focusing on the narrative structure of conspiracy theory. I will begin by focusing on the narrative theory of Ricardo Piglia, in order to show that conspiracy theory emerges whenever a secret story (a "complot") destabilizes the continuity of a visible story (a "plot"). Piglia's narrative theory suggests that a conspiracy theory always tells the story of a conflict between a secret story and a visible story, regardless of the content of the narrative. However, to read for the complot does not mean that one simply unveils this secret story, as a detective might reveal the secret at the end of a mystery novel. To reveal the secret in this way would be to conjure away the secret, in effect resolving the conflict between a secret story and a visible story. Instead, by comparing Ernest Hemingway's "Big Two-Hearted River" and Ishmael Reed's *Mumbo Jumbo*, I will argue that conspiracy narratives always posit a reader who can never fully reveal or know the secret story. In the end, to read for the complot is to wait for a threatening secret that never fully emerges.

THE COMPLOT EFFECT (PIGLIA)

By focusing on the strange narrative structure of conspiracy theory, I am following the path indicated by the Argentine novelist Ricardo Piglia in his literary and cultural theory. As I noted in the Introduction, Piglia explicitly inscribes his own fiction in a tradition that includes Don DeLillo, Thomas Pynchon, Philip K. Dick, and Jorge Luis Borges, and which he calls "a fiction of paranoia."[8] He does not mean "paranoia" in the clinical sense, but rather refers to a certain structure that defines the essential movement of these narratives, what he calls "a strange manipulative movement."[9] By highlighting this manipulative movement, Piglia suggests that "paranoia" or "conspiracy" is not so much a theme in fiction as it is a particular formal element that produces political effects. To quote Piglia again from his "Afterword" to *The Absent City*:

> [P]olitics enters the contemporary novel through the model of a con-spiracy, through the narration of an intrigue—even if this conspiracy is devoid of any explicitly political characteristics. The form itself consti-tutes the politicizing of the novel. The conspiracy does not necessarily have to contain elements of a political intrigue (although it may, as is the case with Norman Mailer) for the mechanism of utilizing a conspir-acy to be political.[10]

A narrative is "political," for Piglia, not because of this or that subject matter, but rather because of a particular mechanism within the "form" of the conspiracy story. Unfortunately, Piglia does not explicitly develop this idea further.[11] For that reason, the task ahead is to develop an idea of what this "form" would look like and why this form points to a certain definition of the "political."

Even though Piglia has never fully developed his notion of the politi-cal form of conspiracy theories, in effect he develops a theory of the "complot" in his essays on the *cuento* or short story. In fact, the form of the *cuento* allows Piglia to suggest an implicit relation between storytell-ing in general (the art of telling a story, *contar un cuento*) and the paradox-ical mechanism of conspiracy theories. In "Tesis sobre el cuento" ("The-ses on the Short Story") and "Nuevas tesis sobre el cuento" ("New Theses on the Short Story"), Piglia argues that the structure of every *cuento* promises the emergence of a secret.[12] At the same time, he suggests that the form of the *cuento* produces the effect of conspiracy (or "complot"), since a secret story ends up conspiring against a visible story. Although Piglia does not explicitly relate his theses to conspiracy theories as such, I will argue that the structure of the *cuento* models the paradoxical form of the conspiracy narrative.

In Piglia's first essay, "Theses on the Short Story," first published in the 1986 edition of *Crítica y ficción*, he sketches out his theory that the secret is a structural principle of the *cuento*. Starting from a diary entry in one of Chekhov's notebooks, Piglia finds that all *cuentos* tell, in fact, two stories. Chekhov's brief note tells the story of a man who goes to a casino, wins a million, then returns home and commits suicide. In this undevel-oped story, Piglia focuses on the paradoxical nature of its intrigue: "La anécdota tiende a desvincular la historia del juego y la historia del suici-dio" (The anecdote tends to disconnect the story of the game from the story of the suicide).[13] Rather than the conventional story of a man gam-bling, *losing* a million, and going home to commit suicide, this story intro-duces a strange fork in the narrative: the man *wins*. By focusing on this split between two stories, Piglia points to the double character of the *cuento* and states: "Un cuento siempre cuenta dos historias" (*FB*, 105) (a short story always tells two stories). For instance, the classical *cuento*, which he associates with Edgar Allan Poe and Horacio Quiroga, tends to narrate the story of the gambler as its primary focus, but at the same time constructs a second story—the story of the suicide—"in secret" (*FB*, 106).[14]

In effect, Piglia's theory of the secret relies on—but also fundamentally reinscribes—Borges's theory of the *cuento*.[15] In the prologue to a book of short stories by María Esther Vázquez, Borges states: "el cuento deberá constar de dos argumentos; uno, falso, que vagamente se indica, y otro, el auténtico, que se mantendrá secreto hasta el fin" (the short story ought to consist of two plots: a false one, that is vaguely indicated, and another, the authentic one, that is kept in secret until the end).[16] The second story is therefore not only a secret, but is also *authentic*, especially in comparison to the *false* story, or surface narrative. The conclusion of a *cuento* produces the revelation that, among other things, the reader has been duped for the length of the story, until the end is reached. Borges's theory here tends to make the ending of a *cuento* somewhat reassuring, even if it involves the momentary embarrassment that one "didn't get it" from the beginning. Although it would now be clear that the reader had been taken in by the first (false) story, at least at the end the reader would finally know the truth and would now have possession of the authentic story.[17]

As we will see, Piglia's theory does not allow such a comfortable conclusion, although he initially has recourse to a rhetoric of encryption that would suggest a binary between the visible (or false) and the invisible (or true). The challenge for the short-story writer is "saber cifrar la historia 2 en los intersticios de la historia 1" (*FB*, 106) (to know how to hide story 2 within the cracks of story 1). Like the Minister D—in Edgar Allan Poe's "The Purloined Letter," the trick is to know how to hide things within the interstices of the visible. As the word *"intersticio"* suggests, the problem has to do with *setting* something *within* the visible, in such a way that the hidden object appears as nothing. To encrypt this second story is therefore no easy matter; after all, to cipher something is to make it appear as zero or empty. The second story must therefore appear literally as nothing, as the word *"cifrar"* suggests. The first story is then "[u]n relato visible [que] esconde un relato secreto, narrado de un modo elíptico y fragmentario" (*FB*, 106) (a visible tale that hides a secret tale, narrated in an elliptical and fragmentary way). The second story only takes place as silence or absence, and therefore seems to take place by not quite taking place at all.

This emphasis on a hidden story might seem to suggest that Piglia is discussing a hermeneutic process, as if an act of interpretation were necessary to reveal the hidden story, or as if this second story were the meaning of the first story. This hermeneutic process would necessitate the task of enclosing one tale within another. Piglia indeed goes in this direction, when he states that the cuento *encloses* a secret tale: "El cuento es un relato que encierra un relato secreto" (*FB*, 107). This model of the enclosed narration might therefore suggest that the secret in the *cuento* is simply a hidden meaning that a reader could voluntarily open up through a process of interpretation. Nevertheless, Piglia warns against this way of reading his notion of the secret. Immediately after suggesting the enclosed quality of the second story, Piglia states: "No se trata de un sentido oculto que depende de la interpretación: el enigma no es otra cosa que una historia que se cuenta de un modo enigmático. La estrategia del relato está puesta al servicio de esa narración cifrada. ¿Cómo contar una historia mientras se está contando otra?" (*FB*, 107–8) (It is not a question of a hidden sense that would depend on interpretation: the enigma is nothing but a story that is told in an enigmatic way. The strategy of the tale is placed in the service of the encrypted narration. How to tell one story while another one is being told?). The secret is then not the meaning of the *cuento*, but rather its structural principle. The task of the writer is to find a way of encrypting some *other* story in the very folds of the first story. The secret tale, however, is never there and is not actively told by the narrator. Rather, the other story is *being told*, "*se está contando otra*." In fact, one could say that the other story is never told by the narrator because this secret story is always in the process of *telling itself*, as if there were another agency at work beyond the intentions of the storyteller. The second tale is "secret" to the extent that it is absent, and yet this absence gives the *cuento* as a whole an enigmatic quality that allows one to feel the presence of something secret. The end of the *cuento* therefore does not produce the reassuring effect implied by Borges's notion of a secret but *authentic* story. Nothing is fully revealed at the end of the *cuento*, according to Piglia. Instead, one is left with a complex, enigmatic quality, an effect that he will later relate to conspiracy.

Piglia emphasizes this point because his task is to show that this enigmatic presence (the "secret") is not an accidental quality limited to certain *cuentos*. To a certain extent, one could say that Piglia's theory is a generalization of Tzvetan Todorov's reading of Henry James's work, in "The Secret of Narrative": "Thus the secret of Jamesian narrative is precisely the existence of an essential secret, of something not named, of an absent and superpowerful force which sets the whole present machinery of the narrative in motion."[18] Piglia's point, however, is that his theory is not limited to this or that short story; rather, the existence of a secret is a structural necessity of the narrative form that he calls the *cuento*. Without the secret, there is no *cuento*: "la historia secreta es la clave de la forma del cuento y de sus variantes" (*FB*, 108) (the secret story is the key to the form of the short story and its variants). The secret therefore not only makes itself felt by its very absence but also ends up defining the form of the short story. Piglia's task in these essays is to locate the structural principle of *all cuentos*, not only those that are "classical" (Poe) or "modern" (Hemingway) (*FB*, 108). Piglia names this principle "the secret" and proceeds to define its formal effects.

If the secret is an essential part of a *cuento*'s form, then this form suggests a strange temporal structure. The problem begins when Piglia insists that every *cuento* is the narration of two stories, but that these two stories are told *at the same time*. The *cuento* is then the *simultaneous* narration of two different tales. How is this simultaneity possible if the two stories are in fact distinct? Piglia explains:

> Cada una de las dos historias se cuenta de modo distinto. Trabajar con dos historias quiere decir trabajar con dos sistemas diferentes de causalidad. Los mismos acontecimientos entran simultáneamente en dos lógicas narrativas antagónicas. Los elementos esenciales de un cuento tienen doble función y son usados de manera diferente en cada una de las dos historias. (*FB*, 106)

> [Each of the two stories is told differently. To work with two stories means to work with two different systems of causality. The same events enter simultaneously into two narrative logics that are antagonistic. The essential elements of a short story have this double function and are used differently in each of the two stories.]

According to Piglia, then, the second story could be called a repetition of the first. After all, the essential events are the same in both stories. In other words, the fact that there are two stories does not mean that there are two sets of different events: the same material is contained in both. The difference, then, lies not in the material, but rather in how those events connect in order to create a logical order. It is important to note that Piglia is not talking about the formalist distinction between *fabula* (or *histoire*, story) and *sjuzet* (or *récit*, plot). For example, Boris Tomashevsky, in his essay "Thematics," points out: "Plot is distinct from story. Both include the same events, but in the plot the events *are arranged* and connected according to the orderly sequence in which they were presented in the work."[19] In the Russian Formalist distinction, the story is not arranged but rather has to do with the question: what happened? Plot, on the other hand, is the arrangement of the events as they are ordered in the text. Piglia, however, does not distinguish between the arrangement of events (plot) and the material used for formulating the plot (story), but rather focuses on two plots (although he calls them *"historias"*) that are antagonistic. Piglia's distinction is between two different arrangements that are nevertheless told at the same time. But this seems paradoxical: how can there be a repetition according to a different syntax if Piglia insists that this repetition does not take place sequentially but rather *at the same time*, simultaneously? The second story would be the *simultaneous repetition* of the first story, only structured according to a different causality. How is this possible?

It helps to go back to the note from Chekhov that Piglia uses to illustrate his theses on the *cuento*. According to Piglia, Chekhov writes: "'Un hombre, en Montecarlo, va al Casino, gana un millón, vuelve a su casa, se suicida'" (*FB*, 105) (A man, in Monte carlo, goes to the Casino, wins a million, returns home, commits suicide). As mentioned earlier, Piglia generalizes this undeveloped *cuento* in order to say that the first story is the tale of a man winning, while the second (secret) story would be the tale of a man committing suicide. In other words, Piglia marks the first or visible tale as the story of a gain (winning a million), whereas the second or hidden tale is the story of a total loss (committing suicide). However, Piglia now says that the second story is in fact a repetition of the first story; that is, it is told simultaneously and uses the same material but according to a different logic. If in the first story the man wins, in the second story that logic is not only reversed (he does not simply lose the game). Rather, in the second story the man kills himself, thereby enacting an essential loss that cannot be recuperated in the game told in the first story. For this reason, Piglia suggests that the two stories are completely antagonistic: "The same events enter simultaneously into two narrative logics that are antagonistic" (*FB*, 106). This antagonistic relation means that one story cannot simply replace or assimilate the other story. Instead, the two stories are irreducible: a radical split divides the two stories, even though they happen at the same time and use the same material, even though they are strictly speaking repetitions of each other. Piglia therefore suggests that the secret of the *cuento* lies precisely in the incommensurability of the two stories that constitute the genre in the first place. The *cuento* would be something like an impossible structure that creates two simultaneous tales that radically negate each other. The possibility of reading one tale thus always means the impossibility of reading the other tale. This incommensurability is what produces the enigmatic quality that marks the form of the *cuento*.

If the two stories are radically antagonistic and yet take place simultaneously, this means that there is a necessary delay that separates the two acts of reading. In other words, to say that the stories are told "simultaneously" is to refer to the way they are articulated *simul*, that is, "together." The inherent duplicity of this structure means also that one story always *simulates* the other story—one story repeats the other story but *feigns* exact repetition, and therefore creates a kind of counterfeit doubling. This logic of the *simul* (simulate, simulation, simultaneous) produces an antagonistic struggle between the two stories. This struggle is not only a battle between two stories, but also between two temporalities: the *cuento* produces a fold in time that divides the first story from its counterfeit. The temporal structure of the *cuento* is therefore constitutively split between two moments of reading, even though these two moments are articulated together (*simul*) in the *cuento*.

The mark of the "simultaneous" thus points to the strange temporality of this narrative structure: it creates the effect of a thick temporal structure without relying on a traditional storytelling practice that could only be produced through multiple retellings of the same story over time. In effect, Piglia is arguing against Walter Benjamin's assertion, in his 1936 essay "The Storyteller," that storytelling is in danger of passing away. Or rather, Piglia's essays intervene in the debate on storytelling in order to show how the *cuento* rearticulates traditional storytelling but in a simulated fashion. Piglia does not necessarily disagree that modernity marks a moment when experience is in decline, especially the capacity to share experiences.[20] In fact he would agree with Benjamin's assertion that the short story is a symptom of this historical process, as when Benjamin remarks: "We have witnessed the evolution of the 'short story', which has removed itself from oral tradition and no longer permits that slow piling up, one on top of the other, of thin, transparent layers which constitutes the most appropriate image of the way in which the perfect narrative is revealed through the layers of various retellings."[21] For Benjamin, the condition that allows a traditional story to exist is precisely the way a story gets repeated from storyteller to storyteller. These countless retellings in effect define the story as such, since the traditional story is not only the transmission of one storyteller's experience, but rather the transmission of an entire culture reaching back into an archaic past. The short story, for Benjamin, necessarily cuts short this link to tradition and therefore reduces the thick temporal structure of the traditional story to the instantaneous moment of the short story.[22] Although Piglia does not allude explicitly to Benjamin in his essays, his theory of the *cuento* nevertheless responds to Benjamin's denigration of this short form in order to ask: how does the *cuento* produce the *effect* of a traditional tale, given the fact that the *cuento* is by definition severed from tradition? Piglia's answer is that the *cuento* produces the enigmatic effect of an accumulation over time, except that this accumulation happens not through multiple retellings over many generations (as in the traditional story), but rather through the double structure of the short story. The *cuento* is therefore constituted as a split structure that creates a temporal depth through the artificial mechanism of the *simul*, a mechanism that not only produces two antagonistic stories, but also two antagonistic durations.

Piglia goes further to define the specific *effect* produced by the double structure of the *cuento*. In fact, to say that there is an "enigmatic quality" produced by this structure is to understate the case. In the later essay, "New Theses on the Short Story" (originally given as a lecture in 1998), Piglia reads this effect as an event that happens within the form and that ends up troubling its structure. The emergence of the secret story is described as an effective event, as something that *happens*. He writes: "Una historia se puede contar de manera distinta, pero siempre hay un doble movimiento, algo incomprensible que sucede y está oculto" (*FB*, 127) (A story can be told differently, but there is always a double movement, something incomprehensible that happens and is hidden). The short story is precisely this transmission of an event, but this event takes place as a secret: there is a double movement that resists understanding, an event that happens incomprehensively and remains incomprehensible. The secret is now precisely the event that bifurcates the *cuento* into two, incommensurable stories in the first place.

In the process of redefining the secret as a destabilizing event, Piglia returns to his discussion of a hidden "sense": "El sentido de un relato tiene la estructura del secreto (remite al origen etimológico de la palabra *se-cernere*, poner aparte), está escondido, separado del conjunto de la historia, reservado para el final y en otra parte" (*FB*, 127) (The sense of a tale has the structure of the secret [which goes back to the etymological origin of the word *se-cernere*, to place apart]: it is hidden, separated from the totality of the story, reserved for the end and in some other part). Strangely, Piglia places these two seemingly contradictory phrases together: the secret is reserved for the end *and* in some other part. On the one hand, he seems to suggest that the secret is indeed a textual figure, only that it is hidden until the end of the story. But precisely right at the end of the story, when it appears, it appears not there, at the end where you would expect it, but rather somewhere else, in an unspecified elsewhere, *en otra parte*. What, then, is the nature of this appearance? Especially when, in one of his most paradoxical formulations, Piglia states that the secret is indeed a figure, but that it is a *hidden* figure, a figure that hides itself away: "No es un enigma, es una figura que se oculta" (*FB*, 127) (It is not an enigma, it is a figure that is hidden). This formulation needs some explanation, of course. In the first place, how can a figure be hidden? After all, a figure is precisely that which, in the text, seems to be pointing to something else: a figure would be any linguistic element that substitutes for something that is not explicitly said. A figure *points* to something hidden, but normally cannot be hidden itself. Otherwise, if the figure itself were hidden, how would one know that a substitution was in fact taking place?[23]

The end of "New Theses on the Short Story" provides a way to approach this paradox. We have already seen how Piglia is now thinking about the secret as something like an event that is not accessible to understanding. He then develops this idea by talking about this figural event as a movement or mechanism that happens only at the conclusion of a story:

> Hay un mecanismo mínimo que se esconde en la textura de la historia y es su borde y su centro invisible.
> Se trata de un procedimiento de articulación, un levísimo engarce que cierra la doble realidad.
> La verdad de una historia depende siempre de un argumento simétrico que se cuenta en secreto. Concluir un relato es descubrir el punto de cruce que permite entrar en la otra trama. (*FB*, 135)

[There is a minimal mechanism that is hidden in the texture of the story and is its edge and its invisible center. It has to do with a procedure of articulation, an extremely delicate linkage that encloses a double reality. The truth of a story always depends on a symmetrical plot that is told in secret. To conclude a tale is to discover the crossing point that allows one to enter into the other plot.]

The possibility of concluding a *cuento* thus depends on the discovery of a secret *linkage*, a crossing point or minimal mechanism. Piglia now defines the secret as a hidden connection, a crossing point from one reality to another, from one logic to another. Although Piglia states that this passage is symmetrical, we have already seen that this does not mean that one story can simply be assimilated by the other story. Rather, the "symmetrical plot" is "secret": this means that the crossing point (*punto de cruce*) which produces this "symmetrical" structure is not only hidden for the time being, but in fact is incomprehensible, as Piglia noted earlier in the essay: it is a "double movement, something incomprehensible that happens" (*FB*, 127). This sudden movement resists understanding and is for that reason "secret"—it cannot be known as such. In fact, this hidden linkage (*engarce*) is not always there, but rather *happens* as a turn at the end of the first story. At that concluding moment, Piglia notes, "[e]l argumento, en un instante, gira y encuentra su forma" (*FB*, 128) (the plot, in an instant, turns and finds its form). In other words, the end of the first story is only the beginning of the *cuento*: in that instantaneous event of a turn, the *cuento* finds its form as a sudden configuration that takes place between two stories. The happening of this configuration is what Piglia calls the hidden figure or secret; it is a turn or trope that makes its presence known as a founding force that constitutes the *cuento* as such. Piglia thus redefines what it means to conclude the *cuento*'s first story: the *desenlace* (the outcome, but also the dis-connection) is not simply a clever ending but is in fact the "secret" or constitutive trope of the *cuento*, the hidden figure that creates an incommensurable relation between two stories.

Piglia further thinks of this trope as a voice that suddenly comes to the surface toward the end of the first story. However, this voice is not the voice of the traditional storyteller, let alone the voice of tradition itself that speaks through the archaic figure of the storyteller. In Benjamin's account of the decline of storytelling in his 1936 essay, "the voice of Nature" appears as a gentle reminder that allows a character to remember something lost through a slow, layered revelation.[24] This voice of nature has a fundamental connection to memory or *Erinnerung*, the interiorized "chain of tradition which transmits an event from generation to generation."[25] In contrast, the "voice" in Piglia's essay has an artificial and mechanical quality; it is the "minimal mechanism" that serves as the hinge of the form of the *cuento*. Piglia writes:

Esa estructura de caleidoscopio y de doble fondo se sostiene sobre una pequeña maquinación imperceptible: la íntima voz que ... ha marcado el tono y el registro verbal de la historia se identifica y se hace ver y define desde afuera el relato y lo cierra.

Su entrada es la condición del final; es el que ha urdido la intriga y está del otro lado de la frontera, más allá del círculo cerrado de la historia. Su aparición, siempre artificial y compleja, invierte el significado de la intriga y produce un efecto de paradoja y de complot. (*FB*, 133–34)

[This kaleidoscopic and double-bottomed structure is sustained by an imperceptibly small machination. The intimate voice that . . . has marked the tone and verbal register of the story is identified and becomes visible; this voice defines the tale from the outside and concludes it.

The arrival of this voice is the condition of the ending. It is the one that has plotted the intrigue from the other side of the frontier, beyond the closed circle of the story. Its appearance, always artificial and complex, inverts the meaning of the intrigue and produces an effect of paradox and conspiracy.]

The voice that suddenly appears at the end of a *cuento* is therefore not the storyteller's voice, but rather an "imperceptibly small machination," a set-up that has been operating since the beginning of the tale. The sudden appearance of this "voice" produces an effect of paradox and conspiracy (or "complot"): the second story conspires against the first story, completely reconfiguring it, although the second story never appears as such. For that reason, the second story is not only incompatible with the first story; rather, the second story ends up machinating against the first story, undermining and inverting it even as the first story reaches its end and goal. This antagonistic battle then retroactively posits the existence of a voice or "imperceptibly small machination" that seems to have plotted the intrigue from the beginning. In this way, the antagonistic relation between two stories produces a prosopopoeia: the structural antagonism is given a voice and an agency (an "intimate voice . . . becomes visible"). In Piglia's theory, the antagonistic relation constitutive of the *cuento* is figured as the voice of the enemy, a secret agent who threatens the stability of the first story. If the conspiratorial effect of the *cuento* produces an image of the enemy, then ultimately the form of the *cuento* tells the story of an internal relation between two enemies engaged in a conspiratorial struggle, even if the enemy is figured as an outside agent that threatens a stable, interior space. The "plot," in other words, is continually besieged by the "complot," an outside force that nevertheless undermines the interior space from within.

In this way, Piglia suggests that conspiracy theory is an effect produced by a certain kind of narrative, the *cuento*. But "*cuento*" now means any story that encloses a destabilizing secret. The constitutive trait of this structure is the formation of an antagonistic frontier between two discourses. This antagonism is not thematic, but rather structural: a visible or official discourse is steadily undermined by an *other* discourse that cannot be assimilated by the first discourse. The two discourses are therefore irreducible, in part because the *other* discourse is never "there" as such, but rather takes place as an obscure agency that brings about the subversion of the official discourse. Piglia figures this overturning movement as "suicide," as in the story by Chekhov, but also as a "hidden figure" that disrupts the very visibility of the first story. The effect of this disruption is the "voice" of the *cuento*: the constitutive antagonism produces the effect of paradox and complot. The storyteller, Piglia suggests, must bear witness to this *complot effect*. If Walter Benjamin insisted that the "shock experience" (*Chockerlebnis*) defines modern-day experience,[26] Piglia suggests that the *cuento* reproduces this shock as an effect of narration: now the shock takes place as the sudden emergence of a second story that disrupts the first story. To tell a story after the passing away of the storyteller is thus to tell a double story that produces the shock of the complot effect.

We can now see that "conspiracy theory" is in fact any story that is haunted by the possible emergence of a secret story and that this double structure produces the effect of complot (or conspiracy). Piglia privileges the *cuento* because it allows him to isolate this moment and the way it duplicates something like an essential experience, that is, the experience of searching for a unique experience. As Piglia notes at the end of his first essay: "El cuento . . . [r]eproduce la busca siempre renovada de una experiencia única que nos permita ver, bajo la superficie opaca de la vida, una verdad secreta" (*FB*, 111) (The *cuento* . . . reproduces the always-renewed search for a unique experience that would allow us to see, beneath the opaque surface of life, a secret truth). This unique experience is, to paraphrase Benjamin, a capability to which we no longer have access—it is the ability to experience a kind of epic truth that is always about to arrive. However, the "secret truth" that the *cuento* offers is a *simulated* epic truth; rather than the interweaving of "counsel" into life as it is lived (*Erlebnis*), which would be the image of the traditional story, the *cuento* simulates the layering effects of a story, as if the invisible story were transmitted by multiple storytellers through the ages.[27] The form of the short story intimates a depth, but this depth is produced not through the multiple retellings of a tale, but rather by means of an artificial mechanism. Nevertheless, this artificial mechanism has a didactic purpose that precisely supplements the death of storytelling. As Piglia explains, this kind of narration entails "el arte de presentir lo inesperado; de saber esperar lo que viene, nítido, invisible, como la silueta de una mariposa contra la tela vacía. . . . En la experiencia siempre renovada de esa revelación que es la forma, la literatura tiene, como siempre, mucho que enseñarnos sobre la vida" (*FB*, 137) (the art of sensing the unexpected, of knowing how to wait for what comes, clearly, invisibly, like the sil-houette of a butterfly against an empty canvas. . . . In the always-renewed experience of that revelation which is form, literature has, as always, much to teach us about life). The idea is not only to wait for the unex-pected, but more precisely to wait for that which you are *not* waiting for (or *esperar lo inesperado*). In this way, the *cuento* always contains a hidden pedagogical purpose: it is a training mechanism that artificially dupli-cates the experience of waiting for something completely other. The *cuen-to* (or "conspiracy theory") therefore teaches what it means to read for the complot, which is now defined as the art of waiting for the disruptive emergence of something completely other.

THE UNSAID (HEMINGWAY)

But what would it mean to bear witness to the arrival of this kind of threatening other? Piglia provides a number of examples to show how this complot effect can be produced, but perhaps one of the most impor-tant figures in his essay (besides Jorge Luis Borges) is Ernest Hemingway. Piglia insists that Hemingway's theory of the iceberg is the clearest ex-pression of his notion of the double story that defines all *cuentos*. He writes: "La teoría del iceberg de Hemingway es la primera síntesis de ese proceso de transformación: lo más importante nunca se cuenta. La histor-ia secreta se construye con lo no dicho, con el sobreentendido y la alusión" (*FB*, 108) (Hemingway's theory of the iceberg is the first synthe-sis of this process of transformation: the most important thing is never told. The secret story is constructed with what is left unsaid, by means of inference and allusion). In this way, Piglia takes up Hemingway's em-phasis on silence as a mode of narration: what is important is not what is said, but what is left unsaid.[28] Absence, then, is the primary material by means of which a true storyteller weaves a narrative. It is important to note that this absence is not simply an allegorical meaning that is indi-rectly signaled by the narration, nor is this absence an enigma that is momentarily obscure until the end. Rather, Piglia emphasizes the way that the unsaid is radically not there: *lo no dicho* means precisely some-thing that language never utters. There might be "something" there, but this "something" is not a thing at all but rather merely a neuter pronoun: *lo* (*lo más importante, lo no dicho*). The presence of that absent "thing" only makes itself known through the vaguest of allusions, through a language that, far from referring to reality, instead continually defers any reference to reality. Nevertheless, it is by means of this constant deferment of refer-ence that one senses the absent presence of that other "thing."

Piglia names Hemingway's "The Big Two-Hearted River" as the ex-emplary story of this iceberg theory of narration. Piglia writes: "[Hem-ingway] cifra hasta tal punto la historia 2 (los efectos de la guerra en Nick

Adams) que el cuento parece la descripción trivial de una excursión de pesca. . . . Usa con tal maestría el arte de la elipsis que logra que se note la *ausencia* del otro relato" (*FB,* 109) (Hemingway hides story 2 [the effects of the war on Nick Adams] to such an extent that the story seems to be the trivial description of a fishing excursion. . . . He uses the art of ellipsis with such mastery that one only notes the *absence* of the other story). By using Hemingway's Nick Adams story from *In Our Time,* Piglia rehearses the theory that he develops throughout "Theses on the Short Story" and "New Theses on the Short Story." He notes that "Big Two-Hearted River" contains two stories. The first story is the step-by-step description of Nick's fishing trip: each action takes place as if there were no relation to preceding actions. In fact, the narration persistently describes the way Nick leaves everything behind him, as if he were constantly turning his back on any event that did not have to do with his immediate desires or fears: "[H]e walked along the road that paralleled the railway track, leaving the burned town behind in the heat, and then turned off around a hill with a high, fire-scarred hill on either side onto a road that went back into the country. . . . His muscles ached and the day was hot, but Nick felt happy. He felt he had left everything behind, the need for thinking, the need to write, other needs. It was all back of him."[29] Nick's entire trajectory is turned away from the past, so that as soon as he passes through one experience (the vision of the burned town), he immediately leaves it behind him, turns his back on it, in order to burrow further into the country. Not only has he left everything behind him as it all passes by, but he also leaves behind the very processes of meditating on what has happened: he leaves behind the need to think, write, or more generally to reflect on the past and its relation to the future. The first story is therefore merely the step-by-step narration of Nick's trip into the country in order to fish. Not only does it avoid any reference to the past, but the narration explicitly remarks that any meditation on the past and the possible future is now thoroughly behind him. The first story, in other words, is locked inside of its own closed system. Piglia remarks: "Hemingway pone toda su pericia en la narración hermética de la historia secreta" (*FB,* 109) (Hemingway puts all of his expertise into the hermetic narration of the secret story). To block off any notion of the past and the future is to keep this first story locked within a hermetic narration.

Strangely, however, Piglia undermines the radical nature of *lo no dicho* by isolating and thereby claiming to know whatever it is that is not said in Hemingway's tale. On the one hand, Piglia again notes that this "second story" ("historia secreta") is radically absent from Hemingway's story: "He uses the art of ellipsis with such mastery that one only notes the *absence* of the other story" (*FB,* 109). The other story is never there: it becomes "present" only because of the gaps in the narration (the art of ellipsis), and these gaps point not to a presence but rather to an absence of something else, "the other story." On the other hand, Piglia strangely *names* this absent story and calls it "the effects of the war on Nick Adams" (*FB*, 109). By naming the second story in this way, Piglia is following a general trend in Hemingway criticism, a tradition that began when Malcolm Cowley, in his 1944 introduction to *The Portable Hemingway*, explicitly linked the fishing expedition of "Big Two-Hearted River" to the war wounds that Nick Adams suffered during World War I.[30] In other words, there is nothing strange about Piglia's interpretation of the story, especially if one reads it in relation to the other stories in *In Our Time*. What is strange, however, is the fact that Piglia chooses this interpretation as an example of *"lo no dicho,"* the unsaid. After all, the unsaid in Piglia's theory has to do with "something" radically absent, a gap in the text that is never uttered as such. Although Piglia insists that this gap or ellipsis presents the sense that there is something hidden (a secret story), nevertheless the first story cannot give any explicit sense that this other story in fact exists. The very notion of the "second story" depends on the sense that *there is something else there*, but that the precise *what* of this second story can never be fully brought into the light of day. Therefore, to name this second story "the effects of the war on Nick Adams" seems to go against the rigor of Piglia's own theory. Rather than the constant deferment of reference, Piglia strangely insists on a direct relation between the story and an outside event (the war).

More recent criticism has noted that, at best, we can only say that *something* is happening in the "background" or behind Nick's back, and that it is only possible to note the various figurations of this absence. For instance, Sarah Mary O'Brien focuses on the way the image of the swamp, in Hemingway's story, functions as a gradual interruption of a pastoral scene (the fishing expedition). She notes that the swamp does not come up suddenly (like a train whistle) but rather emerges slowly, in a haunting way: "the swamp does not pierce the tranquility of the pastoral retreat with any suddenness but, rather, creeps up on Nick and the reader."[31] O'Brien goes on to note that in those moments when the swamp emerges as a significant figure in the text, Nick is suddenly filled with an unaccountable dread that also disturbs the tranquility and "objectivity" of the narration.[32] For instance, the swamp suddenly becomes "tragic" for Nick:

> Nick did not want to go in there now. He felt a reaction against deep wading with the water deepening up under his armpits, to hook big trout in places impossible to land them. In the swamp the banks were bare, the big cedars came together overhead, the sun did not come through, except in patches; in the fast deep water, in the half-light, the fishing would be tragic. In the swamp fishing was a tragic adventure. Nick did not want it. He didn't want to go up the stream any further today.[33]

Although the swamp continually besieges Nick's mind, he is able to keep it at bay. The swamp never grows in figuration to the point that it might be possible to link it explicitly to World War I or even the sense of a wound. At best, the swamp is a figure that remains hidden throughout: it "becomes visible" only as it "appears" as darkness, potential drowning, the tragic, and the inability to find sure footing. The swamp is certainly an image of danger that gradually makes its presence felt, and therefore suggests a second story that is never told. However, this second story never fully emerges as such; it remains buried in the narration at the same time that it haunts the sense of the present. The swamp therefore allows a hidden force to speak: it is the prosopopoeia of something that is "there" but never seen.

In this way, the "hermetic narration" of story 1 is continually threatened by the emergence of story 2, even though the latter never appears as such. The narration of story 1 is therefore something like a locked room that is nevertheless continually besieged by something outside of it, something that lies on the margins of the story, beyond the borders of Nick's contained space. The swamp is always described as a space that lies on "the other side of the stream" or "the other side of the river."[34] At best, then, we can say that the swamp represents the beyond itself: it is the "other side" that threatens to cross borders and infect the closed space that Nick has built and the hermetic narration that Hemingway has written. Nick registers this haunting presence at first by refusing it ("Nick did not want it") and then, at the end of the story, by deferring its presence: "There were plenty of days coming when he could fish the swamp."[35] Nick bears witness to this haunting presence by remaining silent about it, that is, by not facing it, by turning away from it. By turning his back on the swamp, Nick registers the negative impact of the swamp's presence.[36] Therefore, if there is a second story, then this story is addressed to Nick, or rather, to Nick's back: he is the one who feels the impact of this threatening force that lies just on the other side of his locked room. He is the one who both turns his back on this force and awaits its full emergence, when he would be able not only to fish in the swamp, but to fish the swamp itself, to cast about for it in order to catch it by indirect means.

In this way, "reading for the complot" is not simply a method of reading that one would apply to a text. Rather, Hemingway's short story demonstrates Piglia's suggestion that there is always a reader within these narrations who is addressed by this other voice from beyond the closed circle of the story. In "Big Two-Hearted River," this other voice is the swamp that lies just beyond the border, but which nevertheless threatens the hermetic space that this reader (Nick) has built. To name directly that voice from beyond would be to use a catachresis for that which has no proper name. Nick calls it the swamp, Piglia and others call it "the effects of the war on Nick," but ultimately this space is unnamable and threatening precisely because it cannot be named, because it exceeds any attempt to name it. For that reason, to "read for the complot" within Hemingway's story means, paradoxically, to turn away from a direct presentation of this outside force that is seeking to come inside the hermetic narration of the first story. To read for the complot is to bear witness to the threatening other by allowing it to remain an unvoiced, haunting presence that never fully comes to light.

Hemingway's short story therefore serves as an exemplary "conspiracy theory" that nevertheless does not contain the theme of conspiracy. Instead, "Big Two-Hearted River" presents a structure that both models and demands a mode of reading I am calling "reading for the complot." This mode of reading is not only applicable to those narratives that contain explicit allusions to conspiracies, but rather may take place whenever there is a visible narrative line that is undermined by a secret story. In other words, even a short story by Hemingway, which normally would be difficult to fit within the rubric of "paranoid fiction," can be read according to the paradoxical logic of the complot effect. To read Hemingway's story is to read with Nick Adams as he waits for the disruptive emergence of something completely other.

WAITING FOR SOMETHING OR OTHER (REED)

At this point I would like to turn to a more explicitly "paranoid" narrative—Ishmael Reed's 1972 novel *Mumbo Jumbo*—in order to illustrate how this same structure and this same mode of reading operates within a text that contains overt allusions to conspiracies. At first glance it should seem bizarre that I am attempting to compare Hemingway's terse short story with Reed's exuberant postmodern narrative. After all, *Mumbo Jumbo*, which takes place primarily in the 1920s but also alludes to thousands of years of history, is the story of a strange "anti-disease," called Jes Grew, that is infecting America with the desire to dance, sing, and speak in tongues. At the same time, Reed's novel tells the story of a constellation of secret societies that attempts to stamp out this hidden force before it completely infects the world. For that reason, *Mumbo Jumbo* is often read as a conspiracy novel that presents a fantastic alternate history of race relations. It therefore seems difficult to compare Hemingway's reticent style of narration to the exuberance presented in Reed's novel. However, I will argue that *Mumbo Jumbo*, like Hemingway's short story, emphasizes the narration of a secret that never fully emerges. At the same time, I will show that this secret is not a momentarily concealed piece of knowledge that may be revealed through a detective-like search. On the contrary, the very notion of "discovery" changes in the conspiracy narrative offered by *Mumbo Jumbo*. To "discover" the mysterious force of Jes Grew is to bear witness to the way it can never be fully revealed in the light of day.

Mumbo Jumbo is, in its own words, the story of a struggle of secret societies. On the one hand, there is the Wallflower Order, which is the military arm of the Atonist Path. This ancient secret society seems to have only one purpose: to fight against a mysterious force called "Jes Grew" and all of its manifestations.[37] On the other hand, then, is Jes Grew, which is difficult to call a secret society per se, if only because it is rather amorphous and more closely resembles a disease than a full-fledged society.[38] Jes Grew manifests itself at the beginning of the novel as a sudden conflagration which necessitates an emergency response by the "front men"—the mayor of New Orleans, doctors, and scientists—of the Wallflower Order (*MJ*, 18). As one of the doctors remarks: "What was once dormant is now a Creeping Thing" (*MJ*, 3). The first symptoms of this "psychic epidemic" are dancing, shouting, hallucinations, and speaking in tongues (5). The Wallflower Order then seeks to control this epidemic: the rest of the plot, as well as the underlying plot of history, tells the story of this antagonistic conflict between two "societies." For that reason, the narrator vaguely states: "Someone once said that beneath or behind all political and cultural warfare lies a struggle between secret societies" (*MJ*, 18). With this rewriting of *The Communist Manifesto* by Karl Marx and Friedrich Engels ("The history of all hitherto existing society is the history of class struggles"), Reed suggests that this conflict between secret societies may stand as a cipher for understanding all of world history.

However, unlike the well-defined terms in Marx's theory of class conflict, Reed's vision of history leaves at least one of the terms undefined and indefinable. As Henry Louis Gates Jr. notes, the exact definition and purpose of Jes Grew remains a mystery, even at the end of the novel.[39] In effect, there are two underlying questions throughout *Mumbo Jumbo*: 1) What is Jes Grew? 2) What is its Text and where can this Text be found? In effect, these questions are never fully answered, and Jes Grew remains a mystery even for those who would like to support it, such as PaPa LaBas, the voodoo healer who stands as the primary detective of the novel. LaBas would like to reveal all of the mysteries surrounding Jes Grew, so that it may manifest itself fully in the light of day. It is for that reason that Gates insists that *Mumbo Jumbo* has the structure of detective fiction: "The form the narration takes in *Mumbo Jumbo* replicates the tension of the two stories which grounds the form of the detective novel, defined by Tzvetan Todorov as 'the missing story of the crime, and the presented story of the investigation, the role justification of which is to make us discover the first story.'"[40] Todorov's theory is useful because it offers an explanatory apparatus for describing an otherwise fantastical novel about a conflict between secret societies that traverses historical periods and national boundaries. If it were possible to describe *Mumbo Jumbo* as detective fiction (even a parodied detective fiction or a pastiche of the genre), then it would be possible to contain the threatening mystery surrounding Jes Grew and inoculate *Mumbo Jumbo*'s open-ended structure.

At first glance, Reed's novel indeed seems to follow the kind of structure Todorov outlined in "The Typology of Detective Fiction," in which he notes that all detective fiction tells two stories, "the story of the crime and the story of the investigation."[41] Todorov then generalizes this schema by explaining that "the first—the story of the crime—tells 'what really happened,' whereas the second—the story of the investigation—explains 'how the reader (or the narrator) has come to know about it.'"[42] By generalizing the form of detective fiction in this way, Todorov can then explicitly compare this structure to the theory of narrative developed by the Russian formalists: "They distinguished, in fact, the *fable* (story) from the *subject* (plot) of a narrative: the story is what has happened in life, the plot is the way the author presents it to us."[43] Detective fiction takes this more generalized description of narrative as its very form, so that the story of the crime (the first story) is retold, as it were, as the story of an investigation into how the crime happened (the second story). According to Todorov, then, the two stories that constitute all detective fiction correspond exactly to the Russian formalist distinction between story and plot. By referring to Todorov's typology, Gates insists that the story of "what happened?" (the *fabula* or story) precedes the narration of the investigation. The detective's task is then to reconstitute this story of the crime by leading an investigation. In a true detective story, the story of the crime is revealed toward the end of the plot, when the mystery is finally clarified and narrative closure is thereby attained.

As detective fiction, then, *Mumbo Jumbo* should have two stories. The story of the "crime" would address the two central questions of the novel: what is Jes Grew and what is its text? The story of the investigation would be the story that details all the attempts (by LaBas and the Wallflower Order) to reveal Jes Grew to the light of day and to discover its text. Gates argues that this structure, with mild variations, is precisely the structure of Reed's novel. He locates the revelation scene in the thirty-page historical narration in which the detective, PaPa LaBas, omnisciently tells the story of the struggle between Osiris and Set and the machinations of Moses. Thus, rather than immediately clarify the two mysteries of the novel (what is Jes Grew and what would it mean to discover its text?) the revelation scene instead goes back thousands of years to a previous struggle between those who serve Jes Grew (the Jes Grew Carriers) and those who seek to steal its power (the Atonists). Gates explains: "The myth, of course, recapitulates the action of the novel up to this point of the narrative, but by an allegorical representation through mythic discourse."[44] By repeating the action of the novel, Gates notes, the myth takes the narration to another level: it allegorically represents the story of the investigation as a constant battle between secret forces. At this point, the plot of the novel is repeated (allegorically) as the underlying plot of

history. This means that beneath or behind the political and cultural warfare that we witness in the plot of the novel stands a historical struggle
between secret societies that spans thousands of years. For Gates, this
moment signals an allegorical impulse in Reed's fiction: "The Atonists
and the Jes Grew Carriers ('J.G.C.s') reenact allegorically a primal, recur-
ring battle between the forces of light and the forces of darkness, between
forces of the left hand and forces of the right hand, between the descendants of Set and the descendants of Osiris."[45] Thus, Gates himself is
compelled to recognize that the story of the past, which should clarify the
mysteries (what is Jes Grew? What is its text?), instead re-narrates the
story of the investigation but on a different historical level: instead of
PaPa LaBas, we have Osiris and Jethro; instead of Hinckle Von Vampton,
an agent of the Wallflower Order, we have Set and Moses. With this
"allegorical" scene, *Mumbo Jumbo* seems to present yet another coded
history that demands another act of deciphering.

Although Gates recognizes the way *Mumbo Jumbo* frustrates the narrative conventions of detective fiction, he suggests that this frustration is
part of the parodic nature of Reed's novel. In the first place, Gates argues,
Mumbo Jumbo is not a simple whodunit, but rather represents what Todorov calls a "suspense" or "noir" fiction, in the way that the story of the
present (PaPa LaBas's investigation and Von Vampton's machinations) is
emphasized more than the story of the past (the story of Set, Osiris,
Moses, and Jethro). But Gates also notes that Reed presents a parody of
this form: "The crucial exception to [Todorov's] typology, however,
whereby Reed is able to parody even the mode of the two stories themselves and transform the structure into a self-reflecting text or allegory on
the nature of writing itself, is *Mumbo Jumbo*'s device of drawing upon the
story of the past to reflect upon, analyze, and philosophize about the
story of the present."[46] In effect, Gates reads LaBas's mythical story about
Set and Osiris as an allegory of reading, in that it reads the story of the
investigation as a literary critic would read a text. However, this allegor-
ization of the story of the investigation leaves a key aspect of the detective genre—the mystery of Jes Grew—mysterious throughout the novel.
Even in the discontinuous and fragmentary moments of the novel, when
the story is interrupted by an italicized omniscient narrator or by images
and graphs (what Gates calls the novel's "antithetical narration"), the
central mysteries concerning Jes Grew remain in the dark: "The only
mysteries this antithetical narration does not address are the text's first
two mysteries: what exactly Jes Grew is and what precisely its text is."[47]
For Gates, this antithetical narration, along with the allegorical story of
Set and Moses, points to the way *Mumbo Jumbo* signifies upon other traditions in a relation that continually differs and defers from the source
material.[48] However, by focusing on the extended historical explanation
and the investigation that preceded it, one must be blind to the very
mysteries established at the beginning of the novel and which do not get

answered at the end: what is Jes Grew and what is its text? Unlike the situation of the suspense novel, in which the mystery is merely a "point of departure," the mystery of Jes Grew is still the main interest of Reed's novel.[49] If the mystery concerning Jes Grew is never clarified, and yet the mystery remains the crucial motor of the novel at every moment, then it would seem that *Mumbo Jumbo* bears a very different relationship to the canonical forms of detective fiction.

The point here is not to counter Gates's emphasis on the double story that structures *Mumbo Jumbo*, but rather to rethink what it means to say that there are two stories in the first place. The problem again is that the story of Set and Moses does not clear up the mystery of Jes Grew. Using Piglia's terms, we could refer to the story of the investigation (now including the "allegorical" scene as well) as the *visible* story of the novel. If there is a second story, then this second story must have to do with the appearance of Jes Grew, which is the true mystery or secret that haunts *Mumbo Jumbo*. However, this secret story is never told or explained, although the narration constantly alludes to the missing presence of this secret story. Like the swamp in Hemingway's story, we "see" Jes Grew all the time, but it nevertheless remains continuously inaccessible. As one of the Atonists complains at the beginning of the novel, Jes Grew, in its very secrecy, is "nothing we can bring into focus or categorize; once we call it 1 [sic] thing it forms into something else" (*MJ*, 4). Jes Grew never remains a one; whenever anyone tries to categorize or count Jes Grew as something (a number 1), it immediately multiplies and becomes at least two. Jes Grew is never singular, but rather slips into a doubled entity that always becomes something else.[50] This "something else" is the absent center of Reed's novel: Jes Grew is the empty name of a secret force that haunts the novel, taking a momentary configuration only to transform into something else.

In fact, Jes Grew itself (although we do not really know what it is) could be said to be looking for the secret story, or at least the text that will give form to the emptiness of Jes Grew. The omniscient voice explains Jes Grew's "motivation" at the beginning of the novel: "So Jes Grew is seeking its words. Its text. For what good is a liturgy without a text?" (*MJ*, 6). However, the attempt to reveal this text remains frustrated toward the end of the novel.[51] After PaPa LaBas has narrated the allegorical story, everyone in the room is waiting for the big reveal. But instead of a blinding revelation of the text, the novel produces literally nothing: "T Malice places the box [that is said to contain the text] down in the center of the floor and removes the 1st box, an iron box, and the 2nd box, which is bronze and shines so that they have to turn the ceiling lights down. And within this box is a sycamore box and under the sycamore, ebony, and under this ivory, then silver and finally gold and then . . . empty!!" (*MJ*, 196). The series of boxes within boxes reveals layers of precious metals or other materials, thus suggesting a series of transformations into an always-metamorphosing "something else," until finally the text itself is revealed to be exactly nothing, an empty cipher that again points to something else or somewhere else. Strangely, then, the revelation of the presence of the Text is itself revealed to be the presentation of its absence: Jes Grew's story, its Text, is never revealed. It can therefore be said that the story of Jes Grew is not an allegorical story that refers to something else, that is, one story that is really speaking about another story. Rather, Jes Grew is itself this "something else" that never presents itself as such in the narration of the first story; Jes Grew is a continual speaking-otherwise (recalling the etymological sense of allegory as "to speak otherwise in the agora or marketplace"). If there is a second story, as all detective fiction must inevitably have, then this second story never appears as such, but nevertheless makes its presence known as a disruptive force throughout the novel.[52]

Thus, although *Mumbo Jumbo* cannot be adequately explained by alluding to the genre of detective fiction, Gates is nevertheless right to focus on the existence of two stories. However, Reed's novel does not follow Todorov's model that fits together a story of an investigation and the story of a crime that is momentarily hidden. Rather, the novel tells a visible story that is continuously undermined by a secret story. This secret story does not appear as such, but rather takes place as a figure that haunts the main narrative line. *Mumbo Jumbo* therefore displaces the genre of detective fiction and, in doing so, produces a narrative with a radically different structure. If for Gates this structure still resembles the structure of detective fiction (albeit an ironic version), I would like to argue that Reed's novel emphasizes an entirely different relation between the two stories. In short, *Mumbo Jumbo* tells the story of a plot that is steadily undermined by the complot, that is, a secret story that produces a series of destabilizing effects that undermine the solidity of the first narrative line. Reed's novel suggests that conspiracy narratives cannot be read as a simple variation on the structure of detective fiction, since they enact a complete displacement of its form. The "secret" in conspiracy narratives is radically secret, meaning that it produces effects only insofar as the second story maintains its secrecy.

Mumbo Jumbo theorizes this secrecy as a kind of ineloquence, a speaking that cannot fully articulate itself. Early in the novel, PaPa LaBas explains the way Jes Grew is always haunted by ineloquence as it searches for its text. He notes:

> [Jes Grew is] up to its Text. For some, it's a disease, a plague, but in fact it is an anti-plague. You will recall . . . that in the past there were germs that avoided words. . . . Being an anti-plague I figure that it's yearning for The Work of its Word or else it will peter out as in the 1890s, when it wasn't ready and had no idea where to search. It must find its Speaking or strangle upon its own ineloquence. (*MJ*, 33–34)

Here PaPa LaBas is repeating the explanation of Jes Grew as a mysterious force that is searching for its text. As we have seen, this text is never found; Jes Grew remains a secret story that never fully emerges. However, this failure to emerge is in fact a necessary condition that allows Jes Grew to produce effects. After all, if Jes Grew emerged as such, it would then be possible to isolate it or lock it in, as one of the Atonists hopes to accomplish at the beginning of the novel (*MJ*, 4). Therefore, if Jes Grew is to continue to produce its effects, it cannot find its "Speaking" once and for all, but must rather "strangle upon its own ineloquence." In other words, if Jes Grew is to continue to speak in some way, it cannot fully speak (it cannot find its Speaking), or it cannot speak as itself, in its own name. Paradoxically, then, Jes Grew's very ineloquence is what allows it to speak in the first place, although this kind of speaking (a strangling) cannot be called a "Speaking." Rather, if Jes Grew speaks at all, it speaks through a variety of effects that are never fully allowed to flourish, since whenever Jes Grew "manifests" itself it is actually "appearing" as something else.

While lecturing on the origin of the name "Jes Grew," PaPa LaBas notes that this continual transformation into something else is a necessary condition of Jes Grew's "appearance." He first notes that Scott Joplin, the ragtime musician and composer, "has healed many with his ability to summon this X-factor, the Thing that Freud saw, the indefinable quality that James Weldon Johnson called 'Jes Grew'" (*MJ*, 211). PaPa LaBas then explains what he means by this indefinable quality by quoting Johnson and by citing other examples of this power to summon Jes Grew:

> "It belonged to nobody," Johnson said. "Its words were unprintable but its tune irresistible." Jes Grew, the Something or Other that led Charlie Parker to scale the Everests of the Chord. Riff fly skid dip soar and gave his Alto Godspeed. Jes Grew that touched John Coltrane's tenor; that tinged the voice of Otis Redding and compelled Black Herman to write a dictionary to Dreams that Freud would have envied. Jes Grew was the manic in the artist who would rather do glossolalia than be "neat clear or lucid." (*MJ*, 211)

For LaBas, Jes Grew has no story and no name of its own (it is just *called* 'Jes Grew' by catachresis); it is the unknown force or "X-factor" that "tinged the voice" of historical agents throughout the nineteenth and twentieth centuries and which in fact constituted these people as historical agents in the first place. Jes Grew does not have its own "Speaking," but its very ineloquence can tinge other voices. For that reason, Jes Grew is figured as something that is always other, "Something or Other," an unavoidable vagueness that is nevertheless capitalized (on). In other words, Jes Grew is not simply an absence, since whenever it appears it appears as if it were a proper noun: "Jes Grew," "Something or Other." But this presence never remains present, since it is continually transform-

ing into something else or choking on its own ineloquence. This strangling phenomenon simply means that Jes Grew is moving from one agent
to another. As Gates notes: "Jes Grew's text, in other words, is not a
transcendent signified but must be produced in a dynamic process and
manifested in discrete forms, as in black music and black speech acts." [53]
Gates goes on to note that Reed in effect reinscribes the voicelessness of
Bigger in Richard Wright's *Native Son*, in order to suggest an ineloquence
that is nevertheless powerful, a power that takes place precisely because
of its ineloquence. In this way, the only "presence" of Jes Grew is the way
it manifests itself as an ineloquence, as a "Something or Other." In fact,
Gates notes that the political significance of Jes Grew lies in what he calls
its indeterminacy. Jes Grew is not simply absent, as in the way "blackness" has traditionally been figured as an absence or shadow[54]; at the
same time, Jes Grew is not simply present, as if it were another transcendental signified taking the place of "whiteness" in American culture.
Rather, Jes Grew remains as a non-present presence that "speaks" by
strangling on its own ineloquence.[55] The blankness of blackness (to echo
Gates who was echoing Melville) produces an inexplicable force, not despite its blankness, but precisely because of it.

Jes Grew is therefore not a sign that refers to something else, but
rather a "Something or Other" that is always turning into "something
else." This kind of vague language is strangely necessary in order to bear
witness to the unpresentable nature of this hidden figure. In *Mumbo Jumbo* Jes Grew haunts every visible narrative line, every official story, and
stands as the very significant emptiness about which every character
must talk or theorize, or through which artists create. Jes Grew reveals
itself not as something knowable, but rather as an event to which one
must bear witness. This necessity to witness the event of Jes Grew is
something even PaPa LaBas sometimes forgets: "PaPa LaBas thinks to
himself . . . *Perhaps I have been insular, as Berbelang said, limiting myself to a
Mumbo Jumbo Kathedral, not allowing myself to witness the popular manifestations of The Work*" (*MJ*, 139). The Haitian Benoit Battraville also alludes to
the necessity of witnessing: "[The Americans] know this process for they
have synthesized the HooDoo of VooDoo. Its bleeblop essence; they've
isolated the unknown factor which gives their loas their rise. Ragtime.
Jazz. Blues. The new thang. . . . What you have here is an experimental art
form that all of us believe bears watching" (*MJ*, 152). This "watching," or
this necessity "to witness" Jes Grew, is what I have called "reading for
the complot." To quote Piglia again, it is "the art of sensing the unexpected, of knowing how to wait for what comes, clearly, invisibly, like
the silhouette of a butterfly against an empty canvas" (*FB*, 137). Therefore, if *Mumbo Jumbo* still bears any relation to the detective genre, it is in
the way it still maintains a *certain* demand that a secret be "discovered."
However, it should now be clear that the verb "to discover" is changing
its meaning in conspiracy narratives. To discover "Jes Grew," for exam-

ple, is to discover the way it is always changing into something else. Discovery is more of a patient watchfulness, a way to bear witness to a secret that never fully speaks, to an event that is always not quite taking place.

In this way, Piglia's narrative theory and the fictions of Hemingway and Reed suggest that the "complot" (or "conspiracy") is not a visible agent, but rather takes place as an effect of narration: it is the paradoxical disruption of the agency of the main narrative line. This disruption produces the "feeling" that there is a second plot just beneath the surface, an invisible plot that refuses to come to light completely. Conspiracy theory therefore has a bifurcated form that is strangely asymmetrical: the first story cannot be assimilated to the second story, for the simple reason that the second story always remains "set-apart," secret, or is always taking place "somewhere else." It is precisely for that reason that we should avoid assimilating conspiracy theories to detective stories, precisely because conspiracy theories end up transforming what it means to read the secret and even how we define secrecy. After all, conspiracy theories do not simply reveal a secret, as in detective fiction; rather, they present the demand that we bear witness to an incomprehensible event that never fully happens. This means that conspiracy theories define "reading" not as an epistemological exercise (to know and therefore control the secret), but rather as a way to register the force of something unrecognizable. "Conspiracy theory," now understood as the narration of a secret that never fully emerges, teaches the art of reading for the complot, of knowing how to wait for the arrival of something completely other.

NOTES

1. David Wise and Thomas B. Ross, *The Invisible Government* (New York: Bantam Books, 1964), 1.

2. Ibid.

3. Ibid., 4.

4. Ibid., 371.

5. Ibid., 370.

6. Peter Brooks, *Reading for the Plot: Design and Intention in Narrative* (Cambridge: Harvard University Press, 1984), 12.

7. Ibid.

8. Ricardo Piglia, "Afterword," in *The Absent City*, Trans. Sergio Waisman (Durham, NC: Duke University Press, 2000), 145.

9. Ibid. In an interview from 2003, Piglia clarified what he meant by "paranoid fiction": "Lejos de entenderlo en el sentido psiquiátrico, para mí es un modo de definir el estado actual del género policíaco. Después de pasar por la novela de enigma y la novela de la experiencia, por llamarla así, nos topamos con la figura del complot, que me atrae especialmente: el sujeto no descifra un crimen privado sino que se enfrenta a una combinación multitudinaria de enemigos" (Far from understanding [paranoia] in the psychiatric sense, for me it is a way of defining the current state of detective fiction. After passing through the mystery and the novel of 'experience,' we find the figure of the complot, which attracts me especially: the subject does not decipher a

private crime but rather confronts a massive combination of enemies) (Ricardo Piglia, "De la tragedia a la conspiración. Entrevista con Mauricio Montiel Figueiras." *La nación*, May 18, 2003. Accessed October 6, 2005. http://www.lanacion.com.ar/496728-de-la-tragedia-a-la-conspiracion). Unless otherwise noted, all translations are my own.

10. Piglia, "Afterword," 145.

11. Piglia has recently written a more extensive treatment of the relation between conspiracy and literature in "Novela y complot." While his essay focuses explicitly on the relation between conspiracy and state power, it does not develop this theme in relation to his narrative theory.

12. In order to avoid confusion, I will use the Spanish term *cuento* to refer to the "short story" in Piglia's theory. Generally, when I speak of a first or second story, I am translating Piglia's term *historia*.

13. Ricardo Piglia, *Formas breves* (Barcelona: Editorial Anagrama, 2000), 105. Hereafter cited in text as *FB*. Unless otherwise noted, all translations are my own.

14. Critics have often been intrigued by Piglia's theses over the years (especially the earlier "Tesis sobre el cuento"), but critical treatments of the theses have generally focused only on the relation between Piglia's theories and his own *cuentos*. For instance, Alejandro Solomianski, in his article "El cuento de la patria," is one critic who provides an intriguing reading of how Piglia himself practices the technique of weaving together two stories in his own *cuentos*.

15. Pablo A. J. Brescia notes that Piglia at least implicitly develops his theory of the *cuento* from Borges's theory of the *cuento* (Pablo A. J. Brescia, "Ricardo Piglia y el cuento ausente: El género en la posmodernidad," in *Memorias: Primer congreso internacional: Medio siglo de literatura latinoamericana, 1945–1995*, ed. Ana Rosa Domenella et al. [México, D.F.: Universidad Autónoma Metropolitana, 1997], 172). It should also be noted that the idea of the double plot (*la doble trama*) is a motif that often appears in many critics from Piglia's generation. Piglia himself focuses on the double plot in an early essay from 1979, this time in terms of a double heritage (or double lineage, what Piglia calls *"los dos linajes"*) that Borges inscribes in his work and that represents not only a familial genealogy but also a national heritage (Ricardo Piglia, "Ideología y ficción en Borges," in *Ficciones argentinas: Antología de lecturas críticas* [Buenos Aires: Grupo Editorial Norma, 2004], 36–37). Piglia's contemporary, Beatriz Sarlo, discusses her own version of this *"doble linaje"* in her book on Borges (Beatriz Sarlo, *Jorge Luis Borges: A Writer on the Edge* [London: Verso, 1993], 47).

16. Jorge Luis Borges, *Prólogos con un prólogo de prólogos* (Madrid: Alianza Editorial, 1975), 257.

17. Eva Horn, in her essay "Borges's Duels: Friends, Enemies, and the Fictions of History" (in *Thinking with Borges*, eds. David E. Johnson and William Egginton [Aurora, CO: The Davies Group, 2009]), implicitly relies on Borges's theory of the *cuento* while reading the structure of enmity in Borges's tales. While she intriguingly notes that Borges's short stories suggest that history is fundamentally determined by secrecy, she ultimately insists that the visible story or official history is merely a fiction: "Beneath the whitewash of seemingly evident identities, clear-cut distribution of light and shadow, *fama* and *infamia*, lies the smirch of necessary lies and dirty secrets, protected by history's 'sense of shame'—and the discretion of the historiographer" (175–76). Here the visible story of the struggle between light and shadow, between official story (*fama*) and unofficial story (*infama*, in her reading), is revealed to be a fiction ("whitewash"), leading to the revelation that history is constituted by dirty secrets. She more forcefully puts forward this thesis in her excellent observation that Borges's theory of enmity undermines the theory of the enemy found in theorists like Carl Schmitt: "The distinction between friends and enemies, Schmitt's benchmark in the realm of 'the political,' is simply a fiction in Borges's view, a simulacrum of order, of clear-cut opposites designed to spite the confused contingencies of reality" (177). Here again Horn suggests that Borges presents a dual history: on the one hand, there is a visible story that involves clear-cut identities; on the other hand, this visible story is finally revealed to be simply a fiction. While the visible story is revealed to be false,

the secret story, in her view, turns out to be true or authentic. As I will show in what follows, Piglia's theory of the *cuento* suggests that the secret story is not true or authentic, even if it undermines the official or visible story. On the contrary, the secret story, if it is to produce its effects, must be constitutively counterfeit and must remain hidden.

18. Tzvetan Todorov, *The Poetics of Prose*, trans. Richard Howard (Ithaca, NY: Cornell University Press, 1977), 145.

19. Boris Tomashevsky, "Thematics," in *Russian Formalist Criticism: Four Essays*, trans. Lee T. Lemon and Marion J. Reis (Lincoln: University of Nebraska Press, 1965), 67.

20. Benjamin insists that, if the storyteller is increasingly becoming a thing of the past, this means that something has happened to experience in the modern age. He writes: "It is as if a capability that seemed inalienable to us, the securest among our possessions, has been taken from us: the ability to share experiences" (Walter Benjamin, "The Storyteller: Observations on the Works of Nikolai Leskov," in *Selected Writings, Volume 3: 1935–1938* [Cambridge: Harvard University Press, 2002], 143).

21. Benjamin, "Storyteller," 150.

22. I develop Benjamin's theory of the short story—especially this emphasis on what Benjamin calls the *"abkürzen"* or cutting-short of traditional storytelling—in my article "The Afterlife of Storytelling: Julio Cortázar's Reading of Walter Benjamin and Edgar Allan Poe."

23. Jean-François Lyotard addresses the problem of the hidden figure in similar ways in "The Sublime and the Avant-Garde": "What can remain of rhetoric (or of poetics) when the rhetorician in Boileau's translation [of Longinus] announces that to attain the sublime effect 'there is no better figure of speech than one which is completely hidden, that which we do not even recognize as a figure of speech'? Must we admit that there are techniques for hiding figures, that there are figures for the erasure of figures? How do we distinguish between a hidden figure and what is not a figure?" (Jean-François Lyotard, "The Sublime and the Avant-Garde," in *The Inhuman: Reflections on Time*, trans. Geoffrey Bennington and Rachel Bowlby [Stanford, CA: Stanford University Press, 1991], 95). My emphasis on the hidden figure is indebted to Benjamin's reading of the *verborgene Figur* (or hidden figure) in the poetry of Charles Baudelaire. For a discussion of Benjamin's notion of the hidden figure in relation to Roland Barthes's *Camera Lucida*, see Elissa Marder's *Dead Time*. In "The Inactuality of Aura," I try to show that Benjamin's notion of a hidden figure, which he develops in the 1930s, goes back to his work on baroque drama from the 1920s.

24. Benjamin, "Storyteller," 159.

25. Ibid., 154.

26. Walter Benjamin, "On Some Motifs in Baudelaire," in *Selected Writings, Volume 4: 1938–1940*, trans. Edmund Jephcott and others (Cambridge: Harvard University Press, 2003), 329.

27. For Benjamin, a traditional story is one that is still connected to an "epic" truth, what he also calls "wisdom." He notes that the traditional storyteller weaves counsel into the fabric of real life, *gelebten Lebens*, life as it is lived (Walter Benjamin, *Gesammelte Schriften* [volume 2], eds. Rolf Tiedemann and Hermann Schweppenhäuser [Frankfurt. Suhrkamp, 1972], 442). "Counsel" is not a meaning or an answer to a question; rather, it is "a proposal concerning the continuation of a story which is in the process of unfolding" (Benjamin, "Storyteller," 145–46). To be able to take counsel therefore means that one must already be able to tell or retell a story; one must still be connected to tradition and long-term unconscious experience. A real story then comes about through the interweaving of counsel into the stuff of *Erlebnis* (or lived experience) in order to create "wisdom," that is, a kind of epic truth (146). For this reason, a real story is always "true," in the sense that it connects to tradition and the wisdom that comes with tradition.

28. This emphasis on silence—both as a thematic element and as a mode of construction—is something that Piglia explores in his earlier novel *Respiración artificial*

(*Artificial Respiration*). One character, speaking of the act of writing, notes: "In a poem about the artist, the word artist should not appear and least of all in the title. Is that a rule or not? In literature . . . the most important thing should never be named" (Ricardo Piglia, *Artificial Respiration*, trans. Daniel Balderston [Durham, NC: Duke University Press, 1994], 142). This "rule" is clearly Piglia's own in *Artificial Respiration*, which addresses, without ever naming, the constant threat of being disappeared by the military during the "Dirty War" in Argentina. This vague but always real threat is insinuated in everyday conversations, for example, when two characters pointedly do not talk about a third character (the Professor): "if we have talked this entire night, it was so as not to speak, or rather, so as not to say anything about him, about the Professor" (212). Recent critics have sought to mobilize Piglia's emphasis on the unsaid in order to interpret the fragmentation of his novels, for instance, in Pablo Lazcano's "Historias de la argentina secreta" and Idelber Avelar's "Cómo respiran los ausentes." For a more general treatment of the unsaid in Piglia's work, see José Sazbón, "La reflexión literaria."

29. Ernest Hemingway, *In Our Time* (New York: Scribner, 1958), 134.

30. Robert Paul Lamb notes that the "war wound" thesis first begins with Cowley's essay, which "implicitly linked 'Big Two-Hearted River' to Nick's experience of war. Five years later in the first major, full-length study of Hemingway, Philip Young further developed this 'war wound' thesis," thereby canonizing this interpretation until the 1980s (Robert Paul Lamb, "Fishing for Stories: What 'Big Two-Hearted River' Is Really About," *MFS: Modern Fiction Studies* 37.2 [Summer 1991]: 162).

31. Sarah Mary O'Brien, "'I, Also, Am in Michigan': Pastoralism of Mind in 'Big Two-Hearted River,'" *Hemingway Review* 28.2 (Spring 2009): 73.

32. Ibid., 74.

33. Hemingway, *In Our Time*, 155.

34. Ibid., 138, 145.

35. Ibid., 156.

36. This emphasis on the "presence" of a negative image is one way to link Hemingway to other writers of modernity, such as Charles Baudelaire. Elissa Marder emphasizes the force of the negative image in her reading of Benjamin's Baudelaire: "Only by reading [Baudelaire's] 'A une passante' as a negative image, presented in relief, can Benjamin read the crowd as the primary (albeit negative) figure of the poem" (Elissa Marder, *Dead Time: Temporal Disorders in the Wake of Modernity (Baudelaire and Flaubert)* [Stanford, CA: Stanford University Press, 2001], 80). Benjamin himself suggests that this attempt to represent modernity through a negative image is what connects Baudelaire to later writers, such as Henri Bergson. Benjamin points to "the alienating, blinding experience of the age of large-scale industrialism" as the primary matrix from which Bergson's philosophy emerged, even though Bergson himself tried to shut out that experience. "In shutting out this experience," Benjamin writes, "the eye perceives a complementary experience—in the form of its spontaneous afterimage, as it were. . . . His philosophy thus indirectly furnishes a clue to the experience which presented itself undistorted to Baudelaire's eyes" (Benjamin, "Motifs," 314).

37. Ishmael Reed, *Mumbo Jumbo* (New York: Simon & Schuster, 1972), 15, 132–33. Hereafter cited in text as *MJ*.

38. It should be pointed out that Thomas De Quincey, in his essay "Secret Societies," notes that secret societies always have the form of a disease, specifically, cancer. In order to portray his first childhood image of what a secret society would look like, he first defines the image of cancer, drawing on the word's origin as "crab": "[cancer] drew its name from the horrid claws, or spurs, or roots, by which it connected itself with distant points, running underground, as it were, baffling detection, and defying radical extirpation" (Thomas De Quincey, "Secret Societies," in *The Collected Writings of Thomas De Quincey*, Vol. 7, ed. David Masson [Edinburgh: Adams and Charles Black, 1890], 174). De Quincey then relates the image of cancer to a conspiracy theory that circulated widely in his childhood: "What I heard read aloud from the Abbé gave that dreadful cancerous character to the plot against Christianity. This plot, by the Abbé's

account, stretched its horrid fangs, and threw out its forerunning feelers and *tentacles*, into many nations, and more than one century. *That* perplexed me, though also fascinating me by its grandeur. How men, living in distant periods and distant places—men that did not know each other, nay, often had not even heard of each other, nor spoke the same languages—could yet be parties to the same treason against a mighty religion towering to the highest heavens, puzzled my understanding" (174).

39. Henry Louis Gates Jr., *The Signifying Monkey: A Theory of African-American Literary Criticism* (Oxford: Oxford University Press, 1988), 229.

40. Ibid., 227.

41. Todorov, *The Poetics of Prose*, 44.

42. Ibid., 45.

43. Ibid.

44. Gates, *The Signifying Monkey*, 226.

45. Ibid., 225.

46. Ibid., 229.

47. Ibid., 232.

48. In Gates's earlier essay on *Mumbo Jumbo*, he summarizes his definition of "signifying": "Kochman argues that signifying depends upon the signifier repeating what someone else has said about a third person in order to reverse the status of a relationship heretofore harmonious; signifying can also be employed to reverse or undermine pretense or even one's opinion about one's own status. This use of repetition and reversal (chiasmus) constitutes an implicit parody of a subject's own complicity in illusion" (Henry Louis Gates Jr., "The 'Blackness of Blackness': A Critique of the Sign and the Signifying Monkey," *Critical Inquiry* 9.4 [June 1983]: 691). In *The Signifying Monkey*, Gates goes on to note the significance of Kochman's use of the term "signifying": "Kochman argues that the function of this sort of claim to repetition is to challenge and reverse the status quo" (Gates, *The Signifying Monkey*, 79).

49. Todorov, *The Poetics of Prose*, 51.

50. Gates notes that the Atonists and the members of the Wallflower Order are obsessed with unity and the number 1, whereas Papa LaBas is consistently related to the number 2 (Gates, *The Signifying Monkey*, 234).

51. Richard Swope notes that Reed's novel in effect does "find" the text of Jes Grew, thereby resolving at least one of the central mysteries of the novel: "*Mumbo Jumbo* itself can, in fact, be regarded as Reed's contribution to this 'future Text' and a product of Jes Grew. . . . That is to say, against the backdrop of the 'neat clean and lucid' detective novel and its adherence to rational explanation and definitive closure, Reed's open-ended, multi-textual, polyvocal 'glossolalia' calls attention to its *own* un-solvability" (Richard Swope, "Crossing Western Space, or the HooDoo Detective on the Boundary in Ishmael Reed's *Mumbo Jumbo*," *African American Review* 36.4 [Winter 2002]: 618). Of course, by interpreting Reed's text as the Text, Swope's argument manages to imitate the "neat clean and lucid" structure of detective fiction: the novel presents itself as its own answer and therefore the search for the book has been resolved. This way of reading the novel, while clearly justified by the text, nevertheless threatens to take away the very un-solvability that *Mumbo Jumbo* seems to encourage.

52. Patricia Merivale and Susan Elizabeth Sweeney include *Mumbo Jumbo* under the rubric of "metaphysical detective story," which is often "composed in equal parts of parody, paradox, epistemological allegory (Nothing can be known with any certainty), and insoluble mystery" (Patricia Merivale and Susan Elizabeth Sweeney, "The Game's Afoot: On the Trail of the Metaphysical Detective Story," in *Detecting Texts: The Metaphysical Detective Story from Poe to Postmodernism*, eds. Patricia Merivale and Susan Elizabeth Sweeney [Philadelphia: University of Pennsylvania Press, 1999], 4). They go on to note that Reed's novel presents the "metaphysical detection of cultural history" (19). Richard Swope follows Merivale and Sweeney by noting that "Reed's novel is no conventional piece of detective fiction. It is, rather, a metaphysical detective story which evokes [according to William Spanos] the 'impulse to "detect" . . . in order to violently frustrate it'" (Swope, 612). While I agree with these critics in their description

of this deliberate frustration of detective fiction conventions, I want to emphasize the way writers like Reed reinscribe the double story of detective fiction in order to focus on the *effects* of secrecy (and not just the question of whether knowledge is possible).

53. Gates, *The Signifying Monkey*, 235.

54. Toni Morrison analyzes the way blackness is traditionally figured in American literature in her classic essay *Playing in the Dark*: "The ways in which artists—and the society that bred them—transferred internal conflicts to a 'blank darkness,' to conveniently bound and violently silenced black bodies, is a major theme in American literature" (Toni Morrison, *Playing in the Dark: Whiteness and the Literary Imagination* [New York: Vintage Books, 1992], 38). Santiago Juan-Navarro, who places Reed's novel within an "inter-American" context, has noted that *Mumbo Jumbo* "refutes the traditional charges that blacks in the Americas have always lacked a tradition and that their 'high' cultural manifestations have been modeled after those of the white world" (Santiago Juan-Navarro, *Archival Reflections: Postmodern Fiction of the Americas (Self-Reflexivity, Historical Revisionism, Utopia)* [Lewisburg, PA: Bucknell University Press, 2000], 142–43). In what follows, I argue that Reed's novel does not refute the notion of "lack" (or what Morrison calls "blank darkness"), but rather reinscribes this blankness as a strangely productive site of political struggle.

55. This ineloquent voice can be compared to the way Jean-François Lyotard, in his essay "Voix" from *Lectures d'enfance*, theorizes "voice" (or *phônè*) as opposed to *lexis*. Speaking of this inarticulate "voice," Lyotard writes: "C'est du son continu, il n'est pas décomposable en ce que nous appelons des phonemes. . . . La voix est sourde, ell est même muette (le silence est une voix)" (Jean-François Lyotard, *Lectures d'enfance*, [Paris: Éditions Galilée, 1991], 134). Claire Nouvet explains: "In contradistinction to the voice of logos, the phonè is a confused, continuous, and inarticulate voice that does not let itself be articulated or cut up in phonemes, the building blocks for the signifying units of the words" (Claire Nouvet, "The Inarticulate Affect: Lyotard and Psychoanalytic Testimony," *Discourse: Journal for Theoretical Studies in Media and Culture* 25.1 and 2 [Winter and Spring 2003]: 237). However, although *phônè* is distinct from *lexis*, Lyotard goes on to suggest that the inarticulate voice—what he also calls "affect"—always haunts articulate language: "Les affects *squattent* en silence les significations référentielles et les destinations les plus explicites" (Lyotard, *Lectures d'enfance*, 139). Nouvet helpfully explains that this "squatting" means that affect "can inhabit articulated language, but as a squatter, a clandestine guest, an 'outside within,' the presence of which articulated language does not even suspect or hear. It is, within articulation, that which cannot be articulated and therefore heard. The affect is mute, claims Lyotard. Muteness does not mean that the affect is simply voiceless. It is not the absence of voice but the condition of a voice condemned to remain unheard" (Nouvet, 239). It is for this reason that Lyotard speaks of the voice as a kind of blank noise, or even a strangulation: "[La voix] s'étrangle, elle éclate, elle est blanche, elle geint, soupire, bâille, pleure" (Lyotard, *Lectures d'enfance*, 134). The voice is not only blank (*blanche*), but is also choked, *s'étrangle*, that is, the voice *is* precisely this choking or clenched sighing; it is the continuous strangulation of breath in the very moment of articulation. Voice therefore remains in all articulate language as an affect that is not heard, but which nevertheless produces unaccountable effects.

TWO

Politics in the Age of the Imaginative Leap

In a scene from Don DeLillo's 1978 novel *Running Dog*, the editor of a countercultural magazine provides an ironically glib statement of purpose that nevertheless also points to one of the major "themes" of contemporary fiction in the Americas: "Conspiracy's our theme. . . . Connections, links, secret associations."[1] The editor, Grace Delaney, goes on to chide her reporter for not including this theme in a new story about a senator's secret pornography collection: "The whole point behind the series you're doing is that it's a complex and very large business involving not only smut merchants, not only the families, not only the police and the courts, but also highly respectable business elements, mostly real estate interests, in a conscious agreement to break the law. Or haven't you heard."[2] To tell a story about a conspiracy, for Grace Delaney, would be to focus on the secret connections that link multiple levels of society, all within a complex, criminal arrangement. The problem with the reporter's story is that it does not investigate these secret connections. The reporter herself recognizes this later on: "Maybe Grace Delaney was right. [The pornography story] lacked ramifications. It wasn't political."[3] For a story to be "political," it has to tell the story of *ramifications*: not only the story of complex arrangements that branch out into multiple segments of society, but also one that reveals startling consequences or produces a multiplication of effect. A political story takes place by dividing itself, spreading out into various branches, and especially by bearing witness to surprising relations: "Connections, links, secret associations."

While Grace Delaney explicitly notes that conspiracy is a "theme," she also suggests that this "theme" has more to do with the way a conspiracy story is told. In her theory, *relation* is key: everything depends on the way a series of isolated events come together in a secret configuration. This mode of relation is, according to Grace Delaney, what makes a story political. However, this conclusion contradicts some of the main currents of political theory over the last fifty years. In fact, it is precisely this way of constructing ramifying relations that Richard Hofstadter objects to in his essay "The Paranoid Style in American Politics." In that 1964 essay, Hofstadter viewed this "style" as suspect precisely because of the links and associations that conspiracy theories inevitably posit. Thus, while Hofstadter and others insist that the style of conspiracy theory disqualifies this kind of narrative as political discourse, Grace Delaney insists that only a narrative that posits secret connections can be considered political. This, then, is the mystery that I will address in this chapter: What is the *political* significance of the secret associations posited in conspiracy theories? In other words, why is the "presence" of a secret necessary for political narratives? Or to put it in the terms of the last chapter, what would it mean to read for the complot and how would this mode of reading be "political"?

In order to address these questions, I will focus on a tradition that views all conspiracy narratives with suspicion, precisely because of the unreliability of the links posited by these narratives. This tradition crosses national borders, including not only discussions of the assassination of John F. Kennedy but also events in other countries, such as the 1994 assassination of Luis Donaldo Colosio, the Mexican political leader. While this tradition blames conspiracy theory for introducing leaps in the narration of events, there is another tradition that tends to emphasize the way political events are themselves constituted by an incomprehensible leap. Through a close reading of Don DeLillo's *Libra* (the American novelist's fictionalization of the Kennedy assassination) and Jorge Volpi's "The Second Conspiracy" (the Mexican novelist's essay on the Colosio assassination), I will argue that this leap is not applied to the event after the fact, but rather constitutes the event as political in the first place. My reading will suggest that a political event must always be a kind of "Kennedy assassination," that is, an event that takes place as the explosion of relations. Furthermore, I will argue that conspiracy theories are an attempt to bear witness to the political event in the age of the imaginative leap. My argument is that the imaginative leap is not a symptom of a paranoid mind or a failure to act politically, but is rather the condition for political storytelling in the first place. In other words, my purpose is not to argue against those, like Hofstadter, who insist that the imaginative leap is simply the sign of illegitimacy. Rather, if the "paranoid style" is "ineradicable," as Hofstadter also suggests, then this means that this style is presenting a condition of possibility, not an accidental aberration.[4] I will argue, then, that illegitimacy is a necessary moment in the narration of political events, a moment that cannot be overcome dialectically.[5] In fact, without the imaginative leap it would be impossible to bear witness to the severing of relations that necessarily happens with any political event. Conspiracy narratives therefore testify to this constitutive gap in relations—to tell the story of conspiracy is to tell a political story in the age of contingent relations.

THE IMAGINATIVE LEAP (HOFSTADTER AND THE HSCA REPORT)

I would like to begin by returning to Hofstadter's "The Paranoid Style in American Politics," since his essay is the first major discussion of the relevance of conspiracy theories for politics. In effect, Hofstadter argues that conspiracy narratives should be relegated to the pathological margins of "normal" political discourse. Of course, by using the term "paranoid," he does not mean that conspiracy theorists are clinically paranoid, but rather that the discourse articulated by conspiracy theorists is similar to the delusions of persecution that one might witness in a paranoid subject. Nevertheless, Hofstadter intends this term "paranoid" to be "pejorative" and employs it strategically to suggest the way a conspiracy narrative is a "distorted style" that signals "a distorted judgment."[6] Hofstadter therefore seeks to protect political discourse from the distortions of conspiracy theory; any political discourse that includes a story about a conspiracy would necessarily find itself marginalized from the world of politics.

Many critics have already noted the way that Hofstadter's account of conspiracy tends to mimic the narrative form of conspiracy theories. Mark Fenster, in his study *Conspiracy Theories*, usefully summarizes this tendency and argues that Hofstadter's theory ends up creating a pathological other (the conspiracy theorist, the paranoid politician, etc.) who lies outside the limits of the political.[7] Fenster concludes:

> By labeling as pathological any challenge or resistance to "consensus," the notion of the "paranoid style" serves as an excuse for neglecting, equating, and even repressing political protest of all sorts. A symbolic, stylistic, and pathological anxiety [as expressed by conspiracy theory] represents little more than an irksome but temporary cry from the margins that must be either defused or incorporated within a pluralistic consensus. This condemnation of conspiracy theory is thus limited in its ability to analyze, challenge, and redirect the populism of conspiracy theory.[8]

Fenster implicitly suggests that Hofstadter's theory ends up mimicking the very tendencies that he ascribes to the "paranoid": the location and figuration of a small group (the "paranoid" group) that threatens the legitimacy of the established discourse (in this case, "politics" as such). Just as the paranoid always works with an image of "a vast and sinister conspiracy, a gigantic and yet subtle machinery of influence set in motion to undermine and destroy a way of life,"[9] Hofstadter views the conspira-

cy theorist as similarly poised to undermine "a way of life," specifically
the consensus mode of engaging in politics. The paranoid politician is
thus figured in Hofstadter's essay as the other of politics. If the conspiracy theorist wins, Hofstadter's theory seems to suggest, politics itself will
disappear.

For Fenster, Hofstadter's theory is itself an aberrant way of theorizing
politics, since it tends to silence the true political crisis expressed by
conspiracy theories. I would like to build on Fenster's reading of Hofstadter, in order to focus on a moment in "The Paranoid Style" that has
not received as much critical attention. I would like to argue that, although Hofstadter's valuation of conspiracy theory mimics the object of
his study, his analysis of the form of conspiracy theory is in fact quite
precise. Furthermore, the problem that Hofstadter outlines, namely that
the imaginative leap ends up disqualifying the paranoid style as legitimate politics, has plagued not only fictional accounts of conspiracies, but
also non-fictional attempts to grapple with unresolved events. The problem, for Hofstadter, is always a particular *style* of narration (which he
calls "paranoid"). Hofstadter makes it clear that this style is not simply
the expression of an obsession with conspiracies, but is rather a particular
way of writing history. He notes that, for the conspiracy theorist,
"[h]istory *is* a conspiracy, set in motion by demonic forces of almost
transcendent power, and what is felt to be needed to defeat it is not the
usual methods of political give-and-take, but an all-out crusade." [10] The
conspiracy theorist views history not only as the visible and recognizable
record of humans in action, but also as the invisible and secret machinations of shadowy figures. History, for a conspiracy theorist, has as
much—or more—to do with the gaps in history than with those moments
that are accountable in some way. Every moment in history is a potential
"X-File" or unexplained phenomenon, due to the way history is constructed out of the gaps in the historical record. For Hofstadter, this way
of viewing history leads to an aberrant politics, or rather it leads to the
end of politics as negotiation or "give-and-take." The paranoid politician
replaces rational consensus with the crusade-like mentality that gives up
nothing and expects everything in return.

If history, for the conspiracy theorist, is constituted by invisible events
and hidden manipulations, the job of the conspiracy theorist is to narrate
the secret histories that have been "disappeared." Hofstadter writes:
"What distinguishes the paranoid style is not, then, the absence of verifi-
able facts . . . but rather the curious leap in imagination that is always
made at some critical point in the recital of events." [11] For Hofstadter, the
"paranoid style" is clearly not a theme at all, but is rather a particular
way of telling a story, a way of linking events. Hofstadter argues that a
conspiracy theorist tends to accumulate factual details which ultimately
stand as "the careful preparation for the big leap from the undeniable to
the unbelievable." [12] In this way, the conspiracy theorist always presents

a narrative that is sustained by a continuous disruption of the narrative. This disruption is the "big leap" or "the curious leap in imagination": it is posited both as the "proof" of the conspiracy and as the very leap that denies the believability of the conspiracy story. The curious leap of imagination is therefore a constitutive interruption that founds the discourse of conspiracy theory. However, for Hofstadter, this "big leap" also interrupts the official economy of the political: it interrupts the rational give-and-take that defines a politics of consensus. The conspiracy theorist, for Hofstadter, destabilizes the very grounds for political discussion by introducing the groundless leap in imagination.[13]

The problem of the imaginative leap is echoed in many attempts to account for events (or crimes) that are still unresolved. In general, this problem emerges as an attempt to ask what it would mean to constitute a "significant association" between events that seem unrelated. This phrase appears in the *Report of the Select Committee on Assassinations of the U.S. House of Representatives* (1979), within a section on what it would mean to prove the existence of a conspiracy to kill President John F. Kennedy. The House Select Committee on Assassinations (HSCA) was convened in 1976 to study not only the Kennedy assassination, but also the assassination of Martin Luther King Jr. The primary mission of the HSCA was to respond to the increasing skepticism regarding the *Warren Report*. However, as Peter Knight notes, this new investigation resembled in many ways the earlier Warren Commission, by including "a mixture of public and private hearings; the commission of elaborate scientific/forensic testing; and a lengthy final report (716 pages), twelve volumes of accompanying transcripts of hearings and appendices, together with hundreds of thousands of pages of evidence to be kept sealed at the National Archives."[14] Nevertheless, the HSCA's *Report* remains an important document, and not only because it found that there is indeed reason to believe that there was a conspiracy to kill the president. Rather, what makes this report stand out is its way of explaining the stakes involved in investigating a conspiracy, especially what it would mean to use the word "conspiracy" in relation to an assassination attempt.

The *Report* explains that, even if there were no evidence at the scene of the assassination to allege a conspiracy, a conspiracy could be said to exist if others assisted Oswald in the act. However, this question of Oswald's possible "associates" brings up a troubling semantic question: what does the term "associate" mean? The *Report* explains:

> It is important to realize, too, that the term "associate" may connote widely varying meanings to different people. A person's associate may be his next door neighbor and vacation companion, or it may be an individual he has met only once for the purpose of discussing a contract for a murder. The Warren Commission [in its 1964 report] examined Oswald's past and concluded he was essentially a loner. It reasoned, therefore, that since Oswald had no significant associations

with persons who could have been involved with him in the assassination, there could not have been a conspiracy. [15]

The *Report* therefore finds that a critical hinge in the Warren Commission's investigation into the existence of a conspiracy is the term "significant associations." Of course, this should come as no surprise, since a "conspiracy," etymologically speaking, already alludes to an act (breathing, respiration) that happens in association with others (*con*, together). Given this etymological definition, the *Report* asks, what then does it mean to talk about an association that is significant enough to establish a criminal relation? As the HSCA explains, the earlier *Warren Report* was able to discredit the idea of conspiracy by presumably showing that Oswald was a "loner" both psychologically and sociologically—he was a man who needed no one and always acted alone. The term "loner" is then crucial for any attempt to discredit the supposition of conspiracy: if a man is a loner, if he acts alone by definition, then there can be no significant associations that would demonstrate the existence of a conspiracy.

Nevertheless, the HSCA does indeed find evidence that there was a second shooter in the assassination of President Kennedy, thereby pointing to the fact that Oswald could not have been as isolated as the *Warren Report* made him out to be. But the committee immediately stumbles upon the problem that has always plagued investigations into Kennedy's assassination: there are gaps in the evidence that do not sufficiently prove the existence of this other gunman. The *Report* admits: "There was a high probability that a second gunman, in fact, fired at the President. At the same time, the committee candidly stated, in expressing its finding of conspiracy in the Kennedy assassination, that it was 'unable to identify the other gunman or the extent of the conspiracy.'" [16] This gap in the available evidence produces an interruption in the committee's rigorous investigative efforts; from then on, the committee confronts the problem of speculation: "It is possible, of course, that the extent of the conspiracy was so limited that it involved only Oswald and the second gunman. The committee was not able to reach such a conclusion, for it would have been based on speculation, not evidence." [17] The HSCA then concludes that even a severely limited notion of conspiracy—the association of Oswald with another shooter—is difficult to prove due to a lack of evidence. Certainly, the lack of evidence does not *completely* disrupt the investigation into the assassination. However, it does instantly change the sign under which the investigation is carried out: rather than an investigation based on evidence, the investigation is now about to fall into the baseless ground of speculation. In this way, the term "speculation" marks the moment when evidence fails to keep up with the narrative of events. Even though the account of a conspiracy to kill the president can easily continue, such a story would remain at the level of speculative fiction.

   Therefore, the question of what precisely constitutes a "significant association" is not only a simple matter of semantics, but rather tends to disrupt the very nature of a rigorous investigation, thereby causing the investigation to slide into speculation. The term "speculation" points to the moment when knowledge reaches its limit and can no longer support the claims and relations that the conspiracy theory would like to put forward. At this point, even a supposedly rigorous investigation—for instance, one commissioned by the U.S. Congress—could fall into speculation, thereby leading to the suspension of knowledge. In general, then, any narrative of a conspiracy must face the problem of what constitutes a "significant association." If the narrative begins to introduce an "imaginative leap" in the recitation of events, the narrative immediately falls into a "paranoid style" and begins to slide into the speculative genre. In the case of the assassination of President Kennedy, there is a high "probability" that a conspiracy existed, but the story of this conspiracy always remains at the level of speculation because of the gaps in the historical record.

CATACHRESTIC TALES, OR WHAT IS A POLITICAL EVENT? (DELILLO)

Don DeLillo's *Libra* includes a character who represents this tendency to define conspiracy theory as a paranoid, imaginative way of viewing history. One of the narrative lines of DeLillo's 1988 novel is the story of Nicholas Branch, a CIA-affiliated researcher who is trying to write a sc cret history of the Kennedy assassination. Branch is figured as the one who has access to all available information at his fingertips, and who is therefore *supposed* to be able to bring all the relations together into a satisfying whole. With this kind of inside history, there should be no gaps in the historical record; all evidence should be transparent and should present an unobstructed view of the event. Nevertheless, Branch feels that, regardless of the amount of information he receives, the evidence leaves him in a state of indecision: while he would like to throw out seemingly unbelievable relations between historical events and actors, he remains fascinated by the *suggestiveness* of these significant associations. For instance, he cannot help but notice the significance of what he calls "a roster of the dead," that is, the "printout of the names of witnesses, informers, investigators, people linked to Lee H. Oswald, people linked to Jack Ruby, all conveniently and suggestively dead."[18] Branch notices that all of these people, who seem to have no immediate relations among themselves, nevertheless form a significant constellation when it is noted that they all connect to either Oswald or Ruby, and that they are all bound together in death. These two relations—connections to the main actors in the assassination and a connection to death—are suggestive,

Branch admits. They suggest a meaning that goes beyond random associations and beyond the random happenings of death. However, Branch
also notes that Congress already concluded that these relations are mere
coincidence: "In 1979 a House select committee determined there was
nothing statistically abnormal about the death rate among those who
were connected in some way to the events of November 22," the day
when Kennedy was shot (*L*, 57). For that reason, Branch feels the need to
resist the kind of significant associations that the 1979 House Select Committee on Assassinations found to be untenable, since these connections
remain mere speculation. The narrator notes, for example, that Branch
insists he "is writing a history, not a study of the ways in which people
succumb to paranoia" (*L*, 57). As in Hofstadter's account of the paranoid
style in politics, "paranoia," for Branch, names the illegitimate way of
making connections between events, connections that may be due to
mere coincidence. Paranoia names a possible way to explain the connection between events, but this possibility is immediately thrown out, dismissed as pathological, "paranoid."

The term "paranoia" therefore names an illegitimate way to account
for a specific historical event: the assassination of President Kennedy.
Paranoia must be rejected because it inevitably seeks to connect two *coincidental* events or historical actors. The problem is that this kind of significant association cannot be made without the imaginative leap, precisely
the mode of narration that the HSCA dismissed as "speculation." As the
Report stated, a conspiracy or a significant association would be based on
speculation, not evidence. In this way, paranoia (or "speculation") is figured as a mode of interpretation that necessarily lies outside the event
itself; it is an unnecessary, and therefore illegitimate, way to account for
the Kennedy assassination. This mode of narration—"paranoid style,"
"speculation," "conspiracy theory"—must be rejected by Branch because
it presumably cannot bear witness to the very happening of this important event.

It is for that reason that Branch becomes suspicious of coincidence,
that is, the seemingly random coinciding of two or more events. Toward
the end of the novel, the narrator notes: "Branch has become wary of
these cases of cheap coincidence. He's beginning to think someone is
trying to sway him toward superstition. He wants a thing to be what it is.
Can't a man die without the ensuing ritual of a search for patterns and
links?" (*L*, 379). The problem with coincidence, for Branch, is that *too
much* coincidence begins to feel significant, as if these accidental happenings were actually being controlled by a hidden figure. Branch therefore
feels overwhelmed by these seemingly accidental connections between
events and tries to throw out the meaningful interpretation of coincidence—what he calls "superstition"—as a ground for a history of the
assassination. In other words, Branch wants to see coincidence as simply
that: events that *happen* to fall together. To view the accident as simply an

accident (and not the sign of a significant relation) is to be left with only a dead body: *mere* coincidence would mean that death is equal to itself and means nothing other than what it is. Death, which here suggests a fullness of meaning, would not be related to a before and an after, and therefore would not be inscribed in a history: it is what it is. Branch would prefer to define coincidence, not as the significant coinciding of two or more events, but rather as the random occurrence of an unrelated happening. If "coincidence" were to name a *significant* association, then he would be faced again with the problem of paranoia: the formation of a speculative link or imaginative leap between events that might otherwise be viewed as simple random occurrences.

However, Branch's attempt to forget the dead by viewing death as an isolated occurrence ultimately fails. The dead begin to haunt him in his office, coming together in a conjuration that ends up paralyzing him with the power of this kind of conspiracy of the dead.[19] The narrator notes: "He feels disheartened, almost immobilized by his sense of the dead. The dead are in the room. . . . The case will haunt him to the end" (*L*, 445). This conjuration of the dead weighs down on Branch, producing the feeling of "growing old," as if the room itself were built specifically for his own fall into death (*L*, 445). Strangely, then, the attempt to avoid a paranoid reading of the dead only ends up converting Branch into one more dead body in this conjuration of the dead. It is therefore already clear that it is difficult to avoid the "paranoid style." After all, if the significant association between seemingly random events were indeed an aberration that had no bearing on the case, why does the paranoid style keep coming back like the dead, haunting and thereby infecting even those researchers who should have access to all possible information concerning Kennedy's death? If the paranoid style is labeled pathological by Hofstadter, why does he also insist that it is ineradicable? If the imaginative leap characteristic of the paranoid style were simply outside the event itself, why the *constant* need to conjure it away, to dismiss it as pathological (paranoid) or illegitimate (mere speculation)? Why, in DeLillo's novel, is this supposedly outside element continually infecting any attempt to understand the event itself?

If, for Hofstadter, the imaginative leap is applied to events after the fact by the conspiracy theorist, *Libra* ultimately reads the event of Kennedy's assassination as itself constituted by a necessary imaginative leap. In various interviews, DeLillo speaks of the way he tends to approach the event of Kennedy's assassination not as an origin moment that is fully present and therefore knowable, but rather as a lack that disrupts knowledge. In an interview given after the publication of *Libra*, DeLillo points out that the Kennedy assassination should be thought of as an event that is constitutively conspiratorial. The assassination presupposes conspiracy, he notes, not because he believes there was certainly a conspiracy to kill the president, but rather because the event is itself constituted by the imaginative leaps typical of conspiracy theories. He notes: "There's the shattering randomness of the event, the missing motive . . . the uncertainty we feel about the basic facts that surround the case—number of gunmen, number of shots and so on. Our grip on reality has felt a little threatened. Every revelation about the event seems to produce new levels of secrecy, unexpected links."[20] The assassination is, for DeLillo, defined by a lack that threatens the very meaning of reality. In other words, the assassination is clearly an *event* in the most rigorous definition of the word: a non-cognitive happening that cannot be linked to a before or an after except by a violent act of will.[21] On the one hand, it is certainly possible to say that the shot in Dealey Plaza annihilated the very reality of a community: "our grip on reality has felt a little threatened." On the other hand, in the very moment of stating that the reality of this community has been annihilated, DeLillo has recourse to a "we" that is strangely constituted by that constant threat of annihilation: he emphasizes the uncertainty "we" feel, the way "our" grip on reality has been threatened. If it is true that the reality of a community has been annihilated by the Kennedy assassination, nevertheless a new "we" emerges in the wake of the event, a "we" that paradoxically can no longer constitute itself as a fully present community since the very nature of relation has been unraveled by this event, that is, by the shattering randomness of the event. In fact, the aftermath of the event ends up producing a number of new links as a constant effect, but these new links are irreducibly illegitimate insofar as they remain secret and unexpected ("new levels of secrecy, unexpected links"). As an event, the Kennedy assassination is defined by a constitutive lack that nevertheless *produces* unexpected associations.

DeLillo's *Libra* then takes up the Kennedy assassination in order to ask: What is a political event? In other words, how does an event intervene in the very constitution of a community, a *polis*? Is a political event defined by the way it offers itself up for understanding, or is it rather defined by the way it precisely resists understanding? In what follows, I will argue that *Libra* is DeLillo's attempt to account for the way political events happen as a gap or lack that both suggests significant associations and resists any attempt to fix those relations into a believable narrative.

In the current "Author's Note" that serves as a short afterword to *Libra*, DeLillo notes that his novel is only possible because of the way the event is constituted by historical gaps: "Any novel about a major unresolved event would aspire to fill some of the blank spaces in the known record. To do this, I've altered and embellished reality, extended real people into imagined space and time, invented incidents, dialogues, and characters" (DeLillo, *Libra*, 458). *Libra* therefore takes place within the very blank spaces of the historical record, filling them up with various strategies of invention. Because the historical record is itself lacking, DeLillo's novel is, as he says, "a work of imagination" (*L*, 458). Imagination is what fills out the blank spaces that constitute the historical event of the assassination. However, an earlier Author's Note—now rescinded by the author—states that the novel should not be thought of as a mere fictional-ization of the event. Rather, the "fictional variations,"[22] as he calls his imaginary interpolations in an interview, should be viewed as an attempt to provide "refuge" for readers.[23] DeLillo uses the word "refuge" here because he hopes to provide "a way of thinking about the assassination without being constrained by half-facts or overwhelmed by possibilities, by the tide of speculation that widens with the years."[24] DeLillo's task is to think about the event, not by avoiding speculation, but precisely by taking speculation and the imaginative leap as a starting point. *Libra* will not try to avoid the gaps in the historical record, but will rather tell a story that incorporates those gaps as a structural principle, that is, through the construction of "significant associations" that come together unforeseeably. In other words, DeLillo posits the need for *imaginative leaps* in order to approach the event of Kennedy's assassination in the first place. As he notes: "This is a work of imagination" that aspires "to fill some of the blank spaces in the known record." His novel therefore does not seek to avoid the imaginative leaps that Hofstadter described as the essential characteristic of conspiracy theory. In fact, I will argue that *Libra* takes these curious leaps in imagination as constitutive of the event itself. Speculation is not simply a moment external to the event, but rather constitutes the event itself in all of its unknowability.

If a strange leap in imagination governs the event in the first place, this would seem to suggest that the conspiracy to kill the president is not as consciously motivated as one would normally believe. Of course, the beginning of DeLillo's novel seems to suggest otherwise: one of the major narrative threads of the novel details the machinations of a few current and former CIA operatives who intentionally seek to construct an event that would push the nation into a war against Castro's Cuba. In fact, the conspirators seem to know in advance what makes a good conspiracy. Win Everett, the mastermind behind the initial plan, wants to set up an orchestrated attempt on the life of the president, an attempt that crucially would just barely miss Kennedy, in order to set up the political condi-tions for a military intervention into Cuba. He tells his co-conspirators:

> We want to set up an attempt on the life of the President. We plan every step, design every incident leading up to the event. We put to-gether a team, leave a dim trail. The evidence is ambiguous. But it points to the Cuban Intelligence Directorate. Inherent in the plan is a second set of clues, even more unclear, more intriguing. These point to the Agency's [the CIA's] attempts to assassinate Castro. I am designing a plan that includes elements of both the American provocation and the Cuban reply. (*L*, 27–28)

The key to Win's plan is a double story that the orchestrated evidence will narrate. On the one hand, there will be the story of Cuba's involvement in the attempted assassination, thus leading investigations toward an outside enemy that can be localized and destroyed (Castro's Cuba). On the other hand, the conspirators will plant evidence of the CIA's own attempts to assassinate Castro, thus giving the story psychological motivation: Castro's attempt on the president will be seen as retaliation for the American attempts on Castro. The point of the plan is, according to Win, to "electrify" the American people to go to war with Cuba, "to get Cuba back" (*L*, 27, 28). Win's plot is thus deeply embedded within an economy of give and take: in return for a negative moment (the assassination attempt), the United States will get Cuba.

Win therefore plans to construct a kind of detective story based on a crime and an investigation that leads to a culprit and a motive. In other words, Win's plan simulates the double story that takes place in every detective fiction[25]: the story of the investigation will produce a second story, which is the story of the framed culprit (Castro) and his motivation (to retaliate against the CIA's assassination attempts against Castro). Win remarks: "It would all require a massive decipherment, a conversion to plain text. He envisioned teams of linguists, photo analysts, fingerprint experts, handwriting experts, experts in hairs and fibers, smudges and blurs. Investigators building up chronologies. He would give them the makings of deep chronos" (*L*, 78). The double structure that constitutes Win's plan is therefore not only important for its political effects, but also for its narrative strength: it produces that suspension of disbelief that constitutes poetic faith, as Coleridge put it.[26] Like a good detective story, Win's plan will lead the detectives after the event along a seemingly fortuitous path to the planned revelation at the end. And just as in any good detective story, apparent coincidences are in fact all part of the controlled series of incidents planned by the author in order to produce a believable fiction. As Win puts it: "You have to leave them with coincidence, lingering mystery. This is what makes it real. . . . Create coincidence so bizarre they have to believe it" (*L*, 147). The structure of the detective story is therefore mobilized as a way to create a controlled event that could be used to produce specific policy objectives.

However, the power of Win's story is predicated on the ability to *control all events*, to produce belief in a certain version of events. As Win makes clear, a crucial aspect of his plan is that the narrator (Win and his co-conspirators) should control every incident relating to the attempted assassination, even those incidents that will appear as coincidental. But this element of control is precisely what troubles Win: even in the moment of developing his plan, he worries that another element might enter into his plan, an element that is always there but that keeps itself hidden until the end. At first he thinks of this troubling element in a joking manner, and names it "coincidence," that is, a coincidence that remains outside of his control. He notices that the school where he teaches—and where the CIA placed him to look for potential agents—once changed its name to the College of Industrial Arts, which therefore gives it the acronym "CIA": "He was too tired to appreciate the irony, or coincidence, or whatever it was. There were too many ironies and coincidences. A shrewd person would one day start a religion based on coincidence, if he hasn't already, and make a million" (*L*, 79). This meditation on irony or coincidence ("or whatever it was") quickly leads Win to think about his general anxieties about the possibility of some accident that might befall him or his wife: "The house was a terrible place when his wife and child were not there, when they were late coming home in the car. He imagined accidents all the time. . . . It was all part of the long fall, the general sense that he was dying" (*L*, 79). What bothers Win is the idea of a sudden, uncontrollable fall that disrupts the normal plot of his life. This sudden fall—which is equated with the operations of irony and coincidence—is thematized as death or "dying."[27] Win is therefore bothered by all those possibilities related etymologically to the event of a fall (*cadere*, in Latin): the accident, the coincidence, and the long fall into decay.

These meditations on the event of a fall emerge directly from his admiring thoughts about his plan and later link up in Win's mind to a more troubling realization about the nature of all plots. He begins to sense that he is no longer in complete control of the incidents as planned, and that a worrisome degree of uncontrollable *coincidence* has entered into his plot. Win then theorizes this eventuality in terms of an element that is always there within any plot, even if it is momentarily invisible:

> Plots carry their own logic. There is a tendency of plots to move toward death. He believed that the idea of death is woven into the nature of every plot. A narrative plot no less than a conspiracy of armed men. The tighter the plot of a story, the more likely it will come to death. . . . He worried about the deathward logic of his plot. . . . He had a foreboding that the plot would move to a limit, develop a logical end. (*L*, 221)

Within a novel that necessarily must end with the assassination of President Kennedy, it is naturally assumed that Win is foreseeing the possibility that other characters might take matters into their own hands and actually assassinate the president. On the level of plot, this assumption is, of course, correct: for instance, T. J. Mackey plays his part in pushing the plot away from Win's control so that it would focus instead on the *successful* assassination of Kennedy (*L*, 219).[28] However, according to the rhetoric of Win's own meditations, what worries him is not specifically the death of Kennedy, but rather the way his plot carries within it an element of chance or coincidence. It is precisely this element—the event of a fall—that he fears: the ironic uncontrollability of his plot. Although he recognizes (retrospectively) that all plots are in fact constituted by this deathward logic (the tighter the plot, the more likely it will tend toward death), Win nevertheless fears this introduction of a "fall" within the narrative he has carefully constructed, since it suggests that he will *not* be

able to "design every incident leading up to the event." The inner structure of Win's tale is constituted—and troubled—by coincidence and
death.

The conspiracy to kill the president is therefore not constituted by
Win's conscious intentions, but rather by something within the plot that
is invisible but makes its presence felt.[29] This "something" is called at
times "coincidence," "irony," "death," but more often simply stands as
something unnamable ("or whatever it was"). This "something" is a destabilizing element in the plot (conspiratorial or narrative) that produces
unreliable relations, such as the link that eventually places the conspirators in relation to Lee Harvey Oswald. After all, there can be no conspiracy to kill President Kennedy without these "significant associations" between Oswald and his co-conspirators. These connections are not immediately given in *Libra*, and in fact there does not seem to be any necessary
reason for Oswald's role in the conspiracy to kill the president. The plot
of the novel emphasizes the way Oswald's life parallels but does not
immediately connect to the conspirators: *Libra* alternates between chapters dealing exclusively with Oswald's life and those that deal with the
machinations of conspirators. In effect, DeLillo's novel puts forth two
stories about the connection between the conspirators and Oswald. The
first story narrates the way people like David Ferrie consciously attempt
to seduce Oswald into the role of the assassin on behalf of the conspirators. This story line would therefore suggest that the conspiracy indeed
follows a plot that is conscious and intentional. However, Ferrie, the
character who most obviously connects the conspirators and Oswald, is
also the one who theorizes another story, a story that depends on something that is again called "coincidence." In fact, Ferrie is the student of
coincidence, the one who chases after coincidence in all of its unknowability. Speaking to Oswald, Ferrie notes that the conspirators are searching for "[s]igns that you exist. Evidence that Lee Oswald matches the
cardboard cutout they've been shaping all along. You're a quirk of history. You're a coincidence. They devise a plan, you fit it perfectly. . . .
There's a pattern in things. . . . I chase it discreetly" (*L*, 330). Ferrie goes
on to theorize the emergence of this "pattern" or "coincidence" as a disruptive event that nevertheless connects two narrative lines:

> Think of two parallel lines. . . . One is the life of Lee H. Oswald. One is
> the conspiracy to kill the President. What bridges the space between
> them? What makes a connection inevitable? There is a third line. It
> comes out of dreams, visions, intuitions, prayers, out of the deepest
> levels of the self. It's not generated by cause and effect like the other
> two lines. It's a line that cuts across causality, cuts across time. It has no
> history that we can recognize or understand. But it forces a connection.
> It puts a man on the path of his destiny. (*L*, 339)

As John Johnston has noted, this "third line" is more of a "superlinear event," a line that does not function in a linear manner.[30] Rather, this third line functions more as an interruption that disrupts the linearity of the other two lines. Nevertheless, it is the very force of this disruption that produces a connection between these two lines, between the machinations of the conspirators and the life of Oswald.

Libra therefore emphasizes the fact that there is nothing inherently significant about Oswald's life that would make it somehow necessary for the structure of conspiracy to take place. "Coincidence" should not be taken as another word for an intentional pattern that we have not *yet* understood. Rather, "coincidence" is, as Ferrie notes in his first meeting with Lee, the way "patterns emerge outside the bounds of cause and effect" (*L*, 44). There is therefore no inherent cause that would predispose Oswald for the role of assassin as an effect. Nevertheless, the very fact that Oswald is a "zero in the system," "a complete nothing, a zero person in a T-shirt," and a "cardboard cutout" sets the grounds for the event to take place (*L*, 151, 330, 421). As Patrick O'Donnell has noted in *Latent Destinies*, Oswald is an empty place-holder, a name that allows everything to fold into it, a cipher: "the fabrication of Oswald by many parties whose intentions are at odds might be thought of as a fractal equation: something that, empty in itself—a mere cipher—gathers to itself seemingly random elements reconstituted into fluid patterns typified by the phrase 'orderly disorder.'"[31] O'Donnell goes on to note that Oswald, as a zero, easily transforms into a one in the novel: "[Oswald] is also the paranoid subject at the center of the plot available both to himself and those who fabricate him as the receptacle of hermeneutic value, potentially full of meaning as the one to his own zero."[32] Although O'Donnell does not mention Paul de Man's "Pascal's Allegory of Persuasion," that 1981 essay clearly seems implied in O'Donnell's account here. As de Man notes, a zero is "radically not a number, absolutely heterogeneous to the order of number," but the naming of this absence of number inevitably turns the zero into a number, into a *one*.[33] De Man writes: "There can be no *one* without a zero, but the zero always appears in the guise of a *one*, of a (some)thing. The name is the trope of the zero. The zero is always *called* a one, when the zero is actually nameless."[34] Similarly, Oswald has no value (he's a zero in the system), but this absence, when named, performs crucial effects.

In fact we can go on to say that it is precisely Oswald's status as a zero in the system that allows the system to function in the first place. Ernesto Laclau, in "The Politics of Rhetoric," notes that de Man's reading of the zero in fact articulates the mechanism of politics, which he calls "hegemony." In the first place, he notes the paradox that the zero is outside the system (it is radically not a number). At the same time, however, the zero is necessary to articulate the system of numbers as a whole: it becomes a "one" that begins the enumeration of numbers. Similarly, hegemony is "the representation, by a particular social sector, of an impossible totality with which it is incommensurable."[35] Laclau clarifies this operation in *On Populist Reason*, where he notes that a leader like Juan Domingo Perón comes to represent multiple popular demands precisely when the leader's name is emptied out, as it were, in order to hold within it a variety of sometimes competing demands.[36] In this way, Perón's very emptiness (the fact that his discourses could appeal to so many different sectors) is also the condition of Perón's potential fullness: the name "Perón" is the "empty signifier" "of what is heterogeneous and excessive in a particular society" and thus "will have an irresistible attraction over *any* demand which is lived as unfulfilled."[37] "Perón" therefore names the possibility that all demands may one day be fulfilled.[38] Similarly, "Oswald," in DeLillo's *Libra*, is a zero that is both inside and outside the system: precisely because of his emptiness, he becomes a one that is able to signify a wide range of ideological positions. "Oswald," as a zero, comes to signify the very notion of lack; but by signifying in this way, "Oswald" becomes, in Laclau's words, "the signifier of the absent communitarian fullness."[39] "Lee," a zero that is inscribed within the system, becomes "Lee Harvey Oswald." Again, there is no necessary reason for this transformation to take place. As Laclau notes in his essay on de Man, "[w]hat is constitutive of a hegemonic relation is that its component elements and dimensions are articulated by contingent links."[40] Oswald becomes an "empty signifier" simply because of his availability as the right zero at the right time, but this availability predisposes him to play the role of a political agent. Lee's transformation into a political actor—his transformation into "Lee Harvey Oswald"—is therefore nothing but a coincidence: it is a contingent happening that might not have happened at all.

And yet the relation between Oswald and the conspirators does happen and is, in its own way, "inevitable," as Ferrie notes. Although Ferrie is a student of coincidence, he confesses his own amazement at the coincidence that forced the president's entourage to pass underneath Oswald's window at the Texas School Book Depository. He tells Oswald (whose name is here "Leon"):

> There's no such *thing* as coincidence. We don't know what to call it, so we say coincidence. It happens because you make it happen. . . . We didn't arrange your job in that building or set up the motorcade route. We don't have that kind of reach or power. There's something else that's generating this event. A pattern outside experience. Something that *jerks* you out of the spin of history. I think you've had it backwards all this time. You wanted to enter history. Wrong approach, Leon. What you really want is out. Get out. Jump out. Find your place and your name on another level. (*L*, 384)

As Ferrie explains, this "something else that's generating the event" is something we sometimes call coincidence, a movement that is in excess of what can be understood. This motive force has no name ("We don't know what to call it"); it is an unnamable excess that generates the connection between two "lines." The only thing that does determine Lee's place in this process is the fact that he was born, by coincidence, under the sign of Libra. This means, according to Ferrie, that Oswald is "[p]oised to make the dangerous leap" (*L*, 315). His unsteady and impulsive nature—again, determined by the coincidental fact that he was born a Libran—drives him toward the dangerous leap that would make the connection. One can say, in fact, that the event of Kennedy's assassination is constituted in the moment that Oswald takes this leap—what we could call, with Hofstadter, "a curious leap in imagination." The event takes place precisely when Oswald suddenly leaps into relation with the conspirators. The leap is not taken by the conspiracy theorist, after the event; rather, the leap is something internal to the event. Even though this leap is internal to the event, this does not mean that the leap happens consciously or intentionally. In other words, the actors are not fully present to their own actions: there is something else, something outside of their own experience, that allows a connection to happen, even though this connection is pure coincidence, even though the event happens through a contingent relation.

Libra therefore suggests that the event of Kennedy's assassination is itself the event of a leap. It is a moment that interrupts understanding, just as it interrupts any attempt to create a before and an after or a fluid line between cause and effect. For this reason it no longer makes sense to suggest, with Hofstadter, that conspiracy theories *introduce* "the curious leap in imagination . . . in the recital of events," or that this leap is "made" by the conspiracy theorist alone.[41] Hofstadter's claim is that this curious leap in imagination ends up positing a spurious relation between events. *Libra*, on the other hand, suggests that this spurious relation between events is inevitable, since the event itself was constituted by a leap. Conspiracy theory bears witness to this leap by naming precisely what cannot be named. As Ferrie remarks, we don't know what to call it, although it is evoked by various names in DeLillo's novel: coincidence, the long fall, death, or simply "whatever." Conspiracy theories are therefore formed through a catachresis, a term that rhetoricians use to refer to any leap of imagination that links something that has no name to another term that seems similar (for instance, the "leg" of a table, the "face" of a clock). Unlike a metaphor, which links two objects that both have names, a catachresis is often figured as an abuse: it stretches the meaning of one term in order to cover over a gap or lack (an object without a name). A catachresis cannot permanently cover over the gap, but rather forever marks the fact that we do not know how to name this gap or what to call it. The gap is therefore a constitutive condition of the catachresis, which thus always threatens the stability of the relation in the first place. Although we do not have another word to describe the "leg" of a table, the word "leg" is clearly inappropriate, since it does not allow the table to walk. For that reason, catachreses often fall into the realm of fantasy, producing monstrous figures like a table that dances or a mountain that speaks (since it has a face).[42] "Coincidence," in DeLillo's novel, is in this way a catachresis: it covers over a gap, not because we are temporarily unable to name the event, but rather because the event is itself defined by a leap that cannot be understood. Conspiracy theories "introduce" this imaginative leap (or catachresis) in order to bear witness to a gap that can never be fully covered over.[43]

In this way, DeLillo's novel suggests that this speculative leap is not something brought in from the outside to interpret the event; rather, the speculative leap is what defines the event in the first place. This is what Win theorized as the deathward logic of every plot. "Death" is a catachresis; as I suggested above, "death" names the moment when a narrative veers away from the control of the plotters. Although Win's conspiracy was indeed a coherent story that left nothing to chance, there was nevertheless another element, something that Win could not possibly plan for, that pushed his plot in a different direction, thereby ruining the very careful attempt to change official policy toward Cuba. DeLillo suggests that an event is constituted by a kind of "secret" that we can only *call* coincidence. But coincidence here simply means the way we lose control of all plots: to read the event of the Kennedy assassination would be to bear witness to the moment when the plot swerves away from any kind of conscious or intentional control. To read for this narrative moment—to read for the complot—is to read for the event that undoes the narrative as a whole. The speculative leap is therefore not only within the event, making it happen, but also prevents any full understanding of the event. In effect, the event remains, for all the agents involved, as something we can only call "coincidence." But this word "coincidence" is a catachresis: it is just the name we give to something that has no proper name. This event cannot be *properly* named, which means that, in order to do justice to the event, you would have to do justice to the unnamability of what happened. You would have to leave the story of the event with a leap.

Conspiracy theories therefore mark the emergence of an event that can never be properly named or resolved in a conclusive manner. This event, I will argue, is the moment of the political: it is the gap that prohibits any closure of the case. A political event is a happening for which no one is fully prepared and which no one is able to witness completely. This gap in knowledge demands that some sort of "name" be given to the event in order to cover over the gap, and it demands that this name be inscribed within a sequential narrative. However, this "name" will always have the appearance of an "imaginative leap," a speculative moment that cannot be fully grounded once and for all. Conspiracy theories bear witness to the way an event, if it is to be political, must contain an element that goes beyond the control of all agents. This means, then, that the imaginative leap must take place not only in conspiracy narratives, but in any political story. Even consensus politics (what Hofstadter would call the properly "political") necessarily bases itself on the constitutive gap that defines political events. After all, if it were possible to bring closure to an event, then negotiation would be a farce, since the solution would be already decided in advance (even if momentarily occluded). This situation is what Win hopes to construct in his plot to miss Kennedy and get Cuba back: the plan is to control all incidents to such a degree that the result follows mechanically from the cause. In such a situation, there is no political negotiation, no element that is beyond the total control of the actors. However, as DeLillo's novel demonstrates, every plot contains within it an element that goes beyond the conscious control of the plotters. This moment of "death" or "coincidence" is a necessary moment of politics: if an event is to produce any give-and-take at all, it must be an event that cannot be fully and conclusively controlled. This means that any political decision (that is, the construction of a new plot) would necessarily be a "leap" away from a prior narrative line; without this leap, there would never be any change of course and therefore no new events. In other words, without the imaginative leap, history itself would end, since there would be no way for an event to take place.

Conspiracy theory, I would like to argue, is the narrative form that responds to these gaps or leaps that constitute history. To bear witness to a political event is necessarily to construct a "conspiracy theory," that is, a story that incorporates the imaginative leap as part of its narrative technique. The disruption produced by the imaginative leap is thus also necessary, since without this disruption the leap would not seem like a leap at all, but would rather seem like some sort of natural connection. As Laclau notes, "if there is going to be hegemony, the traces of the contingency of the articulation cannot be entirely effaced."[44] In this way, DeLillo's novel suggests that the Kennedy assassination produces the grounds for political discourse, that is, it sets the stage for the possibility of a new hegemonic formation.

KENNEDY ASSASSINATIONS, OR WHAT (UN)MAKES A POLITICAL EVENT? (VOLPI)

In order to develop further the way a political story must incorporate the "imaginative leap," I would like to turn away from the United States and focus instead on a more recent historical moment in Mexico: the assassination of the presidential candidate Luis Donaldo Colosio in 1994. This event stands, according to the novelist Jorge Volpi, as a defining moment in the history of Mexico's political system and its ruling party at the time, the Institutional Revolutionary Party (PRI). For over sixty years, the transition from one president to another followed a stable and predictable trajectory: each president would hand-pick his successor in such a way that power always remained with the PRI. However, Colosio's candidacy had a hint of unpredictability from the beginning, since the incumbent president, Carlos Salinas, did not explicitly tap Colosio as his successor. On March 23, 1994, Colosio was shot while campaigning in Tijuana, a few weeks after he had pushed for reforms that promised to do away with all "vestigio de autoritarismo" (remnants of authoritarianism) in the country.[45] Volpi, a contemporary Mexican novelist whose works have been linked to the "Crack" movement, reads this assassination as a watershed moment in Mexican history, as it indicates a crisis that would shake the PRI-led regime that had ruled Mexico for over sixty years.[46]

While at first it might seem arbitrary to move from the assassination of John F. Kennedy in 1963 to an event and a context that are radically different (Mexico, 1994), nevertheless I would like to argue that the Kennedy assassination is strangely inscribed within the event of the Colosio assassination. This is not simply because, as Peter Knight has noted, the Kennedy assassination seems to be "an absent presence . . . a ghostly and unspoken moment of hidden causality" in accounts of contemporary events since the 1960s.[47] The point is not to argue that Mexican history should be subsumed under the umbrella of American history; it is not to say that the "cause" of Mexican history turns out to be American history after all. Rather, I would only like to point out the way the Kennedy assassination has indeed become a kind of shorthand in order to talk about any unresolved event that continues to fascinate the public imagination. As Volpi notes in his 1999 essay "La segunda conspiración" (The Second Conspiracy), "los primeros analistas del caso [de Colosio] no dudaron en establecer un paralelismo con los asesinatos de Álvaro Obregón en 1928 y de John F. Kennedy en 1963" (SC, 46) (the first analysts of the Colosio case quickly established a parallel with the assassinations of Álvaro Obregón in 1928 and John F. Kennedy in 1963). The case of Obregón parallels the Colosio case specifically in the way the word "conspiracy" very quickly circulated around the country. But the Kennedy assassination provides the most striking parallel for Volpi, since it was also plagued by the impossibility of coming up with a coherent narration of the crime. The Kennedy assassination therefore indeed stands as "an absent presence," a "ghostly" moment, precisely because this name ("the Kennedy assassination") tends to signify not only itself, but also any event that seems impossible to resolve due to the gaps in the historical record. My point now is not to suggest that the Kennedy assassination is exemplary in any way, but rather quite the opposite. I would like to suggest that a political event is always, in some way, a "Kennedy assassination." This means that a political event happens precisely as a constitutive gap that demands an imaginative leap, but this leap can never fully cover over the lack that constituted the event in the first place.[48]

In "The Second Conspiracy," Volpi notes that the lone gunman theory was posited officially by the government but undermined unofficially by a series of conspiracy theories that circulated throughout the country. As in the Kennedy case, the police immediately found a lone gunman (Mario Aburto) to blame for the murder. However, again like the Kennedy case, the Colosio case remained open despite official reports that supported this initial police investigation. Volpi notes that "la opinión pública se empeñó en leer todos los actos y declaraciones relacionados con el caso como parte de la macabra obra teatral planeada por los conjurados" (SC, 45) (public opinion insisted on reading all the acts and declarations related to the case as part of a macabre performance planned by the conspirators). For that reason, Volpi argues that the story of Colosio's assassination is really the story of two conspiracies. First, it is the story, based on rumors and unconfirmed reports, that there must have been a conspiracy to assassinate Colosio; an important corollary of this first conspiracy is that the plot probably involved members of the government and/or drug cartels. The second conspiracy is the story, based on the very gaps in the evidence, that there must have been a conspiracy to assassinate the truth about Colosio's murder after the fact and that this conspiracy again necessarily involves members of the government and other powerful interests. Volpi's essay is therefore an attempt to tell the story of how this second conspiracy has operated and how it has consistently undermined Mexican politics.

Like the Kennedy case, the Colosio case is defined by the fact that it is impossible to close or conclude. Unlike the traditional detective story, in which the detective finds the guilty party by assembling the clues into a believable story, the problem with the Kennedy and Colosio cases is the fact that "resulta casi imposible seguir los hilos de la conjura que condujo al atentado debido a la existencia de una *segunda* conspiración encargada de enturbiar las pistas, de manipular los testimonios, de silenciar a los inconformes; en unas palabras, de destruir la verdad" (SC, 46) (it is almost impossible to follow the threads of the conspiracy that led to the assassination due to the existence of a *second* conspiracy responsible for confusing the trail of clues, manipulating testimony, silencing those who did not cooperate: in short, destroying the truth). The Colosio case, like the Kennedy case before it, cannot be closed, due to the confusion surrounding the evidence itself. For Volpi, these gaps in the record are not accidental, but rather attest to the existence of a second conspiracy that has mysteriously erased the truth of what occurred during Colosio's assassination. Volpi even asserts that the second conspiracy has been well documented: the conspirators "construyeron una nueva espiral conspiratorial cuya existencia, a diferencia de la primera [conspiración], está plenamente documentada" (*SC*, 46) (constructed a new conspiratorial spiral whose existence, unlike the first conspiracy, is fully documented). This documentation can be viewed, Volpi insists, by anyone wishing to take a

closer look at the four official investigations into the case. Each investigation failed in one form or another because of contradictory evidence.
After the failure of the first investigation, Volpi explains that a new type
of investigation was instigated, what he calls *"metapoliciaco"* (meta-detec-
tive): the attempt to investigate the legitimacy of the previous investigations and to study the very fact that evidence is lacking (*SC*, 49). The goal
of the *metapoliciaco* is therefore not to look for evidence of an original
crime, but to study the lack of evidence, to investigate the fact of secrecy
rather than to investigate in order to reveal secrets. As the final report of
Olga Islas's investigation states, the faults or "deficiencias" in the investigation have left "algunas incógnitas que no ha sido posible aclarar cabal-
mente" (quoted in *SC*, 49) (some unknown factors that have not been
possible to clear up sufficiently). The second conspiracy emerges not as a
presence, but rather as the absence of knowledge, as so many *incógnitas*.
Volpi writes: "La segunda conspiración fue puesta en marcha, quién sabe
si por los propios autores de la anterior o por agentes ajenos a ella, para
ocultar y borrar los rastros de la primera" (*SC*, 49) (The second conspiracy was set in motion, who knows if it was by the authors of the first
conspiracy themselves or by agents unrelated to it, in order to hide and
erase the traces of the first conspiracy). Thus, when Volpi speaks of the
well-documented nature of the second conspiracy ("cuya existencia . . .
está plenamente documentada"), he is really referring to the *lack* of documentation that nevertheless bears witness to a conspiracy responsible for
the destruction of evidence.
   For Volpi, then, the "second conspiracy" can be said to emerge only
when there are insurmountable gaps in the record, that is, when it becomes impossible to arrive at any certainty regarding the perpetrators of
the first conspiracy. As Volpi's language suggests, this second conspiracy
is secondary to the first conspiracy; it should be thought of as a kind of
"meta-conspiracy," just as the investigation into previous investigations
is called *"metapoliciaco."* If the first conspiracy is the very visible spectacle
of Colosio's assassination (like the Kennedy assassination, it was caught
on film), the second conspiracy appears as a phantom: it produces effects
without producing itself, it "appears" as a withdrawal from the scene.
Therefore, even though Volpi would like to think of this conspiracy as
secondary, in fact it begins to define the entirety of the Colosio assassination. He writes: "Más que comprobar la conjura para asesinar al candidato, el Expediente Colosio demuestra la existencia de la segunda
conspiración, articulada a lo largo de estos cinco años, cuyo objetivo—
aparentemente cumplido—ha sido confundir la realidad al grado de hacer imposible cualquier certeza en torno al homicidio" (*SC*, 49) (Rather
than prove the existence of the conspiracy to assassinate the candidate,
the Colosio case demonstrates the existence of the second conspiracy,
articulated over the last five years, whose objective—apparently fulfilled—has been to confuse reality to such a degree as to make any cer-

tainty impossible concerning the homicide). Therefore, if the Colosio assassination is an event at all, then this "second conspiracy" is not secondary in relation to the event, but rather constitutes the event as such. After all, without the gaps in the evidence, without the inability to bring closure to the case, there would be no instability and the event would hardly register as an event at all. Volpi admits as much when briefly discussing another 1994 murder, the death of José Francisco Ruiz Massieu. This case was also linked to powerful figures such as President Salinas, but "se inscribió de modo más inmediato y previsible en una tragedia familiar" (SC, 45) (was inscribed immediately and foreseeably within a family tragedy), since the murder involved the ex-brother-in-law of the victim. Things are different, however, in the Colosio case, since "los disparos que segaron la vida del candidato continuaron—y continúan— siendo inexplicables y, por ello mismo, aterradores" (SC, 45) (the shots that cut down the life of the candidate continued—and continue—to be inexplicable and, for that very reason, terrifying). Thus, if it had been possible to bring narrative closure to the case, it would not have captured the imagination of the public (it would not have terrified the public). The Colosio case becomes a public narrative, not because it is necessarily "spectacular," but rather because it resists a clear view of the events and *therefore* becomes terrifying. The assassination demands to be narrated precisely because it resists narration, precisely because of the *"incógnitas"* (to use Islas's word) or non-cognitive happenings that mark the event as an event in the first place. If the uncertainty regarding the event could be erased, then in effect there would be no event to narrate. In this way, the Colosio case is defined at every moment as a "second conspiracy"; Colosio's murder is an event precisely because of the systematic erasure of certainty, not despite it.

In short, Volpi's essay meditates on the effects of uncertainty in politics. His explicit argument is that uncertainty is used as a tool by governmental forces in order to consolidate their power. For this reason, he insists that conspiracy theories always lead to a dictatorial use of power. He writes: "una conspiración siempre instaura, de hecho, un estado de excepción. Una vez que se la acepta, el Mal se vuelve ubicuo, amenazas desconocidas se precipitan sobre todos y, en un estado de zozobra, no queda más remedio que plegarse a las soluciones de quien ejerce el gobierno" (SC, 50) (in fact, a conspiracy always establishes a state of exception. Once accepted, the Evil becomes ubiquitous, unknown threats are leveled at everyone and, in a state of anxiety, there is no other choice but to submit to the solutions of those who are in control of the government). For Volpi, then, politics of the paranoid style leads inevitably to the state of exception, that is, the state in which the government finds it necessary to pass beyond the realm of legality in order to return the country to a state of "normality." A narration about conspiracy would therefore seem to be a step away from democratic politics, since the use of conspiracy theory seems to lead inevitably to the abuse of executive power. Volpi explains: "el uso de la teoría de la conspiración como *raison d'État* . . . [es] una sintomática inversión de su esencia, la conjura no es tanto un arma *contra* el poder como un arma *del* poder contra sus enemigos" (SC, 50) (the use of conspiracy theory as *raison d'État* . . . [is] a symptomatic inversion of its essence: conspiracy is not so much a weapon *against* power as it is a weapon used *by* power against its enemies). The use of conspiracy theory is therefore a perversion of the original meaning of a conspiracy (Volpi uses the Real Academia definition of "conspirar," "to conspire": "to unite against a superior or sovereign power" [SC, 45]). Instead of fighting against abuse, conspiracy theory is abuse itself, used against anyone who might be designated the enemy.

One can of course sympathize with this warning against the use of conspiracy theory. As Giorgio Agamben notes in *State of Exception*, Hitler's rise to power took place as an "exception" to the rule of law in the Weimar Republic. This exception was made possible by the circulation of a conspiracy theory that stated that the communists were responsible for the burning of the Reichstag. The resulting state of emergency allowed for "the physical elimination not only of political adversaries but of entire categories of citizens who for some reason cannot be integrated into the political system."[49] Clearly, then, conspiracy theory can be used to "solidizar a la sociedad con sus gobernantes para combatir a quienes, desde la oscuridad, alientan el desorden" (SC, 50) (unite society with the government in order to combat those who, from a position of obscurity, encourage disorder). However, the question at hand is not whether conspiracy theory can be used to institute a state of exception, but rather whether conspiracy theory is necessarily a perverted form of politics. Is conspiracy theory an inversion of the essence of "conspirar," and is this inversion *symptomatic* of the way this paranoid style overturns politics itself? Is the uncertainty produced by the "second conspiracy" a perversion of politics, or does it rather produce the necessary conditions for politics?

For Volpi, the uncertainty derived from conspiracy theory is merely a form of power that undermines democratic politics. Volpi insists that the ruling party used the Colosio case in order to argue that a hidden enemy was laying siege to the Mexican state and was therefore responsible for the evils of destabilization. After all, 1994 was not only the year of Colosio's assassination, but was also the year when the North American Free Trade Agreement (NAFTA) was signed, and, almost as a result, the year when the Ejército Zapatista de Liberación Nacional (EZLN) first began its campaigns in Chiapas. The Mexican state was besieged from all sides: from within (the EZLN), from without (North America), and from some other secret place, somewhere set apart but which nevertheless had the power to kill a PRI candidate for the presidency and cover up the traces of that crime. The "second conspiracy" therefore produces a dangerous destabilization that threatens the very survival of the Mexican state. Volpi notes that all certainty was sapped from the state, leading to the erosion of any claim to truth: "al minar la credibilidad de las investigaciones y al derruir cualquier posibilidad de recomponerlas, se garantiza el mejor de los mundos posibles: la incertidumbre. . . . [L]a segunda conspiración apostó por cancelar definitivamente la verdad y, por tanto, la construcción de una visión fiable de los hechos" (SC, 50) (by undermining the credibility of the investigations and by ruining any possibility of rectifying them, the second conspiracy guaranteed the best of all possible worlds: uncertainty. . . . [T]he second conspiracy pledged its firm commitment to cancel out the truth and therefore also any construction of a believable vision of the facts). The second conspiracy here carries out an impossible speech act: it pledged itself to (*apostó por*) the untruth. That is, Volpi is suggesting that we think of conspiracy theory—*la teoría de la conjura*—as also a theory of swearing-together (which is also *"la teoría de la con-jura"*), a theory concerning the performance of speech acts that are secret or that go awry. After all, if the second conspiracy swore with others (*conjurar*: to swear together, to conspire), this act of swearing should necessitate good faith and a commitment to truth. However, Volpi states that the specific goal of this *conjura*—this performative utterance that pledges or swears—is the commitment to cancel out the truth. The second conspiracy utters an impossible speech act, as if stating "I pledge truthfully to cancel out the truth." By using the phrase *"apostó por,"* Volpi highlights the way the second conspiracy is formed as a speech act that undoes the very performance of a speech act. The second conspiracy *happens*, as an event or performative utterance, in the very non-happening of the performance, in the canceling out of the possibility of its felicitous occurrence.[50]

This situation inevitably brings up the primary question again: Did the second conspiracy ever happen? That is, did the *conjura* "swear-together" (*conjurar*) at all if the swearing happened and did not happen at the same time? At this point, there can be no straight answer to this question, since the situation brings about a fundamental uncertainty as to what is happening in the first place. Volpi then interprets this uncertainty as the moment the country is fundamentally destabilized: "la teoría de la conspiración—y la incertidumbre derivada de ella—contaminó todos los aspectos de la vida pública del país" (SC, 51) (conspiracy theory—and the uncertainty derived from it—contaminated all aspects of the country's public life). At the same time, according to Volpi, the governing party (PRI) took advantage of this situation by selling itself as the party of stability, that is, the party that will bring back stability to a fallen world. By taking advantage of this period of instability, Volpi insists, the PRI won the elections but caused a complete meltdown of the system. He notes: "Acorralado por el miedo y la desconfianza, el país se precipitó en el peor de los escenarios posibles: el triunfo indiscutible del PRI que, más que garantizar la estabilidad, retardaba la transición democrática . . . [y provocó] la quiebra financiera" (SC, 51) (Trapped by fear and mistrust, the country fell into the worst scenario possible: the indisputable triumph of the PRI which, rather than guarantee stability, postponed the democratic transition . . . [and provoked] a breakdown of the financial system). Conspiracy theory is therefore the harbinger of doom in Volpi's narrative: it introduces a dangerous destabilization that ruined the country politically and economically. Even though the second conspiracy cannot carry out an uncontaminated speech act (a pledge or commitment secured by a notion of truth), it nevertheless promises a general destabilization of the system.

For Volpi, then, uncertainty seems to be an exception to the normal state of politics. This exceptional state then provokes a state of exception (the authoritarian regime) in order to get rid of this exception (uncertainty) and reinstall the normality of certainty. Volpi therefore thinks of this use of conspiracy theory as a fall from a politics of transparency. He goes on to suggest that the state of exception might even be necessary sometimes, but that more transparency is needed in those moments when illegality is necessary. For instance, he writes that it is time "construir los mecanismos necesarios para que el poder esté permanentemente vigilado aun en situaciones de emergencia" (SC, 51) (to construct the necessary mechanisms so that power will always be permanently watched even in situations of emergency). Through this constant vigilance of the government's actions it might be possible "preservar esa actitud que toda sociedad democrática debe exigir de quien la gobierna: su apuesta por la verdad" (SC, 51) (to preserve that attitude that every democratic society ought to demand of its government: its commitment to the truth). Here Volpi again uses a form of the phrase "*apostar por*," to pledge or be committed: "*su apuesta por la verdad.*" The idea now is that a government should only perform truly felicitous speech acts, as if to say: "I pledge truthfully to be committed to the truth." Any kind of "swearing-together" (*conjurar*) that might happen is to be done out in the open, transparently, so that it may become clear to the watchful eyes of the public that the agents involved are not crossing their fingers behind their backs. Transparency for Volpi would mean a speech act that performs exactly what it promises to enact. Therefore, instead of the opaqueness and uncertainty produced by conspiracy theory, Volpi recommends transparency, which will end the supposedly abnormal state of affairs: uncertainty. If the people have access to the truth, and if the government pledges itself truthfully to the truth, then there would be no reason for uncertainty and the destabilization that uncertainty brings with it.

However, another story emerges from Volpi's argument if one takes into account his earlier comments in the introduction to his essay. In order to set the stage for the Colosio case, Volpi notes that there were three important events in 1994 (NAFTA, EZLN, and the assassination of

Colosio) and that these events in effect "rompieron el equilibrio y la estabilidad que habían caracterizado al sistema político mexicano durante más de 60 años" (SC, 44) (broke the equilibrium and stability that had characterized the Mexican political system for over sixty years). Volpi explains what this destabilization means:

> Desde 1929, los regímenes revolucionarios habían intentado construir en México un sistema cuyas principales virtudes fuesen la permanencia, la estabilidad y la previsibilidad: los conflictos entre los diversos grupos de poder debían resolverse en el interior del partido oficial, bajo el estricto control del presidente de la República, en el cual estaba provisto de un poder cuya única limitación . . . era el tiempo de su mandato. (SC, 44–45)

> [Since 1929, the revolutionary regimes had attempted to construct in Mexico a system whose principal virtues were permanence, stability, and foreseeability: the conflicts between diverse groups of power ought to be resolved from within the official party, under strict control of the president of the Republic, who was given power that had only one limitation . . . his term of office.]

Volpi is therefore clear, at the beginning of his essay, that political "stability" in Mexico means the authoritarian, one-party rule in which all political conflicts become internal party disagreements that could be co-opted and defused. Volpi later admits that, "si algún mérito tuvieron los sacudimientos de 1994, fue terminar de una vez por todas con uno de los mitos fundadores del sistema político mexicano: la omnipotencia y omnisciencia del presidente en turno" (SC, 48) (if the shocks of 1994 had some merit, it was to finish off, once and for all, one of the founding myths of the Mexican political system: the omnipotence and omniscience of the president in power). Uncertainty, far from being the invitation to a state of emergency, is here the very moment when the authoritarian power of the state is undermined for the first time. In effect, the events of 1994 opened up the totalitarian system to the possibility of an outside voice that could not be so readily assimilated into the omnipotence and omniscience of the political system. For the first time, a crack developed in the system that allowed the myth of presidential power to be exposed for what it is: a narrative that could be countered with any number of other narratives. Uncertainty, in other words, is now figured as the potential beginnings of democracy, not its inevitable delay. In this way, politics does not come to an end with the "second conspiracy," but rather only begins at the moment of disequilibrium, at the moment when an event produces a radical destabilization. If the PRI was forced to use conspiracy theory as a mode of politics, this is not necessarily a unique weapon used only by power against its enemies. Rather, if the PRI is suddenly using conspiracy theory and, by doing so, courting destabilization, then this can only mean that this destabilization has already occurred, and that the ruling party is already no longer the well-entrenched institutional power that it had been for over 60 years.[51] Conspiracy theory is not the end of politics, but rather signals the fact that the PRI must use narrative to construct a new hegemony, rather than simply co-opting all conflict from within the party itself.

In effect, then, Volpi's struggle to define the place of uncertainty in politics ends with two stories. On the one hand, "La segunda conspiración" explicitly argues that conspiracy theory spells the end of politics. However, on the other hand, Volpi's essay contains another story that counteracts this explicit argument. This other story ultimately points out that the uncertainty produced by conspiracy theory in fact opens up politics by undermining the credibility of all official statements. If politics only begins with this destabilization, then this means that the basis of politics is not a commitment to truth (*apuesta por la verdad*), but is rather precisely the kind of contaminated speech act that both grounds itself on truth and performs the undoing of that truth (*apuesta por cancelar la verdad*). Politics is the act of pledging to cancel out the truth, not in order to create chaos, but rather to create the very conditions of political negotiation. In effect, there can be no politics without this essential destabilizing of truth as transparency. If political negotiation is to take place, truth must always be in some way obscured, hidden, or simply lacking in general. Volpi's essay, perhaps beyond the author's intentions, suggests that the "second conspiracy" is the name for the constitutive destabilization that is necessary if there is to be politics in the first place.[52]

We can therefore agree with Hofstadter when he notes that all conspiracy theories are constituted by a curious leap in imagination in the narration of events. However, this leap can no longer be theorized as an aberrant mode of representing political events, a view that allowed Hofstadter to dismiss conspiracy theories as merely "paranoid." Rather, conspiracy theory is a mode of storytelling that bears witness to the constitutive gap that marks an event as "political" in the first place. A political event—a "Kennedy assassination"—only takes place as a constitutive gap that both demands the imaginative leap and prohibits any attempt to turn that leap into a fixed relation. After all, an event only *happens* if it happens beyond the control of all agents involved; like Nicholas Branch's notion of conspiracy, a political event is a "rambling affair" that takes place, if it takes place at all, "due mainly to chance" (*L*, 441). If the event were completely under someone's control, it would not appear as an event, but rather as merely a programmable stage in a well-oiled machine. An event must therefore include some uncontrollable or unforeseeable element if it is to be recognized as an event in the first place; there must be a constitutive gap or leap in its unfolding. Insofar as a happening is truly an event, then this means that the event entails the loss of intelligibility. To quote DeLillo again: "There's the shattering randomness of the event, the missing motive . . . the uncertainty we feel about the basic facts that surround the case."[53] An event of this sort must always produce a demand that cannot be fulfilled or satisfied by definition. At the very least, an event inevitably produces the demand that it be witnessed and recognized, that is, that the event be made intelligible. The shattering randomness of the event must be reinserted into an economy that would trade a loss for a gain: the loss of intelligibility must be converted into an understanding of what happened. In this way, to meet the demand of the event (to recognize the event as something important that happened), it would be necessary to give back what has been lost: the event's intelligibility. But this demand to understand the event runs up against the event's own resistance to understanding. In other words, to make the event intelligible is to miss the eventness of the event, the way the event happens by withdrawing from sense, by remaining "secret" (in the sense of "set apart," inaccessible). Thus, to bear witness to the eventness of the event, it is necessary to bear witness to this gap in understanding, that is, the way relations come undone in the happening of the event: the shattering randomness of the event. For this reason, we can say that conspiracy theory is a mode of storytelling that bears witness to the happening of an event, since the imaginative leap that constitutes conspiracy theory fills in the gap in a wholly contingent way. Conspiracy theories cover over the gap by "introducing" the imaginative leap in the narration of events.

In this way, the study of conspiracy theory necessarily leads to the question of the political event. However, the question is no longer, What is a political event? Rather, the question now is: What (un)makes a political event? That is, the question now needs to take into account the constitutive gap that both constitutes an event as political in the first place and prevents a full understanding of the event. This lack of understanding (the *incógnita*, the mystery, the secret) is not a temporary state of our understanding of the event, such that, with time, we would eventually come to a full understanding of the event. Rather, the lack of intelligibility constitutes the event as such, so that if the event were finally fully understood, it would no longer be an event in the first place. For that reason, we can say that events always create *political demands*. In the aftermath of the assassinations of Kennedy and Colosio, the demand could be summarized as: What actually happened, and what steps has the government taken to address this crime? This demand would have disappeared if the government had been able to fulfill the demand by closing the cases in a convincing manner. To close a case is to present a believable narrative, regardless of how horrible the narrative is. In the case of Massieu, who was assassinated the same year as Colosio, a convincing narrative was presented that inscribed the murder as a familial affair (as dysfunctional as this "family" might have been). However, if a convincing narrative cannot be articulated, the murder becomes truly terrifying, not because of the content of the story, but rather because the story cannot be fully told. In this case, the demand for the "truth" cannot be met. Any narrative that tries to answer the demand finds itself blocked, such that the demands continue to emerge like a ghost that cannot be put to rest. In a sense, then, there is no such thing as a political crime that has been *resolved*, since to resolve a political crime would erase the political nature of it. Instead of a *political* crime, it would simply be a crime that has been resolved. The assassinations of Kennedy and Colosio are therefore political events, in the sense that the demand that the crimes be resolved through narrative closure becomes impossible to fulfill. The political event is constituted by the way it presents a demand that can never be fully satisfied. In other words, the demand is not articulated by an already constituted subject; rather, the gap in knowledge is itself the demand: all political demands have the appearance of this gap that can never be fully resolved or covered over.

This situation of a demand that cannot be handled in an institutional way is what Ernesto Laclau calls a "popular demand." In the first place, Laclau explains, the smallest unit of analysis is the social demand, which is not the expression of an already constituted agent; rather, the subject is constituted in the articulation of particular social demands. These demands are always based on some sort of lack, and the point of the demand is to ask for this lack to be rectified by a particular social institution. In *On Populist Reason*, Laclau explains that a *popular* demand is one that cannot be fulfilled by the institutions and, for that reason, connects with a plurality of other demands, thereby creating equivalential links between various demands.[54] The only common element amongst those demands is their shared opposition to the institutional power. In fact, Laclau uses the PRI as an example of the difference between partial demands that can be handled institutionally and larger demands that the system cannot handle: "In Mexico, during the period of hegemony of the Partido Revolucionario Institucional (PRI), political jargon used to distinguish between the punctual demands which the system could absorb in a *transformistic* way (to use the Gramscian term) and what was called *el paquete* (the parcel)—a large set of simultaneous demands presented as a unified whole. It was only with the latter that the regime was not prepared to negotiate—they were usually met with ruthless repression."[55] A popular demand refers to the way a large set of unfulfillable demands (*el paquete*) presents a threat to the regime. The *paquete* presents itself as a threat because the demands cannot be satisfied *within the system*. This momentary interruption therefore posits the experience of a generalized lack that destabilizes the social as such. As Laclau notes, this "experience of a *lack*, a gap which has emerged in the harmonious continuity of the social," is the decisive moment, since "the construction of the 'people' will be the attempt to give a name to that absent fullness."[56] This attempt to give a name to something that is constitutively absent—catachresis—then creates a narrative that pits the "people" against the institutional forces that are against the people. This moment, Laclau argues, is the moment of politics: "the construction of the 'people' is the political act *par excellence*—as opposed to pure administration within a stable institutional framework."[57] It is for this reason that Laclau places so much emphasis on the moment when the social space becomes destabilized: "Without this initial breakdown of something in the social order—however minimal that something could initially be—there is no possibility of antagonism, frontier, or, ultimately, 'people.'"[58] Therefore, the destabilization produced by the "second conspiracy" is not at all the end of politics, as Volpi explicitly suggests, but is rather the inauguration of politics, the opening of political demands. Politics is what threatens the PRI, and for this reason it was necessary for the party to enter into the political fray with its own version of a conspiracy theory.

In this way, conspiracy theories respond to political demands that can no longer be managed within institutional and stable bounds. The primary technique of conspiracy theory is indeed the imaginative leap which seeks to name the gap articulated by the political demand in the first place. This catachresis (the naming of something that has no proper name) is constitutively unstable, since it can never *properly* name the gap. At the same time, however, there would be no politics without this act of naming, that is, without this *contingent* leap that brings together two or more events into a secret configuration or a significant association. After all, if relations were completely fixed and legitimate, the narrative could be fully closed off and the demand could therefore be handled from within the institutional group. But if an event is to remain political, there must be this essential gap that is continuously named and renamed, one catachresis after another, without ever filling up the gap in a finalized or authoritative way.[59] In a sense, then, conspiracy theories "repeat" the constitutive gap that defines all political events by articulating the catachrestic leap. This means, then, that a political event is one that necessarily keeps happening, that never stops happening, even if the content of the event changes. For that reason I have insisted that the Colosio assassination is an unintentional repetition of the Kennedy assassination: even when the theme of the conspiracy theory is no longer the Kennedy assassination, even when it is someone else's assassination entirely (Colosio's, for instance), even then it is still a "Kennedy Assassination." The latter is the name for the way a political event happens as a radical leap that defies understanding. A political narrative must therefore have the form of a conspiracy theory if it is to respond to political demands, that is, if it is to remain a political narrative at all.

NOTES

1. Don DeLillo, *Running Dog* (New York: Vintage Books, 1978), 58.
2. Ibid.
3. Ibid., 80.

4. "Our experience suggests too that, while [the paranoid style] comes in waves of different intensity, it appears to be all but ineradicable" (Richard Hofstadter, *The Paranoid Style in American Politics and Other Essays* [New York: Vintage Books, 1967], 6).

5. Jodi Dean, in *Aliens in America*, argues that conspiracy theories are a necessary form of politics specifically during the age of the Internet. Before the Internet, she suggests, consensus politics might have been possible. But after the culture of the hyperlink, traditional politics can no longer be practiced. She writes: "Historians like Hofstadter write about conspiracy fears and paranoid styles from the presumption of a normal political and social field as one that is constituted by compromise, inclusion, debate, security, and constancy. The terms of politics, the players, the rules, and the ethical position of 'each' of the two sides (for the options are necessarily binary) are clear and known. Subterfuge and secrecy can only be distortions in this world; they aren't necessary. This is a dangerous presumption today. Such a presumption covers over awareness of the invasive, the insecure, the illusory, exposed by abduction, accessible on the Net" (Jodi Dean, *Aliens in America: Conspiracy Cultures from Outerspace to Cyberspace* [Ithaca, NY: Cornell University Press, 1998], 145). While I will agree that the possibility of making connections is a crucial aspect of politics, my argument maintains that the need for links is not only necessary during the age of the Internet, but rather is a condition of political discourse as such. In fact, as I will suggest, even consensus politics would not be possible without the constitutive gap that continually undermines any certainty.

6. Hofstadter, *The Paranoid Style in American Politics*, 5, 6.

7. Mark Fenster, *Conspiracy Theories: Secrecy and Power in American Culture* (Minneapolis: University of Minnesota Press, 1999), 18.

8. Ibid., 21.

9. Hofstadter, *The Paranoid Style in American Politics*, 29.

10. Ibid.

11. Ibid., 37.

12. Ibid., 37–38.

13. It is useful to note that this charge against conspiracy theory is repeated in critical accounts of literary conspiracy narratives. For instance, John A. McClure insists that DeLillo's novels celebrate conspiracies only to reveal that "the new intricacies [promised by conspiracy narratives] are ultimately soulless, the new institutions debased. . . . The jungle of technical and human systems possesses only a spurious and superficial sublimity: it's the stuff of perverse fascinations and cheap thrills rather than awe and wonder" (John A. McClure, "Postmodern Romance: Don DeLillo and the Age of Conspiracy," in *Introducing Don DeLillo*, ed. Frank Lentriccia [Durham, NC: Duke University Press, 1991], 106). McClure therefore reads the motif of conspiracy in DeLillo's novels as a false promise, an empty or debased mystery, "inferior to the effects produced by truer mysteries, more realistic romances" (106). McClure concludes that, ultimately, DeLillo ends up "dismissing conspiracy—the activity, the mode of speech it sponsors, the genre" (115). However, I will argue that conspiracy theories must necessarily include precisely this kind of double gesture: the promise of "new intricacies" and the sense that these systems are "ultimately soulless." If DeLillo's novels both celebrate and repudiate conspiracies, this double gesture alone does not distance his novels from the form of conspiracy theory.

14. Peter Knight, *The Kennedy Assassination* (Jackson: University Press of Mississippi, 2007), 69.

15. *Report of the Select Committee on Assassinations of the U.S. House of Representatives* (H.R. Rept. No. 95-1828, Part 2, 95th Cong., 2nd Sess. [1979]), 96. All quotes from the HSCA report refer to the print edition, as posted online on the webpage of the U.S. National Archives and Records Administration.

16. Ibid., 97.

17. Ibid., 98.

18. Don DeLillo, *Libra* (New York: Penguin Books, 1988), 57. Hereafter cited in text as *L*.

19. As Derrida remarks in *Specters of Marx*, the French word "conjuration" can mean, among other things, the evocation of the dead as well as the notion of a conspiracy. On the one hand, "conjuration" means "the magical incantation destined to *evoke*, to bring forth with the voice, to *convoke* a charm and a spirit. Conjuration says in sum the appeal that causes to come forth *with the voice* and thus it makes come, by definition, what *is not there* at the present moment of the appeal. This voice does not describe, what it says certifies nothing; its words cause something to happen" (Jacques Derrida, *Specters of Marx: The State of the Debt, the Work of Mourning, and the New International*, trans. Peggy Kamuf [New York: Routledge, 1994], 41). On the other hand, a "conjuration" is also "an alliance, to be sure, sometimes a political alliance, more or less secret, if not tacit, a plot or a conspiracy. It is a matter of neutralizing a hegemony or overturning some power. . . . In the occult society of those who have sworn together [des conjurés], certain subjects, either individual or collective, represent forces and ally themselves together in the name of common interests to combat a dreaded political adversary, that is, also to conjure it away" (47–48).

20. Don DeLillo, *Conversations with Don DeLillo*, ed. Thomas DePietro (Jackson: University Press of Mississippi, 2005), 103.

21. See Paul de Man's discussion of the positing power of language in his essay "Shelley Disfigured" (in *The Rhetoric of Romanticism* [New York: Columbia University Press, 1984]). De Man asserts that Shelley's poem "warns us that nothing, whether deed, word, thought, or text, ever happens in relation, positive or negative, to anything that precedes, follows, or exists elsewhere, but only as a random event whose power, like the power of death, is due to the randomness of its occurrence" (122). De Man suggests that the randomness of the event demands recuperative attempts to insert the event into a sequential narrative. For that reason, he asks: "How does a speech act become a trope, a catachresis which then engenders in its turn the narrative sequence of an allegory? It can only be because we impose, in our turn, on the senseless power of positional language the authority of sense and of meaning. But this is radically inconsistent: language posits and language means (since it articulates) but language cannot posit meaning; it can only reiterate (or reflect) it in its reconfirmed falsehood" (117).

22. DeLillo, *Conversations*, 58.

23. Don DeLillo, *Libra* (New York: Viking, 1988), 458.

24. Ibid.

25. As I noted in the last chapter, Tzvetan Todorov's "The Typology of Detective Fiction" argues that all detective fiction tells two stories, "the story of the crime and the story of the investigation." Todorov goes on to note that "the first—the story of the crime—tells 'what really happened,' whereas the second—the story of the investigation—explains 'how the reader (or the narrator) has come to know about it'" (Tzvetan Todorov, *The Poetics of Prose*, trans. Richard Howard [Ithaca, NY: Cornell University Press, 1977], 44, 45).

26. See Samuel Taylor Coleridge's *Biographia Literaria*, in which he emphasizes "that willing suspension of disbelief . . . which constitutes poetic faith" (Samuel Taylor Coleridge, *Biographia Literaria*, eds. James Engell and W. Jackson Bate [Princeton, NJ: Princeton University Press, 1983], II 6).

27. Paul de Man, in "The Rhetoric of Temporality," notes that irony is often associated with the event of a sudden fall. Speaking specifically of Charles Baudelaire, de Man writes: "the division of the subject into a multiple consciousness takes place in immediate connection with a fall. The element of falling introduces the specifically comical and ultimately ironical ingredient. At the moment that the artistic or philosophical, that is, the language-determined, man laughs at himself falling, he is laughing at a mistaken, mystified assumption he was making about himself. . . . The ironic language splits the subject into an empirical self that exists in a state of inauthenticity and a self that exists only in the form of a language that asserts the knowledge of this inauthenticity" (Paul de Man, "The Rhetoric of Temporality," in *Blindness and Insight: Essays in the Rhetoric of Contemporary Criticism* [Minneapolis: University of Minnesota

Press, 1983], 214). In *Unclaimed Experience,* Cathy Caruth relates de Man's rhetoric of falling to his discussion of reference: "What theory does, de Man tells us repeatedly, is fall; and in falling, it refers" (Cathy Caruth, *Unclaimed Experience: Trauma, Narrative, and History* [Baltimore: Johns Hopkins University Press, 1996], 90). Falling here becomes an indirect mode of reference, that is, a way of bearing witness to an event that cannot be coherently narrated or controlled.

28. This moment when the plot moves away from Win's control is figured as a leap, a term that will become even more important when I discuss Oswald: "The second leap was Mackey's. . . . They had to take it one more step" (*L,* 219). It should be noted that Win's original idea is also figured precisely as a leap: "It was [Win] Everett who'd made the leap" to orchestrate a surgical miss (*L,* 219). DeLillo thus suggests that any radical turn from a narrative line is necessarily a leap away from that narrative and therefore potentially uncontrollable: a leap can always turn into a fall.

29. Many critics suggest that Win's lack of control over the plot he has set in motion necessarily indicates that *Libra* is repudiating conspiracy theory as a way to account for the Kennedy assassination. Skip Willman, for instance, notes that DeLillo "departs from the paranoid position by emphasizing the *illusion* of control and mastery that supports the social effectiveness of the CIA" (Skip Willman, "Traversing the Fantasies of the JFK Assassination: Conspiracy and Contingency in Don DeLillo's *Libra,*" *Contemporary Literature* 39.3 [Fall 1998]: 414; hereafter cited as "Traversing"). While it is certainly true that control turns out to be an illusion (Win Everett is the first to admit this), my argument is that *Libra*'s emphasis on plots (both narrative and conspiratorial) and not individual intention suggests that DeLillo is rethinking the intentional structure of conspiracy theory. In effect, DeLillo demonstrates that conspiracy theories are not stories about intentional acts by fully aware agents. Rather, conspiracy theories trace the way political communities are formed precisely because agents lose control of the stories they tell.

30. John Johnston, *Information Multiplicity: American Fiction in the Age of Media Saturation* (Baltimore: Johns Hopkins University Press, 1998), 193.

31. Patrick O'Donnell, *Latent Destinies: Cultural Paranoia and Contemporary U.S. Narrative* (Durham, NC: Duke University Press, 2000), 52.

32. Ibid., 53.

33. Paul de Man, "Pascal's Allegory of Persuasion," in *Aesthetic Ideology,* ed. Andrzej Warminski (Minneapolis: University of Minnesota Press, 1996), 59.

34. Ibid.

35. Ernesto Laclau, "The Politics of Rhetoric," in *Material Events: Paul de Man and the Afterlife of Theory,* ed. Tom Cohen et al. (Minneapolis: University of Minnesota Press, 2001), 244.

36. Laclau takes the social demand as the basic unit of political practice in his study of populism. This means that "political practices do not *express* the nature of social agents but, instead, *constitute* the latter. . . . To put it in slightly different terms: practices would be more primary units of analysis than the group—that is, the group would only be the result of an articulation of social practices. If this approach is correct, we could say that a movement is not populist because in its politics or ideology it presents actual *contents* identifiable as populistic, but because it shows a particular *logic of articulation* of those contents—whatever those contents are" (Ernesto Laclau, *On Populist Reason* [London: Verso, 2005], 33).

37. Ibid., 108.

38. Ibid., 216–17.

39. Ernesto Laclau, "Why Do Empty Signifiers Matter to Politics?" in *Emancipation(s)* (London: Verso, 1996), 43.

40. Laclau, "The Politics of Rhetoric," 237.

41. Hofstadter, *The Paranoid Style in American Politics,* 37.

42. In "The Epistemology of Metaphor," Paul de Man links monsters to catachreses: "They are capable of inventing the most fantastic entities by dint of the positional power inherent in language. They can dismember the texture of reality and reassemble

it in the most capricious of ways, pairing man with woman or human being with beast in the most unnatural shapes. Something monstrous lurks in the most innocent of catachreses: when one speaks of the legs of the table or the face of the mountain, catachresis is already turning into prosopopoeia, and one begins to perceive a world of potential ghosts and monsters" (Paul de Man, "The Epistemology of Metaphor," in *Aesthetic Ideology*, ed. Andrzej Warminski [Minneapolis: University of Minnesota Press, 1996], 41–42). Thomas Keenan develops de Man's emphasis on catachresis in relation to Karl Marx's *Capital*. He suggests that the passage from interpretation to change is political precisely insofar as this passage cannot be conclusively grounded except by "the wild, random, uncontrolled, and utterly arbitrary positing of a status, a relation or a name to be related" through the trope of catachresis (Thomas Keenan, *Fables of Responsibility: Aberrations and Predicaments in Ethics and Politics* [Stanford, CA: Stanford University Press, 1997], 132). For a more specific way that catachreses are used in political discourse, see Viviane K. Namaste's "The Use and Abuse of Queer Tropes," in which she emphasizes the way the name "queer" has been used catachrestically by queer-punk culture: "queer" does not refer to homosexuals in general, but rather takes place as a political act that works against heterosexism. Namaste concludes: "catachrestic deployments of the word draw our attention not merely to what the word 'queer' denotes. Rather, these examples ask us to think about how that sign circulates within various communities—queer, punk, lesbian, gay—and to what political ends" (Viviane K. Namaste, "The Use and Abuse of Queer Tropes: Metaphor and Catachresis in Queer Theory and Politics," *Social Semiotics* 9.2 [August 1999]: 232). For a now-canonical discussion of the way gender is performed, see Judith Butler's "Performative Acts and Gender Constitution."

43. It should be noted that readings of DeLillo's *Libra* often posit a strict difference between conspiracy theories and contingency theories. This dichotomy has led some critics to claim that *Libra* is less a novel about conspiracies than it is a novel about the effects of contingency on history. For instance, Frank Lentricchia notes: "though [De-Lillo] lays out a paranoid plot for our delectation, one calculated to titillate the left . . . DeLillo, by his insistence on the chancy appearance of Oswald, presses us to rethink the question of Oswald outside the framework of conspiracy" (Frank Lentricchia, "*Libra* as Postmodern Critique," in *Introducing Don DeLillo*, ed. Frank Lentriccia [Durham, NC: Duke University Press, 1991], 203). Skip Willman expands on Lentricchia's reading by explaining how it might be possible to differentiate between conspiracy theory and contingency theory: "Conspiracy theories posit a 'fallen' society, the failure of which to constitute itself as a harmonious whole must be explained; the conspiratorial narrative resurrects the possibility of society even as it traces its demise through the agency of hidden forces. Contingency theories, on the other hand, envision a smoothly functioning social system subject only to accidental deviations and deformations introduced by external, corrupting forces" (Skip Willman, "Art after Dealey Plaza: DeLillo's *Libra*," *MFS: Modern Fiction Studies* 45.3 [Fall 1999]: 624). Although Willman notes, in an earlier essay, that contingency theory and conspiracy theory are indeed similar in that they "explain the failure of society to constitute itself as a harmonious whole," he nevertheless insists on their fundamental difference so that he can posit a dialectical relationship between the two: "The difficult task accomplished by DeLillo in *Libra* consists in holding conspiracy and contingency in dialectical tension and examining the ways in which each undermines the other" (Willman, "Traversing," 407, 408). However, I would argue that the difference between contingency theory and conspiracy theory is not as clear-cut as Willman suggests here. Both narratives posit an "outside" force (secret or accidental) that is introduced into the interior of society, thereby ruining the harmonious fullness of society. In both, there is an illegitimate force that destabilizes an established authority. Willman, however, would like to separate these two theories or narratives, so that he can argue that *Libra* combines conspiracy theory and contingency theory through the figure of astrology, which takes from conspiracy theory the idea of a hidden force that guides historical causality, while negating "the malignant valence behind this mysterious agency"

(Willman, "Art After Dealey Plaza," 635). However, I would argue, with Ricardo Piglia, that the clandestine nature of the hidden force points to its illegitimate nature (it is not authorized to speak fully), which therefore already suggests a "malignant" effect, even if there is no conscious motivation behind this effect. As Piglia notes, "el complot . . . es ilegal porque es secreto; su amenaza implícita no debe atribuirse a la simple peligrosidad de sus métodos sino al carácter clandestino de su organización" (Ricardo Piglia, "Novela y complot," *Quimera* 280 [March 2007]: 46) (conspiracy . . . is illegal because it is secret; the implicit threat of conspiracy should not be attributed to the simple dangerousness of its methods, but rather to the clandestine character of its organization).

44. Laclau, "The Politics of Rhetoric," 237.

45. Luis Donaldo Colosio, quoted in Jorge Volpi, "La segunda conspiración," *Letras libres* (March 1999): 48. All translations from Volpi's essay are my own. Hereafter cited in text as SC.

46. For an overview of the *"generación de 'crack,'"* including the *"Manifiesto Crack,"* see *Crack: Instrucciones de uso*, ed. Ricardo Chávez Castañeda (Mexico City: Mondadori, 2004).

47. Knight, *Conspiracy Culture*, 77.

48. It is useful to refer here to the way that Jean-François Lyotard has similarly theorized the "event" in relation to a violent death. Geoffrey Bennington notes that Lyotard first begins to theorize the "event" in an analysis of the story told by the Renault motor company after the death of Pierre Overney during a demonstration in 1972. Lyotard writes: "If this death is an event, this is *above all* as a tensor or intense passage" (Lyotard, quoted in Geoffrey Bennington, *Lyotard: Writing the Event* [New York: Columbia University Press, 1988], 109). Bennington explains: "In other words, says Lyotard, Overney's death is an 'event' not because of its causes and effects, but because of its senselessness or *inanity*: despite the efforts of the Renault company's narrative, and even of the demonstration's organisers, Overney's death is an event insofar as it refuses to be absorbed into the *order* of a classical narrative, brought to book in a narrative *account*, its tension exchanged for other tensions" (Bennington, *Lyotard: Writing the Event*, 109).

49. Giorgio Agamben, *State of Exception*, trans. Kevin Attell (Chicago: University of Chicago Press, 2005), 2.

50. J. L. Austin laboriously sought to elucidate how a speech act (an utterance that performs what it utters) can become "infelicitous," that is, how it might go awry. One such infelicity is the promise stated by someone who has no intention of carrying out the promise (J. L. Austin, "Performative Utterances," in *Philosophical Papers*, ed. J. O. Urmson and G. J. Warnock [Oxford: Oxford University Press, 1979], 239). Austin specifically brings up the phrase "I promise that I shall be there, but I haven't the least intention of being there," and notes: "you can of course perfectly well promise to be there without having the least intention of being there, but there is something outrageous about saying it, about actually avowing the insincerity of the promise you give. . . . [It] makes a peculiar kind of nonsense" (248). It is a peculiar kind of nonsense because the speaker has both promised to be there and stated that she will not be there. I will return to this strange speech act that both produces an event and interrupts an event: both the happening and non-happening of a speech act.

51. The historian Enrique Krauze notes that the Zapatista movement and the Colosio case "broke the system" (Enrique Krauze, *La presidencia imperial: Ascenso y caída del sistema político mexicano (1940–1996)* [Barcelona: Tusquets Editores, SA, 1997], 478). For this reason, he insists that the PRI's electoral triumph in 1994 was "clearly a vote against violence, not in support of the system" (478–80).

52. Volpi has also written a novel, *La paz de los sepulcros* (Mexico City: Editorial Planeta Mexicana, S.A., 2007), that narrates the investigation into a political murder that resembles the Colosio case. In fact, in the 2007 reissue of the novel, Volpi suggested that *La paz de los sepulcros* was rewritten to avoid a close correspondence with reality. The first version was written in 1994 *before* Colosio's murder, and this earlier

version narrated the assassination of a PRI candidate for the presidency. Given the obvious similarities between real life and his fiction, Volpi found it necessary to change the plot so that it would not resemble so closely the Colosio case. Because *La paz de los sepulcros* deals explicitly with the relation between politics and the corpse, I will leave Volpi's novel for a later study, tentatively entitled *The Political Corpus*.

53. DeLillo, *Conversations*, 103.

54. Laclau, *On Populist Reason*, 74.

55. Ibid., 82.

56. Ibid., 85.

57. Ibid., 154.

58. Ibid., 85.

59. One could go on to say that all political events are precisely *traumatic*, and that conspiracy theory is the traumatic response to the political nature of an event. According to Cathy Caruth, a traumatic event happens because the victim is not aware of the event as it happens (the victim of an accident comes away apparently unharmed); the essential aspect of the traumatic event is the way it shatters relations, the way it "appears" as an "incógnita," something unknown. Because traumatic events cannot be known directly, Caruth concludes that they are registered only in their repetition: "The experience of trauma . . . would thus seem to consist, not in the forgetting of a reality that can hence never be fully known; but in an inherent latency within the experience itself. The historical power of the trauma is not just that the experience is repeated after its forgetting, but that it is only in and through its inherent forgetting that it is first experienced at all" (Caruth, 187). Therefore, if an event happens at all, it happens through the repetition of this lack of awareness of the event. Caruth calls this "the inherent latency in the event" (187). Jacques Derrida's discussion of the "event" of 9/11 is instructive in this regard, since he not only notes the way "the event is first of all *that which* I do not first of all comprehend," but also that "the event is first of all *that* I do not comprehend" (Jacques Derrida, "Autoimmunity: Real and Symbolic Suicides," in *Philosophy in a Time of Terror: Dialogues with Jürgen Habermas and Jacques Derrida*, ed. Giovanna Borradori [Chicago: University of Chicago Press, 2003], 90). He goes on to note that "any event worthy of this name, even if it is a 'happy' event, has within it something that is traumatizing. . . . There is traumatism with no possible work of mourning when the evil comes from the possibility to come of the worst, from the repetition to come—though worse. Traumatism is produced by the *future*, by the *to come*, by the threat of the worst *to come*, rather than by an aggression that is 'over and done with'" (96, 97). In effect, then, an event is political only if it is also "traumatic," which means that it opens itself up to a threatening future that cannot be known as such: it is inassimilable or unappropriable (Derrida: "It is the future that determines the unappropriability of the event, not the present or the past" [97]). Conspiracy theories, in turn, respond to political events by narrating the unknowability of this "Something or Other," to use Ishmael Reed's phrase.

THREE

Why Hidden Figures Matter
for Politics

In "New Theses on the Short Story," Piglia narrates a dream (the dreamer was Borges) about a man who encounters a friend whose hand is hidden within his jacket. The man senses that his friend needs help and asks what has happened that he now seems so changed. As his friend slowly takes his hand out of his jacket, he admits that he has indeed changed a lot. The dreamer looks down at his friend's hand, but instead of a hand, the man sees that his friend's arm ends in a bird's claw. With that revelation the story (or dream) ends. Piglia uses this story to illustrate his idea that every *cuento* or short story contains "una figura que se oculta" (a figure that is hidden).[1] The emergence of this hidden figure "reveals" a second story: instead of the story of a man who is down on his luck, this is the fantastical story of a man who is slowly turning into a bird. This second story is never revealed as such, however; it only emerges in that figure that remains hidden throughout most of the story, that hand that is not a hand and which the friend keeps out of sight. With its revelation, it seems that the man can finally understand the secret story, even if the story as such is never told.

Although this story is useful to give a quick illustration of what it might mean to suggest a secret story through the revelation of a hidden figure, it nevertheless does not quite do justice to Piglia's own understanding of the hidden figure. As I noted in the first chapter, the secret is "hidden, separated from the story as a whole, reserved for the end and in some other part."[2] Although the secret is reserved for the end of a story, this secret, Piglia insists, is more on the order of an event and therefore remains fundamentally incomprehensible: "there is always a double movement, something incomprehensible that happens and is hidden."[3] The hidden figure emerges as a happening both at the end and somewhere else, "en otra parte."[4] If the hidden figure "appears" at all, then, it must appear as something that resists understanding (it is "something incomprehensible") and therefore must remain hidden, even in its "appearance."

This notion of a hidden figure that remains incomprehensible is a central element of any conspiracy narrative. By focusing on the interruptive effect of the hidden figure, I will show that the secret story is always the unvoiced demand of a "low type" or "parasite" that illegitimately inhabits an official story. At the same time, by further isolating the formal characteristics of the conspiracy narrative, it will be possible to show that this kind of narrative takes place not only in so-called paranoid fiction, but also in texts that are normally not considered "paranoid." For that reason, this chapter will compare two texts that are usually not read together: Thomas Pynchon's *The Crying of Lot 49* and Rigoberta Menchú's *testimonio* or testimonial narrative, *Me llamo Rigoberta Menchú y así me nació la conciencia*. While Pynchon's novel is the "paranoid" story of a conspiracy that never fully emerges, Menchú's narrative testifies to her community's struggle against a dominant political and economic system in Guatemala. Although these texts emerge from two very different traditions, both emphasize the way hidden figures, while inevitably difficult to pin down, are nevertheless a constitutive part of any political narrative. In fact, it will be clear that politics only takes place when there is a hidden figure that demands to be heard, but which nevertheless is not authorized to speak. Paradoxically, the hidden figure takes place by not taking place, but this not-taking-place is not simply an absence. Rather, the hidden figure opens a gap in the social field which produces, in turn, an interruption or a generalized fall from power, what Menchú calls a *desgaste*. I will argue that this disruptive event is necessary if there is to be politics at all: there must always be a hidden figure that interrupts an authorized discourse and presents an otherness to the way things stand.

PYNCHON'S PARASITE (*THE CRYING OF LOT 49*)

I have already emphasized the strange effect of the hidden figure when I focused on Ishmael Reed's novel *Mumbo Jumbo* in the first chapter. I showed that Reed's novel is structured as a detective novel that nevertheless frustrates this genre by introducing a minimal mechanism, what I am now calling a "hidden figure." In *Mumbo Jumbo*, this hidden figure (Jes Grew) is an inarticulate voice that nevertheless speaks, a figure that never reveals itself as a positive figuration, a presence that is only present when it withdraws. I would now like to return to this notion of the hidden figure in order to develop its political importance. Like Reed's novel, *The Crying of Lot 49* bears a clear relation to the detective novel at the same time that it undermines this structure by introducing a similar kind of minimal mechanism. In Pynchon's 1966 novel, the hidden figure is called the Trystero,[5] the postal conspiracy that Oedipa Maas stumbles upon when executing the will of her former lover, Pierce Inverarity. Oedipa's detective-like search for the Trystero is frustrated by the fact that this secret society is constituted by invisible relationships that reach across large expanses of space and time in order to accomplish a secret communication or to tell a secret story. A large part of the mystery of the Trystero has to do with the way this secret society continuously withdraws from the scene, the way it becomes a kind of (non)figure. By calling the Trystero a "(non)figure," I am emphasizing the way the secret society appears as a name with the promise of meaning (thus a figure), but at the same time the Trystero disfigures itself through a continual withdrawal from the scene (thus a non-figure). In fact, the undecidable nature of the Trystero is what gives this hidden figure its mysterious force. The Trystero is constituted as a (secret) society precisely to the extent that this society never emerges as such. For that reason, I will argue that the Trystero stands as a counterfeit figure that "speaks" to the extent that its voice is not authorized. If Piglia stated that the complot effect is produced whenever there is a visible story that is undermined by a secret story, Pynchon's *Lot 49* suggests that this secret story is a demand to be heard that nevertheless can never be fully heard. This demand to be heard, coupled with the inability to express this demand fully, constitutes the political effect of Pynchon's novel.

In a sense, my argument follows a very traditional line that would emphasize the way *Lot 49* is based on a series of metaphors from which is derived the essential plot mechanism of his novel.[6] However, "metaphor" has a very specific meaning within the context of *Lot 49*; in fact, a close reading of Pynchon's definition of "metaphor" is also an approach to the question of the hidden figure. In a crucial passage in the novel, which I will read in more detail in a moment, "metaphor" appears as a way to theorize both the Trystero and the Nefastis Machine. The latter is named after its inventor, John Nefastis, whom Oedipa Maas finds while pursuing a lead in her search for evidence of a postal conspiracy that seems to be communicating outside of the U.S. Mail system. The Nefastis Machine refers to a utopian device that allegedly can sort heat molecules without expending any energy, with a little help from an invisible "Demon." Nefastis's friend, Stanley Koteks, explains that the Demon is "a tiny intelligence" that sorts fast molecules from slow molecules, thus creating a heat differential, since the fast molecules have more energy and thus more heat.[7] Because the Demon is doing all the work, the machine violates the Second Law of Thermodynamics, "getting something for nothing, causing perpetual motion" (*CL*, 68). The Demon is strange not only because it is a non-human element that exists within the machine as a sorting mechanism, but also because it produces a rupture in a theoretical "law": it allows the machine to produce a pure gain without any corresponding loss. The Nefastis Machine is therefore utopian—in the sense of "perfect"—because nothing falls out of this system as waste. It is the model of a perfectly ordered system in which loss is never needed in order to produce a gain.

It should be emphasized that the Nefastis Machine is made possible by a certain belief in the existence of a non-human sorting element, the Demon. In fact, Nefastis insists that this non-human element is not simply a fiction. Without the Demon the machine is only held together by an accidental event that happened in the 1930s, when it was discovered that the equation for heat entropy happens to look like the equation for information entropy. Nefastis explains that his machine was made possible precisely because of this mere coincidence, but that this coincidence—which he calls a "metaphor"—is literalized, so to speak, by the existence of the Demon. He explains: "Entropy is a figure of speech, then . . . a metaphor. It connects the world of thermodynamics to the world of information flow. The Machine uses both. The Demon makes the metaphor not only verbally graceful, but also objectively true" (*CL*, 85). The important point here is not the way Pynchon's novel puts into play these conflicting theories of entropy (or how they are "resolved" in the fictional Nefastis Machine), but rather the way *Lot 49* theorizes "metaphor." Traditionally, this term in rhetoric has come to mean a figure that mediates between a literal meaning and a "figural" meaning: a word normally used in one context (its literal meaning) is now used in a foreign context (its figural meaning), in order to transfer some of the literal meaning into a new context. For example, to say that the world is a stage is to take a certain aspect of the meaning of "stage" and transfer it (*meta-pherein*, to bear across) to "world," which is now thought of as similar to a stage where one might perform a role. However, in Nefastis's explanation of what makes his machine possible, the literal-figural content is emptied out, and instead what is emphasized is the mechanism of transference that takes place within the figure. Metaphor is therefore a general structure that connects two dissimilar elements, in this case, two equations that refer to two incompatible "worlds." If the Nefastis Machine is a sorting machine, then there is also a prior sorting mechanism that makes this sorting machine possible: the metaphor that transfers heat entropy to information entropy and vice versa. In this founding metaphor there is no distinction between a literal and a figural content; rather, what defines the metaphor is simply this transfer or connection between two different worlds. Regardless of the existence of the Demon, the Nefastis Machine is made possible because of this *metaphorical* connection between two equations.

However, what is indeed strange about this metaphorical connection is that the Nefastis Machine posits the existence of a tiny intelligence that allows this connection to function in reality, and not just as a metaphor. As Nefastis notes, "[t]he Demon makes the metaphor not only verbally graceful, but also objectively true" (*CL*, 85). There are therefore two connections taking place through the Nefastis Machine: if the Demon allows a connection to take place between heat entropy and information entropy, then this metaphorical connection also produces a relation between the world of fiction, or rhetoric, and the real world. What should be emphasized in the Nefastis Machine is not only the supposition that this machine breaks a law of thermodynamics, but also that it produces incomprehensible connections. As many critics have noted in exasperation, Pynchon's use of two theories of entropy in order to model his Nefastis Machine is confusing at best.[8] As we will see, the point is not simply that entropy is a confused and therefore meaningless concept in Pynchon's novel, but rather that the confusion about Pynchon's use of the term "entropy" is in fact a transposition of the constitutive non-relation that enables the Nefastis Machine to "work." The machine *works* precisely because of this confusion between two types of entropy, precisely because of the confusion between the world of rhetoric and the real world. Confusion is therefore productive within Pynchon's novel, even if this same confusion seems to confuse its critics.

I would like to argue that the Nefastis Machine not only models a certain notion of incomprehensible relations, but also stands as a figure for the specific relations that constitute the postal conspiracy that lies at the center of *Lot 49*. In fact, the narrator explicitly compares the Nefastis Machine and the Trystero: both are constituted by incomprehensible relations that come together by coincidence. The narrator explains:

> For John Nefastis . . . two kinds of entropy, thermodynamic and informational, happened, say by coincidence, to look alike, when you wrote them down as equations. Yet he had made his mere coincidence respectable, with the help of Maxwell's Demon.
>
> Now here was Oedipa, faced with a metaphor of God knew how many parts; more than two, anyway. With coincidences blossoming these days wherever she looked, she had nothing but a sound, a word, Trystero, to hold them together. (*CL*, 87)

Thus, Pynchon's minimal definition of conspiracy is that it is a device that makes possible an impossibility: it allows a transfer to take place between accidental events that should have nothing to do with each other. The Trystero conspiracy is therefore a metaphor, in Pynchon's sense of the word: it forges a contingent relation without uniting the two (or more) parts in a unity. The only element holding together the accidental parts of the conspiracy is a name, the "Trystero." This name refers to the agent or "Demon" that invisibly ties everything together and keeps the machine running. At the same time, this demonic agent also lends its name to the organization as a whole: the Trystero is both the invisible demon and the structure of incomprehensible relations held together by the demon. Conspiracy therefore takes place precisely as a metaphor;

however, this phrase ("as a metaphor") no longer means a merely linguistic reality that has no relation to "nonverbal" reality. Rather, "metaphor," as I noted above, designates a connection that is *really* produced
through an incomprehensible relation between dissimilar elements. This
real connection happens because of a name: in the case of the Nefastis
Machine, this name is the "Demon," and in the case of the postal conspiracy, the name is "Trystero." In each case, the name allows an equivalential logic to take place between completely dissimilar elements. In the
Nefastis Machine, the Demon connects the unrelated fields of thermodynamics and information flow; in the postal conspiracy, the Trystero connects a series of heterogeneous elements that normally would not constitute a "community." The Nefastis Machine is therefore not simply an
example of bogus science, but rather functions in the novel as a model for
the secret society.[9]

What complicates this scheme is that the Trystero is not simply a
metaphor that connects dissimilar elements but is also a postal delivery
service that sorts messages.[10] Oedipa notices the structural similarities
when talking with Stanley Koteks about how it is not necessary to introduce work into the Nefastis Machine because of the Demon's sorting
mechanism. Oedipa asks: "Sorting isn't work? . . . Tell them down at the
post office, you'll find yourself in a mailbag headed for Fairbanks, Alas-
ka, without even a FRAGILE sticker going for you" (*CL*, 68). Although
Koteks insists that mental work is not the same as work in the thermodynamic sense, Oedipa's point is clear: there is an analogy between the
operations of the Nefastis Machine and the operations of the Trystero, in
that both operate as a system of communication between heterogeneous
elements. However, the Trystero is not just another postal delivery service, just as the Nefastis Machine is not just another heat engine. In the
latter, the completely unrelated equations that constitute its structure do
not simply join together around the full presence of a name (the Demon),
but rather come together as an oppositional configuration, pitting themselves against a common enemy: they are against the law that says it is
"illegal" to get something for nothing. The second law of thermodynamics sets up an economy of loss and gain: for a thermodynamic engine to
work, energy must be introduced into the machine from the outside. This
means that energy must first be lost in order for any gain to be possible.
The two types of equations within the Nefastis Machine bind together,
not because of their coincidental resemblance, but rather because of the
way they go against the economy of loss and gain. The intervention of the
Nefastis Machine—the innovation that would define it as an "invention"—is that it articulates the possibility (never realized within the novel) of an energy gain without any corresponding loss. In other words, the
Nefastis Machine posits itself as an anti-economy or "countereconomy"
that is not simply different from an economy of loss and gain, but rather
disrupts the possibility of economy as such.[11]

Therefore, the Nefastis Machine only stands as a model for a secret society insofar as both "machines" are *criminal* machines: they constitute themselves through an antagonistic relation to an official economy. After all, the Trystero mail conspiracy is by nature a secret system: the transfers that happen within the system are mysteriously clandestine and operate outside the law. In other words, the Trystero is explicitly not the official sorting machine; it is rather a criminal machine that operates against the official sorting machines (the U.S. Mail, the European Thurn and Taxis system, etc.). For that reason, the Nefastis Machine is again the model for the Trystero. "Nefastis" is not just a name, but also points to the etymology of the word "nefarious": "*ne-fas*" means "unlawful." Both the Nefastis Machine and the Trystero are therefore "criminal" attempts to oppose an official economy.

However, the similarities end here, since Nefastis would like his machine to produce pure presence (a "gain"), even if that presence is momentarily absent for the time being, since it seems that no one can actually get the machine to work. Nefastis, then, is "a believer" in the full presence of his machine (*CL*, 85). The Trystero, on the other hand, shows that this absence of pure presence is not a momentary phenomenon, but is rather the condition of its structure. Even in the case of the Nefastis Machine, the fact that the "metaphor" that connects disparate elements is "objectively true," as Nefastis says, does not mean that its existence can be proven without a doubt (*CL*, 85). The incomprehensible relations put forward by the name ("Demon" or "Trystero") prevent "the metaphor of God knew how many parts" to be verified with certainty. This unverifiability is not a lack that would conclusively argue against the existence of a conspiracy. Rather, as Oedipa finds out, the apocryphal nature of the conspiracy is constitutive of the Trystero's structure. After all, Oedipa's access to the Trystero always happens in the novel by means of apocryphal texts and counterfeit objects. The central "clue" is the stamp collection that Pierce Inverarity left behind after his death and which is therefore part of the estate that Oedipa was originally assigned to execute. Within Pierce's legacy are the stamps that Ghenghis Cohen, the philatelist, finds are filled with "irregularities" and which he judges to be "counterfeit" (*CL*, 75, 78). However, as I will argue in a moment, "counterfeit" in Pynchon's novel does not mean a mere fiction that posits itself as true or believable. Rather, as Ghenghis Cohen notes, each stamp contains an error, "a deliberate mistake . . . laboriously worked into the design, like a taunt" (*CL*, 78). Oedipa finds that these counterfeit products are not simply part of a systematic postal fraud (a trick or sleight of hand), but rather connect to a generalized strategy of counterfeiting (a taunt).

But what does it mean for these counterfeit stamps to act as "a taunt"? It helps to notice that the counterfeit in *Lot 49* is defined as a particular kind of relation: there is a "counterfeit" object only in relation to an original with which it does not quite coincide. The counterfeit object posits a relation to an original that is based on similarity (the stamps look the same at first glance), but which in fact are completely opposed to the original (there are deliberate errors). In the case of the first stamp found by Ghenghis Cohen, the error takes the form of an anarchist attack: "The picture [on the stamp] had a Pony Express rider galloping out of a western fort. From shrubbery over on the right-hand side and possibly in the direction the rider would be heading, protruded a single, painstakingly engraved, black feather" (*CL*, 78). This black feather represents the mysterious Trystero agent who would attack any official postal carrier throughout history. The counterfeit stamp therefore offers this scene of potential violence "as a taunt." This taunt is not only an innocent addition to the stamp, but rather intervenes in a particular relation of power. After all, the power of the state is not only represented by a stamp but rather *happens* as the capacity to authorize written statements (stamps) that, in turn, attest to the power of the state. The counterfeit object interrupts this self-replicating process, but not through simple resistance or even by violent uprising. Rather, the counterfeit disrupts the economy of state power through a kind of false repetition: the counterfeit stamp testifies to its own authority (it "gives faith," to use Ángel Rama's language) at the same time that it introduces these "taunts" that end up undermining the notion of a faithful rendition.[12] The counterfeit stamp establishes an antagonistic relation to the official "writing" of the state and therefore interrupts this economy-power. The counterfeit, it can be said, is defined as a relation to a more official statement that it disfigures and disrupts. In this way, the conspiracy of the Trystero establishes itself as a counterfeit discourse that antagonistically relates to the official documents that certify the power of a centralized form of communication.

Unlike Nefastis's belief in the full presence of his machine, the Trystero is constituted only insofar as it takes place as a counterfeit replication of the official economy. The conspiracy of the Trystero does not simply set itself up as a parallel economy that impossibly produces gain without loss, but rather inserts itself into the official economy as counterfeit. At the same time, the Trystero is not only a loss that the official economy suffers; after all, an economy is defined as this relation between a loss and a gain. Rather, I would like to suggest that the Trystero constitutes itself as a total loss that disrupts the loss and gain of the official economy. This shift in the definition of the Trystero occurs within an appropriately speculative history of the Trystero system, in which the secret society is theorized precisely in terms of this strategy of the counterfeit. Oedipa learns that, as the U.S. Postal Service began to crack down on alternative mail delivery, the Trystero decided to "stay on . . . in the context of conspiracy," which meant a new "emphasis now toward silence, impersonation, opposition masquerading as allegiance" (*CL*, 143). The Trystero conspiracy therefore not only engages in the act of counterfeiting; rather, the secret society *only takes place* as the counterfeiting of any official discourse that authorizes itself as power. Although this might seem a strange way to construct a conspiracy, in fact Pynchon suggests that this structure defines the form of any conspiracy. A conspiracy does not take place through the negation of power by means of power, but rather through the interruption of the economy of loss and gain that structures power. A true conspiracy, it would seem, is one that forges a counterfeit economy: by definition, this kind of "economy" interrupts the official economy and therefore cannot be reappropriated by the official economy as simply another negative moment to be assimilated. In fact, Oedipa realizes that if she ever dreamed of trying to produce a settlement in a court of law between the U.S. government and the Trystero, she would be laughed out of the court (*CL*, 149–50). Between the Trystero and the U.S. Mail there is an incommensurable divide that cannot be resolved through a differential logic, that is, as if the Trystero were a recognizable and isolated group that differed from other distinct groups. The Trystero is therefore not a recognized voice wishing to take power; it is rather a non-conceptual event that takes place as an interruption of the official networks of power.

If the Trystero "appears" as a kind of interruption, this interruption is not thematized as a violent explosion, but rather as a withdrawal, a silence, or a strange kind of absence. Oedipa begins to recognize the Trystero's strange mode of "appearance" as she wanders around San Francisco in the hopes that she would certainly not find—by coincidence—any more signs of the postal conspiracy. Of course Oedipa does not actually see fully visible signs that the conspiracy exists. Nevertheless, everywhere she goes she recognizes the counterfeit signature of the Trystero, especially the muted post horn and the letters WASTE. As the narrator notes during Oedipa's meanderings around San Francisco: "Decorating each alienation, each species of withdrawal, as cufflink, decal, aimless doodling, there was somehow always the post horn" (*CL*, 100). The counterfeit nature of the conspiracy therefore begins to articulate itself as a "visible" withdrawal. The narrator, filtered through Oedipa's consciousness, goes on to note:

> If miracles were . . . intrusions into this world from another, a kiss of cosmic pool balls, then so must be each of the night's post horns. For here were God knew how many citizens, deliberately choosing not to communicate by U.S. Mail. It was not an act of treason, nor possibly even of defiance. But it was a calculated withdrawal, from the life of the Republic, from its machinery. Whatever else was being denied them out of hate, indifference to the power of their vote, loopholes, simple ignorance, this withdrawal was their own, unpublicized, private. Since they could not have withdrawn into a vacuum (could they?), there had to exist the separate, silent, unsuspected world. (*CL*, 101)

The post horn and the withdrawal that this emblem figures are therefore not simply signs of the conspiracy, but rather real intrusions into the machinery of the Republic. Paradoxically, these intrusions take place as a withdrawal into a kind of silence. It should be said that "withdrawal" here does not mean an absolute disappearance. Rather, within the context of conspiracy, *withdrawal means opposition masquerading as allegiance.*[13] This counterfeiting strategy can be seen in the very emblem of the Tryste-ro, the post horn, which resembles the sign of the official European postal service, Thurn and Taxis, except for the introduction of an imperceptible mute within the horn's opening. This imperceptibly small mechanism, to paraphrase Piglia, is itself the mechanism of withdrawal: it stands as an intervention into the power of the centralized or official economy of the post. To "withdraw" from the life and machinery of the Republic is to remain behind and endure within the context of conspiracy, as an opposi-tional force that feigns loyalty or faithfulness. And yet this very imperso-nation is thought in terms of an impossible community: just as the Tryste-ro was figured previously as "a metaphor of God knew how many parts," the postal conspiracy is now figured as "God knew how many citizens, deliberately choosing not to communicate by U.S. Mail." The basis of their community is precisely this antagonistic relation to the power of the official economy, here figured as the U.S. Mail. Conspiracy therefore is not a full presence that can be known or understood, but rather *takes place*, as an event, as the intrusion of a total loss that cannot be recuperated at the level of an economy of loss and gain. The conspiracy takes place in every moment of withdrawal, for instance, in the "rituals of miscarriage" that one 'member' of the 'community' continuously enacts, "dedicated not to continuity but to some kind of interregnum" (*CL*, 100). Conspiracy is this intervention into the reigning power (an interregnum), an event that takes place by not taking place.

We can now summarize the structure of conspiracy as it is narrated in Pynchon's novel. The Trystero is a way of organizing the social field as a kind of positive negativity: it *takes place* as withdrawal, secrecy, waiting, or silence. This positive negativity means that the Trystero operates ac-cording to the logic of the counterfeit by repeating the official system in an antagonistic way. The Nefastis Machine still stands as the figure for this metaphorical structure, only not in terms of the belief that charac-terizes Nefastis's relation to the machine, but rather in terms of Oedipa's own relation of waiting. After all, her experiment with the machine exact-ly corresponds to her attempt to find the Trystero: as the experience of a withdrawal. In terms of the Nefastis Machine, Oedipa sits, "waiting for the Demon to communicate" (*CL*, 85). In relation to the Trystero, Oedipa is left at the end of the novel at the auction of Pierce's counterfeit stamp collection (as lot number 49), hoping that a Trystero agent might appear. The novel ends as "Oedipa settled back, to await the crying of lot 49" (*CL*, 152). Therefore, at the end of the novel, Oedipa herself is inscribed in this experience of withdrawing and waiting, that is, the very experience that constitutes the (non)relation between every member of the WASTE postal conspiracy. After all, the acronym WASTE stands for: "We Await Silent Tristero's Empire" (*CL*, 139). Oedipa steadily finds herself inscribed within this WASTE system, not because she formally joins some sort of official community, but rather because of the experience of withdrawing or waiting for something to appear. This process begins toward the end of the novel, when her "investigation" into the conspiracy slowly turns into something else: "Even a month ago, Oedipa's next question would have been, 'Why?' But now she kept a silence, waiting, as if to be illuminated" (*CL*, 125). At this point, revelation or "illumination" is less a certain goal than a subjunctive possibility: "as if to be illuminated." This is illumination in the mode of the subjunctive (the "as if"), which also means that Oedipa is now recognizing a kind of "counterfeit" illumination, an illumination that is always "contrary to fact" or "opposed to something done or made." The expectation of an illumination gradually loses its revelatory aim and becomes instead an empty and endless structure of waiting.[14] She begins to reply to any sign of evidence with a version of the silence that is now associated with the Trystero: she is marked by a reluctance to act ("Having begun to feel reluctant about following up anything") or a waiting (a feeling that she is "waiting on something truly terrible"; "[t]he waiting above all") (*CL*, 137, 140, 150). As with the Trystero in general, Oedipa's "silence" does not refer to a lack of communication. Rather, it points to another mode of communication, a mode that is characterized as withdrawal and waiting. Her silence is therefore not simply a negative response, but rather the positive announcement of negativity: she is marked by the *expression* of silence. This positive negativity is what defines the Trystero as a secret society or hidden figure.

In this way, the Trystero conspiracy only takes place as withdrawal or silence, as a counterfeit object or counterfeit experience. At the same time, to become a member of this secret society is not to enter into a consensual agreement, but rather happens at the moment of becoming the WASTE of America, that is, those who await Trystero. The waste of America does not refer to those who have been left behind, which is perhaps a constituent feature of any economy of loss and gain. Rather, Pynchon's novel points to an experience of community based on a radical loss or withdrawal that cannot simply be recuperated by the official economy. The community of WASTE is therefore constituted not by any kind of positive appearance, but rather by the experience of waiting for something other to appear. As Piglia notes in his "New Theses on the Short Story," "[t]he art of narration is the art of sensing the unexpected, of knowing how to wait for what comes, clearly, invisibly, like the silhouette of a butterfly against an empty canvas" (*FB*, 137). Pynchon's narration of the secret society takes this kind of waiting as a structural principle. This principle is what Pynchon calls a "metaphor," a structure that produces unbelievable relations and takes place only as absence. The model for this kind of metaphor is the Nefastis Machine, but the structure of the Nefastis Machine can take place at any moment, as long as there are two movements: first, a conjunction of incomprehensible relations; second, an antagonistic repetition of an enemy discourse. This antagonistic repetition is not thematic, but rather structural: an official or visible discourse is steadily undermined by an *other* discourse that cannot be simply assimilated by the first discourse. The two discourses are therefore irreducible, in part because the other discourse is never "there" as such, but rather takes place as an internal "virus" that brings about the subversion of the official discourse. Pynchon's novel figures this overturning as the counterfeit repetition of the official discourse, thereby creating an antagonistic relation that comes together in a voice or name—the Trystero—that serves as the retroactive ground of the conspiracy. In fact, however, this "voice" is continually produced by the antagonistic relation and therefore stands as the unique effect of the conspiratorial figure. Pynchon's novel tells the story of a secret, counterfeit voice that takes place as a constitutive absence.

The Trystero "speaks" then, but as a hidden figure it never speaks with any kind of authority. It is a counterfeit voice that presents a demand that can never be fully heard, if only because the voice lacks authority as a condition of its expression. If the voice were able to speak with full authority, if its demands were fully heard, then there would be no difference between the Trystero and the official institution. If the Trystero is to take place at all, then, it must take place as this strange kind of absence that nevertheless strives to speak in a full voice. This notion of an illegitimate voice that is heard precisely to the extent that its demands are not met is what Ernesto Laclau calls a "popular demand." As I noted in the last chapter, politics begins for Laclau when an institutional power *cannot* meet a particular demand. If the demand were immediately satisfied, then the demand would obviously disappear, since there would no longer be a lack to be addressed. However, if the demand is not fulfilled, then this unsatisfied demand begins to link to other unfulfilled demands through a system of equivalences. As Laclau remarks in his essay on empty signifiers, "all of [these unfulfilled demands] are seen as related to each other, not because their concrete objectives are intrinsically related but because they are all seen as equivalent in confrontation with the repressive regime."[15] Although each demand remains particular, they band together in opposition to the official regime that refuses to listen to their voice. In effect, the only glue that holds these unfulfilled demands together is the experience of waiting to be satisfied, a waiting that can never end. This waiting thus produces an antagonistic frontier between, in Laclau's words, "unfulfilled social demands, on the one hand, and an unresponsive power, on the other."[16] All of these demands then come together in opposition to this unresponsive power. Any new demand that

is similarly waiting to be satisfied (but which continues to be an illegitimate demand) is then added on to this larger unit, thus creating a popular demand that forms around an empty name. This name is empty because it refers to the emergence of the "people," but not the fullness of the
people. Rather, the empty name refers to the endless waiting for the
people to emerge. As Laclau explains: "The 'people' . . . is something less
than the totality of the members of the community: it is a partial component which nevertheless aspires to be conceived as the only legitimate
totality." [17] In Pynchon's novel, this empty name (what Laclau calls the
"empty signifier") is the Trystero, which names precisely the endless
waiting for the emergence of a legitimate people: We Await Silent Trystero's Empire. In this way, Oedipa's act of waiting gets inscribed within a
larger group, thereby forming a conspiracy of waiting, a secret society of
those who wait. This larger group, the Trystero, no longer simply puts
forward a demand, but rather now introduces a claim, as if to say: I claim
the right to speak.

But this claim is now very strange, since the "I" here still has no right
to speak and therefore should not be able to claim the right to speak in
the first place. This paradoxical situation—this strange ineloquence of its
speaking—can be likened to the situation of the "low type," a figure that
J. L. Austin introduces in order to explain why performative utterances
sometimes *do not* perform what they are uttering. Austin gives the example of a "low type" who comes along during the naming of a ship, takes
the bottle out of the hands of the one who was authorized to name it, and
yells "I name this ship the Generalissimo Stalin!" [18] Even though the low
type has uttered a performative statement ("I name . . ."), Austin concludes that the speech act has not occurred, but has rather "misfired,"
since the low type was not authorized to name the ship in this situation.
The speech act can only occur if the agents involved follow the prescribed
conventions. For the same reason, Austin excludes performative utterances that are "said by an actor on the stage, or if introduced in a poem,
or spoken in soliloquy," since "[l]anguage in such circumstances is in
special ways — intelligibly — used not seriously, but in ways *parasitic* upon
its normal use." [19] Like the speech of the "low type," these moments of
theater (or "fiction") have the appearance of a performative utterance,
but nevertheless undermine the intentional effectiveness of the utterance.
Austin insists that such speech acts would be *"in a peculiar way hollow or
void."* [20] If someone gets married on stage, a real marriage cannot be said
to have taken place: it would all be empty theater. However, as in the
case of the "low type," *something* happens when the actor quotes a speech
act or when the low type names the ship without having proper authority, even if in both cases the effect is not the precise action named in the
utterance. The low type and the actor both *counterfeit* the speech act, but
this act of counterfeiting is not without its effects. As Austin goes on to
note in *How to Do Things with Words*, a misfire may make a performative

utterance "void or without effect," but this strangely "does not here mean 'without consequences, results, effects.'"[21]

I would like to argue that one of these effects is in fact the effect of politics. After all, the low type, who has no legitimacy, has nevertheless spoken, not so much in order to name a ship but rather to claim legitimacy. In other words, the unauthorized speaker's claim to speak should not be heard, in fact cannot be heard, but nevertheless happens and produces an effect. Like the unauthorized stamps that are nevertheless sent into circulation in Pynchon's novel, the low type produces an interruption that immediately splits the social space into two camps: an authorized voice and an unauthorized voice. However, it is not as if the unauthorized voice can simply be forgotten at this point. In fact, as soon as the "low type" has uttered his claim, this unauthorized discourse has now lodged itself within the social field and forces the authorized discourse to "hear" its demand in some way, though not as a fully legitimate demand. Like the Trystero, which continually counterfeits the official postal service in order to emphasize its status as the "Disinherited," the constant "theme" of the low type is "disinheritance" (*CL*, 132). In this way, the Trystero, like the low type, is the very definition of the parasite: it is like the guest who has made his way inside the home under false pretenses, and who then lives off the host in a violent way, upending the very economy of the house.[22] The parasite is both inside and outside: not wholly inside, because his presence undermines the integrity of the inside; but not wholly outside, since he cannot be so easily pushed outside the house. As Derrida notes in his extended treatment of speech acts, "*[n]ever quite* taking place is thus part of [the parasite's] performance, of its success as an event, of its taking-place."[23] The parasite never really happens: it is that which threatens to take the place of the rightful heir or owner, but which never quite usurps this place. On the other hand, the owner is forced to defend his own house, which is also to say that he must defend the law of his own house, his economy (his *oikos* + *nomos*). However, in a sense it is too late, since the parasite has made the house *other*, thereby introducing an *other* economy that antagonistically undermines the owner's economy as a continual possibility. In *The Crying of Lot 49*, this parasite takes place as a withdrawal or silence, a not-quite-taking-place, a counterfeit stamp, for example, that constantly disrupts the official performative utterances of the state. The parasite is a constitutive complot that disrupts the main narrative line or official discourse. The Trystero is the empty name for the parasite or low type that attaches itself to an authoritative performative utterance at the same time that it presents itself as an antagonistic threat that destabilizes the fixity of this authority. In what follows I will go on to argue that this parasitic structure is necessary if there is to be politics in the first place: there must always be a parasite that threatens the law and the economy of the home, a hidden figure that interrupts an authorized discourse, a "low type" that presents an otherness to the way things stand.

MENCHÚ'S POLITICAL TRAPS (*I, RIGOBERTA MENCHÚ*)

I would like to turn now to a text that, at first glance, has nothing to do with the kind of conspiracy narrative found in *The Crying of Lot 49*. However, I would like to argue that the model of conspiracy outlined in Pynchon's novel can also be read in any narrative, even those that are not normally considered "paranoid." For that reason, I will argue not only that Rigoberta Menchú's *testimonio* contains a similar model of a complot that undermines the main narrative line, but also that her text demands that one read for the complot in order to bear witness to the political effect of her narrative. In *Me llamo Rigoberta Menchú y así me nació la conciencia*[24] (translated as *I, Rigoberta Menchú: An Indian Woman in Guatemala*),[25] politics takes place as an effect of secrecy. In fact, I would like to argue that Menchú's entire text is built around a certain definition of the secret, and that this secrecy is what defines the political structure of her narrative. This emphasis on secrecy is perhaps not surprising, since many critics have already brought up the fact that Menchú insists on secrecy in her text. However, I would like to suggest that the secret, in Menchú's text, is not about protecting hidden knowledge. In fact, I would like to displace the question of secrecy from this epistemological perspective (what is known or unknown), and instead ask about the way Menchú's rhetoric of secrecy produces specific political effects. I will argue that Menchú's use of secrecy is not something that disqualifies her text as a political document, as if the fact that she has secrets might mean that her politics is somehow without effect. Rather, I will argue that politics happens in this text as precisely an effect of narrating the secret. In short, Menchú's emphasis on secrecy is a performative gesture that produces political effects.

Of course, by referring to *I, Rigoberta Menchú* as Menchú's text is already to enter into some controversy. After all, this *testimonio* is an event in part because it problematizes the notion of a single author that gave birth to the work. On the one hand, this problematic authorship is clearly the result of the particular circumstances involved in producing this text. As the anthropologist Elisabeth Burgos-Debray relates in her introduction to the text, Menchú spent a week with her in January 1982, during which time Menchú transmitted, in fragments, the story about her life and her struggles in Guatemala. Menchú's text is therefore not simply a mediated transcription of an oral story, but rather a narrative that only takes place through mediation: the tape recorder and the anthropologist are in fact essential for the production of this text.[26] Therefore, although Burgos-Debray insists that this text offers up the biological facticity of a body named Rigoberta Menchú ("we actually seem to hear her speaking and can almost hear her breathing" [*IRB*, xii]), in fact the "voice" that speaks to us is a mechanical voice, a voice that counterfeits the presumed singular voice of Menchú: this mechanical voice repeats Menchú's voice while nevertheless withholding the unmediated presence of that voice. However, this counterfeit voice does not hide Menchú's story but rather produces the story in the first place: without this counterfeit voice, without the technological and institutional mediations that thoroughly penetrate the web of this text, there would be no *I, Rigoberta Menchú*. As John Beverley notes about *testimonio* in general, "the assumed lack of writing ability or skill on the part of the narrator of the testimonio, even in those cases where the story is written instead of narrated orally, also combines to the 'truth effect' the form generates." [27] Part of the presumed authenticity of the text (its "truth effect") is due to the way Menchú's voice or signature is constitutively impure. [28]

Therefore, when I speak of Menchú's text, I am not alluding only to the person Menchú, but also to the way her text produces the persona "Menchú," a persona that does not fully coincide with the character narrated in the story ("I"). At the same time, however, the very genre of *testimonio* emphasizes the way the name of the voice not only attests to the experience of one person, but also includes the experience of an entire culture or people. Menchú expresses this tendency right at the beginning of her *testimonio*: "I'd like to stress that it's not only *my* life, it's also the testimony of my people. . . . The important thing is that what has happened to me has happened to many other people too: My story is the story of all poor Guatemalans. My personal experience is the reality of a whole people" (*IRM*, 1). John Beverley finds that this gesture is typical of all *testimonios*: "The narrator in *testimonio* . . . speaks for, or in the name of, a community or group, approximating in this way the symbolic function of the epic hero, without at the same time assuming the epic hero's hierarchical and patriarchal status." [29] Like the traditional storyteller in Walter Benjamin's theory of storytelling, the *testimonio* narrator carries out a metonymical relationship with the community as a whole: the experience of the storyteller is not only her own experience but also the experience of her people. Menchú's experience *embraces* ("*engloba*") the experience of her people, to such an extent that the narration of her own experience is also the narration of the experience of the community of which she remains merely a part (*MLRM*, 21). Menchú, as narrator, is therefore both herself (particular) and her entire community (general), which thus makes it difficult to talk about a singular author of this text.

Doris Sommer, in her article "No Secrets," usefully explains the political consequences of the rhetorical operations at work in Menchú's text. Alluding to the work of Ernesto Laclau and Chantal Mouffe, she notes:

In rhetorical terms, whose political consequences should be evident by now, there is a fundamental difference here between the *metaphor* of autobiography and heroic narrative in general, which assumes an identity-by-substitution, whereby one (superior) signifier replaces another (I substitutes for we, leader for follower, Christ for the faithful), and *metonymy*, a lateral move of identification-through-relationship, which acknowledges the possible differences among 'us' as components of a centerless whole. This is where we can come in as readers, invited to be (*estar*) with the speaker rather than to be (*ser*) her. (Sommer, 146)[30]

It is therefore possible to say that politics is already inscribed in Menchú's text, in that "Menchú" becomes an empty signifier for a host of demands that the text is expressing but which are not fully heard. The text is "authored" by Menchú, but Menchú is not a person but rather the empty signifier that allows unvoiced demands to be expressed. In this way, "Menchú's text" does not refer to the text of a singular author, but to the way a proper name ("Menchú") tells the story of an individual at the same time that it represents an entire people. However, this metonymic representation is not a smooth transition, but rather produces a dissonance between the story of an individual and the story of a community. The story of the community—the story of the *polis*, the story that makes Menchú's text political in the first place—never takes place as such, but rather is produced through the narration of secrets. Therefore, if we are to bear witness, in turn, to Menchú's *political* story, it will be necessary to bear witness to these secrets, especially the way her text is constructed out of disruptive hidden figures. In fact, *I, Rigoberta Menchú* is perhaps unique in the way that it not only demands this testimony, but also teaches us how this testimony might take place. In this way, I will argue that Menchú's text is a pedagogical narrative that helps us understand what it might mean to read for the complot.

For this reason, it should be clear that David Stoll's discoveries, in *Rigoberta Menchú and the Story of All Poor Guatemalans*, are not relevant for my discussion. Stoll argues that his position as an "outside observer" enables him to judge the truth of the events, that is, what really happened during the Guatemalan civil war.[31] In Stoll's view, to take Menchú's story as the only truth of what happened would be to falsify history and thereby to pursue an inauthentic politics. Stoll especially targets intellectuals in the United States for celebrating what he calls Menchú's "fantasies of rebellion": "What makes *I, Rigoberta Menchú* so attractive in universities is what makes it misleading about the struggle for survival in Guatemala. We think we are getting closer to understanding Guatemalan peasants when actually we are being borne away by the mystifications wrapped up in an iconic figure."[32] For Stoll, then, Menchú's text is misleading since it posits the protagonist as the personification of her people. That is, without fully stating it, Stoll is pointing precisely to the way that "Menchú" becomes an empty signifier, a figure that personifies or *engloba* the experience of her people, even if that experience is shot through with "fiction." Menchú's text is therefore emblematic of a host of other texts that speak in the mode of nonfiction (including memoirs, *testimonios*, and autobiographies) but which are nevertheless contaminated by fiction. *I, Rigoberta Menchú* demands that we ask about this relation not only between politics and fiction, but also between legitimate acts and inauthentic or counterfeit acts, between full disclosure and secrecy.

By now it is no secret that Menchú's text brings up secrecy in an almost obsessive way. In fact, critics have long been intrigued by the way Menchú emphasizes secrecy as a central part of her life story and her account of her culture. For example, Sommer asks: "Why should [Menchú] make so much of keeping secrets . . . secrets that don't have any apparent military or strategic value?"[33] Sommer goes on to describe the supposedly inevitable choice when faced with a narrator who is being secretive: "either she is a vulnerable vehicle for truth beyond her control, revealing information that compromises and infuriates the government; or she is exercising control over apparently irrelevant information, perhaps to produce her own strategic version of truth."[34] It is worth pointing out that in both scenarios, what is at stake is the revelation of information or the transmission of knowledge in general: secrecy as a way to control knowledge. I will come back to this point in a moment. For now I just want to emphasize Sommer's argument: she argues that Menchú's "flamboyant refusal of information" is not an obstacle that the reader ought to overcome, but rather marks a fundamental gap between the text and the reader.[35] She writes: "Calling attention to an unknowable subtext is a profound lesson. . . . Not that a reader should want to compete with Rigoberta's text, but that she or he might well want to learn from it how to coordinate intense political engagement, even at national and international levels, with a defense of difference."[36] Sommer therefore puts forward a very convincing thesis: to unite oneself with Menchú or with Menchú's cause is to come up against a secret that acts as a remainder that cannot be assimilated. If the point of this text is to gain supporters and produce a loose coalition, then "support" could not mean assimilation but rather respect for the cultural differences that necessarily exist between two or more agents in a coalition. For a coalition to take place, there must be these "secrets" (in the sense of "refusal of information") that allow each group to maintain its cultural identity. To dissolve the specificity of Menchú's culture (her secrets) would be to dissolve the very foundation of the coalition in the first place.[37]

However, I believe there is something stranger going on with the way secrecy comes up in Menchú's text. I would like to argue that secrecy involves not simply a secret that Menchú—as addressor—refuses to unveil. In fact, I am not even certain that Menchú's references to secrets actually refer to something that is kept from public knowledge. After all, often when Menchú mentions a secret, she immediately reveals as much

as she conceals. In other words, secrecy does not seem to be an epistemological problem in Menchú's text; knowledge, in the sense of "to know a
fact" (*saber*), is not what is at stake. Far from withholding information, it
sometimes seems as if Menchú paradoxically gives information precisely
in the moment when she states she is withholding something. In part, this
is the paradox that Sommer investigates in her article: is there really
"something else" that Menchú is hiding, or is it a rhetorical gesture
meant to distance the reader from Menchú and her culture? However, I
would like to move away from this notion of secrecy as an epistemological problem (the refusal of information) and instead focus on the way
Menchú herself theorizes secrecy in this text.

Toward the beginning of Menchú's narrative, secrecy is linked to the
task of conserving her ancestors' memory in order to preserve tradition
and bring about the survival of culture. For example, when explaining
the necessary steps for integrating a child into the community, there is a
constant interplay between three critical verbs: *guardar*, *conservar*, and
acumular. Early in her narrative, Menchú offers a scene of cultural transmission (that is, a scene of teaching) as well as a scene of storytelling: "el
niño sabrá acumular y guardar todo lo que sea de nuestros antepasados"
(*MLRM*, 33). The child therefore learns a new technique very early on: he
shall know how to accumulate tradition and conserve everything that
belongs to the ancestors. This is not the first task given to a child (the first
task is to know how to respect, and live through, life's sufferings), but it
is a critical task that is emphasized throughout Menchú's account: a double strategy of accumulating (*acumular*) and conserving (*guardar*) all that
remains of the ancestors. With this task in mind, an elder of the community then comes forward to teach the child this new responsibility: "El
señor tendrá que dar su experiencia, su ejemplo, como ha conservado lo
de nuestros antepasados. Allí es donde va a venir una charla, del señor
elegido, de la señora elegida, de sus hijos, cómo han conservado las costumbres de nuestros antepasados" (*MLRM*, 33) (The elder comes and
offers his experience, his example, how he has preserved the customs of
our ancestors. Here is when the elected leader will give a speech about
how they have preserved the customs of our ancestors).[38] The elder of the
community is thus given the task of the storyteller, in a way that recalls
Benjamin's description of this figure in his 1936 essay "The Storyteller."
The elder transmits his or her experience by passing on the accumulations of traditions known to the community. This layered narrative is
crucial to the objective of relaying experience, not only the experience of
the elder, but of the entire community and of the ancestors of the community. As Menchú states, the elder will have to give his experience, *dar su
experiencia*, but also will have to show how this experience encapsulates
the experience of the ancestors ("ha conservado lo de nuestros antepasados"). This description is consistent with Benjamin's remarks about oral
storytelling, which entails "that slow piling up, one on top of the other, of

thin, transparent layers which constitutes the most appropriate image of the way in which the perfect narrative is revealed through the layers of various retellings."[39] To pass on tradition through this scene of teaching is therefore not only a question of keeping or conserving traditions, but also crucially of accumulating these traditions and keeping them tied together within thin, transparent layers, so that the community's experience may be transmitted as a story.

But there is a second task that Menchú relates in this scene of cultural transmission, and it is a task that is mostly absent from Benjamin's description of the task of the storyteller. This task of *guardar, acumular,* and *conservar* (of keeping, accumulating, and preserving) the cultural past is not simply a way to pass on tradition through the *telling* of experience. Rather, there is a second task, at once supplementary and essential to the first task: it is the task of keeping a secret, *guardar el secreto*: "Que los padres tienen que enseñarle al niño . . . que aprenda a guardar todos los secretos, que nadie pueda acabar con nuestra cultura, con nuestras costumbres" (*MLRM*, 33) (The parents should teach the child that he needs to learn to keep all of our secrets, so that no one can put an end to our culture and our customs). There is then a double task that happens through the articulation of the same verbs: keeping, preserving, accumulating the traditions of the past; keeping, preserving, accumulating all of these traditions as secret. We have then *"guardar"* in the sense of holding or maintaining something in place; but also, *"guardar"* in the sense of putting something away, keeping it out of sight. This is the double task that bears on the child, and this double task becomes, in turn, the task of survival: first, preserving through the transmission of experience, and second, keeping this experience a secret.

It is because of this kind of scene of teaching that many critics have focused on the epistemological aspect of secrecy in Menchú's text. After all, teaching, one supposes, has to do with the transmission of knowledge: what else are we doing when we teach but engaging in some sort of transmission of knowledge from one rational being to other rational beings? However, this scene of teaching early on in Menchú's text is a bit strange, and not only because it involves the teaching of secrecy. It is a strange scene because "teaching" here is not predicated on the meeting of two conscious and rational minds, but rather takes place as an event of transmission that flows from the elder to the child. But the "child" here is not the child inherent in the word pedagogy ("to lead a child"); rather, Menchú is speaking of a newborn infant, the *infans,* the one who is incapable of speech and incapable of receiving speech.[40] What kind of knowledge can we really expect to be transmitted in such an asymmetrical relationship? This relationship is in fact figured in the text through an image of this newborn baby, since he is covered up and out of sight: "The child is present for all of this, although he's all wrapped up and can scarcely be seen" (*IRM*, 13). The child is thus not only the recipient of a secret, and is not only being taught secrecy, but is also figured as a secret, as a hidden figure that is never fully revealed at this point. Of course it is true that the child is reminded of these tasks when he reaches ten years of age. Nevertheless, that original scene of teaching is figured in Menchú's text not as the transmission of knowledge (how could the child really receive any knowledge at that point?), but rather as the transmission of an event and the production of an effect. In other words, this moment is, as the chapter indicates, a *ceremony*, an event that happens as the performance of community. The act of teaching knowledge is secondary; what is important is the transmission of the event of secrecy, which means not the transmission of secret knowledge but rather the performance of this secrecy in the figure of the hidden baby. The baby cannot be seen (he is hidden); but the community recognizes this absence as central to the task of survival, that is, to the task of transmitting the secret. This concealed baby is thus not only receiving knowledge but also exemplifying the covering up of the future so that the community may have a future.

Secrecy, in Menchú's text, takes place as this kind of performance that does not depend on the transmission of knowledge, or even the refusal to transmit knowledge. Rather, it has to do with recognizing and distinguishing (*conocer*) and not the faculty of knowing something (*saber*). To develop this idea I would like to focus on a particular figure that comes up in a critical moment in the narration of Menchú's life. If the hidden baby is the exemplary figure of secrecy within the community, this figure becomes something else when Menchú describes her interactions with those who threaten her community from the outside. This new figure is the trap, a hidden figure that exemplifies the rhetorical strategy of secrecy in Menchú's text and which also demonstrates Menchú's political strategy of secrecy.

Before going into the descriptions of these traps, it is necessary to focus on this transitional moment that goes from secrecy in communal ceremonies to secrecy in relation to politics. Menchú articulates this transitional moment through the narration of a conspiracy, that is, by narrating the secret maneuvers of a threatening other that is interrupting the closed circle of her community. She states:

> The Government says the land belongs to the nation. It owns the land and gives it to us to cultivate. But when we've cleared and cultivated the land, that's when the landowners appear. However, the landowners don't just appear on their own—they have connections with the different authorities that allow them to manoeuvre like that. (*IRM*, 105)

In this way, Menchú describes a threatening conspiracy of powers that links together the government of Guatemala with the landowners and their men. Menchú describes this conspiracy as an enigmatic web of relations that can be glimpsed only by their effects: by the power maneuvers (*sus maniobras*) that are set in place by secret agents (*MLRM*, 131). In other words, Menchú is careful already to point out that secrecy is not, by itself, something to valorize, since the oppositional forces also put into practice a technique of secrecy to achieve their own ends.

Menchú later calls this conspiracy of relations "the system," and begins to understand that the root of the problem comes down to who holds the land, "la tenencia de la tierra" (*MLRM*, 142). This realization that there is a systemic enemy that threatens her community (and not simply an accidental threat that can be avoided) is, for Menchú, the beginning of her political formation. In fact, she gains a certain political clarity right at the moment when she is finally able to name the enemy, even if the enemy is a vague idea that simply goes by the name "enemy." She first understands that her enemy is not simply the landowners, but rather the entire system, "todo el sistema" (*MLRM*, 142). Nevertheless, this introduction of a certain vagueness in her description of her enemies does not prevent her from articulating a political discourse. In fact, it is precisely the *naming* of an invisible force "enemy," and the ability to fit a variety of different actors into that name, that begins Menchú's political formation. She explains:

> The moment I learned to identify our enemies was very important for me. For me now the landowner was a big enemy, an evil one. The soldier too was a criminal enemy. And so were all the rich. We began using the term "enemies," because we didn't have the notion of enemy in our culture, until those people arrived to exploit us, oppress us and discriminate against us. (*IRM*, 122–23)

The defining political moment, for Menchú, is not only that instant of being able to see or distinguish the enemies ("cuando aprendí a distinguir a los enemigos"), but rather being able to name the enemy as such, to use this term as a way to demarcate between those who are threatening her community and those who are not (*MLRM*, 148). The word "enemy" is not only a new term for Menchú, but also names a concept that has no proper name in her culture. Naming the enemy is therefore not simply a moment of discovery but rather takes place as a catachresis: it allows Menchú to group together a series of seemingly unrelated entities under the umbrella of one name ("enemy"). This moment of naming or "distinguishing" the enemy therefore leads to the beginnings of a political organization: "I threw myself into my work and I told myself we had to defeat the enemy. We began to organize" (*IRM*, 123). Thus the work of politics begins when Menchú is able to *"distinguir a los enemigos,"* but this ability to locate the enemy paradoxically does not correspond to a precise definition of who the enemy is. In fact, it is precisely the vague referent of the word "enemy" that allows this word to name any force that threatens the community and which therefore demands that the community come together politically.

It is right at this point, precisely when Menchú is trying to figure out who her enemy is and what it would mean to create a politics that would combat this enemy, that she speaks of the traps that her ancestors passed down as a kind of testimony. These traps become crucial in her narration of how she defended her community from the enemies. Menchú begins to mobilize a rhetoric of security and secrecy that links up with the previous rhetoric of conserving and keeping the secrets of the ancestors. She begins this rhetoric even before she gains a critical political insight into the system, before she is able to identify her enemies: "Yo sin tener una claridad política, de quiénes eran exactamente nuestros enemigos. Empezamos a utilizar nuestros medios de seguridad en la aldea. Empezamos a practicar las trampas que usaban nuestros antepasados, según nos contaron nuestros abuelos. Nuestros antepasados que nos las han dejado como un testimonio" (*MLRM*, 145–46) (Without having any political clarity, without having a clear idea who exactly our enemies were, we began using safety measures in the village. We started putting into practice the traps that our ancestors used, according to our grandparents. Our ancestors passed them down to us like a testimony). The traps are figured as one of the many secrets handed down over the years, from grandparent to child, from past to future, through a technique of storytelling that is also a mode of testifying. The traps themselves serve as a testimony to this process of passing on tradition and of keeping tradition as a secret. It is at this point that the ceremonies of the community, which relied on storytelling, witnessing, and the transmission of secrets, now join up with Menchú's story of her political formation. This secret inheritance from the past will be used by Menchú's community as a means for security, thereby linking the task of security to the task of secrecy.

Thus, before having developed a sense of politics through the construction of the enemy, Menchú's community begins to put into practice this technique of security/secrecy: the traps of her ancestors. And it is this technique of using the "armas populares" that helps Menchú clarify her sense of politics (*MLRM*, 158). Menchú's politics begins at the moment when her community suddenly *remembers* one of the secrets from the ancestors: "We began to organize. Our organization had no name. We began by each of us trying to remember the tricks our ancestors used. They say they used to set traps in their houses, in the path of the conquistadores, the Spaniards" (*IRM*, 123). The act of political mobilization happens in this moment of remembering these secret traps from her community's past. Still without a name, the organization of her political community begins by telling a story about the traps the ancestors used to make ("hacían trampas"), about their trickery ("hacer trampas" can mean both "to set a trap" and "to trick") (*MLRM*, 149). Menchú emphasizes that this moment of the trap is the originary moment of her politics by articulating a series of sentences that include the idea of a beginning: "Empezamos a utilizar," "Empezamos a recordarnos," "Empezamos a organizarnos,"

"Empezamos a implementer nuestras medidas de seguridad," and so on (*MLRM*, 149–53). This rhetoric of beginnings intensifies in this moment of her narrative, when she describes the beginning of her political formation, and this rhetoric especially clusters around the rediscovery of these traps. Menchú's political formation finds its origin point when her community engages in an act of memory and tells the story of the traps of their ancestors.

At the same time that Menchú's community is remembering this secret from their ancestors, she notes that they are also bringing forward these traps *as secrets*. Again using her rhetoric of origins, Menchú remarks: "Así fue también cuando empezamos a incrementar los secretos que tenemos que hacer secretamente, las trampas" (*MLRM*, 152) (That's when we started preparing things we had to do secretly, like the traps [*IRM*, 126]). She therefore notes that these traps are, of course, a secret that comes down to them from the past, from tradition. At the same time, she notes that this is the moment when her community begins to increase these secrets in a secretive way, or that they begin to hatch these traps secretly, *secretamente*. It is not only that the trap comes down to them as a secret, but also the way they use these traps must remain a secret. But what does it mean to use a trap secretly? Menchú explains: "Que nadie tiene que conocer las trampas que hacemos en nuestras aldeas. Teníamos que conocer cada uno de nosotros las trampas del otro vecino, porque si no, en lugar de prensar a uno del ejército o a uno de los guardaespaldas de los ricos, era a uno de nuestra comunidad" (*MLRM*, 153) ("No-one must know about the traps in our villages. But we all had to know where our neighbour's traps were, otherwise they might capture one of us instead of a soldier or a landowner's bodyguard [*IRM*, 126]). At this point in Menchú's text, to know the secret has nothing to do with the faculty of knowing (*saber*), but rather pertains to a mode of recognition (*conocer*). The secret is to be able to recognize the trap, because the problem with these traps is that they are not visible, as Menchú explains: "They were usually large ditches with invisible nets so that neither animals nor soldiers could see them" (*IRM*, 127). The trap functions precisely because it marks an absence, here an absence of road; it is a ditch in the road that is covered over by these invisible threads. The traps capture unsuspecting visitors (the enemy), precisely because the traps cannot be distinguished from the surrounding landscape. The traps are "secret" because the enemy cannot *recognize* the traps as traps, and it is for that reason that it is necessary to be able to *recognize* the neighbor's secret traps. In fact, the enemy can be defined precisely as the one who cannot recognize a trap, and the definition of community is this common ability to recognize a trap for what it is. Menchú's notion of security begins with the use of a trap that is a secret precisely to the extent that the enemy does not know it, *no la conoce*. In this way, a *political* community forms around a hidden figure that traps anyone who does not belong to the community, who cannot recognize the traps in the road.

Secrecy therefore happens not because knowledge has been withheld, but rather happens as a result of not being included within the community of those who know or recognize (*conocer*). The political community is defined, then, as a secret society, a network of those who are able to distinguish what cannot readily be seen. In fact, if the faculty of *saber* comes up at all in Menchú's text, it is as a way to describe this faculty of knowing, a kind of counsel or *know-how*. The last lines of Menchú's text, also quoted by Sommer in her article "No Secrets," alludes to this kind of know-how. Menchú concludes: "Sigo ocultando lo que yo considero que nadie sabe, ni siquiera un antropólogo, ni un intelectual, por más que tenga muchos libros, no saben distinguir todos nuestros secretos" (*MLRM*, 271) (I'm still keeping secret what I think no-one should know. Not even anthropologists or intellectuals, no matter how many books they have, can find out all our secrets [*IRM*, 247]). At first, of course, it sounds as if Menchú is referring to a lack in knowledge, a *saber* that the intellectuals do not possess: she refers to what no one *knows*, "*que nadie sabe.*" But in fact, Menchú goes on to clarify that she is speaking more specifically of a know-how, a technique, a *saber hacer*: no one *knows how* to recognize all of our secrets, "*no saben distinguir todos nuestros secretos.*" The word she uses now, as she did earlier, is "*distinguir*," which in this context means "to see despite any difficulty in seeing this object."[41] It therefore seems that secrecy is not the withholding of information as such, but rather has to do with the creation of a hidden figure that disables those who fall into its trap. The secret is a trap for those who are not able to recognize the invisible threads of a hidden figure. The enemy cannot see the hidden trap not because it is invisible per se, but rather because it is camouflaged, indistinguishable from everything else.

I would like to argue that this rhetoric of secrecy in Menchú's text is in fact what defines her political strategy as well. I will call this political strategy "the triumph of our secrets," a phrase that comes out of the scene when a trap is used to catch a soldier for the first time. In that moment, an older woman stays behind when others from the community flee and manage to escape the soldiers. However, instead of passively dying, the old woman scares the soldiers with an ax and causes one of the fleeing soldiers to fall into a trap. After the soldier falls into the trap, the community comes back to the village and is able to convince the soldier to desert the military and return to his own community. Menchú declares this moment a victory, specifically, a triumph of her community's secrets: "Para mí era un gozo que gozaba tanto, tanto. Y yo decía, esto es el triunfo de nuestros secretos que nadie ha descubierto" (*MLRM*, 173) (I was so overjoyed, so overjoyed. I said: "This is a great victory for our secrets, no one has discovered them" [*IRM*, 147]). What has triumphed, then, is not necessarily the old woman or even Menchú's community as a whole, but rather this "testimony" or inheritance from the past: it is "the triumph of our secrets." This triumph of the secrets comes up repeatedly in Menchú's text, specifically in moments when discussing the political strategy of employing traps or hidden figures against the maneuvers of the landowners and the government. After all, the trap is versatile precisely to the extent that it appears as nothing: it is an absence, a hole that captures and therefore leads to an interruption in the forces of the enemy. In the scene with the old woman and the soldier, the trap in effect converts the soldier, allowing Menchú and others to convince him to desert the army which thereby drains the army of its manpower. The hidden figure triumphs by instigating a sudden fall, which is also a sudden fall from power. In fact, I will argue that Menchú's politics—her political violence—is defined by this notion of an interruption of the enemy's power.

One such "trap" is what she also calls "propaganda bombs." Menchú describes the individual strategies that her political organization has sought to introduce amongst the people. She states:

> Our idea is to put into practice the methods initiated by the masses when they evolved their "people's weapons." . . . What we use most in Guatemala are propaganda bombs. . . . We wanted to weaken the government economically, politically and militarily. We weaken them economically by our actions in that, although the workers carry on working, they tamper with their machines or break parts. Small things that drain economic resources. (*IRM*, 231–32)

Menchú states that the political goal of her organization is to produce a generalized *"desgaste"* (*MLRM*, 256). It is the attempt to create an interruption in power by wearing down the system economically, politically, and militarily. As Menchú describes it, one such *desgaste* can be produced through small interventions, such as when the workers sabotage their own machines. This minimal mechanism or imperceptibly small machination, to use Piglia's terms, represents a hidden kind of work, since the workers continue to work even as they unwork the system. Menchú describes a situation, during one week in May 1981, when it would have been impossible to undertake a general strike, since the government would have attacked any mass demonstration. Therefore, instead of producing that kind of manifestation or protest, Menchú's organization began to call in a series of bomb threats located at a number of factories. Although Menchú states that there were no bombs, the factories were forced to let all the workers leave, thus allowing many workers to get a week's vacation, since Menchú's organization continued with these threats all week. However, the true goal of this strategy is not simply to get time off, but rather to produce an interruption by means of an "invisible" display of power. She states: "This was one way to get rest for the workers. But above all, what we achieved was that the government had

to recognize that our strength lies in the strength of the people themselves, who step by step are learning to do things better" (*IRM*, 233). The
idea is therefore not simply to produce a short delay but rather to produce a radical interruption through hidden sabotage and anonymous
phone calls. This specific strategy of calling in a bomb threat ends up
wearing down the police forces, in that the police cannot tell the difference between a real bomb threat and a fake one: the bomb threats wear
down the government's capacity to *distinguish* the real from the fake, to
recognize the traps that are lying in wait.

This strategy therefore produces a greater interruption than simply a
vacation from work: it produces a weakening of power through a strategy of secrecy. Because the exact origin of these attacks is unknown, it
begins to seem as if the entire populace is the source of the interruption.
Through a metonymic displacement, these attacks are ascribed to the
invisible masses, what Menchú refers to as the capacity of the people
itself. According to this strategy of secrecy, a populist politics arises from
the use of hidden traps which cannot be given a clear origin. This is not,
Menchú says, a clandestine struggle that takes place from the security of
the mountains. Rather, this is a *secret* struggle that is secret precisely to
the extent that it takes place out in the open, but hidden amongst the
masses. As Menchú explains: "It is secret, but not a clandestine movement. We are the people and we can't hide completely. What we call
'clandestine' are the armed *campañeros* who live, not among the people,
but up in the mountains. What we call 'secret' is all the work which we
do secretly among the people" (*IRM*, 245). Menchú therefore describes a
secret work that takes place out in the open: it is any kind of work that is
carried out while hidden amongst the people. This anonymous work is
sustained through the formation of a number of hidden figures or traps,
and the effect of this anonymous work produces a double tale. On the
one hand, we have the narration of a number of traps: acts of small
sabotage, a series of bomb threats, sudden barricades that disperse when
the police arrive. These acts are above all acts of narration: they succeed
to the extent that they are narrated repeatedly, for instance in reports or
rumors. This first tale is therefore an explicit act of narration. On the
other hand, this first tale of a series of traps suggests the existence of
another tale, a secret tale, a story about a vast popular conspiracy that is
able to produce a military, economic, and political interruption or *desgaste*. As I noted above, Menchú figures this second story as a capacity
that comes directly from the people: "logramos que el Gobierno reconoz-
ca *nuestra capacidad* que es la del mismo pueblo" (*MLRM*, 257; my emphasis) (we made the Government recognize our capacity, an ability that
comes from the people). Menchú's politics depends on the successful
narration of this double tale. Strangely the second tale is a story without a
telling: it is never told as such, but is rather secretly transmitted through
the performance of these secrets or traps. At the same time, the second

tale no longer refers only to the specific act in question (the sabotage of a factory) but rather takes on a broader scope that *figures* the intervention of a "people" that otherwise would have no possible voice.

Secrecy is therefore a political strategy in Menchú's text, not because the text withholds information, but rather because it tells the story of a series of hidden figures or traps. Politics here is not based on the *manifestation* of power, and it is not the declaration of a single, unified subject. Menchú's concept of the *desgaste* is a refusal of that form of power, and rather entails the gradual and continual interruption of power. Menchú describes this strategy as a kind of political violence, what she continually calls "*la violencia justa,*" a just violence that consists in the interruption of power. And this violence has more to do with the confusion that it produces, the *desgaste*, than it does with the loss of life or even of property. It has to do with the nature of its secrecy, the fact that it takes place out in the open, but is nevertheless hidden or invisible. Therefore, to proclaim, as Menchú does, the triumph of her secrets, is in fact to talk about the triumph of her hidden figures, the traps that produce a generalized loss of power and introduce the beginning of a political intervention.

In this way, politics begins in Menchú's text by falling into a trap. This "fall" is a necessary moment, since it reproduces the way that politics, if it is to be politics at all, must be a contingent happening. For example, the soldier captured by the old woman is in fact an "indio," an indigenous man who nevertheless has no ties with Menchú's community. The soldier is therefore not "naturally" part of the political uprising, as if his categorization as "indigenous" would necessarily place him within Menchú's camp. Menchú's politics does not take place on the site of a stable ground, a fixed identity that is simply waiting to be expressed. Rather, Menchú demonstrates that politics, if it happens at all, is contingent and happens in the event of a fall; the soldier must first *fall into the trap of politics*. Menchú's notion of politics takes place precisely to the extent that it is invisible, secret, an absence that is continually undercutting any stable ground. This hidden figure is therefore not a body of knowledge that is kept secret, but rather an act that produces an effect precisely to the extent that it fails to be recognized. This sudden fall is a *desgaste*, a fall from power, a draining or weakening of the system.

Menchú therefore theorizes politics on the basis of the hidden figure. This "secret" is not simply the result of a momentary lack of knowledge, but is rather constitutively incomprehensible and unrecognizable. If it were possible to understand or recognize these hidden figures, then one would already be within the community and there would be no frontier between two antagonistic camps. The hidden figure is therefore the (non)ground for the articulation of any political story that pits an institutional discourse against an anti-institutional discourse that upends the system. As Menchú shows, it is not the content of the hidden figure that produces this constitutive split; rather, it is precisely its "emptiness" that accounts for the political effects of this figure. A hidden figure is therefore "hidden," not necessarily because it is literally invisible, but rather because its inaccessibility demands that it withdraw from representation. It is indistinguishable from what surrounds it—it counterfeits the landscape, as it were—up until the moment when it produces a fall or *desgaste*. If the hidden figure were to appear fully, if it were to reveal itself completely to the light of day, we would have a merely differential relationship between the people and the enemy: in that situation, the group of demands could be addressed and effectively erased. Instead, the hidden figure must always remain hidden, must always remain as a secret if politics is to take place.

It is therefore possible to conclude that the secret "complot" that constitutes the conspiracy narrative is also the necessary "hidden figure" that conditions *any* political narrative. As Ernesto Laclau has noted in relation to populism, a narrative becomes political when there is an unauthorized voice that antagonistically relates to the status quo. Laclau explains:

> Populism means putting into question the institutional order by constructing an underdog as an historical agent—i.e., an agent which is an *other* in relation to the way things stand. But this is the same as politics. We only have politics through the gesture which embraces the existing state of affairs as a system and presents an alternative to it (or, conversely, when we defend that system against existing potential alternatives). That is the reason why the end of populism coincides with the end of politics. We have an end of politics when the community conceived as a totality and the will representing that totality become indistinguishable from each other.[42]

In this way, the hidden figure—or the "underdog"—can never appear as such, because this kind of appearance would spell the end of politics: the hidden figure would no longer be a threat that undermines the status quo. Politics takes place only to the extent that the underdog discourse stays hidden. But "hidden" now no longer refers to the realm of visibility, but rather has to do with the way that the underdog discourse or low type "speaks" even though this figure is not authorized to speak. The speech of the low type does not produce an *intended* effect, but rather, like a misfired performative utterance, ends up performing an interruption, a *desgaste*. This moment of interruption is the event of politics, when a low type effectively intervenes in the social field precisely because this figure is not authorized to intervene. In this way, the underdog discourse is not only a figure that is hidden, but also presents itself as an antagonistic other that threatens the way things stand. This play of legitimacy between an authorized speech act and an unauthorized speech act is therefore not only the form of so-called paranoid fiction, but also describes the necessary form of any political narrative.

NOTES

1. Ricardo Piglia, *Formas breves* (Barcelona: Editorial Anagrama, 2000), 127. Unless otherwise noted, all translations are my own.

2. Ibid.

3. Ibid.

4. Ibid.

5. Pynchon uses two spellings to refer to the postal conspiracy: "Trystero" and "Tristero." Because I begin my reading of the postal conspiracy from the narrator's comparison of the Nefastis Machine and what is called the "Trystero," I will use this spelling throughout, except for those cases when the narrator explicitly uses "Tristero." In other words, I will be consistent in the spelling of this name, but not to the point of misquoting the text.

6. For example, N. Katherine Hayles, in "'A Metaphor of God Knew How Many Parts': The Engine That Drives *The Crying of Lot 49*" (in *New Essays on* The Crying of Lot 49, ed. Patrick O'Donnell [Cambridge: Cambridge University Press, 1991]) asserts that metaphor is the "engine" that drives the novel. However, Hayles's approach relies on the definition of metaphor presented by George Lakoff and Mark Johnson, whereas my argument will focus on the way Pynchon's novel provides its own idiosyncratic definition of metaphor.

7. Thomas Pynchon, *The Crying of Lot 49* (New York: Harper & Row, 1966), 68. Hereafter cited in text as *CL*.

8. J. Kerry Grant provides a useful overview of the critical reaction to Pynchon's use of the term "entropy" (J. Kerry Grant, *A Companion to* The Crying of Lot 49 [Athens: University of Georgia Press, 1994], 81–95). Thomas Richards, in *The Imperial Archive: Knowledge and the Fantasy of Empire* (London: Verso, 1993), suggests the ways in which theories of entropy were already mobilized during the Victorian era (and beyond) as a metaphorical matrix for discussions of state power.

9. Thomas Schaub notes that the metaphorical connections described in the Nefastis Machine also pertain to the description of Oedipa's *search* for the conspiracy "Trystero": "Many of the connections which Oedipa establishes are bogus. Like the metaphor of 'entropy' in the Nefastis machine, the links created by her on the basis of 'sound' . . . often join realities which bear no literal relation to one another. On a metaphorical level, however, they do. . . . Language, as metaphor, becomes the source of connection; and the connection has reality only in the language itself" (Thomas Schaub, "Open Letter in Response to Edward Mendelson's 'The Sacred, the Profane, and *The Crying of Lot 49*,'" *Boundary 2: An International Journal of Literature and Culture* 5 [Fall 1976]: 98). While I agree with Schaub that the metaphorical structure defines the way conspiracy is presented in Pynchon's novel, I do not find that this structure only obtains at the level of Oedipa's search, or that the connections only take place at the level of language (if language is, as he suggests, in opposition to "reality"). Rather, as we will see, conspiracy—that is, a structure that produces and is produced by incomprehensible relations—happens in "reality"—that is, as a political fact—precisely because of its linguistic nature.

10. For a discussion of the way politics is inextricably linked to postal institutions, see Geoffrey Bennington's "Postal Politics and the Institution of the Nation," in *Legislations: The Politics of Deconstruction* (London: Verso, 1994). While Bennington's article is not a direct reading of *The Crying of Lot 49*, he briefly suggests that Pynchon's novel "might be read as an allegory of all the issues raised here," including the relation between politics and secrecy (255).

11. In part, I owe this notion of a political countereconomy to Piglia's reading of the Argentine writer Roberto Arlt: "*Hacer* dinero: Arlt toma esta frase como esencia de la sociedad y la interpreta literalmente. Hacer dinero quiere decir fabricarlo: la falsificación es la estrategia central de la contraeconomía arltiana" (Ricardo Piglia, "Roberto Arlt: La ficción del dinero" in *La Argentina en pedazos* [Buenos Aires: Ediciones de la Urraca, 1993], 124) (To *make* money: Arlt takes this phrase as the essence of

society and interprets it literally. To make money means to fabricate it: counterfeiting is the central strategy of the Arltian countereconomy). I develop Piglia's notion of a "countereconomy" or counterfeit economy in "The Theme of the Traitor: Disinheritance in Ricardo Piglia's *Artificial Respiration*."

12. In *The Lettered City*, Ángel Rama describes the way writing is associated with the imperial power that began with the first colonies in the Americas. He notes that writing's function was to give faith (*dar fe*), a kind of "faith" that bears witness to its own authenticity or authority (Ángel Rama, *La ciudad letrada* [Hanover, NH: Ediciones del Norte, 1984], 8–9). This authority then enacts the network of power that stands as the condition of empire. I will return to Rama in the epilogue.

13. Although Pynchon is very explicit about the way resistance is tied to withdrawal ("Their entire emphasis now toward silence, impersonation, opposition masquerading as allegiance" [143]), some critics have fought against this insight. For example, Samuel Thomas insists that the Trystero-like group Inamorati Anonymous (or IA) "is a form of *withdrawal* rather than a form of *resistance*" (Samuel Thomas, *Pynchon and the Political* [New York: Routledge, 2007], 122). Thomas strangely goes on to say that withdrawal is a kind of substitute resistance: "withdrawal can become a displaced form of resistance under the most extreme circumstances" (125). Thomas's study more generally is a laudable attempt to rethink the political in Pynchon, often with reference to the work of Theodor Adorno. In fact, the stated goal at the beginning of his study seems to share my interest in the cryptological nature of politics, as when he writes that "it is this 'secret' [the secret of a legacy, of an inheritance] that I wish to explore, through Pynchon, as politics" (9). However, although he states that "politics, in this sense, 'is never a given' but 'a *task*,'" it becomes clear later in his study that politics for Thomas has to do with the revelation of full presence and the legitimization of a secret that has now come to light: "Perhaps . . . there is a habitable, legitimate space emerging from this process—something hidden becoming visible, something fugitive taking root, something oblique drawing closer in" (150). In the end, Thomas argues that the political, in Pynchon, is merely the moment of empathy or "unmediated human contact," when one already-constituted subject becomes fully present to another (130).

14. Pynchon emphasizes this subjunctive mode more explicitly in *Mason & Dixon*: "Does Britannia, when she sleeps, dream? Is America her dream?—in which all that cannot pass in the metropolitan Wakefulness is allow'd Expression away in the restless Slumber of these Provinces, and on West-ward, wherever 'tis not yet mapp'd, nor written down, nor ever, by the majority of Mankind, seen,—serving as a very Rubbish-Tip for subjunctive Hopes, for all that *may yet be true*" (Thomas Pynchon, *Mason & Dixon* [New York: Picador, 1997], 345).

15. Ernesto Laclau, "Why do Empty Signifiers Matter to Politics?" in *Emancipation(s)* (London: Verso, 1996), 40.

16. Ernesto Laclau, *On Populist Reason* (London: Verso, 2005), 86.

17. Ibid., 81.

18. Austin writes: "Suppose you are just about to name the ship, you have been appointed to name it, and you are just about to bang the bottle against the stern; but at that very moment some low type comes up, snatches the bottle out of your hand, breaks it on the stern, shouts out 'I name this ship the *Generalissimo Stalin*,'and then for good measure kicks away the chocks. Well, we agree of course on several things. We agree that the ship certainly isn't now named the *Generalissimo Stalin*, and we agree that it's an infernal shame and so on and so forth. . . . We might say that here is a case of a perfectly legitimate and agreed procedure which, however, has been invoked in the wrong circumstances, namely by the wrong person, this low type instead of the person appointed to do it" (J. L. Austin, "Performative Utterances," in *Philosophical Papers*, ed. J. O. Urmson and G. J. Warnock [Oxford: Oxford University Press, 1979], 239–40).

19. J. L. Austin, *How to Do Things with Words*, ed. J. O. Urmson and Marina Sbisà (Cambridge: Harvard University Press, 1975), 22.

20. Ibid.

21. Ibid., 17.

22. As J. Hillis Miller notes, Austin's speech act theory explicitly brings up the question of what belongs inside and what must be excluded. Responding to Austin's remark that an actor's performative utterance is parasitic upon its normal use, Miller explains: "Parasitic certainly means 'dependent on,' as a parasitic plant is dependent on, lives off of its host. The word 'parasitic' originally referred to a man who eats you out of house and home: the man who came to dinner and stayed. . . . The question is whether the parasite may not belong in the home, or come to be at home there, that is, whether literature [an utterance said by an actor on stage, introduced in a poem, or spoken in a soliloquy] may not after all be an essential part of the economy of speech acts" (J. Hillis Miller, *Speech Acts in Literature* [Stanford: Stanford University Press, 2001], 36). See also Bonnie Honig's work, especially when she shows that Hannah Arendt's theory of political action can be read in relation to Austin's theory of performatives and Derrida's reading of Austin. Honig is especially useful since she emphasizes (following Derrida) the necessity of the *infelicitous* speech act, if an act is going to be political: "on [Arendt's] account as on Derrida's, the possibility of infelicity is a structurally necessary possibility of action (hence Arendt's insistence that contingency is a necessary condition of action). Speech action would be something else if it could not go awry. . . . If speech action was only felicitous, we would be in a realm of process and predictability where calculation, but not action, would be the appropriate modus operandi. . . . [W]hen action works, it is not in spite of but partly because of the risk, infelicity, and dissemination that are action's characteristic features" (Bonnie Honig, *Political Theory and the Displacement of Politics* [Ithaca, NY, and London: Cornell University Press, 1993], 91–92). Recently, Thomas Keenan has developed the political significance of the "low type." He notes that the low type, not only in Austin's theory but also in events such as the Fifth Annual AIDS Conference in Montreal, teaches "a difficult lesson: there could be no politics without irony, without copying, without enigma, and without drift" (Thomas Keenan, "Re JD: Remembering Jacques Derrida (part 2)/Drift: Politics and the Simulation of Real Life," *Grey Room* 21 [Fall 2005]: 107).

23. Jacques Derrida, *Limited Inc.*, trans. Samuel Weber (Evanston, IL: Northwestern University Press, 1988), 90.

24. Rigoberta Menchú, *Me llamo Rigoberta Menchú y así me nació la conciencia*, ed. Elizabeth Burgos (Mexico City: Siglo Veintiuno Editores, S.A., 1985). Hereafter cited in the text as *MLRM*.

25. Elisabeth Burgos-Debray, *I, Rigoberta Menchú: An Indian Woman in Guatemala*, trans. Ann Wright (London: Verso, 1984). Hereafter cited in the text as *IRM*.

26. Arturo Arias notes that Menchú's narrative is constitutively hybrid, in that "she visualized a double task: to explain Mayan culture and subjectivity to the outside world and to argue for its rightful place in the Guatemalan opposition. These undertakings forced her into an inevitable duality. She had to embrace elements of Western discourse to make herself heard by her target audiences, but she also had to guarantee the preservation and continuity of her Mayan identity, which was the validating element of her discourse. This is why she performs her identity as she does, mediating Mayan 'secrets' and Western parameters of understanding" (Arturo Arias, "Authoring Ethnicized Subjects: Rigoberta Menchú and the Performative Production of the Subaltern Self," *PMLA* 116 [January 2001]: 80). It is precisely because of the hybrid nature of Menchú's text that critics like David Stoll have attacked Menchú for not truly representing the voice of subaltern groups in Guatemala. Arias summarizes this view: "Burgos-Debray attempted to subordinate the 'subaltern' Mayan component (as Spivak defines it), turning the text into a hybrid Western-Mayan document with clear Western legibility" (Arias, "Authoring," 81). As Arias notes, this problem of representing the subaltern was famously developed in Gayatri Chakravorty Spivak's essay "Can the Subaltern Speak?" John Beverley summarizes Spivak's view by noting that "the subaltern cannot speak in a way that would carry any sort of authority or meaning for us [the Western intellectual] without altering the relations of power/knowledge that constitute it as subaltern in the first place" (John Beverley, "Theses on Subalter-

nity, Representation, and Politics," in *Postcolonial Studies* 1.3 [November 1998]: 306). In what follows I will address what Beverley calls the "'silence' of the subaltern" by reading Menchú's own account of silence or secrecy in her necessarily hybrid text (Beverley, "Theses," 306).

27. John Beverley, *Testimonio: On the Politics of Truth* (Minneapolis: University of Minnesota Press, 2004), 33.

28. Of course, this could also be argued through a reading of Jacques Derrida's "Signature Event Context," especially when he notes that a signature only possesses its force—and produces an event—if it is always a "counterfeit" signature: "In order to function, that is, to be readable, a signature must have a repeatable, iterable, imitable form; it must be able to be detached from the present and singular intention of its production. It is its sameness which, by corrupting its identity and its singularity, divides its seal" (Derrida, *Limited*, 20). For that reason, Derrida signs his text by noting the counterfeit nature of his signature: "That dispatch [the original conference paper] should thus have been signed. Which I do, and counterfeit, here" (Derrida, *Limited*, 21).

29. Beverley, *Testimonio*, 33.

30. Doris Sommer, "No Secrets," in *The Real Thing: Testimonial Discourse and Latin America*, ed. Georg M. Gugelberger (Durham, NC: Duke University Press, 1996), 146. Alberto Moreiras is not as optimistic that the critic can form such a coalition with Menchú: "The voice that speaks in testimonio—I am referring to the testimonial voice, and not to the paratextual voice of the author or mediator—is metonymically representative of the group it speaks for. But this is not true for the critic of testimonio, who is at best—in this sense not unlike the paratextual voice of testimonio—in a metaphoric relation with the testimonial subject through an assumed and voluntaristically affirmed solidarity with it" (Alberto Moreiras, "The Aura of Testimonio," in *The Real Thing: Testimonial Discourse and Latin America*, ed. Georg M. Gugelberger [Durham, NC: Duke University Press, 1996], 197).

31. David Stoll, *Rigoberta Menchú and the Story of All Poor Guatemalans* (Philadelphia: Westview Press, 2008), 217.

32. Ibid., 247. It is worth noting that John Beverley, among others, has located the *efficacy* of *testimonio* precisely in the way that it relies on "inauthentic" modes of knowledge. After all, the radical nature of *testimonio* is that it intervenes in the way the subaltern is constituted through a certain mode of knowledge. As Beverley notes, studying the subaltern "points to a new register of knowledge where the power of the university to understand and represent the world breaks down or reaches a limit" (Beverley, "Theses," 306). In other words, to study or "know" the subaltern from the position of the university ends up intervening in the way that the university produces knowledge. This intervention can take place, in part, because of a narrative like *testimonio*, which no longer relies on the authority of the lettered city. Beverley writes: "Because of the presence of the voice in its narrative form, *testimonio* tends to affirm the authority of orality against processes of cultural modernisation that privilege literacy and written literature as norms of expression. In societies of primary orality, cultural-political transmission depends primarily on rumour and storytelling. Rumour (as opposed to 'news') operates according to a fluid dynamic of anonymity, improvisation, and transitivity" (Beverley, "Theses," 311). Rumor can be privileged, for Beverley, because of the way that it produces a different kind of knowledge. More specifically, it produces an *unauthorized* knowledge, a type of knowledge that is constitutively uncertain. As Spivak notes, "it is more appropriate to think of the power of rumor in the subaltern context as deriving from its participation in the structure of illegitimate writing rather than the authoritative writing of the law" (Gayatri Chakravorty Spivak, *In Other Worlds* [New York: Methuen, 1987], 213). I would therefore have to disagree with Beverley's suggestion that *testimonio* privileges the *authority* of orality. While it certainly privileges discourses like rumor, these discourses or modes of storytelling present themselves precisely as unauthorized. We could even say that *testimonio*, as a discourse, "Stoll-ifies" itself right from the beginning: it is constitutively

counterfeit and lacking authority, long before historians like David Stoll began to investigate the authority of a narrative like Menchú's. As I will argue in what follows, *testimonio* depends on this de-authorizing gesture to produce political effects.

33. Sommer, "No Secrets," 130.

34. Ibid.

35. Ibid., 142.

36. Ibid., 142–43.

37. Menchú's insistence on secrecy has more generally been used to help guide debates on how to approach subaltern discourses. An exemplary document is the "Founding Statement" of the Latin American Subaltern Studies Group, which alludes to Menchú precisely at a moment in the manifesto that serves as both a send-off and a warning: "We need to conclude this statement, however, with a recognition of the limits of the idea of 'studying' the subaltern and a caution to ourselves in setting out to do this. Our project, in which a team of researchers and their collaborators in elite metropolitan universities want to extricate from documents and practices the oral world of the subaltern, the structural presence of the unavoidable, indestructible, and effective subject who has proven us wrong—she/he who has demonstrated that we did not know them—must itself confront the dilemma of subaltern resistance to and insurgency against elite conceptualizations. Clearly, it is a question not only of new ways of looking at the subaltern, new and more powerful forms of information retrieval, but also of building new relations between ourselves and those human contemporaries whom we posit as objects of study. Rigoberta Menchú's injunction at the end of her famous testimonio is perhaps relevant in this regard: 'I'm still keeping secret what I think no-one should know. Not even anthropologists or intellectuals, no matter how many books they have, can find out all our secrets'" (Latin American Subaltern Studies Group, "Founding Statement," *Boundary 2* 20.3 [Autumn 1993]: 121). I will return to this quote from Menchú toward the end of this chapter.

38. Because the English translation of Menchú's work often summarizes crucial passages, and because Menchú's specific rhetoric is crucial for my argument, I have provided my own translations of the Spanish, unless otherwise noted.

39. Walter Benjamin, "The Storyteller: Observations on the Works of Nikolai Leskov," in *Selected Writings, Volume 3: 1935–1938* (Cambridge: Harvard University Press, 2002), 150.

40. Jean-François Lyotard defines the *infans* as that which has a voice, but which does not articulate: "cela a de la voix, mais n'articule pas. Non référentielle et inadressée, la phrase infantile est signal affectuel, plaisir, douleur. . . . On ne dira pas que *infans* parle une autre langue, puisqu'une langue est par définition traduisible dans une langue connue. Il n'est donc pas non plus une autre personne" (Jean-François Lyotard, *Lectures d'enfance* [Paris: Éditions Galilée, 1991], 138).

41. La Real Academia Española defines "distinguir" as "Ver un objeto, diferenciándolo de los demás, a pesar de alguna dificultad que haya para ello, como la lejanía, la falta de diafanidad en el aire, la debilidad de la vista, etc."

42. Ernesto Laclau, "Populism: What's in a Name?" in *Populism and the Mirror of Democracy*, ed. F. Panizza (London: Verso, 2005), 47–48.

FOUR

The Discovery of Politics

On August 21, 2007, President Bush addressed rumors that the United States, Canada, and Mexico were establishing a super-state called the North American Union, complete with its own laws, regulations, and even a new currency (the "Amero"). In effect, the North American Union, if it existed, threatened to dissolve the sovereignty of each of the three member nations. In a press conference with President Felipe Calderón of Mexico and Prime Minister Stephen Harper of Canada, President Bush states:

> We each respect each other's sovereignty. You know, there are some who would like to frighten our fellow citizens into believing that relations between us are harmful for our respective peoples. . . . I'm amused by some of the speculation, some of the old—you can call them political scare tactics. If you've been in politics as long as I have, you get used to that kind of technique where you lay out a conspiracy and then force people to try to prove it doesn't exist. That's just the way some people operate.[1]

Not only does Bush insist that there is no threat to the sovereignty of the three nations, but he also condemns rumors about a secretive North American Union as "political scare tactics." The "Amero Conspiracy" (as it has been called) is part of a "technique," Bush notes, that has long been a part of politics, even if it should be placed on the margins of what really happens in the political world. In his statement to the press, President Bush goes on to explain what this "technique" usually entails: "I'm amused by the difference between what actually takes place in the meetings and what some are trying to say takes place. It's quite comical, actually, when you realize the difference between reality and what some people are talking on TV about."[2] Although the conspiracy theorists in the media would like to insist that there is a secret threat to the sovereign-

121

ty of the nation, President Bush dismisses this threat as merely the amus-
ing ramblings of "some people." However, as comical as these rumors
may be, they are also very serious since they threaten to derail political
discussion and ultimately force politicians to respond to a controversial
scenario that does not correspond to the real world. For Bush, there
would be a clear difference between the real story that actually takes
place and the fake story (the conspiracy theory disseminated by the media) that, he suggests, does not exist. This second story—"what some are
trying to say takes place"—is simply the way "some people" operate:
they lay out a conspiracy as a taunt, hoping to ensnare serious political
leaders in an illusory debate.

Counterfeit Politics has argued, however, that this is not simply the
way "some people" operate, but rather defines the way political narratives necessarily operate. After all, even when President Bush explicitly
argues against conspiracy theories, he nevertheless has recourse to the
structure of conspiracy theory in order to make his argument. In effect,
Bush replaces one secret with another: instead of postulating a secretive
super-state that threatens the sovereignty of traditional nation-states,
Bush posits the existence of a nebulous community—"some people"—
that is *always* on the outside of politics looking in: these people do not
know "what actually takes place," but their conspiracy theories nevertheless infect the inner sanctum of politics by forcing politicians like President Bush to respond to this fantasy about power. Bush's statement is
therefore itself part of what he calls "political scare tactics": his tactic is to
counter one conspiracy theory (the "Amero Conspiracy") with his own
conspiracy theory about the way unauthorized discourses are invading
the very essence of politics.[3]

This "technique" is consistent with the structure I have isolated
throughout this book: a "conspiracy theory" always tells the story of a
secret that continually undermines the main narrative line. In each chapter, I have shown how this secret has been given different names: "coincidence," "complot," hidden figure," "counterfeit," or simply "secret story." In whatever guise, this secret is always presented in conspiracy theories as a *threat* to the stability of a political community. It is for that reason
that critics of conspiracy theories like Richard Hofstadter have attacked
them as pathological in the first place. As I noted in chapter two, Hofstadter's 1964 essay "The Paranoid Style in American Politics" argues that the
narration of a conspiracy theory marks the moment when "normal" politics disappears and is replaced by an extremist or "paranoid" understanding of history.[4] In fact, Hofstadter notes that, for the conspiracy
theorist, "[h]istory *is* a conspiracy, set in motion by demonic forces of
almost transcendent power, and what is felt to be needed to defeat it is
not the usual methods of political give-and-take, but an all-out crusade."[5]
For Hofstadter, as soon as one admits to the presence of a hidden figure
(a demonic force), the "paranoid" politician then forgets the "normal"

give-and-take of politics and instead begins an antagonistic crusade intent on annihilating that hidden enemy. In other words, conspiracy theories willfully suspend the "normal" procedures of politics in order to combat an internal enemy that is threatening to destroy the stability of the *polis*.[6] For Hofstadter, the precise moment when conspiracy theories are voiced is clearly the end of politics, since this kind of discourse signals the end of negotiation and the beginning of violence.[7] The "paranoid style" of politics would therefore be part of what Bush calls a political scare tactic that is employed only to produce terror.

In what follows, I will agree, to a certain extent, with Hofstadter's concerns about conspiracy theories. Indeed, it is possible to argue that conspiracy theories, by attempting to save the *polis* from the subversions of a hidden agent, end up dissolving the norms of consensus that constitute the political community in the first place. The "paranoid" politics of conspiracy theories therefore would seem to threaten the very possibility of politics. However, I will go on to argue that this is true only if we also say that any political narrative necessarily threatens the possibility of politics. In other words, the threat to politics is not an exception but rather stands as the conditions of political discourse.[8] In what follows, I will focus on two conspiracy narratives—Jorge Luis Borges's short story "Tlön, Uqbar, Orbis Tertius" and Thomas Pynchon's novel *Gravity's Rainbow*—to suggest that politics takes place only when the *polis* itself is at stake, that is, whenever the story of a community (a "we") is invaded by the story of an enemy (a "they") that threatens the future of politics. This also means that the "Invasion narrative" that is so common in conspiracy theories is not simply an element of the fantastic that has been wrongfully grafted onto political narratives. On the contrary, I will argue that all political narratives necessarily contain this moment of invasion, that is, the moment when the *polis* is truly threatened by a shadowy figuration that seems to come from the outside. Conspiracy theory, then, is the paradoxical narrative that produces politics at the very same moment that it narrates an imminent threat to politics.

THE TLÖNIAN INVASION, OR POLITICS AT RISK (BORGES)

In Jorge Luis Borges's 1941 short story "Tlön, Uqbar, Orbis Tertius," the Argentine writer narrates the discovery of a conspiracy or secret society that has introduced a series of counterfeit objects into the real world, thereby confusing the relation between reality and fiction. This conspiracy, according to the narrator, is figured not only as a general invasion of the world, but rather more specifically as a threat that is besieging any notion of a political community. However, Borges's story not only narrates the discovery of this destabilizing conspiracy, but also destabilizes, in turn, the very notion of a "discovery." In effect, Borges asks: what would it mean to *discover* the event of a conspiracy? The problem is that, throughout "Tlön," there is a fundamental confusion over whether a reader is discovering an event or producing an event. I would like to argue that politics only takes place when a discovery is also the production of an effect that cannot be controlled by the main narrative line. Thus, even though the narrator seems to discover the end of politics, I will show that this statement of discovery also *produces* politics in its very utterance.

The short story that begins Borges's collection *Ficciones* (1944) is, as Borges himself remarks in the "Prologue," a note on an imaginary book. However, his procedure in "Tlön, Uqbar, Orbis Tertius" is different from his other stories that purport to be commentaries on another text. "Tlön" is not a book review of a novel or a commentary on a philosophical text (as are, for example, "The Approach to Al-Mu'Tasim" or "Three Versions of Judas," respectively), but rather tells the story of a man (the narrator) who discovers a conspiracy to take over the world by means of an apocryphal encyclopedia. A large part of the story therefore indeed functions as a commentary on the encyclopedic texts that describe various imaginary lands. The first encyclopedia describes "Uqbar," an imaginary region that is perhaps located in the Middle East. The later encyclopedias then describe the planet "Tlön," which presumably exists only in the fantastic literature of Uqbar. Because the narrator fortuitously finds an apocryphal encyclopedia of Tlön, the majority of the tale consists of a commentary on this imaginary world as it appears in a fake reference book. The last section of Borges's tale, however, shifts from the mode of commentary to the mode of the jeremiad: the narrator complains that the real world has now been infected by the contagious logic of Tlön and claims that the real world—and implicitly the possibility of democracy—will disappear as a result. Borges therefore combines the scholarly mode of commentary with the fantastic narration of an alien invasion (by the logic of Tlön) in order to produce a miniaturized conspiracy narrative.

In this sense, Borges crystallizes in "Tlön" the central mechanism of the twentieth-century conspiracy narrative: it is the story of the discovery of a secret (though apocryphal) history that threatens to overturn a more official history. In fact, there are three major discoveries, which correspond to the three sections of the text. In the first section, the narrator describes the conditions of the first discovery and the problems that this discovery opens up. The narrator and Adolfo Bioy Casares (an actual friend of Borges's and the author of *The Invention of Morel*, among other texts) stumble upon the existence of an imaginary country named Uqbar. They find the description of Uqbar in an article of an encyclopedia that only Bioy seems to own. This discovery not only leads them to the idea of a fictional world within the context of the real world (the rest of the encyclopedia seems more or less similar to the 1902 edition of the *Encyclopedia Britannica*), but also introduces the mystery of a "pirated" encyclopedia. At the same time, the narrator notes in passing that the literary works written in the imaginary land of Uqbar all fit within the genre of the fantastic and take place on two imaginary planets: either Mlejnas or Tlön. The section ends with the narrator's attempt to find other references to Uqbar in other encyclopedias, but all of his investigations point to the fact that Bioy's pirated volume is unique.

The second section begins with the narration of a second discovery. A friend of the narrator's father, Herbert Ashe, leaves upon his death volume XI of *A First Encyclopedia of Tlön*, which the narrator happens to find. This discovery opens up the "book review" section of the story, in which the narrator describes the main characteristics of Tlön that can be divined from volume XI of the encyclopedia. Beyond the fantastic nature of the Tlönian universe, the narrator is also bewildered by the sudden discovery of this detailed description of an imaginary planet thought up by an imaginary country (Uqbar). This second-order fiction (a fiction of a fiction) disturbs the narrator enough to begin an investigation into the reasons for the sudden appearance of this encyclopedia. The best he can do, however, is conjecture that it must be the work of a secret society. I will return to this conjecture later on.

In the third section of the story, which appears as a postscript dated 1947 (an anachronistic addition, since Borges's story, with its postscript, was first published in 1941), the narrator supplements his previous article in order to speak of what has happened since the discovery of the XIth volume of the Tlönian encyclopedia. He relates that a letter was found in a book owned by Herbert Ashe, in which is explained the origins and task of the secret society that was only conjectured in the second section. The narrator also relates that Tlönian objects have now been "discovered" throughout the world, thus leading to a gradual erosion of the real world in favor of this imaginary world thought up by a fictional country. Thus begins the mode of the jeremiad: the narrator foresees a future in which the real world will be completely overtaken by this counterfeit world. At the same time, he notes that the task of the conspirators has already been accomplished: the very legitimacy of the real world has been undermined by the introduction of elements from the counterfeit world of Tlön.

In this way, Borges's story is constructed as a series of discoveries, with a final complaint that these discoveries are threatening the very substance of the real world. However, in a procedure characteristic of many of Borges's fictions, it turns out that the notion of discovery is itself problematized by the world of Tlön. It is therefore necessary to turn briefly to the "book review" section of the story, in order to focus on the way "discovery" becomes radically unstable within Tlönian logic. The first signs of this destabilization take place when the narrator relates a troubling feature that arises as a result of Tlönian idealism. According to the Encyclopedia that the narrator discovers, the duplication of lost objects regularly takes place in Tlön. In fact, accidental duplication happened for years. For instance: "Two people are looking for a pencil; the first one finds it and says nothing; the second finds a second pencil, no less real, but more in keeping with his expectation. These secondary objects are called *hrönir* and, even though awkward in form, are a little larger than the originals."[9] These secondary objects—*hrönir*—are discovered in the context of a search: after an object has been lost, the search for the object somehow can produce two versions of the same lost object. A search for the lost object therefore doubles it. However, the secondary object is produced in distorted form: it is *"desairada"*—awkward, but also devalued, disesteemed, even humiliated.[10] The *hrön*—as the duplicated objects are known in the singular—can therefore be called a counterfeit object: through duplication, the object is distorted and devalued. To say that the *hrönir* are counterfeit objects is also to say that they are *made against* the form of the original lost object (counterfeit comes from the French word *contrefaire*, which literally means "to make against"). The duplication of lost objects is therefore also a counterfeiting process that works against the original form of the object.[11]

This fantastic procedure is certainly startling, but it is entirely in keeping with the logic of Tlön. Again, Tlönian thought is the result of a certain idealism. The narrator explains: "Su lenguaje y las derivaciones de su lenguaje—la religión, las letras, la metafísica—presuponen el idealismo. El mundo para ellos no es un concurso de objetos en el espacio; es una serie heterogénea de actos independientes" (*OC*, 435) (Their language, with its derivatives—religion, literature, metaphysics—presupposes idealism. For them, the world is not a concurrence of objects in space; it is a heterogeneous series of independent acts [*F*, 23]).[12] The idealism that controls the languages of Tlön posits language as a continual parataxis: every act of language takes place without relation to every other act of language. It is worth noting that Paul de Man, in an early international review of Borges's fiction, claims that much of Borges's own language takes place as parataxis: Borges prefers "what grammarians call parataxis, the mere placing of events side by side, without conjunctions."[13] For that reason, de Man hastily concludes that Borges's stories are constructed out of "a finite number of isolated events incapable of establishing relations among one another."[14] However, in Borges's depiction of Tlönian language, the absence of a mediated relationship between events does not mean that relations do not happen. Rather, relations happen all the time, but these relations take place as events that are strangely productive. As the narrator explains, a noun in the language of one of the southern regions of Tlön can only be formed by an accumulation of adjectives (*OC*, 435). This accumulation of adjectives indeed corresponds to a real object, but this correspondence is on the order of an event, a coming-together that is purely fortuitous. Borges writes: "la masa de adjetivos corresponde a un objeto real; el hecho es puramente fortuito" (*OC*, 435).

Tlönian language therefore fortuitously comes together in an event, an "*hecho*" that cannot be foreseen in advance. Nevertheless, this conglomeration or accumulation produces a correspondence with a real object. In this way, parataxis not only rules the relation between clauses, but also the very connections that produce the possibility of *sustantivos*, of nouns. Because of Tlönian idealism, the mere fact of producing a noun through these accumulations is tantamount to producing a correspondence to a "real object." In Tlön, relations not only happen, they also *produce reality* in their coming together.

This form of idealism, explains the narrator, is present in all of Tlönian thought and therefore invalidates the possibility of science as an authoritative discipline or series of disciplines. The narrator explains: "Este monismo o idealismo total invalida la ciencia. Explicar (o juzgar) un hecho es unirlo a otro; esa vinculación, en Tlön, es un estado posterior del sujeto, que no puede afectar o iluminar el estado anterior. Todo estado mental es irreducible: el mero hecho de nombrarlo—*id est*, de clasificarlo—importa un falseo" (*OC*, 436) (This monism or complete idealism invalidates science. To explain [or judge] an event is to unite it with another; this connection, in Tlön, is a later state of the subject and cannot affect or illuminate a prior state. Every mental state is irreducible: the mere event of naming it—*id est*, classifying it—introduces a falsification). Because the narrator defines the possibility of science as the possibility of linking and therefore forming a narration, there can be no *authoritative* science or knowledge if connections are merely fortuitous. In other words, in Tlön, *all* relations are artificial relations. The usual causal connections between events—for instance, between a cloud of smoke, the countryside on fire, and a half-extinguished cigar (*F*, 24)—do not apply in Tlön, since every event is irreducible to every other event. If one were to try to posit a causal chain between the cigar and the forest fire, a Tlönian would call that connection a mere "association of ideas" (*F*, 24). Each mental state—or each event—stands on its own and cannot be led back to any other event or mental state: each event is irreducible. Between one "*hecho*" and another is always a gap that cannot be bridged in a legitimate way. To try to bridge the gap between events is always illegitimate: either it belongs to the spurious association of ideas, or it is labeled as a falsification. As the narrator explains, to name something (to relate one event to another) is always to introduce a falsification or disfiguration: "*importa un falseo*" (*OC*, 436). It is worth noting that the verb form of "*falseo*," "*falsear*," is not simply "to make false," which would be "*falsificar*." Rather, according to the Real Academia Española, *falsear* is: "to taint or corrupt something, for example coins, writing, doctrine, or thought."[15] Thus to "false" something, "*falsear*," refers to a generalized process of reproducing something so that it comes out corrupted, as in counterfeit money, plagiarism, or apocryphal writing. This effect of artificiality is the result of the way a relation, in Tlön, always introduces a constitutive disfiguration (*importa un falseo*): as soon as there is relation, there is also falsification. To relate (*vincular*) is always to counterfeit, but there would be no relations without the *falseo*.

For this reason, the search for a lost object in Tlön can lead to the discovery (or production) of *hrönir*, secondary objects that are distorted in some way. In the search for a lost object, the act of searching is posited as an event that is arbitrarily connected to the event of losing the object in the first place. In other words, on the one hand there is a lost object, and on the other hand there is the search for the lost object. To try to bring the two together would be to *bring in* a distortion or falsification: *importa un falseo*. This falsification is not simply a judgment, but in itself constitutes an act or event. In other words, the conjunction of two acts or events (*hechos*) produces a third act or event (*hecho*) that takes place as a falsification or corrupted form. Therefore, the act of discovering an object in fact *produces* a counterfeit object. And we can generalize this to say that the logic of discovery/production not only counterfeits lost objects, but also counterfeits anything that is buried, hidden, or not immediately visible. In Tlön, to discover or unveil a secret is actually to produce an endless series of replications in distorted form.

It should be said that within the Tlönian world, there is no confusion here: to discover an object is never simply an act of finding something that was lost, but rather is always an act of producing these *hrönir*. However, from the narrator's point of view (that is, the view from "our world"), to be confronted with the Tlönian logic is to be infected with a fundamental confusion about the very act of finding a *hrön*. For instance, while describing what happens when a group of students in Tlön try to find, that is, produce *hrönir*, the narrator notes his confusion explicitly: "los discípulos exhumaron—o produjeron—una máscara de oro . . . [y otros objetos 'perdidos']" (*OC*, 439) (the students unearthed—or produced—a gold mask . . . [and other 'lost' objects]). The narrator therefore notes the radical uncertainty that haunts the activity of searching for a lost object: the *hrön* is *either* unearthed *or* produced, but the narrator cannot say for sure which is happening here. Therefore, from the narrator's point of view, the search for *hrönir* always takes place within this undecidability between discovery (exhumation) and production.

In this way, Tlönian logic troubles the very idea of "discovery" and introduces an undecidable relation between "discovery" and "production." In fact, it is precisely this undecidability that defines the conspiracy in "Tlön, Uqbar, Orbis Tertius." In the third section of the story, the narrator discovers a document that tells "la espléndida historia" of the development of this conspiracy (*OC*, 440). According to this splendid story/history, a mysterious secret society had worked in relative secrecy since the early 1600s with the mission to create an imaginary country (*F*, 31). This relatively simple mission was completely revamped in the nineteenth century, when the American Ezra Buckley suggested that only the invention of another *planet* would do. He promised to give his fortune to the enterprise, as long as it worked against the idea of God as it appears in Christianity: "Buckley did not believe in God, but nevertheless wished to demonstrate to the nonexistent God that mortal men were capable of conceiving a world" (*F*, 31). The conspiracy to create a secret society—which is now to be called Orbis Tertius—therefore comes about as an attempt to create a counterfeit world, that is, a world that would form itself in an antagonistic relation to "God's world." This task necessitates not only a world in which counterfeiting is a common activity, but rather a world that is itself constituted by the very act of counterfeiting (and the counterfeiting of counterfeits). Tlön is then necessarily counterfeit, since it must work against the "making" or creation found in "God's world." For that reason, the building blocks of Tlön—its language and thought—are characterized by the construction of only artificial relations that in turn create counterfeit events: duplicated objects that in turn can be multiplied. This multiplication of events constitutes the task of the conspirators: to build a world that would not only parallel the real world (the world of God's creation), but would relate to it antagonistically.

This antagonistic relation is the task that continues at the end of the narrator's tale: "Una dispersa dinastía de solitarios ha cambiado la faz del mundo. Su tarea prosigue" (*OC*, 443) (A dispersed dynasty of solitaries has changed the face of the world. Its task continues). The secret society—a dispersed group of loners, a society constituted by a relation without relation—thus surreptitiously continues the work of disseminating objects from Tlön throughout various countries, thereby "saturating" ("*abarrotando*") the real world with elements from the false planet (*OC*, 442). The net effect of this saturation is a gradual undermining of the legitimacy of the real world: "Almost immediately, reality gave ground on more than one point" (*F*, 34). As fragments of Tlön begin to invade the real world, it becomes clear that the task of the conspirators is to work toward the delegitimization of the real world through the introduction of a counterfeit world. The "complaint" that arises from the narrator's jeremiad is that the world will be infected by the logic of Tlön. However, this eventuality has already come to pass: the task of the conspirators has already been accomplished through the introduction of Tlönian logic into the real world and the subsequent delegitimization of the real world. The immediate result is the overthrow of history as it was known before the invasion of the Tlönian world: "Now, in all memories, a fictitious past occupies the place of any other. We know nothing about it with any certainty, not even that it is false" (*F*, 34). The narrator makes it clear that the artificial memory produced by the invasion of Tlönian logic is not *simply* false or wrong, but rather that its counterfeit nature undermines the possibility of certainty. Of course, this would not be a problem for a native of Tlön. It is rather the continual juxtaposition of two different logics or two different systems—the world of Tlön and the narrator's

world—that produces the dissonance of uncertainty. The task of the conspirators is therefore to infect the real world with a lack of certainty about
any stable reality, including the stories it tells about its past.[16] This sudden emergence of a destabilizing plot that undermines the solidity of a
first narrative line is what I have called the complot effect. This effect
emerges as an antagonistic relationship—not to God necessarily, but to
whatever appears as legitimate. Borges's conspiracy theory is therefore
not the story of an already recognized voice that is publicly opposed to
the status quo, but rather takes place, as an event, whenever there is a
secret plot that undermines the legitimacy of the main narrative line. The
voice of Tlön is "secret" because it never appears as such, but rather takes
place as a counterfeit world that duplicates and undermines everything
"legitimate."

In this way, the complot effect of Borges's story opens up the following question: are we dealing with the *discovery* of an object or event from
the past, or the *production* of an object or event from the past? But this
very question opens up another problem: if the notion of "discovery" has
been destabilized, then it is now necessary to go back to those moments
when the narrator speaks about anything that has been discovered, especially the discovery of a conspiracy or secret society.[17] As I noted earlier,
"Tlön" is the story of a narrator who *discovers* the existence of a conspiracy to undermine the real world in favor of a counterfeit world. However,
it is now clear that the conspiracy of Tlön destabilizes the very notion of
"discovery." After all, the imaginary planet "Tlön" is described essentially as a logic that produces counterfeit objects in the very moment of
discovering "lost" objects. To what extent, then, is the narrator's language *already* infected by the logic of Tlön, even at the beginning of the
story? What if the Tlönian logic—this uncertain relation between discovery and production—is already at work whenever the narrator describes
the discovery of Tlön? This would mean that each moment when the
narrator *discovers* an element of the conspiracy must also be considered a
moment when the narrator *produces* the conspiracy. This is not to say that
we must discard the idea of discovery in favor of production. The problem, rather, is that the conspiracy of Tlön takes place *in the narrative* as
discovery/production, not as one or the other.

This undecidable relation between discovery and production is figured in the text as conjecture. In fact, conjecture marks the very existence
of the secret society in the first place; the idea of such a society *occurs* to
the narrator as if the secret society were a *hrön* of some lost object. This
"lost object" is thematized as the apparent loss of the full series of volumes that would make up *A First Encyclopedia of Tlön*. As I noted earlier,
the discovery of Tlön is originally only based on the encounter with
volume XI of *A First Encyclopedia of Tlön*, thus causing the narrator and
associates to begin an investigation into the existence of the other volumes. However, the narrator admits that his "patient investigations have

proved fruitless" (*F*, 22). The investigators are therefore looking for the other encyclopedias as if together these texts would constitute a lost object. Nevertheless, this apparent "lost object" is in fact a transposition of a deeper loss: the inability to account for an encyclopedia that seemingly does not pertain to this world. The relevant "loss" is therefore the inability to tell a story that would understand this anomaly: the first investigators are at a loss to account for the secret relations that would ultimately explain this event. It is within the context of this search for a lost object that the notion of a secret society first comes up.[18] The narrator proposes—as a *conjecture*—the idea that there is a secret society that is responsible for this event: "Se conjetura que este brave new world es obra de una sociedad secreta de astrónomos, de biólogos, de ingenieros, de metafísicos, de poetas, de químicos, de algebristas, de moralistas, de pintores, de geómetros . . . dirigidos por un oscuro hombre de genio" (*OC*, 434) (It is conjectured that this brave new world is the work of a secret society of astronomers, biologists, engineers, metaphysicians, poets, chemists, algebraists, moralists, painters, geometers . . . all led by an obscure man of genius). The narrator finds this conjecture inevitable, since the encyclopedia suggests a mastery of various disciplines that would be impossible for one person alone to achieve. The secret society is therefore posited by an inevitable conjecture, a *throwing-together* (from *conjicere*, to throw together) of individual agents, thereby producing an always expandable series that is held together by the empty figure of an obscure genius. The narrator therefore brings up the idea of a secret society as a proposition articulated through the formation of relations that cannot add up to a complete whole: within the mark of the ellipsis can be added an infinite number of other agents. At the same time, the logic of conjecture takes place precisely at the moment when events cannot be coherently related to form a convincing thesis; instead, relations are simply thrown together, as the etymology of "conjecture" suggests. This notion of conjecture, in fact, describes precisely the way events are merely thrown together in Tlönian logic. To quote the narrator again: "To explain (or judge) an event is to unite it with another; this connection, in Tlön, is a later state of the subject and cannot affect or illuminate a prior state. Every mental state is irreducible: the mere event of naming it—*id est*, classifying it—introduces a falsification" (*OC*, 436). As in the world of Tlön, the construction of a series of contingent relations (what the narrator also calls "conjecture") could be said to have produced a *falseo* or counterfeit event: the secret society itself seems to be a *hrön*, a counterfeit object that was produced as a result of a search for a lost object.

However, we need not assume that the conspiracy to inundate the world with counterfeit objects in fact does not exist, or that it is simply a hoax. Borges's narrative does not offer this kind of certainty either. While it is true that a secret society was in some way produced through its "discovery"—the letter detailing its existence only "came to light" after the conjecture was proposed—nevertheless the prior existence of a secret society is not necessary for a conspiracy to produce effects. The only necessary element is the constitutive confusion between discovery and production. In that moment of confusion, the secret society has *effectively* happened, not only in the past, but also in the present moment of narration. The effects of the conspiracy can be felt even if it is not clear whether the narrative is discovering a previous referent or producing the secret society in the very moment of articulation. In other words, the conspiracy takes place as a discursive event: it takes place whenever a "conjecture" appears, that is, whenever a narrator throws together two or more events.[19] The notion of "conspiracy" is thrown together in this discursive act, thereby producing a destabilizing confusion between discovery and production.

This confusion appears in the narrator's language right from the beginning of Borges's story, when the narrator admits: "I owe the discovery of Uqbar to the conjunction of a mirror and an encyclopedia. . . . The whole affair happened some five years ago" (*F*, 17). Curiously enough, the confusion of the narrator's language is smoothed over in the excellent English translation. Alastair Reid's translation ("the whole affair happened some five years ago") certainly gets the general sense of Borges's "[e]l hecho se produjo hará unos cinco años" (*OC*, 431). However, the rhetoric of an event (*hecho*) that is produced (*se produjo*)—a rhetoric that runs throughout the section on Tlönian logic—is too strong to ignore the specificity of Borges's language. The narrator is suggesting that "Uqbar" is then an "event," an "*hecho*," that was discovered due to the fortuitous conjunction of a mirror and an encyclopedia, but also produced in that same moment five years ago. The conjunction of the mirror and the encyclopedia is fortuitous because, as it turns out, the conjunction happens simply because the narrator's friend is reminded of an encyclopedia entry: "From the far end of the corridor, the mirror was watching us; and we discovered . . . that mirrors have something grotesque about them" (*F*, 17). It is precisely at this point that Bioy Casares recalls a saying from one of the heresiarchs of Uqbar, namely that there is something monstrous about mirrors and copulation, since both end up reproducing human beings and therefore are complicit in the logic of reproduction (*F*, 17). Here, the narrator's friend happens to relate the monstrosity of mirrors (the mirrors have something monstrous about them, "algo monstruoso") to an encyclopedia that talks about the monstrous nature of mirrors and copulation (*OC*, 431). The accidental conjunction of two thoughts is therefore something of an "association of ideas," which is the phrase used to describe how relations might come together *artificially* in Tlön. As we noted earlier, in Tlön there can be no true relation between one event and another, and any attempt to do so is an example of the association of ideas or implies a mere falsification. We can therefore rephrase this opening scene from the perspective of Tlön: Bioy Casares links one phrase-event (mirrors are monstrous) to another phrase-event (mirrors and cop-ulation are monstrous). This linkage, in turn, allows the narrator to dis-cover—or produce—the land of Uqbar.

Borges's story therefore introduces right from the beginning this un-decidable play between discovery and production. These moments of discovery/production recur throughout the story, thereby problematizing the series of discoveries I noted at the beginning. In fact, the logic of the Tlönian conspiracy seems to infect every moment when the conspiracy of Tlön is discovered. After all, the narrator uses the same verb (*"exhumar"*) to describe both the discovery of *hrönir* in Tlön and the discovery of the other volumes of *A First Encyclopedia of Tlön*: "Hacia 1944 un investiga-dor . . . exhumó en una biblioteca de Memphis los cuarenta volúmenes de la Primera Enciclopedia de Tlön. Hasta el día de hoy se discute si ese descubrimiento fue casual o si lo consintieron los directores del todavía nebuloso *Orbis Tertius*" (*OC*, 442) (About 1944, a reporter . . . uncovered, in a Memphis library, the forty volumes of the *First Encyclopedia of Tlön*. Even now it is uncertain whether this discovery was accidental, or whether the director of the still nebulous *Orbis Tertius* condoned it [*F*, 33]). Of course, we can now read the narrator's paranoia about the appar-ently accidental nature of the discovery or exhumation, not in terms of whether a secret society condoned the discovery, but rather whether the volumes were *discovered* by the investigator or *produced* precisely through the search for a "lost object."

This confusion between discovery and production then produces two possible stories. On the one hand, "Tlön, Uqbar, Orbis Tertius" tells the story of a series of discoveries that point to a conspiracy bent on over-throwing the real world in favor of a counterfeit world. However, a sec-ond reading tells the story of a series of productions that counterfeit the real world, either through mirrors and pirated encyclopedias, or through the introduction of counterfeit objects that produce an artificial memory and a false past. At this point it is impossible to decide which story is being told: a story about the discovery of a conspiracy, or a story that enacts and disseminates Tlönian logic. In fact, the confusion produced by the emergence of two contradictory stories is described by the narrator at the beginning of the story, as the topic of a conversation between him and Bioy: "Bioy Casares había cenado conmigo esa noche y nos demoró una vasta polémica sobre la ejecución de una novela en primera persona, cuyo narrador omitiera o desfigurara los hechos e incurriera en diversas contradicciones, que permitieran a unos pocos lectores—a muy pocos lectores—la adivinación de una realidad atroz o banal" (*OC*, 431) (Bioy Casares had dined with me that night and we found ourselves detained by a vast polemic about the execution of a novel in the first person, whose narrator would omit or disfigure the events and would fall into various contradictions, which would permit a few readers—a very few readers—the supposition of an atrocious or banal reality). This discussion surprisingly describes the logic of Tlön, but this passage takes place *before* that logic was manifest in the story. The narrator and Bioy discuss a story that carries within it its own disfigurement, and which allows a certain kind of reader to discover another reality behind the apparent reality. This "discovery" is not a full revelation, but rather a supposition, an *"adivinación,"* a judgment based on conjecture. The exact nature of the other reality "divined" by these few readers is unknown: it might be banal or atrocious, the narrator states. The point is rather that the other story takes place as the disfigurement of the first story, thereby producing the Tlönian effect: what is remembered of the novel is put forward as an artificial memory, since the authority of the first story is now put into question. After all, the events (*"los hechos"*) of the first story are repeated in the "second story," but now those *hechos* seem disfigured or strangely altered in their repetition. What seemed banal in the first story now turns out to be atrocious when repeated. In this way, the second story is not just a different interpretation of the projected novel, but is rather the disfigurement of the first story, thereby producing an effect of confusion and illegitimacy. The question now will always be: which is the *real* story?

This narrative confusion might seem to have little to do with the realm of the political. After all, how does politics relate to this fiction that tells two mutually exclusive stories?[20] Strangely, the narrator himself suddenly brings up the topic, when he compares the Tlönian invasion to certain populist movements in the twentieth century. The narrator writes: "Almost immediately, reality gave ground on more than one point. The truth is that it hankered to give ground. Ten years ago, any symmetrical system whatsoever which gave the appearance of order—dialectical materialism, anti-Semitism, Nazism—was enough to fascinate men. Why not fall under the spell of Tlön and submit to the minute and vast evidence of an ordered planet?" (*F*, 34). The narrator therefore implicitly compares the Tlönian invasion to the kinds of populism often associated with totalitarianism. The introduction of Tlön into our world is then, for the narrator, similar to the way Nazism managed to exert its influence in Germany. For that reason, the narrator's story about the Tlönian invasion seems to be a warning: the invasion of Tlön will spell the end of democratic politics. Thus, when the narrator insists that "reality" longed to give ground, he is in fact referring to the way "men" were taken in by these systems of "order." The inevitable conclusion seems to be that the invasion of Tlön has undermined the *demos* just as Nazism and other "ordered" movements undermined the people by fascinating them with the specter of order.[21]

However, by now this reference to an "ordered planet" should seem odd, if only because Tlön produces anything *but* order: it produces a fundamental confusion about the very order or logic of things. After all, it is not just that one system is dominating, but rather, as seen through the eyes of the narrator, the two systems are being juxtaposed at every moment: on the one hand, the logic of discovery; on the other hand, the logic of production. The only sure thing we know is the coexistence of these two stories which are indeed doubles of each other, but not in a way that one story could simply fold onto the other. The two stories are rather mutually exclusive, irreducible. In this way, Borges's text both describes and enacts the division between two antagonistic stories: an authentic story (the real world) that is continually being invaded by a counterfeit story (the logic of Tlön). On the one hand, the first story is constantly trying to battle against this antagonistic other (the second story). On the other hand, the first story is constantly being invaded by the second story (the first story is always losing ground). "Tlön" is the story of a plot that is fundamentally disrupted by a complot. This antagonistic relation between a plot and a complot is not an accidental feature of the story, nor is it simply a theme of Borges's fiction. Rather, this antagonistic relation is constitutive of the very form of "Tlön, Uqbar, Orbis Tertius."

The narrator's comments therefore seem strange: although the invasion of Tlön clearly signals a radical confusion, the narrator nevertheless figures this confusion as the introduction of order. We could even say that the narrator himself is confused or is part of this more generalized confusion: he confuses the radical instability introduced by Tlön (the threat of disorder) with the introduction of order by Tlön (the threat of order). And just as the narrator figures a moment of confusion as the introduction of order, so he views the confusion of relations as the threat of fixed relations, of totalitarianism. After all, the invasion of Tlönian logic introduces a fundamental instability into the narrative, as if an illegitimate discourse (a counterfeit discourse) were overturning a legitimate discourse. This overturning never fully happens, but rather takes place as a continual invasion. At that point, the very legitimacy of the status quo is put in question, thereby leading to the claim that the continued existence of the political order is under attack. However, this "confusion" is not simply an error on the narrator's part that could be rectified, but rather remains as a condition of any conspiracy narrative: if the mysterious force were not threatening the reigning political order, then this mysterious force could not be figured as an interruption at all. For the mysterious force to be felt as an event, it must be figured as the overturning of the established political order. For that reason, the narrator ends his conspiracy theory about the invasion of Tlön with the lament that democracy too is about to be invaded by its other.

However, I would like to argue that this invasion story is in fact a necessary condition of politics. After all, democracy only begins when there is an effective alternative to the established order. As Ernesto Laclau has argued, "[w]e only have politics through the gesture which embraces the existing state of affairs as a system and presents an alternative to it (or, conversely, when we defend that system against existing potential alternatives)."[22] For Laclau, a story becomes political only when it tells two stories: the story of the existing state of affairs and an effective alternative to that system. The alternative is truly effective only if it is completely other and if this otherness in itself presents a real threat to the status quo. For that reason, Brett Levinson, in his reading of Laclau and Chantal Mouffe, states that politics has to do with the attempt to defend oneself from the constant invasion of an outside force: "For Laclau and Mouffe, political practice involves, on the one hand, the endless opening of a group or self to more of itself, to the more than the self, the antagonism, the overdetermination, or the constitutive outside; and on the other hand, the refusal to open, to struggle to hold one's ground."[23] There are therefore two necessary conditions in this political articulation: first, an invasion of the wholly other, and second, the attempt to counter this other in an antagonistic way. If the alternative to the status quo is not continually invading the system, then there is no reason to take this outside discourse seriously. At the same time, if the status quo were able to listen to the demands without the creation of the antagonistic frontier, then there would be no difference between the system and an alternative system. For that reason, politics can only be said to take place when the wholly other is constantly invading a closed system, when a complot or secret plot is constantly undermining the visible plot.

The narrator of Borges's story exemplifies this movement in his conclusion, when he states that the invasion of Tlön no longer interests him; instead, he decides to withdraw into a hotel room in Adrogué and continue working on a translation of Thomas Browne's *Urn Burial* into Spanish (*F*, 35). In effect, the narrator hopes to hide from the invasion of Tlön by closing himself off in a small room (the hotel in Adrogué) and burying himself in a translation of a literary text. However, this act of closing himself off from Tlön must inevitably fail, since he is smuggling the logic of Tlön into this closed space. After all, translation—especially an *uncertain* or indecisive translation (*"una indecisa traducción"*)—discovers a text by duplicating it, but this duplication is not simply a repetition of the original, but rather stands as a continual becoming-other of the text (*OC*, 443).[24] The same logic of discovery/production follows the narrator into that closed room, in fact follows him into the apparently closed-off sphere of literature (a Quevedian translation of Browne), and shows that its uncertainty is continually invading even these hermetic spaces. In order to produce his translation, the narrator must enter into the logic of Tlön, the very logic that he seeks to escape.[25]

In this way, Borges's story is a conspiracy theory that is also a political articulation: it is marked both by an "endless opening" of itself onto an antagonistic other and by the refusal to open up to this other force.[26] This "invasion narrative" is therefore not simply an element of the fantastic that has nothing to do with politics. Rather, politics only takes place in this moment of invasion, that is, when the political community is truly threatened by a hidden figure that seems to come from the outside. In this way, political narratives depend on this confusion between discovery and production: the discovery of the invasion of Tlön ends up producing a new political articulation.

THE RUINS OF POLITICS (PYNCHON'S *GRAVITY'S RAINBOW*)

The accusation that there is a dangerous other that threatens the possibility of politics is not only a theme in conspiracy theories and fictions such as Borges's short story. It also happens to be a continual complaint in many critical accounts of the political significance of conspiracy theories in general. It seems that whenever conspiracy theories come up, whether they arise in a fictional text or in a critical study, the question of the future of politics becomes inevitable. In fact, even those critics who would like to view conspiracy theories in a positive light end up suggesting that this kind of narrative still threatens the future of politics or the constitution of a political community. In these critical accounts, conspiracy theories are viewed as an attempt to mimic the operations of politics at the same time that they subvert the very possibility of politics. Conspiracy theories therefore function like a hidden figure that is inside political discourse (it mimics its operations), even as it invades political discourse as if it were coming from the outside. However, if conspiracy theories present this kind of internal subversion of politics, then the same would have to be said about any political narrative. In what follows I will show that Pynchon's *Gravity's Rainbow* strangely responds to these critics of conspiracy theories. His novel suggests that the threat that politics will end is always also the moment of discovering the political.

I have already noted the way Richard Hofstadter has condemned conspiracy theory as "paranoid" precisely because of the way these narratives suspend the "the usual political methods of give-and-take" in order to pursue a crusade against a shadowy threat to the *polis*.[27] I have also suggested that Hofstadter's attempt to exclude conspiracy theory from politics tends to repeat the very procedures of the conspiracy theorist. Peter Knight, for instance, links Hofstadter's analysis to the studies of Elaine Showalter, Richard Pipes, Robert S. Robins, and Jerrold Post, in order to show that these critics end up creating a shadowy other that must be driven out of the *polis* before conspiracy theory manages to contaminate the entire community. Knight states that "the figuration of the spread of paranoid thinking as an 'epidemic' (Robins and Post) or a 'plague' (Showalter) likewise renders it an inscrutable and virtually unstoppable force that infiltrates innocent minds."[28] Knight argues that "these commentators thus end up replicating the very mode of paranoid thinking they seek to condemn."[29] Mark Fenster, in *Conspiracy Theories*, is even more critical of Hofstadter and his followers. He writes: "By labeling as pathological any challenge or resistance to 'consensus', the notion of the 'paranoid style' serves as an excuse for neglecting, equating, and even repressing political protest of all sorts."[30] For Fenster, then, the attempt to exclude conspiracy theory becomes an attempt to exclude a range of political protest. He therefore upends the thesis of Hofstadter: rather than state that conspiracy theories are the end of politics, Fenster insists that Hofstadter and his followers, by attempting to exclude conspiracy theories, are in fact extinguishing political speech.[31]

I would like to return now to the way that these attempts to redeem conspiracy theory and cast it as a legitimate politics often end up repeating this tendency to view conspiracy theories as a failure to engage politically. For Frederic Jameson, whose work is clearly important for critics such as Fenster and Knight, conspiracy narratives are a valiant attempt to map the confusing terrain of postmodern culture, even if this valiant attempt ultimately fails. Jameson relates the "conspiratorial text" to "the desire called cognitive mapping" — the desire "to figure out where we are and what landscapes and forces confront us in a late twentieth century whose abominations are heightened by their concealment and their bureaucratic impersonality."[32] For Jameson, the conspiratorial text attempts to map out this confusion with its speculations about hidden forces and secret associations. In *The Geopolitical Aesthetic*, Jameson notes that the conspiratorial text is at least a courageous attempt to represent the hidden forces of global capitalism, even if it falls short of its goal. Speaking specifically of film, he writes: "Conspiracy film takes a wild stab at the heart of all that [late-twentieth-century capitalism], in a situation in which it is the intent and the gesture that counts. Nothing is gained by having been persuaded of the definitive verisimilitude of this or that conspiratorial hypothesis: but in the intent to hypothesize, in the desire called cognitive mapping—therein lies the beginning of wisdom."[33] For Jameson, conspiracy narratives are certainly on the right track, even if the speculations within these stories remain only "wild stabs" at the truth.

In his more extended treatments of the concept of "cognitive mapping," Jameson is even less generous in his judgment of conspiracy narratives. Ultimately, he writes, "[c]onspiracy . . . is a degraded figure of the total logic of late capital, a desperate attempt to represent the latter's system, whose failure is marked by its slippage into sheer theme and content."[34] This emphasis on the "degraded" and "desperate" nature of conspiracy narratives is repeated in *Postmodernism, or the Cultural Logic of Late Capitalism*, where he notes that the conspiracy narrative is, at best, a *substitute* for a truly engaged politics. He finds that conspiracy narratives in literature and popular culture are of interest precisely to the extent that they present "labyrinthine conspiracies of autonomous but deadly interlocking and competing information agencies in a complexity often beyond the capacity of the normal reading mind."[35] At best, however, the kinds of relations posited in conspiracy narratives are merely figures of

the truth: "I want to suggest that our faulty representations of some im-
mense communicational and computer network are themselves but a distorted figuration of something even deeper, namely, the whole world
system of a present-day multinational capitalism."[36] Conspiracy theories
can be read or viewed, Jameson insists, only if they are continually read
for what they are *not* presenting: the narrative of global capitalism. But
even then conspiracy narratives are poor substitutes for a more engaged
political text: "[C]onspiracy theory (and its garish narrative manifestations) must be seen as a degraded attempt—through the figuration of
advanced technology—to think the impossible totality of the contemporary world system. It is in terms of that enormous and threatening, yet
only dimly perceivable, other reality of economic and social institutions
that, in my opinion, the postmodern sublime can alone be adequately
theorized."[37] Conspiracy theory is again useful, but ultimately it stands
as a substitute text that is displacing a successful attempt to map the
cognitive dimensions of global capitalism.[38]

Both in the essay "Cognitive Mapping" and the study *Postmodernism*,
the key adjective describing conspiracy narratives is *degraded*. This word
is associated, in Jameson's text, with postmodern culture more generally:
"The postmodernisms have in fact been fascinated precisely by this
whole 'degraded' landscape of schlock and kitsch, of TV series and *Readers' Digest* culture, of advertising and motels, of the late show and the
grade-B Hollywood film, of so-called paraliterature with its airport
paperback categories of the gothic and the romance, the popular biogra-
phy, the murder mystery and science fiction or fantasy novel."[39] By placing the word "degraded" in quotes, Jameson is suggesting that this
"landscape" is clearly not degraded for those postmodern artists who
take this culture as a starting point. However, the word "degraded"
comes up again when Jameson describes one such postmodern work, E.
L. Doctorow's *Ragtime*. The problem, for Jameson, is that the postmodern
historical novel does not represent the historical past, but rather assem-
bles stereotypes about the historical past. He writes: "Cultural production is thereby driven back inside a mental space which is no longer that
of the old monadic subject, but rather that of some degraded collective
'objective spirit': it can no longer gaze directly on some putative real
world, at some reconstruction of a past history which was once itself a
present; rather, as in Plato's cave, it must trace our mental images of that
past upon its confining walls."[40] Here the word "degraded" is linked to
the world of images, as opposed to the "real world": the postmodern
historical novel is degraded to the extent that it refers to the fallen world
of sheer images, of stereotypes, the ruins of culture and history.

It is therefore clear that the problem with conspiracy theory—which
stands as an exemplary postmodern text for Jameson—is that it is *a step
down* from a true political narrative, as the word "degraded" implies. In
other words, conspiracy theory *falls short*: it is a degraded form of politics,

meaning that it has been reduced in rank, demoted, or ruined. Conspiracy theory is the fall of politics, Jameson suggests: it falls away from politics precisely in the moment when it seems most desperate to find politics (precisely when it attempts that "wild stab" at the truth). The conspiratorial text fails to be political to the extent that it does not offer a stable view of the relations that make up global capitalism. If cognitive mapping is to work, Jameson insists that a postmodern text must allow us "to grasp our positioning as individual and collective subjects and regain a capacity to act and struggle which is at present neutralized by our spatial as well as our social confusion."[41] Like the Bonaventura Hotel in Los Angeles, which Jameson describes as a space of confusing movement, the conspiracy narrative cannot give an already-constituted subject a stance from which to figure out spatial coordinates or trajectories to follow in the future. For that reason it is important for Jameson to designate conspiracy narratives, with their wild stabs and hypothetical relations, as "degraded," not only in the sense of a demotion or being inadequate to the task, but also in the sense of a destabilization, the way conspiracy narratives continually fall away from a mappable reality.[42]

This emphasis on the failure of conspiracy narratives is repeated in more recent studies on the subject. For instance, Fenster seems to agree with Jameson by noting that the conspiracy narrative may be "simplistic and wrong," but at least it symbolically attempts a confrontation with and representation of totality.[43] Fenster then goes on to explain why conspiracy theory nevertheless fails to be political:

> Beyond its shortcomings as a universal theory of power and an approach to historical and political research . . . conspiracy theory ultimately fails as a political and cultural practice. It not only fails to inform us how to move from the end of the uncovered plot to the beginning of a political movement; it is also unable to locate a material position at which we can begin to organize people in a world divided by complex divisions based on class, race, gender, sexuality, and other social antagonisms.[44]

For Fenster, conspiracy theory is always failing to do what it sets out to do, unable to become the politics that it longs to perform. Conspiracy theory therefore comes to be figured as a fallen politics, a ruined politics, precisely because it is always marked by a constant falling away from politics. In what follows I would like to take seriously the assertions that conspiracy narratives in some way *fail* to be political. However, unlike critics such as Peter Knight, who chastises Fenster for assuming that conspiracy narratives are intending to be political in the first place,[45] I am not concerned with the original intentions of conspiracy theorists. Rather, I would like to focus on the way politics emerges as a surprise even (and especially) for those actively engaged in the narrations of conspiracy theories. Strangely, conspiracy theories demonstrate that the failure of politics is also the uncertain emergence of the political.

In order to develop this notion of the *necessary* failure of politics, I would like to turn to a short passage from Thomas Pynchon's novel *Gravity's Rainbow*. Even though this 1973 novel was written before some of the major works on conspiracy theory narratives (Jameson, Fenster, Knight, etc.), it is possible to read *Gravity's Rainbow* as precisely a *reading* of those critics. In other words, even though there is clearly a relationship of reading that moves from Fredric Jameson to Pynchon (Jameson, for example, engages in a reading of Pynchon's *The Crying of Lot 49*), I am more interested in the way Pynchon's novel produces an anticipatory reading of Jameson. The task ahead is therefore to show that Pynchon *in effect* reads the tendency—evidenced in Jameson and others—to rehabilitate conspiracy theory only in order to dismiss it in the end as non-political.

For the most part, the action of *Gravity's Rainbow* takes place among the ruins of Europe at the end of World War II and dramatizes the way these ruins seem to provoke a generalized paranoia. In what follows, I will focus on a passage that involves Enzian, one of the many characters searching for a mythical rocket during the last years of World War II. He is passing through a particularly war-torn part of the "Zone," that unregulated region of Europe that opened up after the fall of the Third Reich and before the Allied powers took control.[46] Enzian suddenly has a revelation of sorts as he passes by an oil refinery that has been bombed into ruins during the last air raids of the war.[47] This short passage is useful because it develops a conspiracy theory out of these ruins, thereby suggesting that ruins are exemplary material for the construction of conspiracy theories. Conspiracy theories hold fast to the ruins, to echo Walter Benjamin on allegory, precisely because ruins represent a gap in knowledge that needs to be filled by narrative.[48] This gap in knowledge is a result of the fact that a ruin, by definition, refers to the state of having fallen. The ruin is anything that remains after a fall, after an act of destruction that predates the ruin. The ruin is therefore not a presence but rather always presents the image of lack: not only is its structure no longer whole, but the ruin also refers back to an event (a "fall") with which it cannot coincide. Precisely for that reason, a ruin demands to be witnessed, that is, it demands a supplementary act that might reconstitute the ruin's presence. At the same time, however, it is never clear what it would mean to bear witness to something that cannot be fully reconstituted, since to reconstitute the ruin would be the attempt to erase not only its incomplete structure but also the act of ruination that constituted the ruin in the first place. This double movement—the demand for restitution and the impossibility of this act of restitution—is what I have been calling a "political demand," following Ernesto Laclau. As Laclau notes in *On Populist Reason*, the decisive moment in any popular demand is the

"experience of a *lack*, a gap which has emerged in the harmonious continuity of the social."[49] Political demands are not the fully conscious expressions of already constituted entities, but rather emerge out of any
destabilizing gap or lack. As I discussed in the second chapter, conspiracy theories seek to address this constitutive lack with the imaginative
leap, a catachresis that names something that by definition cannot be
properly named. Similarly, ruins produce political demands that call out
for the kinds of allegories presented by conspiracy theories.

This constitutive lack is highlighted in Enzian's conspiracy theory,
especially the way his ideas seem incomprehensible even to himself, as if
they came from the outside. As he rides into the ruins, the narrator describes Enzian's experience of seeing double: he sees both the ruins themselves and something else that simply occurs to him, beyond his intentions: "*Zoom* uphill slantwise toward a rampart of wasted, knotted, fused,
and scorched girderwork, stacks, pipes, ducting, windings, fairings, insu-
lators reconfigured by all the bombing, grease-stained pebblery on the
ground rushing by a mile a minute and wait, wait, say what, say '*reconfigured*', now?" (*GR*, 520). In the very process of narrating Enzian's vision of
the ruins something else occurs, something that surprises Enzian himself:
the word "reconfigured." This word produces an interruption in the narrative itself, a stumbling or stuttering ("wait, wait") that drags the narration of ruins to a standstill. What had been a simple enumeration of the
ruined parts of the structure ("stacks, pipes, ducting, windings," etc.)
suddenly becomes a different kind of narration altogether. At that moment, the entire notion of "ruin" seems to be overturned, since the oil
refinery is no longer simply a non-functioning *lack,* an enumeration of
disconnected parts, but rather appears as something that has taken on a
new figuration: a reconfiguration. The word "reconfigured" is Enzian's
word, but it also shocks him, as if he is not in control of his own thoughts.
This word suddenly turns the "silence" of the ruins into a loud, articulate
speech with intention, a language that seems to posit some other conscious agent behind the scenes who has set up this language and made it
speak in the first place.

The word "reconfigured" therefore marks the moment of a surprising
discovery. The narrator, from Enzian's point of view, tries to make sense
of this revelation: "There doesn't exactly dawn, no but there *breaks*, as
that light you're afraid will break some night at too deep an hour to
explain away—there floods on Enzian what seems to him an extraordinary understanding" (*GR*, 520). Enzian's understanding is not only figured here as a revelation, but is also presented as the difficulty in figuring
this understanding in the first place. The discovery happens to him first
like a natural event, something like the dawn, but then this natural
understanding falls away before the violence of a rupture, when the revelation now seems to *break* upon him as something that cannot be ignored
but which nevertheless threatens him with its overwhelming force, a ver-

itable *flood* of revelation. Therefore, the discovery itself is not simply a natural event, but rather happens more on the order of a catastrophic event that seems to overturn nature itself (a flood). This ruinous event nevertheless brings about a new understanding of what he is witnessing: "This serpentine slag heap he is just about to ride into now, this ex-refinery . . . *is not a ruin at all. It is in perfect working order*" (*GR*, 520). Enzian suddenly understands that this reconfigured ruin—which he now thinks is not a ruin at all—is a "holy Text," and that perhaps this ruin is the holy Torah that he has been searching for (*GR*, 520). The ruin has therefore undergone a complete transformation in Enzian's mind. Rather than simply a gap in knowledge that can only be approached through a careful depiction of its component elements (stacks, pipes, ducting), the ruin now becomes a reconfigured and therefore articulated language, a new text that is also, *perhaps*, a holy text, a transcendental signified, the text that gives everything else meaning.

But Enzian's excitement is short-lived, since he soon realizes that this transcendental signified presents more mysteries than certain answers. He realizes, for instance, that the refinery ruined by Allied planes was built by IG Farben, the German conglomerate that was actually instrumental in the rise of Nazi power, and that the Allied planes themselves must have been built by IG Farben. At this point the narrator's voice seems to disappear and Enzian's thoughts are given directly:

> [I]f what the IG built on this site were not at *all* the final shape of it, but only an arrangement of fetishes, come-ons to call down special tools in the form of 8th AF bombers *yes* the "Allied" planes all would have been, ultimately, IG-built, by way of Director Krupp, through his English interlocks—the bombing was the exact industrial process of conversion, each release of energy placed exactly in space and time, each shockwave plotted in advance to bring *precisely tonight's wreck* into being thus decoding the Text, thus coding, recoding, redecoding the holy Text. (*GR*, 520–21)

Now not only is the ruin not really a ruin, but the violence produced by the war is also not violence at all, but rather a process of conversion that corresponds to a flirtatious address by the refinery itself, as if asking to be bombed in the first place. Now "bombed" no longer means destruction, but is rather a necessary intervention that allows the refinery to take on a "final shape." This final shape, however, does not give Enzian any answers, since he must still figure out what this new configuration is designed to do: "If it is in working order, what is it meant to do? The engineers who built it as a refinery never knew there were any further steps to be taken. Their design was 'finalized', and they could forget it" (*GR*, 521). Enzian's revelation then concerns the reconfiguration not only of the ruin itself, but also of the intentions of those who built or rebuilt the ruin in the first place. Rather than the known intentions of the refin-

ery engineers, Enzian posits the mysterious machinations of a secret
agent that has other intentions.

In this way, Enzian's ruin seems to tell two stories. On the one hand, it
tells the story of a simple oil refinery now in ruins; that is, it is something
that can still be recognized as an oil refinery, but it can no longer be used
for that purpose because of what has befallen it. According to this first
story, the fact that this oil refinery cannot perform its primary task (refin-
ing oil) means that the bombing, while strategically important, was in the
end accidental: it *befell* the refinery, it *happened to* the refinery accidentally,
as it were. This ruin is a ruin not only because it has fallen down, but also
because this fallen state has befallen it as an accident that came from the
outside. But this first story is ruined by a second story. In this second
story, the ruin is not a ruin at all, which means that it is not a fallen-down
version of an oil refinery, but rather something completely other. Nothing has befallen the oil refinery from the outside as an accident; rather the
oil-refinery itself called down "special tools" that were used to reconfig-
ure the building into its final shape. If the "ruin" is in complete working
order *after* the bombing, this means that Enzian is observing something
that bears no relation to an oil-refinery, except to the extent that the oil-
refinery was the raw material for this *other thing*. In short, this second
story narrates the becoming-other of the ruin.

The ruin therefore splits into two, incommensurable stories, a plot that
is undermined by a complot, an official story that suddenly falls away to
reveal a secret story. It is impossible to read the two stories at the same
time, since, in effect, the second story ruins the first story, and the first
story ruins the second story. However, even if it is impossible to read the
two stories at the same time, the condition of possibility of a conspiracy
narrative is that it must have this antagonistic relation between two stories. Is it just a ruin, or is it a reconfiguration? Is it an accident, or is there
a secret intentional structure at work? These questions remain undecidable: even though Enzian has discovered or uncovered this second story,
this second story is nothing if it is not continually conspiring against the
first story. If the second story is to exist at all, then, the first story must
also be posited; likewise, the first or official story only becomes a story to
begin with (and not simply "the truth" or something "obvious") when
this first story is threatened by a second story. In this way, the two stories
are continuously in conflict, but this conflict is constitutive and not a
momentary problem.

Therefore, the second story cannot be viewed as the conclusive deter-
mination of what Enzian is witnessing in the ruined oil refinery. In fact,
even though the second story seems to be revealed at this point, its revelation only leads to more mystery, more secrecy. For instance, Enzian
realizes that this reconfigured ruin is hiding a more essential secret about
the events he has been witnessing in the Zone:

It means that this War was never political at all, the politics was all theatre, all just to keep the people distracted. . . . [S]ecretly, it was being dictated instead by the needs of technology . . . by a conspiracy between human beings and techniques, by something that needed the energy-burst of war, crying "Money be damned, the very life of [insert name of Nation] is at stake," but meaning, most likely, *dawn is nearly here, I need my night's blood, my funding, ahh more, more.* . . . The real crises were crises of allocation and priority, not among firms—it was only staged to look that way—but among the different Technologies, Plastics, Electronics, Aircraft, and their needs which are understood only by the ruling elite. (*GR*, 520; all ellipses, brackets, and italics are Pynchon's)

At this point, the second story begins to expand and infect other concerns, such as World War II itself. Enzian realizes that, if this ruin is not in fact a ruin, then this War is not a war at all, in the sense of a military struggle that carries out national policy by other means. It would mean that this "war" has nothing to do with separate sides, of Allied and Axis powers, but rather entails the secret configuration of *interlocking* interests. This word "interlock" was mentioned earlier in this same scene, when Enzian realized that the Allied planes that bombed the oil-refinery would have been built by Director Krupp of IG Farben, "through his English interlocks" (*GR*, 520). This interlocking relationship would mean that the distinction between Allied and Axis powers is meaningless, since a secret configuration of business interests—all interlocking—was carrying out its own plan. But here it gets a bit strange, since the conspiracy is not the result of any one conscious and willful conspirator or society of conspirators, but rather has to do with the "needs of technology." While it is true that members of the "ruling elite" are a crucial part of this conspiracy—they are specially placed to be able to understand the needs of technology—nevertheless the conspiracy itself is not the result of merely human machinations. Rather, it is dictated by machination itself: the inhuman work of the machine. In other words, if there is a "They" with a capital "T," that "T" also stands for the Technological in general, the machine that allocates and prioritizes, but does not allow for the accidental, for the event. Pynchon will later call this the "They-system," and this "They-system" ultimately does away with politics: in this "war," politics is just theatre or a series of stagings ("it was only staged to look that way"). If the politics is merely theatre, this means that it is, as J. L. Austin noted about speech acts performed on stage, hollow or void.[50] Those public acts that are normally considered "political" are now viewed by Enzian as only hollow performances, quotations of politics rather than the real thing, and therefore without any true effect. Instead of politics we have the dictations of the machine, and one form of this machine would be a kind of global technocratic state that rules by administration and always needs the spark of funding.

Of course, this "They-system" is only half the story. After all, what is a "They-system" without a "We-system"? Pynchon explicitly brings up this problem later in the novel, when one experienced paranoid, Pirate Prentice, tells "a novice paranoid," Roger Mexico: "Of course a well-developed They-system is necessary—but it's only half the story. For every They there ought to be a We. In our case there is. Creative paranoia means developing at least as thorough a We-system as a They-system" (*GR*, 638). The problem with this explanation is that Prentice here thinks of this "We-system" as a choice, as if one could simply choose to create a "They-system" without a "We-system," or as if one could willfully create a We-system and maintain it indefinitely. But in Enzian's narrative, it seems that this "We-system" is not developed as a choice, but rather takes place as soon as a "They-system" has been posited. Immediately after the revelation about the needs of technology, the narration abruptly moves to the first-person plural ("we"): "We have to look for power sources here, and distribution networks we were never taught, routes of power our teachers never imagined, or were encouraged to avoid. . . . [W]e have to find meters whose scales are unknown in the world, draw our own schematics, getting feedback, making connections, reducing the error, trying to learn the real function . . . zeroing in on what incalculable plot?" (*GR*, 521). The pronoun "we" punctuates Enzian's thoughts and accrues a mission that is always antagonistically positioned against the secret plot. In this way, the first binary between two stories—is it a ruin or a reconfigured ruin?—then secretes, as it were, a second binary between two stories or articulations. This second binary hinges on this division between a "we" and a "they." First a "they-system" is "discovered," "revealed," or posited as the secret agent or hidden figure that manipulates everything. This manipulation is figured as the usurpation of a site that does not legitimately belong to the "They-system," but which belongs rather to an implied "we." The narrator alludes to this "usurpation" at the end of the paragraph right before the "we" appears. Through a prosopopoeia, the They-system itself speaks: "Go ahead, capitalize the T on technology, deify it if it'll make you feel less responsible—but it puts you in with the neutered, brother, in with the eunuchs keeping the harem of our stolen Earth for the numb and joyless hardons of human sultans, human elite with no right at all to be where they are" (*GR*, 521). The They-system is figured here as Technology itself, which speaks precisely in order to dismiss any claims of conspiracy. Nevertheless, Technology finds itself continuing the narrative of usurpation: the They-system has usurped a position that does not belong to it. The earth itself has been stolen and reconfigured by this conspiracy between technology and human "sultans." The conspiracy is figured as a parasite that takes and takes without ever paying back. And it is precisely at this moment that the "We-system" emerges as a counterforce or anti-institutional articulation that struggles against an illegitimate usurpation: "We have to look for power sources here" (*GR*, 521). The We-system constitutes itself as a lack, that is, as a response to a usurpation that has already taken place. The "we" is therefore an empty place-holder for a community that binds together in order to oppose the ruining effect of a They-system.

In this way, two sets of binaries emerge out of Enzian's ruin. The first binary is the story of an accidental ruin and the story of a reconfiguration of a ruin into something other. This "something other" then produces, as an effect, a second binary: a They-system that is pitted against a We-system. This second binary is the story of "the people" (the "we") in its struggle against a debilitating power (a "they"). I would like to argue that this abstraction of the social field into binary poles ("we" and "they") is not simply a moment of extremism, but rather constitutes the moment of politics. *Gravity's Rainbow* makes this point at various moments in the novel, but none as explicit as the scene when Enzian receives his "extraordinary understanding" about the hidden story behind the ruins. At first it might seem paradoxical to locate the moment of the political in this discovery of a conspiracy; after all, as in Borges, Enzian here identifies the moment of conspiracy as precisely the *end* of politics. Enzian realizes that the fact that there is a conspiracy at work "means that this War was never political at all, the political was all theatre, all just to keep the people distracted. . . . [S]ecretly, it was being dictated instead by the needs of technology" (*GR*, 521). Here politics is defined negatively: politics *ends* (becomes something else, becomes mere "theatre") when everything is dictated by the needs of technology, which means here a kind of mechanical administration of funds and resources. This "conspiracy" or "They-system" is constructed through a series of interlocking relations between different conglomerations, governments, special interests, and so on. If politics *ends* when relations are totalized in this way, when all connections become interlocking, then a positive definition of politics would be the moment when these interlocking relations have come undone. The idea here is not that politics would be the moment of no-relation, but rather that politics would be the emergence of an always-ruined relation, a relation that is always on the verge of coming undone, and in fact might fail to form in the first place.

This notion of a relation that is always already ruined is precisely the way that *Gravity's Rainbow* describes the "We-system." The problem, of course, is that the We-system has no other cohesion than this anti-institutional discourse against a They-system. In other words, a community is formed—a "we"—but the content of this "we" is constituted negatively: the "we" exists only insofar as it is opposed to a "they." If the "we-system" is so dependent on the "they-system" for its cohesion, this means that this minimal community is continually threatened by its own disintegration. In fact this eventuality is exactly what happens in the narrator's description of Enzian's "extraordinary understanding." At the moment when the "They-system" begins to stretch too thin, the understanding dissipates, as does the voice of the "we-system":

> And if it isn't exactly Jamf Ölfabriken Werke? what if it's the Krupp works in Essen, what if it's Blohm & Voss right here in Hamburg or another make-believe "ruin," in another city? Another *country*? YAAAGGGGHHHHH!
>
> Well, this is stimulant talk here, yes Enzian's been stuffing down Nazi surplus Pervitins these days like popcorn at the movies, and by now the bulk of the refinery . . . is behind them, and Enzian is on into some other paranoid terror, talking, talking, though each man's wind and motor cuts him off from conversation. (*GR*, 521–22)

Clearly this moment—the idea that this is all just stimulant talk—would seem to undercut the validity of Enzian's "extraordinary understanding." It would seem necessary to say that instead of a true insight into the workings of power, Enzian has fallen into yet another delusion about the world, even as his mind falls into ruin ("Enzian is on into some other paranoid terror"). Likewise, it would follow that the community of the "we" that he had just built has also just disintegrated. Enzian has been cut off from all conversation, not only because of the noise of the motors and wind, but more generally because he no longer speaks as part of a "we": he is now an isolated voice stuck within a drug hallucination. Fenster would therefore seem to be correct when he noted that conspiracy theory is "unable to locate a material position at which we can begin to organize people in a world divided by complex divisions."[51] In fact, Fenster views conspiracy theories as problematic precisely because of the way they seem haunted by "the continual threat of falling apart":

> If, however, the structures of the classical conspiracy narrative offer a utopian promise of knowledge and resistance, a cognitive map of power, then they also contain within them the undoing of that promise, the unraveling of that map. Their narrative desire might be to make some order out of the chaos of history and to provide some answer to the riddle of power, but the conspiracy narrative itself offers no programmatic response or emergent politics to replace the conspiracy it so intricately uncovers and explains.[52]

Fenster's discussion of conspiracy theories would therefore seem to be easily applicable to Enzian's momentary revelation. The "we," almost as soon as it is constituted, fizzles away into nothing.[53] In the end, it seems unable to locate a material position that could actually bring people together.

In fact, this critique of the political efficacy of conspiracy theory is mentioned by one of the characters in *Gravity's Rainbow*. After hearing about the necessity of creating a We-system, Roger Mexico, the "novice paranoid," remarks: "It's a little bewildering—if this is a 'We-system', why isn't it at least thoughtful enough to interlock in a reasonable way, like They-systems do?" (*GR*, 638). The problem with We-systems, for Mexico, is precisely the way they do not interlock in the same way that They-systems interlock. If the We-system cannot form such interlocking links, this means that this minimal community can indeed fall apart at any moment, just as Enzian's "we" disintegrates when he reaches the end of his revelation. The We-system is therefore always a potential ruin, or is in fact always on its way to ruination, or is always about to fall apart. As Fenster notes, "[as] easy as it is to construct such a [conspiracy] narrative, this construction is always already relatively incoherent, moving forward with the continual threat of falling apart."[54] One could ask, as Peter Knight does in his study on conspiracy culture, why Fenster would assume that conspiracy theories should be political in the first place, but this kind of question seems to ignore the fact that political theory continuously finds it necessary to throw conspiracy theory outside the realm of politics. Why is it necessary to repeat this exclusion of conspiracy theory if this kind of narration were already safely outside the political realm? Why does political theory feel so threatened by conspiracy theory if the latter is indeed nothing more than a kind of "everyday paranoia," far from "proper political thought and action"?[55] What is it about this kind of narrative that not only finds itself falling apart, but also threatens politics itself with a critical destabilization?

Everything depends, then, on the way the We-system precisely does *not* interlock in the way that They-systems supposedly interlock. In fact one could argue that it would not make sense to talk about the We-system as interlocking, since this interlocking system is the definition of a They-system. A We-system that is not continually threatened by the eventuality of its disintegration would simply be yet another They-system: there would be no difference between a "we" and a "they," since it would all be one interlocking conglomerate or system of totalizing relations. In that case you would have no politics, according to *Gravity's Rainbow*; you would only have administration, mere theatre, a situation in which everything would be dictated by the needs of the machine, a mere question of the allocation of resources and services by "experts." Politics only takes place when there is a split between a We-system and a They-system, but this split can only happen if the We-system is constantly being threatened or invaded by the They-system. On the one hand, then, a political community only takes place when there is a radical division between the "people" (the "we") and the enemy (the "They"). If the relations between the "we" and the "They" interlock at all, then a viable "we" cannot form. On the other hand, the They-system must present a threat—a vital usurpation—that prohibits the full constitution of an antagonistic political community. This usurpation is a real threat precisely because the "We-system" does not interlock; it can fall apart at any moment. In fact, if the political community were not threatened by its eventual ruination, then it would not be a political community in the first place. In this way, the condition of possibility of politics is its condition of impossibility: politics only takes place in the continual threat of its dissolution.

Therefore, if conspiracy theory is, as Jameson suggested, a degraded politics, then this would also be true for any kind of politics. The "degraded" nature of conspiracy theory, the "failure" of conspiracy theory to constitute a stable political movement, is the condition of politics in general. As I argued in relation to Borges's "Tlön, Uqbar, Orbis Tertius," politics itself must be at risk if a narration is going to be political. For there to be politics at all, there must be this division between two stories, even if the frontier between the two stories is always unstable, even if one story is constantly being "invaded" by another story. In fact the unstable nature of the frontier between two stories is necessary, because if the frontier were fixed (no invasion, no confusion), you would simply have two already-formed narratives and therefore no political negotiation would be possible. In this way, consensus politics itself rests on the very threat to its possibility; without a complot that threatens the stability of politics, even "the usual methods of political give-and-take"[56] would not be possible. The complot—the Tlönian invasion or They-system—is a necessary moment of politics precisely because it introduces a chasm into the social space without fixing the frontier of this division. This unstable frontier is what Laclau and Mouffe have called hegemony: "the two conditions of a hegemonic articulation are the presence of antagonistic forces and the instability of the frontiers which separate them."[57] Thus, while the antagonistic conflict between two stories is crucial for any hegemonic articulation, these two stories cannot be fixed completely. Rather, one story must continually invade the other in some way; the complot must continually emerge as a threat to the plot. Therefore, the degradation of conspiracy theory is also the degradation of any political narrative. After all, if politics were not degraded in the first place, that is, if politics did not take place as something already exposed to its own dissolution, then you simply would not have politics. All you would have would be the mechanical dictations of technology. If politics is to take place at all, it necessarily takes place in the ruined form of conspiracy theory.

NOTES

1. Office of the Press Secretary, "President Bush Participates in Joint Press Availability with Prime Minister Harper of Canada, and President Calderón of Mexico," *The White House: President George W. Bush*, August 21, 2007. Accessed August 19, 2009. Http://georgewbush-whitehouse.archives.gov/news/releases/2007/08/20070821-3.html.
2. Ibid.
3. Recent critics have sought to relate literary conspiracy narratives to the conspiracy theories about Al-Qaeda narrated by the Bush administration. See, for example, Skip Willman, "Specters of Marx in Pynchon's *Vineland*." It should be noted, however, that President Bush's statement about the problem of conspiracy theories makes it

difficult to blame the Bush administration for reintroducing paranoid politics into American democracy. After all, to say that Bush has contaminated American politics with conspiracy narratives is to imitate Bush's own strategy of demonizing the conspiracy theorists.

4. Seymour Martin Lipset and Earl Raab continue Hofstadter's assessment of conspiracy theory by framing it within the context of "extremist" politics. They write that "extremism means going beyond the limits of the normative procedures which define the democratic political process" (Seymour Martin Lipset and Earl Raab, *The Politics of Unreason: Right-Wing Extremism in America, 1790–1977* [Chicago: University of Chicago Press, 1978], 5). Although Lipset and Raab acknowledge that these procedural norms are always changing, they nevertheless assert that "the unchanging heart of the democratic political process" is "pluralism," that is, "a society which tends to protect and nurture the independent coexistence of different political entities, ethnic groups, ideas" (Lipset and Raab, 5). I will return to this version of consensus politics at the end of this chapter.

5. Richard Hofstadter, *The Paranoid Style in American Politics and Other Essays* (New York: Vintage Books, 1967), 29.

6. See Giorgio Agamben's *State of Exception* for a similar logic of suspension: the state of emergency suspends the laws of government in order to safeguard the law. For Agamben, the state of exception is a legal concept that actually works at the limits of the juridical order: "what is ultimately at issue is the question of the juridical significance of a sphere of action that is in itself extrajuridical" (Giorgio Agamben, *State of Exception*, trans. Kevin Attell [Chicago: University of Chicago Press, 2005], 11).

7. As Hannah Arendt has argued, violence has traditionally marked the limit of political thought: "Where violence rules absolutely, as for instance in the concentration camps of totalitarian regimes, not only the laws . . . but everything and everybody must fall silent. It is because of this silence that violence is a marginal phenomenon in the political realm; for man, to the extent that he is a political being, is endowed with the power of speech. . . . The point here is that violence itself is incapable of speech, and not merely that speech is helpless when confronted with violence. Because of this speechlessness political theory has little to say about the phenomenon of violence and must leave its discussion to the technicians" (Hannah Arendt, *On Revolution* [London: Penguin Books, 1963], 18–19). However, I have tried to argue throughout this book that political theory must take this "speechlessness" into account.

8. Geoffrey Bennington makes a similar point in "Postal Politics and the Institution of the Nation," specifically through a reading of Montesquieu: "As postal network, all politics wants politics to end. The arrival of the letter should erase its delivery. The end of politics is the end of politics" (Geoffrey Bennington, *Legislations: The Politics of Deconstruction* [London: Verso, 1994], 248). In other words, the goal or end-point of politics is what Immanuel Kant calls "perpetual peace," a singular point when politics would no longer be necessary (Geoffrey Bennington, "Kant's Open Secret," in *Theory, Culture & Society* 28.7–8 [2011]: 32–33). In general, I share Bennington's interest in thinking through what has been called "the eclipse of politics": "There would be more to be said about this figure of eclipse, and what happens to it if it is not taken as a historical or even temporal event, but as something originary or constitutive: maybe politics has some more intimate connection with eclipse, or maybe what we most readily call 'politics' always involves the eclipse of what we sometimes call 'the political'?" (Geoffrey Bennington, "Political Animals" in *diacritics* 39.2 [2009]: 23).

9. Jorge Luis Borges, *Ficciones*, ed. Anthony Kerrigan (New York: Grove Press, 1962), 29. Hereafter cited in the text as *F*.

10. Jorge Luis Borges, *Obras completas I* (Barcelona: Emecé Editores, 1989), 439. Hereafter cited in the text as *OC*. All translations are mine unless indicated otherwise.

11. Sylvia Molloy emphasizes this counterfeiting process, though without naming it as such: "In sum, these 'secondary objects' replicate an unnamed 'original' and at the same time diverge from it. Additionally, they are endowed with the power to question and modify, a power that Borges usually associates with the practice of literature"

(Sylvia Molloy, *Signs of Borges*, trans. Oscar Montero [Durham, NC: Duke University Press, 1994], 87–88). As Ricardo Piglia has noted, this emphasis on a doubling/diverging process, which I am calling "counterfeiting," is one of the surprising links that ties Borges's work to the Argentine writer Roberto Arlt. As I noted in chapter 3, Piglia has often suggested that counterfeiting is a central strategy in Arlt's countereconomy (Ricardo Piglia, "Roberto Arlt: La ficción del dinero," in *La Argentina en pedazos* [Buenos Aires: Ediciones de la Urraca, 1993], 124). Piglia expands on this relation between Arlt and Borges in his novel *Artificial Respiration*: "One can read [Borges] in a different way . . . read him, for instance, from Arlt" (Ricardo Piglia, *Artificial Respiration*, trans. Daniel Balderston [Durham, NC: Duke University Press, 1994], 136).

　　12. Translation modified. At times I have modified the elegant translations of Borges's work in order to emphasize certain aspects of Borges's language in Spanish. In this case, Alastair Reid inserted conjunctions such as "and" and "but." My awkward modification of the translation seeks to emphasize the paratactical nature of Borges's language.

　　13. Paul de Man, "A Modern Master: Jorge Luis Borges," in *Critical Writings, 1953–1978*, ed. Lindsay Waters (Minneapolis: University of Minnesota Press, 1989), 128.

　　14. Ibid.

　　15. According to the Real Academia Española, the first definition of "falsear" (from "falso" [false]) means "adulterar o corromper algo, como la moneda, la escritura, la doctrina o el pensamiento."

　　16. In a sense, I am arguing against those who view Tlön as a figuration of empire. For example, Josefina Ludmer reads the emergence of Tlön as the return of empire, especially since this fantastic world emerges specifically out of encyclopedias, that is, out of the ordering impulse of "the imperial archive," a term she borrows from Thomas Richards (Josefina Ludmer, *The Corpus Delicti: A Manual of Argentine Fictions*, trans. Glen S. Close [Pittsburgh: University of Pittsburgh Press, 2004], 258–59). Roberto González Echevarría similarly views the significance of the encyclopedias in Borges's story in terms of empire and its legitimating discourses (including ethnography): "the presence of the encyclopedia . . . and the role played by the English engineer, clearly point not only to the literary nature of ethnographic writing, but also to the source of such discourse in institutions fostered by the British Empire. As we know, growth of the *Brittanica* during the nineteenth century paralleled the expansion of the Empire" (Roberto González Echevarría, *Myth and Archive: A Theory of Latin American Narrative* [Durham, NC: Duke University Press, 1998], 164–65). However, if empire is an important concern in Borges's story, as González Echevarría and Ludmer suggest, the question proposed by "Tlön, Uqbar, Orbis Tertius" has to do with a certain *intervention* in imperial discourses. In effect, Borges is asking: What would it mean to *counterfeit* empire? After all, the first mention of the word "Tlön" appears in relation to a *pirated* encyclopedia, that is, a counterfeit version of the imperial archive. As the narrator explains at the beginning of the story, the encyclopedia is a literal reprint of the *Britannica*, but it's also "morosa" (*OC*, 431), which suggests not only "inadequate"(*F*, 17), as the Reid translation states, but "delinquent" or "doubtful," as one says of a debt that has not been paid back. Therefore, it is difficult to maintain that Tlön is *only* part of the imperial archive, the goal of which is, according to Ludmer, "the organization of all knowledge into a coherent imperial whole" (Ludmer, *The Corpus Delicti*, 259). Far from a coherent whole, Tlön represents the moment when two incommensurable logics are placed in juxtaposition—a real world and a false world—thereby producing dissonance and the destabilization of any coherent knowledge. Therefore, if Tlön should be included within the imperial archive, it remains as a parasite that counterfeits the archive, repeating it and destabilizing it at the same time.

　　17. Cristina Parodi offers a helpful overview of the way variations of the word "discovery" end up infecting the narrator's language: "La confusión de universos en 'Tlön' se refuerza por las opciones léxicas y semánticas del narrador. . . . En realidad, todo el campo semántico de 'descubrir,' 'buscar,' 'encontrar' (y los derivados . . .)

configura una red intrincada de puentes y túneles que vuelven porosas las fronteras entre los diferentes mundos de la ficción y entre los niveles de enunciación" (Cristina Parodi, "El intrincado cronotopo de 'Tlön,'" in *El fragment infinito: Estudios sobre 'Tlön, Uqbar, Orbis Tertius' de J. L. Borges*, ed. Iván Almeida and Cristina Parodi [Zaragoza, Spain: Prensas Universitarias de Zaragoza, 2006], 22).

18. Piglia makes a similar point in his reading of "Tlön" in his recent book of essays: "'Tlön, Uqbar, Orbis Tertius'—the story that defines Borges's oeuvre—begins with a lost text, an encyclopedia article; someone has read it but now can no longer find it. What emerges is not the real, but rather absence, a text that one does not have and the search for which drives toward an encounter with another reality, as in a dream. This lack is immediately assimilated to what has been removed. There is something political here that goes back to conspiracy [*al complot*], to an evil and secret logic [*una lógica malvada y sigilosa*] that alters the order of the world. Someone has what is lacking, someone has erased it. It is not an enigma, nor a mystery; it is a secret, in its etymological meaning (*secernere* means 'to put apart,' 'to hide'). A page—a book—is no longer there, a letter has been stolen, meaning begins to falter, and in that vacillation the fantastic emerges" (Ricardo Piglia, *El último lector* [Barcelona: Editorial Anagrama, 2005], 27; my translation). Here Piglia is returning to his notion of secrecy (developed in "Tesis sobre el cuento" and "Nuevas tesis sobre el cuento") in a way that explicitly links politics and the complot effect ("There is something political here that goes back to conspiracy"), though without fully developing this relation.

19. Didier T. Jaén suggests a similar point when discussing the relevance of the esoteric tradition in Borges, but limits the result of this conjunction to an intuition or at best a metaphorical embodiment: "Tlön is a concept of the universe . . . an intuition which could suddenly seize us in the course of daily experience (the sudden discovery of the surrealists) due to the unexpected conjunction of disparate objects. . . . Borges' story, in a certain sense, dramatizes the discovery of that intuition and illustrates how the mysterious (poetic) conjunction or juxtaposition of an encyclopedia and a mirror may produce the intuition. The story proposes the discovery of that intuition . . . at the very beginning, and the rest of it suggests how an encyclopedia and a mirror are concrete expressions, that is, metaphorical or symbolic embodiments, of the intuition" (Didier T. Jaén, "The Esoteric Tradition in Borges' 'Tlön, Uqbar, Orbis Tertius,'" *Studies in Short Fiction* 21.1 [Winter 1984]: 37). Jaén also proposes that Borges's notion of "conspiracy" does not depend on a conscious act among rational agents: "[I]t is obvious that, not the Rosicrucian society itself, but the principles from which it sprang have been gaining ground. But if the different works and minds that independently work toward that transformation obey the same principles, do they not constitute, in a sense, a secret society, secret even to themselves?" (Jaén, "The Esoteric Tradition," 36).

20. We could conceivably answer this question by turning away from Borges and toward a more "theoretical" text. For instance, it would be possible to compare the undecidability between discovery and production in Borges to the kind of undecidability that Jacques Derrida finds in the American Declaration of Independence. In "Declarations of Independence," Derrida focuses on the "fabulous retroactivity" of the signatures of the Declaration (Jacques Derrida, "Declarations of Independence," trans. Tom Keenan and Tom Pepper, in *Negotiations: Interventions and Interviews, 1971–2001*, ed. Elizabeth Rottenberg [Stanford, CA: Stanford University Press, 2002], 50). He notes, first of all, that there is a constitutive confusion between a constative utterance (which states something as true or false) and a performative utterance (which enacts what it states): "One cannot decide—and this is the interesting thing, the force and 'coup de force' of such a declarative act—whether independence is stated or produced by this utterance. . . . Is it that the good people have already freed themselves in fact and are only stating the fact of this emancipation in [*par*] the Declaration? Or is it rather that they free themselves at the instant of and by [*par*] the signature of this Declaration?" (Derrida, "Declarations of Independence," 49). Derrida goes on to note that this undecidability is not a momentary confusion: "It is not a question here of an obscurity or of a difficulty of interpretation, of a problematic on the way to its

(re)solution. . . . This obscurity, this undecidability between, let us say, a performative structure and a constative structure, is *required* to produce the sought-after effect. It is essential to the very positing or position of a right as such" (Derrida, "Declarations of Independence," 49). Although Derrida refers to this operation—the effective confusion between a constative and a performative utterance—as "a sort of fabulous retroactivity," he also insists that this is the condition of possibility of entering into the *polis* of the United States of America: "The signature of every American citizen today depends, in fact and by right, on this indispensable confusion" (Derrida, "Declarations of Independence," 49–50). Bonnie Honig develops Derrida's ideas in her reading of Arendt: "Arendt resists this undecidability because she seeks in the American Declaration and founding a moment of perfect legitimacy. Insofar as the authority of the founding derives from a constative, it is rooted not in power but in violence. This undecidability, then, delegitimates the republic and so, for the sake of her moment of pure legitimacy, Arendt must do away with it. What she does not see is that the American Declaration and founding are paradigmatic instances of politics (however impure) because of this undecidability, not in spite of it" (Bonnie Honig, *Political Theory and the Displacement of Politics* [Ithaca, NY, and London: Cornell University Press, 1993], 107). In other words, politics opens up only in this undecidability between a constative utterance (the discovery that one already has rights) and a performative utterance (the production of rights that did not exist before the Declaration and its signatures). As I will show in what follows, the word "discovery," in Borges's story, becomes an exemplary political word, precisely because of the confusion it produces. On the one hand, "discovery" is a constative utterance, since the statement that someone has discovered a conspiracy can be stated as true or false. On the other hand, the word "discovery" is a performative utterance, since the statement that someone has discovered a conspiracy ends up *producing* the effects of that conspiracy.

21. This conclusion would be in keeping with a tendency in Borges criticism to view "Tlön" as *only* the introduction of an ordered world. For example, Beatriz Sarlo thinks of "Tlön" as a utopian gesture that seeks to impose its unique order onto the disordered world: "The languages of Tlön have a transparent relationship to the ideal concept of reality: they can never suffer from the disorder of experience" (Beatriz Sarlo, *Jorge Luis Borges: A Writer on the Edge* [London: Verso, 1993], 69). For that reason, Sarlo suggests that Borges's story can be read "as another strategy for establishing order for a society whose old orders were vanishing" (Sarlo, *Jorge Luis Borges*, 70). However, as I suggest in what follows, the narrator's comparison of Tlön and totalitarian movements is only one side of the story, since Borges's text emphasizes not only Tlön's invasion of this world, but also the continued antagonistic relationship between the two worlds.

22. Ernesto Laclau, "Populism: What's in a Name?" in *Populism and the Mirror of Democracy*, ed. F. Panizza (London: Verso, 2005), 48.

23. Brett Levinson, *Market and Thought: Meditations on the Political and the Biopolitical* (New York: Fordham University Press, 2004), 147.

24. See Walter Benjamin's discussion of translation as the afterlife of texts in "The Task of the Translator": "It is evident that no translation, however good it may be, can have any significance as regards the original. Nonetheless, it does stand in the closest relationship to the original by virtue of the original's translatability; in fact, this connection is all the closer since it is no longer of importance to the original. . . . Just as the manifestations of life are intimately connected with the phenomenon of life without being of importance to it, a translation issues from the original—not so much from its life as from its afterlife" (Walter Benjamin, "The Task of the Translator," in *Selected Writings: Volume 1, 1913–1926* [Cambridge: Harvard University Press, 1996], 254). A translation must therefore not seek a likeness to the original: "For in its afterlife—which could not be called that if it were not a transformation and a renewal of something living—the original undergoes a change" (Benjamin, "The Task of the Translator," 256).

25. Efraín Kristal notes that Borges himself translated Browne's *Urn Burial* with Bioy Casares. Interestingly, Kristal finds that the translation not only doubled Browne's text (by transferring it from English to Spanish), but also transformed it by adding one passage that does not exist in the original. Kristal remarks: "Borges's interpolation underscores not only the fragility of memory, but the dark origin and conclusion of matters destined for oblivion. The interpolation is consistent with other changes he made to the *Urn-Burial* that resonate directly with the ethos of 'Tlön, Uqbar, Orbis Tertius'" (Efraín Kristal, *Invisible Work: Borges and Translation* [Nashville, TN: Vanderbilt University Press, 2002], 92). Kristal's interpretation of this "ethos" is part of the more general tendency to view Borges's text as a resistance to ordered, totalitarian systems: "The narrator protests stoically against a transformation he fears and abhors. While all the Indo-European languages are being replaced by languages based on Tlön's *Ursprache*, he decides to translate Sir Thomas Browne's *Urn-Burial* (or *Hydriotaphia*) into Spanish" (Kristal, *Invisible Work*, 91). While Kristal notes that the publication of this translation would be "pointless," he nevertheless continues to see this act as "a quiet protest in the face of obliteration" (Kristal, *Invisible Work*, 91, 93). However, I argue that this act of translation is not *only* a protest, but rather rests uncomfortably somewhere between a protest against Tlön and a contamination by the Tlönian logic that the narrator would like to avoid.

26. Alberto Moreiras interestingly notes that the narrator ("Borges") in fact does *not* undertake the translation of Browne's essay on epigraphs, but rather has instead written the story "Tlön, Uqbar, Orbis Tertius": "de hecho su reacción es escribir 'Tlön,' que es sobre todo traducir la disyunción tlöniana de su mundo, que es el nuestro, como los epitafios traducen la muerte y así articulan una especie de supervivencia. . . . Creo entender el acto traductor de Borges como un acto de resistencia a toda formación totalizante" (Alberto Moreiras, *Tercer Espacio: Duelo y literatura en América Latina* [Santiago: Arcis-LOM, 1999], 76). In effect, Moreiras reads the text itself—"Tlön, Uqbar, Orbis Tertius—as an act of resistance that deauthorizes Tlön (and the Tlönian effect) by 'nounifying' it, that is, by continually naming it, thereby pushing Tlön into the seemingly certain realm of nouns: "Borges concibe expresar a Tlön, sabiendo que afirmar la heterogeneidad es homogeneizarla, proyectar lo irrepresentable es representarlo: nombrando a Tlön, Borges lo destruye . . . al substantivizar lo que se autoconcibe como no-substantivo, encerrando en ello la más violenta de todas las substantivaciones, desautoriza" (Moreiras, *Tercer espacio*, 81). In other words, the narrator's task is to posit his own language—an official, "real" or substantive language—against the counterfeit and illegitimate language of Tlön. While this antagonistic conflict is crucial, the fact remains that the story "Tlön" is itself thoroughly infected or invaded by the Tlönian logic of discovery/production. The narrator must certainly posit his language against that of Tlön, but he must do so precisely because the Tlönian language is continually threatening his own, from the "inside," as it were.

27. Hofstadter, *The Paranoid Style in American Politics*, 29.

28. Peter Knight, *Conspiracy Culture: From the Kennedy Assassination to The X-Files* (London: Routledge, 2000), 7.

29. Ibid.

30. Mark Fenster, *Conspiracy Theories: Secrecy and Power in American Culture* (Minneapolis: University of Minnesota Press, 1999), 21.

31. Jodi Dean goes further when she speaks of the "dangerous" assumptions that rule Hofstadter's overview of the paranoid style (Jodi Dean, *Aliens in America: Conspiracy Cultures from Outerspace to Cyberspace* [Ithaca, NY: Cornell University Press, 1998], 145). See chapter 2, note 5.

32. Fredric Jameson, *The Geopolitical Aesthetic: Cinema and Space in the World System* (Bloomington: Indiana University Press, 1992), 3.

33. Ibid.

34. Fredric Jameson, "Cognitive Mapping," in *Marxism and the Interpretation of Culture*, ed. Cary Nelson and Lawrence Grossberg (Urbana: University of Illinois Press, 1988), 356.

35. Fredric Jameson, *Postmodernism or, The Cultural Logic of Late Capitalism* (Durham, NC: Duke University Press, 1991), 38.

36. Ibid., 37.

37. Ibid., 38.

38. Jon Simons uses Pynchon's *The Crying of Lot 49* and *Gravity's Rainbow* to critique Jameson's understanding of conspiracy theory and its relation to global capitalism. Simons notes that "A Jamesonian reading of postmodern novels or films understood as embodiments of high-tech paranoia should then reinterpret conspiracies as oblique, distorted figurations of the totality of global capitalism" (Jon Simons, "Postmodern Paranoia? Pynchon and Jameson," *Paragraph: A Journal of Modern Critical Theory* 23.2 [July 2000]: 211). Simons compares this either/or scenario (either a full understanding of global capitalism or a deluded understanding of global capitalism) to the scenarios in which Pynchon's characters often find themselves: either total knowledge of reality or just an illusion (Simons, "Postmodern Paranoia," 215, 216). For that reason, Simons concludes that Jameson, like Pynchon's characters, never fully engages in politics: "The strategic, political consequence of this position is that social change seems to be a matter of all or nothing. Resistance would be postponed until the correct revolutionary moment" (Simons, "Postmodern Paranoia," 218). In what follows, I will similarly attempt to counter Jameson's proposals through a reading of Pynchon. However, I argue that the failure to engage in politics (specifically in this sense of a continual delay that would seem to prohibit political action) is paradoxically the condition of possibility of political discourse.

39. Jameson, *Postmodernism*, 55.

40. Ibid., 71.

41. Ibid., 92.

42. Fran Mason points out that Jameson's denigration of conspiracy theory is difficult to maintain, especially if one applies Jameson's own theory of cognitive mapping to his insistence that conspiracy theory is a "poor person's cognitive mapping." Mason notes that "cognitive mapping needs a subjectivity capable of the 'critical distance' that Jameson has often argued is impossible in postmodernity. Jameson's subject is one who has to distance him- or herself from the relationships he or she is trying to map and must therefore exist outside history and society. And yet the subject also has to be inside society and history in order to know what is relevant and legitimate. As a result, conspiracy [theory], rather than being a 'poor person's cognitive mapping', might actually be a paradigm of 'cognitive mapping' and the difficulties it faces in creating a legitimate position of distance between the subject and the global society he or she inhabits" (Fran Mason, "A Poor Person's Cognitive Mapping," in *Conspiracy Nation: The Politics of Paranoia in Postwar America*, ed. Peter Knight [New York: New York University Press, 2002], 47).

43. Fenster, *Conspiracy Theories*, 116.

44. Ibid., 225–26.

45. Knight, *Conspiracy Culture*, 20–21.

46. Thomas Pynchon, *Gravity's Rainbow* (London: Penguin Books, 1973), 518–22. Hereafter cited in the text as *GR*.

47. In "Rubbish, Rubble, Ruins: The Allegorical in *Gravity's Rainbow*," Giuseppe Costigliola contrasts the images of ruins in Pynchon with the ruins one finds in modernist texts. If the modernist text employed ruins to address the breakdown of values and traditions, Pynchon's postmodern novel emphasizes instead the inability of the subject to locate his or her place in the landscape. In this way, Costigliola reads *Gravity's Rainbow* according to Jameson's definition of the postmodern as a space that is difficult to map: "The geographical and political, architectural and literary images of the city reflect the dismemberment of the subject: fictional theme, urban experience and city image are intricately related. If the city is a chaotic heap of rubble, a 'zone' with no hierarchy, with neither centre nor periphery . . . then the human subject is completely lost in it, lacking any sense of spatial and logical progression" (Giuseppe Costigliola, "Rubbish, Rubble, Ruins: The Allegorical in *Gravity's Rainbow*," in *America*

Today: Highways and Labyrinths, ed. Gigliola Nocera [Siracusa, Italy: Grafia, 2003], 562). As I demonstrate in what follows, not only are Pynchon's ruins no longer recognizable landmarks, but they are also not even recognizable as ruins. These scenes of misrecognition occur throughout the novel, for instance when Slothrop thinks he is viewing King Kong, "or some creature closely allied, squatting down, evidently just, taking a shit, right in the street!" (*GR,* 368). This image quickly disappears, revealing instead a ruin from the war: "On closer inspection, the crouching monster turns out to be the Reichstag building, shelled out" (*GR,* 368).

48. See, for instance, Benjamin's "Central Park": "That which the allegorical intention has fixed upon is sundered from the customary contexts of life: it is at once shattered and preserved. Allegory holds fast to the ruins. It offers the image of petrified unrest" (Walter Benjamin, "Central Park," in *Selected Writings, Volume 4: 1938–1940,* trans. Edmund Jephcott and others [Cambridge: Harvard University Press, 2003], 169). For a more direct discussion of Pynchon and allegory, see Maureen Quilligan, "Twentieth-Century American Allegory," in *Thomas Pynchon,* ed. Harold Bloom (Philadelphia: Chelsea House Publishers, 2003), and Deborah L. Madsen, *The Postmodernist Allegories of Thomas Pynchon* (New York: St. Martin's Press, 1991).

49. Ernesto Laclau, *On Populist Reason* (London: Verso, 2005), 85.

50. As I noted in the last chapter, Austin excludes particular situations from his speech-act theory: "Secondly, as *utterances* our performatives are *also* heir to certain other kinds of ill which infect *all* utterances. And these likewise, though again they might be brought into a more general account, we are deliberately at present excluding. I mean, for example, the following: a performative utterance will, for example, be *in a peculiar way* hollow or void if said by an actor on the stage, or if introduced in a poem, or spoken in soliloquy. . . . Language in such circumstances is in special ways—intelligibly—used not seriously, but in ways *parasitic* upon its normal use—ways which fall under the doctrine of the *etiolations* of language. All this we are excluding from consideration" (J. L. Austin, *How to Do Things with Words,* ed. J. O. Urmson and Marina Sbisà [Cambridge: Harvard University Press, 1975], 21–22).

51. Fenster, *Conspiracy Theories,* 226.

52. Ibid., 140, 141.

53. Leo Bersani has expressed a similar view by means of the figure of paranoia: "The self-protective suspicions of paranoia are, therefore, already a defeat. The paranoid We *must* lose out to the enemy They" (Leo Bersani, "Pynchon, Paranoia, and Literature," in *Thomas Pynchon,* ed. Harold Bloom [Philadelphia: Chelsea House Publishers, 2003], 156). Although Bersani does not go in this direction, it would be useful to link this self-defeating self-protection ("The self-protective suspicions of paranoia are . . . already a defeat") to what Jacques Derrida calls "autoimmunity": "an autoimmunitary process is that strange behavior where a living being, in quasi-*suicidal* fashion, 'itself' works to destroy its own protection, to immunize itself *against* its 'own' immunity" (Jacques Derrida, "Autoimmunity: Real and Symbolic Suicides," in *Philosophy in a Time of Terror,* ed. Giovanna Borradori [Chicago: University of Chicago Press, 2003], 94). Derrida goes on to say in *Rogues* that autoimmunity "consists not only in compromising oneself [s'*auto-entamer*] but in compromising the self, the *autos*—and thus ipseity. It consists not only in committing suicide but in compromising *sui-*or *self-*referentiality, the *self* or *sui-*of suicide itself" (Jacques Derrida, *Rogues: Two Essays on Reason,* trans. Pascale-Anne Brault and Michael Naas [Stanford, CA: Stanford University Press, 2005], 45). At this point it is tempting to say, with Richard Hofstadter, that the structure of conspiracy theory indeed ruins politics *itself,* but only if the emphasis is on the "itself" of politics. As I have argued throughout this book, politics (as conspiracy theory) is a split structure that is constituted precisely in its own ruination. There is therefore no "itself" of politics, no "politics itself."

54. Fenster, *Conspiracy Theories,* 140.

55. Knight notes that Fenster tends to "judge conspiracy theory by unreasonably strict standards of proper political thought and action which it will never live up to. Some conspiracy theorists do make claims for their radical politics, but most forms of

everyday paranoia are rarely so grandiose or programmatic. . . . The problem with Fenster's approach is that he implicitly requires conspiracy theory to fulfill a political function which it is always going to fail at" (Knight, *Conspiracy Culture*, 21).

56. Hofstadter, *The Paranoid Style in American Politics*, 29.

57. Ernesto Laclau and Chantal Mouffe, *Hegemony and Socialist Strategy: Towards a Radical Democratic Politics* (London: Verso, 2001), 136.

Epilogue

Counterfeit Politics

If conspiracy theory entails the emergence of a secret or complot that never fully emerges, an event that never really happens, then this kind of narrative might seem to be particularly useless for politics. After all, how can the story of a complot be a legitimate ground for political action? This is the question that implicitly emerges from the story about Macedonio Fernández that I outlined in the introduction to this study. In Borges's anecdote about his mentor, Macedonio decided to undertake two projects: first, to run for president of Argentina; second, to write a conspiracy novel about his attempt to run for president of Argentina. The projected novel was supposed to have a split structure: "In the work, two plots would be woven together: one, visible, Macedonio's curious efforts to become president of the Republic; and another, secret, the conspiracy plotted by a sect of neurasthenic and perhaps insane millionaires, in order to achieve the same goal."[1] Even though Piglia, in his narrative theories, does not mention Macedonio's project,[2] it is clear that this unfinished novel bears the same structure as the form of the *cuento*: a visible story is steadily undermined by a secret story. As in the structure of the *cuento*, the two plots in Macedonio's project are antagonistic repetitions of each other. The first story is Macedonio's visible attempt to campaign for office. The second story, while it theoretically hopes to achieve the same goal, nevertheless only takes place as the proliferation of counterfeit objects. To read for the complot would be to read for the way these hidden figures produce an interruption, the point at which "nothing means anything in this anarchic world."[3] This moment of anarchic disruption is what I have called the "complot effect." The secret story, although it never fully emerges, nevertheless breaks the social field into contingent relations, where nothing automatically means anything, where no relation can be taken for granted.

As I mentioned in the Introduction, this story about Macedonio's projects could be taken to suggest that the conspiracy narrative is merely a substitute politics. After all, instead of running for office and actively participating in politics, Macedonio and friends channel their energy into a novel that is never completed. Rather than the active life, they retreat into an imaginary world of intrigue. The very fact that conspiracy theories only discover an event that never fully comes to light suggests, for critics like Mark Fenster, that the conspiracy narrative represents a kind of "failed politics." In *Conspiracy Theories*, Fenster notes that the "history of twentieth-century conspiracy theories . . . demonstrates that the interpretive practice does not in fact end but continues to engage in the search for more connections in the present and in the past. Totalizing conspiracy theories notoriously 'fail'; they do not, and cannot, adequately find a final order. The future, when the secret will be revealed, never arrives."[4] The problem, for Fenster, is that conspiracy theories fail to bring closure to interpretation, since these narratives always allude to a conspiracy that never fully comes to light. For this reason, Fenster insists that conspiracy narratives do not come up with a stable position from which to produce authentic political statements: "individual conspiracies may be exposed and condemned by society on a regular basis, but conspiracy as a totalizing phenomenon, as a whole way of life, is a practice that seems continually to be frustrated in its inability to persuade and affect political order."[5] Conspiracy theories fail to be political because they always end up in an illegitimate space of indecision: they cannot firmly attest to the existence of the conspiratorial agents, or they do not give convincing proof that there is actual opposition to the dominant political order. Using Fenster's theoretical model, it would be possible to argue that Macedonio's transition from political engagement to the writing of a conspiracy narrative is necessarily a step backward politically. Rather than remain in the realm of action that either takes place or does not take place, Macedonio writes about a realm in which events never quite take place.

Contrary to this theoretical model, I have argued that conspiracy theory's "failure" is in fact the very condition of any kind of political relation. As I noted at the beginning of *Counterfeit Politics*, Piglia suggests that politics is a narrative form that takes place even in those narratives that do not seem particularly "political," that is, in those narratives that have not located a stable position from which to engage in politics. Piglia's argument about the political form of conspiracy theories appears in the afterword to his novel *La ciudad ausente* (*The Absent City*). In this 1992 novel, Piglia rewrites Macedonio's life as the life of a mad scientist, a version that in fact is not far from some of the biographical accounts of Macedonio. But Piglia takes this motif to science-fiction proportions, and in fact places Macedonio within a conspiracy novel that takes the significance of storytelling as its theme. Thus, although he never mentions Macedonio's project in his narrative theory, Piglia nevertheless secretly inscribes this project within the plot of his novel. At the same time, he suggests a way to theorize the political form of conspiracy narratives. However, to say that conspiracy narratives are always political is not to say that these narratives should be given legitimacy. In fact, Piglia suggests that conspiracy narratives necessarily include a "counterfeit" story and therefore can never stand as fully legitimate or authoritative statements. In other words, the point now is not to say that conspiracy narratives are "truly" political, thereby replacing any other narrative that purports to be political. Rather, the idea is to read the paradoxical structure of conspiracy narratives, in order to show that all political statements—even if they do not seem to narrate a conspiracy—have the form of conspiracy theory. This "form" necessarily includes an illegitimate element, a counterfeit story that produces a complot effect. As I will argue in what follows, Piglia models the way that politics, if it takes place at all, only takes place in the counterfeit form of the conspiracy narrative.

The Absent City is about the circulating stories produced by a clandestine machine or cyborg. This machine contains, in fact, the implanted memory of Macedonio's wife, Elena Obieta. In reality, Macedonio lost his wife in 1920, and mourned her death through his poem "Elena Bellamuerte." However, Piglia creates an alternative history for this event and its aftermath. In *The Absent City*, Macedonio tries to interrupt death by placing Elena's memory in a machine. This machine ultimately outlives Macedonio: Elena lives on, "translated" or transferred into a machine that now can only reproduce stories. The action of the novel takes place in the near future, when a journalist, Junior MacKensey, tries to learn more information about the hidden machine. Through a series of tips and investigations, Junior navigates his way through the city in order to find the machine. At the same time, however, it is not quite accurate to say only that the novel is *about* this machine or even *about* the circulating stories produced by the machine. Rather, these stories are included within the fabric of the novel, and sometimes it is difficult to tell if a chapter is a story about the machine or if it is one of the *cuentos* produced by the machine.

One way to get a brief sense of the way Piglia posits his novel within the conspiratorial tradition is to read the implicit context of this literary text. In effect, I would like to follow Piglia's own suggestion (in the "Afterword" to *The Absent City*) that criticism should always attempt to reconstruct the context of a literary work. However, to "reconstruct the context" does not mean that one should refer back to the discourses of history, political science, sociology, and so on, in order to narrate a context that would exist prior to the text. Rather, to reconstruct the context means to read the way the novel itself posits a possible milieu for the action of the plot. Piglia takes as his model James Joyce's *Finnegans Wake*:

> What I have tried to do with [the short story] "The Island" . . . is create a society that might constitute the context for *Finnegans Wake*. Not the society within which Joyce wrote the *Wake*, which would point to Ireland in tension with England, and everything else that makes up the context of the real text. But rather: what would be the imaginary context in which the *Wake* could function? Or: in what society would *Finnegans Wake* be read as a realist work? The answer is a society in which language is constantly changing. This approach has interested me for a long time as a possible model of literary criticism. I believe literary

criticism should try to imagine the implied, fictional context of works of literature.[6]

Piglia goes on to say that this model could be used as a way to read his novel as a whole. The idea, then, is to read *The Absent City* according to its implicit context, which would include not only the literary texts that make Piglia's text possible (for instance, novels by Don DeLillo or Philip K. Dick, mentioned explicitly in the "Afterword"), but also the conditions and limits of the world established by his novel.

In a sense, *The Absent City* takes place within a situation in which any relation to the *polis* is impossible, since all relations must pass through a mechanism that I will now call the "pliant-machine." With this term I am referring to the figuration of an apparatus of control that inscribes the subject within a system of totalized relations. For instance, in Don DeLillo's 1988 novel *Libra*, the CIA man Win Everett imagines the day when the Agency will give him a polygraph test in order to force him to tell the truth about his plans to make an attempt on the life of President Kennedy. Regardless of one's intentions, the polygraph machine always forces a response from the subject: "His body would do the rest, yield up its unprotected data. The machine intervenes between a man and his secrets. . . . It allows you to give yourself away."[7] Like the "Voigt-Kampff testing apparatus" that tests for androids in Philip K. Dick's 1968 novel *Do Androids Dream of Electric Sheep?*, the polygraph machine does not rely on verbal response; it lets the body speak its truth. However, language is crucial for evoking the body's response. As the bounty hunter Phil Resch explains in *Do Androids*, the machine works by testing "[r]eflex fluctuations. . . . But not to the physical stimulus. . . . It'll be to the verbal questions; what we call a flinch reaction."[8] The verbal cues are said to produce a reflexive response—an empathetic response in this case—to the questions put forward by the bounty hunter, and these reactions can be measured. The affective reactions—which do not depend on intention or even meaning—inscribe the subject within the control of the state. However, *Libra* goes on to suggest that the pliant-machine not only extracts truth from the body; it also extracts a verbal confession. Win generalizes his relation to the polygraph test: "Devices make us pliant. We want to please them. The machine was his only hope of deliverance after what he'd done, what he'd loosed into the crowd. . . . He would go beyond yes and no. Tell them about the deathward-tending logic of a plot."[9] The polygraph machine therefore makes the subject pliant, makes him pliable or foldable, and turns him into a subject that can be easily manipulated. The pliant-machine forces a re-ply, but it also forces a response, which is always a "vow-back," a "pledging-back," etymologically. Any kind of response is already to pledge oneself to the truth of the state.[10] How then to respond, how to reply, when a response to the pliant-machine is already to be inscribed within its totalized relations?

This is the "paranoid" question that hovers around *The Absent City*. As in DeLillo's *Libra*, these pliant-machines are in the hands of a disciplinary intelligence agency, here an oppressive police force that seeks "the truth" by means of medical or clinical techniques. One such technique depends on the idea that there are certain *"nudos blancos"* buried in the bones of human skeletons.[11] These "white/blank knots" contain the secret to the subject's experience, according to the clinical police, and the role of the police is to work directly on these "white nodes," as they are called in Sergio Waisman's translation. In one chapter, we are introduced to an avatar of Elena, who at this point believes she is only hallucinating that she is a machine. Elena is in a clinic, and she tells the doctors that she wants to stop hallucinating. One of the doctors then explains to Elena:

> It will be necessary to work on your memory. . . . There are areas of condensation, white nodes, which can be untied, opened up. They are like myths . . . they define the grammar of experience. Everything the linguists have taught us about language also applies to the core of living matter. The genetic code and the verbal code present us with the same characteristics. That is what we call the white nodes. The clinic neurologists can attempt an intervention. It will be necessary to work on your brain.[12]

Strangely, the "clinical" intervention appears in the narrative not as surgery, but rather as a dialogue between Elena and the doctors. The intervention begins with a question on the part of the interrogators, which Elena then answers. It soon becomes clear that the content of her replies does not matter, since the question and answer process is itself the clinical intervention: Elena falls into a dream state in which her memories take on the form of images that can be downloaded. For this reason, Elena begins to fear sleep, since in her dream-state the doctors are able to force a response from her, beyond her intentions.

Therefore, to be conscious and to speak at all in these situations—or even not to speak, to keep the secret to oneself—is already to answer the questions of the police. The state knows how to force the subject to tell stories. As Junior finds out toward the end of the novel, one can learn more about the art of narrative by studying this apparatus of control than by reading literature: "narrative is an art that belongs to the police . . . they are always trying to get people to tell their secrets, to narc on other suspects, to tell on their friends, their brothers. That is why the police and the so-called justice have done more for the progress of narrative . . . than any writer in history" (*AC*, 130). It is not only that the state has taken the place of the storyteller; the citizen, too, is constituted as a storyteller who tells her truth to the state, regardless of intentions. Storytelling is here a form of social control, a way of ending politics by defining the subject as an extension of the state. If there is no way to engage in storytelling

outside the apparatus of the state, if there is no difference between the
state and the people, then there is no way to tell a truly political story.

With this "paranoid" backdrop, Piglia is clearly placing his novel
within the context of U.S. conspiracy narratives. At the same time, however, he is also placing *The Absent City* in dialogue with Latin American
cultural theorists such as Ángel Rama. In *La ciudad letrada*, published in
1984, the Uruguayan critic introduces the term "the lettered city" in order
to describe the apparatus that produces and distributes power by means
of writing. The basis of the lettered city is the scribe, the one who "pub-
lishes" (or makes public) the legal statements of the government. The
function of the scribe is to *"dar fe"*: to "give faith" or attest to the authenticity of a statement. [13] Rama writes: "The [Spanish] conquerors still as-
serted territorial claims . . . but now they required a writer of some sort (a
scribe, a notary, a chronicler) to cast their foundational acts in the form of
imperishable signs. The resulting scripture had the high function reserved to notarial documents, which according to the Spanish formula,
give witness or 'faith' to the acts they record." [14] In Rama's historical
analysis, writing (*escritura*—translated as "scripture" above) [15] is associated with the imperial power that began with the first colonies in the
Americas. He goes on to explain that the written word took on an onto-
logical precedence over the spoken word: "In Latin America, the written
word became the only binding one—in contradistinction to the spoken
word, which belonged to the realm of things precarious and uncertain." [16]
The written word is then the condition for anything binding or valid
(*valedera*). [17] The content of the statement is secondary to this function of
"giving faith" or testifying that something is true.

However, the fact that a statement is "true" has no bearing on whether the statement refers to a referent that exists in the real world. In fact,
Rama thinks of the Latin American city as living something like a *"doble
vida"* (a double life): on the one hand, there is the physical city which
suffers accidental transformations over time; on top of that one there is
another city that takes place on the order of signs, which in turn imprints
its potentiality over the real one ("el orden de los signos imprimió su
potencialidad sobre lo real"). [18] The written city does not *refer* to the real
city, but rather exists only according to its own laws of order, without
being dependent on the real city that lies below it. At the same time, the
lettered city writes upon the surface of the real city and therefore,
through this writing, imprints its power over the real city, as if the lettered city were a kind of "carbon paper" that produced impressions on
the real city. Thus, while the lettered city seems to be secondary in relation to the real city, in fact the lettered city is the condition of the order of
the real city, and therefore determines its political order. The function of
the scribe is to produce statements that structure and authenticate the
lettered city, and the lettered city in turn structures the order of the real
city. Writing is therefore *performative* in Rama's theory, since it does not

refer back to a state of affairs that is true or false, but rather works according to the legitimacy or illegitimacy of the statement. For Rama, the scribe is the true unacknowledged legislator of the world.

Therefore, whether one is jotting down an inventory of goods or composing a poem, one is always taking up the position of the scribe. By basing writing on the figure of the scribe, Rama shows how a felicitous act of writing in the lettered city is always produced as *authentic*. The scribe gives faith and the reader, by being able to read it, automatically returns this faith or belief in the authenticity of the writing. To give faith is always already the give-and-take of faith, an economy of faith that takes place whenever there is "writing." By theorizing writing in this way, Rama suggests that it is not that power simply uses writing in order to publish its power. Rather, writing is constitutive of power; power is produced through a network of belief that is grounded in writing. To escape this system of power one would have to be "illiterate"—that is, one would have to be unable to give faith to any repeatable mark set in a system of differences. However, to be truly illiterate in the lettered city would mean that the subject would be in a state of complete muteness or silence. In fact, it would be difficult even to call this illiterate position a "subject." Instead, we would be dealing with what J. L. Austin called a "low type," that is, an illegitimate figure who "speaks" without authorization and who therefore cannot be heard.[19] This "low type" would have no relation to power, politics, or the community.

It is therefore possible to sketch out the two options that Rama's theory of the lettered city suggests: either one writes for the lettered city or one does not write at all; either one completely relates to the *polis* or one does not relate at all. These options tend to have the same effect: to write within the lettered city is to be subsumed into the lettered city, and to be subsumed into the city thereby dissolves the notion of relation since there is no difference between the writer and the lettered city. After all, one is a subject of the lettered city precisely because one writes; the very condition that permits a "relation" to the *polis* (writing as giving faith) is precisely what annuls any notion of relation. Strangely, then, a "successful" act of writing or performative utterance (one that gives faith or is written in good faith) is essentially *inoperative*, since it would have no effective impact on the lettered city: a successful performative utterance, in this sense, would continue to authorize what has already been authorized. In other words, *nothing* happens in a successful (or felicitous) act of writing. Rama's theory suggests a situation of total control, in which there is no room for resistance because there is no effective political relation. How then to write *politically* when to write at all is already to inscribe oneself within the totalizing relations of this *polis*? How to write a political story and tell the story of politics that would create a non-totalizing relation to the political?[20]

In effect, these are the questions that Piglia's *The Absent City* brings up in relation to the clinical and military power of the police. In fact, I would argue that Piglia's novel responds to the problematic that Rama sets up, implicitly developing a point that Rama suggests toward the end of *The Lettered City*. In the early part of the twentieth century, Rama notes, the new "revolutionized city" produced the conditions for a new writer: the autodidact who is now informed by anarchist and socialist thought. While it is certainly important that this new figure comes into its own in relation to these radical political theories, for Rama the crucial factor is also the very grammar of experience of this new figure: the fact that the autodidact is forged through a confused conglomeration of knowledge. Rama explains:

> Partly under the influence of anarchism, there emerged in the early twentieth century a group of intellectuals, usually from a lower social class, who could not afford or did not desire a university education. The texts of the self-taught intellectuals were to be found in the free market of books and magazines, and their seminars were conversations in cafés and other informal meeting places. The confused and tumultuous process of democratization was creating a new type of letrado who, lacking contact with the most esteemed instrument of formal education, necessarily developed a less disciplined and systematic, but also more liberated, intellectual vision.[21]

Therefore, although there is an emphasis on a "transparent" style during this period, what nevertheless defines this new writer is a crisis over what it means to organize knowledge. That is, this crisis concerns the relational nature of knowledge, or how phenomena enter into relation in order to constitute a "legible" thought. Rather than produce a disciplined writing that joins other disciplines within a unified order, the autodidact simply yokes together conglomerations of knowledge and scribbles them down in a jumbled way ("una visión . . . más caótica, indisciplinada y asistemática").[22] The autodidact is still a kind of scribe (he is still "scribbling"), but the writing produced by this scribe is almost illegible, a kind of "fake" writing. From the perspective of the lettered city, the autodidact tends to disappear in this mess; he becomes "illegible."

In Piglia's earlier novel *Respiración artificial*, the exemplary figure for this new kind of illegible writing is the Argentine novelist Roberto Arlt. For Piglia, Arlt produced an anarchist writing that both gives faith and paradoxically takes it away. As one character insists in Piglia's 1980 novel (published before Rama's study), Arlt stands as the first modern Argentine writer *precisely* because his writing is "illegible":

> [Arlt] wrote badly: but in the moral sense of the word. His is *bad* writing, perverse writing. . . . His is a criminal style. Arlt writes against the idea of a literary style, or rather, he writes against what they taught us should be understood as good writing, namely to write tidy precise

prose without any gerunds—right?—and without repeated words. That's why the highest praise one can give Arlt is to say that at his best moments he is unreadable; at least when the critics say that he is un-readable they mean they cannot read him, using their system they cannot read him.[23]

According to Piglia, then, Arlt's writing is "criminal" to the extent that he writes *against* the established norms of good prose. To read Arlt from the perspective of *their* system or code (*"código"*)—that is, from the perspec-tive of the rules of the scribes and their notion of polished prose—is to recognize the illegibility of Arlt: he is unreadable, *"ilegible."*[24] His writing goes against the very codes that inscribe the norms for connecting to the lettered city. Strangely, these codes are disrupted in the very moment of writing: Arlt disrupts his connection to the lettered city in the very mo-ment of "connecting" to the lettered city, that is, in the moment of writ-ing. Arlt's writing therefore disappears—becomes illegible—if read from the perspective of *their* code. For this reason, it is necessary to read Arlt, not simply from outside of "their" rules, but rather as an attempt to *counter* their system: his writing takes place as a struggle against the lettered city from within the system of the letter. Arlt's writing is a "countereconomy" that intervenes in the give-and-take of any authentic act of writing in the lettered city.

Piglia's later novel, *The Absent City*, generalizes this Arlt-effect and places it within the agency of a storytelling machine. Piglia's novel tells the story of Macedonio's wife, Elena Obieta, whose memory has been downloaded into a machine after the death of Elena's body. The machine seems to offer a way to intervene in the situation of the pliant-machine or the lettered city. If storytelling (or "writing") is a form of social control in *The Absent City*, if there is no way to engage in storytelling outside the apparatus of the state, then how is it possible to tell a political story in this situation? Like Arlt's writing, the machine offers the possibility of a "writing" that is illegible, a writing that gives faith while taking it away. After all, the machine in Piglia's novel is not only a "something" (the memory of Macedonio's deceased wife), but also has a function: it per-forms as a kind of counterfeiting machine, that is, a machine that repli-cates stories and introduces differences into the replication. The narrator notes that the first incarnation of the machine was a translating machine, in which one would insert a text like Edgar Allan Poe's "William Wil-son," and the machine would simply translate the text into Spanish. However, according to legend, the machine would modify the text to an unrecognizable degree. Even the title would change: "William Wilson" became "Stephen Stevenson." The narrator explains: "We had wanted a machine that could translate; we got a machine that transforms stories. It took the theme of the double and translated it. . . . It takes what is avail-able and transforms what appears lost into something else" (*AC*, 37). The first machine begins, then, as a technique for translation. However, the translating machine takes this "loss" and makes it return as something else, or makes it turn into something other (*"en otra cosa"*) (*CA*, 41–42). The new machine therefore describes a certain economy of translation in which it takes part, but which it also dismantles: instead of producing merely a "loss," the machine produces a difference, *"otra cosa."* This technique of difference through repetition is figured as a transposition of a theme from Poe's short story. It is not simply that the machine translates "William Wilson"; it also takes the story's theme of the double and translates this theme, transposes it, and converts it into a technique of storytelling. This storytelling machine therefore always works by translation, if "translation" is now understood as a doubling technique that produces not simply difference, but rather an antagonistic logic between the "original" and the "translation."[25] Between these two versions—which can no longer be thought along the lines of a pure origin and a mere copy—there is a radical divide, as the transforming process of the machine creates versions that are always *"otra cosa,"* something other.

Furthermore, the narrator notes that the machine is also able to learn. "Learning" is defined here as the capacity to remember what it has already narrated: "Learning means that it remembers what it has already done, it accumulates experience as it goes along. It will not necessarily make better stories each time, but it will know the stories it has already made, and perhaps give them a plot to tie them all together at the end" (*AC*, 38). Piglia thus fictionalizes the theory he had already developed about the way the *cuento* can stand as a kind of artificial storytelling technique that supplements the function of traditional storytelling. In fact, the narrator notes that Macedonio thought this invention would be very useful, precisely because "there were very few old men left to tell ghost stories in the countryside at night" (*AC*, 38). Macedonio therefore hopes that the storytelling machine would substitute for the loss of the traditional storyteller, even if this position is already being invaded by state power.[26] Macedonio's storytelling machine has the capacity, it seems, to produce not only an individual memory and experience, but also a kind of collective memory that would artificially tie together all the stories into some sort of whole.

However, this storytelling machine does not produce authentic experience, but rather persists within the task of the translator: it produces an afterlife, an artificial respiration that produces a virtual world.[27] This virtuality is literalized after the death of Macedonio's wife, when he realizes that he can plug her memory into the storytelling machine in order to "save" her: "When it transformed 'William Wilson' into the story of Stephen Stevenson, Macedonio realized that he had the basic elements from which he could build a virtual reality" (*AC*, 41–42). The storytelling machine is therefore an apparatus for living off of storytelling, but the resulting "life" is in fact an afterlife, a virtual world. At the same time, this virtual reality both replicates and opposes the state, since the linked stories that circulate throughout the city are not the stories of the state (by the state or to the state), but rather take place as *replicating replies* to the state. The narrator explains: "Macedonio was not trying to build a replica of man, but rather a machine that could produce replicas. His goal was to nullify death and construct a virtual world" (*AC*, 52) (Macedonio no intentaba producir una réplica del hombre, sino una máquina de producir réplicas. Su objetivo era anular la muerte y construir un mundo virtual [*CA*, 60]). Here Piglia is explicitly asking us to hear the double meaning of *réplica*: on the one hand, "*réplica*" can mean "copy" or "replica"; on the other hand, "*réplica*" can mean "response," in the sense of "*replicar*" (to reply or respond). As the narrator notes, the machine produces replies (*réplicas*) to the state by producing replicas (*réplicas*) of the stories produced by the state. In this way, the "*réplica*" sets up an antagonistic relation to the state. This antagonism is due to the apocryphal status of these stories, the way they reply to the state as mere copies that repeat *and* disfigure the "original." The idea, then, is not simply to produce an artificial presence or a replica man; to do so would be to ignore the way power is produced through stories, that is, the discursive nature of political power. Rather, the point is to produce a machine that in turn produces a counterfeit reply: a *réplica*. This replicating process produces a virtual world, which means that this world is clearly a replica of the real world at the same time that it is a way of antagonistically replying to the storytelling machine that is state power. The machine replies to the state as an otherness that cannot be assimilated to the stories of the state.

This strategy of the *réplica* is called "resistance" by the man who helped build the machine, an engineer named Russo. This engineer insists that state power is based on a series of electronic devices that allow a small group of conspirators to control the world. He tells Junior, the journalist:

> They build electronic devices and electronic personalities and electronic fictions. . . . The State intelligence is essentially a technical mechanism designed to alter the criteria of reality. We have to resist. We are trying to build a microscopic replica [*réplica*], a female defense machine, against the experiences and the experiments and the lies of the State. (*AC*, 116) (*CA*, 142–43)

The point, for Russo, is to resist the bombardment of state-fictions; however, to resist is not to put forward authentic statements or statements of "truth." After all, in Piglia's novel it is the state that defines itself as the arbiter of truth. As one police officer conveniently explains to Junior: "The police . . . are completely removed from all fantasies. We are reality. We are constantly obtaining true confessions and revelations. We care only about real events. We are servants of the truth" (*AC*, 80).[28] It is the task of the police, then, to produce a believable fiction that will stand as truth. As Russo explains, resistance to this "truth" does not take place as a counter-truth, but rather as a *réplica* to the police: a reply that takes place as a replica, an antagonistic repetition of the machinations of the state.

These replicating stories end up producing a kind of side effect amongst the people: as the stories produced (or replicated) by the machine begin to circulate around the city, the people begin not only to listen to the stories but also to replicate them in turn. Junior realizes that the key to understanding the machine is precisely its first "translation" of "William Wilson": it not only translated the theme of the double but also took this theme as its formal mechanism. Similarly, it is this formal mechanism that is being circulated around the city, along with the stories produced by the machine. It is therefore not actually circulation that is taking place, but rather replication masked as circulation. At the same time, however, precisely because these stories are all replications (replies and copies), it is difficult for the police to pin anything on anyone. For instance, the following story about a character named Hannah is indicative of this process:

> A few suspected that Hannah herself had secret connections with the machine. That she distributed apocryphal stories and false versions, that she was part of the counterinformation groups who sold replicas, copies made in labs mounted in clandestine suburban garages. They had never been able to pin anything on her, but they kept a watch over her and occasionally closed down her business. (*AC*, 86)

Here, Junior thinks about the pure speculations regarding this underground figure, but the perspective slowly shifts from rumors ("A few suspected") to a surveillance perspective in the form of the police ("They had never been able to pin anything on her"). The problem, from the perspective of the police, is that nothing can be "pinned" on her conclusively: the production of replicas produces, as an effect, this absence of certainty. In other words, if the conspiracy of stories appears at all, it appears as the impossibility of knowing for sure whether it is appearing.[29]

The Absent City therefore presents a situation that is never fully resolved: on the one hand we have the discourse of the police, which knows how to extract a reply from the subject; and on the other hand, we have these *other* replies, these replies that are *other*, replies that are antagonistic replications of the stories that the state tells. It is important to note that this situation is never resolved in the novel: it is not the story of a revolution against the state or a final victory over the police. Instead, we have the coexistence of two stories: the stories of the police and the conspiratorial stories. These conspiratorial stories produce the outlines of a "secret society," even though it cannot be stated with any certainty that this secret society actually exists. The secret society "takes place" in *The*

Absent City as the apocryphal or counterfeit repetition of the stories of the state: the secret society is precisely an "absent city." Conspiracy is therefore not quite a theme in Piglia's novel, but rather occurs as the emergence of a secret story that disrupts the main narrative line. This disruption splits the narrative into two stories: a visible story (the stories of the State), and a secret story that never fully appears (the counterfeit tales that are replicated throughout the city). Secrecy is therefore not simply defined as something that does not come to light; rather, secrecy is defined in Piglia's novel as a story that cannot be assimilated by the first story and which interrupts any official discourse (here, the discourse of the police state). The first story is continually undermined by this second story, and this split structure is what defines Piglia's conspiracy novel, just as it defined the projected novel that Macedonio Fernández imagined with his band of conspirators.

At the same time, Piglia suggests that politics is structured according to this same logic: there is always a visible story that is steadily undermined by a secret story that never fully emerges. After all, the problem that confronts the characters in the visible city is the fact that the subject can never enter into a political relation with the state: the subject is always already taken up by the state. Whatever these characters might do or say within this police state, at a certain level they are always replying to the state and *as the state*. There is therefore no *political* relation as such in the police state offered by *The Absent City*. However, politics does happen in Piglia's novel, but it happens as this counterfeit event, an interruption that is difficult to localize because of the way it takes place as an antagonistic repetition of the stories of the state. In Piglia's narrative theory, this paradoxical situation is called the *cuento*, the situation of two stories that are told simultaneously but according to antagonistic logics. This theory of narrative is then given form in Piglia's novel as the story of the way politics takes place, that is, as the necessary narration of two stories: one visible, the other secret or absent. The second story is "absent" precisely because it takes place as a *réplica*, a way of "giving faith" that is also a counterfeiting of faith. This means that the only effective political statement would be one that paradoxically falsifies faith: a successful moment of politics would depend on something like an infelicitous performative utterance, a statement that takes place and does not take place at the same time.[30] For this reason, it no longer makes sense to speak of politics in the mode of "commitment." Instead, Piglia puts forward the notion of a "counterfeit" commitment, a politics that is always infected by "bad faith."

For Piglia, then, politics is this event that "takes place" in narrative: politics can only be said to happen when there is a visible story (the "status quo") that is *continually* threatened by a secret story that can never be fully assimilated by the first narrative line. Without this *réplica*— without this replica of the first story that also replies to the first story—

there would be no political relation, since every "reply" would simply be folded back into state power. This second narrative line (the "complot") is necessary if any kind of political relation is to take place, since it desta-bilizes the pliant-machine and allows a reply that is radically other. The emergence of this complot remains as a continual possibility in every plot: as Peter Brooks noted, the complot threatens the authority or "legal-ities" of the main narrative line *at every moment*.[31] This explains why it seems that everyday occurrences can turn political without warning: pol-itics emerges unforeseeably as a narrative event, whenever a "complot" interrupts the authorized story or undermines the official discourse.

If the most obvious form of this double narrative is conspiracy theory, this is only because conspiracy theory thematizes this constitutive antag-onistic relation when it tells the story of a treacherous enemy that threat-ens the people. But this structure conditions any moment of politics, even those moments that do not seem to be narrated in a "paranoid" way. For instance, a paradigmatic moment of politics might be the 2006 demon-stration of millions of people who protested against proposed anti-immi-grant legislation in Congress.[32] While this protest movement seems to have little to do with conspiracy theories, nevertheless it models the way *politics takes place as conspiracy theory*.[33] The historian Jason Frank notes about this movement: "Many of the participants in these actions were formally noncitizens who nonetheless enacted a claim to speak on behalf of the (authorized and enfranchised) people; they, 'the undocumented' and their supporters, enacted a political power that they did not yet officially have."[34] The participants in this demonstration are situated in the position of the "low type": they have no authority to speak (their "demonstration" cannot be legitimately demonstrated), and yet they en-act a claim that simulates an authentic speech act. In fact, Frank interest-ingly relates this type of claiming to Austin's discussion of felicitous and infelicitous speech acts: "At such times political claims to speak in the people's name are felicitous, even as they explicitly break from the estab-lished procedures or rules for representing popular voice."[35] In general, then, Frank notes that it is precisely the "underauthorization" of these speech acts "that oddly grants them a higher authorization, their ability to enact claims that can only be retrospectively vindicated."[36] While I agree with Frank that moments like these attest to the power of this kind of infelicitous speech act, the "illegitimate" nature of conspiracy theory has taught us that this speech act must *remain* "infelicitous" and irredu-cibly "invisible": there can be no expectation that these acts will become retrospectively felicitous.[37] In fact, I would argue that the illegitimate speech of the "undocumented" protesters can remain political only if this speech *remains* illegitimate. This would mean that the protesters could never *fully* appear within the *polis*: their "appearance" must always be tainted by an irreducible "invisibility" or "disappearance." This is not to say that the claims of those who are "undocumented" can never reach their goal; it only means that their claims are no longer *political* if they are able to speak with a fully legitimate voice or if a future legitimacy is programmed in advance. For a statement to be political, it must use the infelicitous language of the *réplica*: a reply that replicates and thereby counterfeits the "writing" of the state.

In this way, the play of legitimacy that defines the *theme* of conspiracy theory is also the very form of the political: there is no politics without a secret narrative that undermines the legitimacy of an official narrative. However, this conclusion does not mean that conspiracy theories, instead of other types of narratives, are the only authentic expressions of politics. After all, conspiracy narratives only take place when there is an illegitimate or counterfeit story that undermines any claim to authenticity. Conspiracy theories are *constitutively* counterfeit. They demand that we confront the illegitimate form of politics, that is, the way politics always takes place as the emergence of an illegitimate force—the complot—that conspires against a legitimate discourse. To read for the complot would therefore be to read for the emergence of the political.

NOTES

1. Jorge Luis Borges, *Prólogos con un prólogo de prólogos* (Madrid: Alianza Editorial, 1975), 86. All translations from Borges's essay on Macedonio Fernández are mine.

2. In a 2007 essay ("Novela y complot"), Piglia indeed comments on Borges's famous anecdote about Macedonio, but his comments stay focused on Macedonio's campaign to run for president. Piglia notes that even in this visible attempt to engage in politics, Macedonio's campaign showed "todas las características de una práctica conspirativa destinada a producir en la realidad efectos mínimos, pero muy metafóricos" (Ricardo Piglia, "Novela y complot," *Quimera* 280 [March 2007]: 49) (all the characteristics of a conspiratorial practice destined to produce minimal but very metaphorical effects in reality). Piglia goes on to say that this campaign is in fact "una crítica práctica del funcionamiento de la política" (Piglia, "Novela y complot," 49) (a practical critique of the functioning of politics). As mentioned earlier, Piglia's essay develops some intriguing theses on the role of conspiracy narratives in novels, but he does not relate these ideas to his narrative theory. All translations are mine unless noted.

3. Borges, *Prólogos*, 87.

4. Mark Fenster, *Conspiracy Theories: Secrecy and Power in American Culture* (Minneapolis: University of Minnesota Press, 1999), 89.

5. Ibid., 90.

6. Ricardo Piglia, "Afterword," in *The Absent City*, trans. Sergio Waisman (Durham, NC: Duke University Press, 2000), 144.

7. Don DeLillo, *Libra* (New York: Penguin Books, 1988), 361–62.

8. Philip K. Dick, *Do Androids Dream of Electric Sheep?* (New York: Ballantine Books, 1968), 139.

9. DeLillo, *Libra*, 362–63.

10. The disciplinary power of the examination is described in Michel Foucault's *Discipline and Punish*. He writes that "one should look into the mechanisms of examination, into the formation of the mechanisms of discipline, and of a new type of power over bodies. . . . The disciplinary methods [exemplified by the examination] . . . lowered the threshold of describable individuality and made of this description a

means of control and a method of domination. It is no longer a monument for future memory, but a document for possible use" (Michel Foucault, *Discipline and Punish: The Birth of the Prison*, trans. Alan Sheridan [New York: Vintage Books, 1977], 191). In the first volume of *The History of Sexuality*, Foucault describes a more general incitement to speak, specifically in relation to the discourse of sex: "It was here, perhaps, that the injunction, so peculiar to the West, was laid down for the first time . . . the nearly infinite task of telling—telling oneself and another, as often as possible, everything that might concern the interplay of innumerable pleasures, sensations, and thoughts which, through the body and the soul, had some affinity with sex. . . . An imperative was established: Not only will you confess to acts contravening the law, but you will seek to transform your desire, your every desire, into discourse" (Michel Foucault, *History of Sexuality: Volume I, An Introduction*, trans. Robert Hurley [New York: Vintage Books, 1978], 20–21). Foucault therefore calls this the "great subjugation," beyond the secondary devices of control: "ways of rendering it [sex] morally acceptable and technically useful" (Foucault, *History of Sexuality*, 21).

11. Ricardo Piglia, *La ciudad ausente* (Barcelona: Editorial Anagrama, 2003), 71. Hereafter cited in the text as *CA*.

12. Ricardo Piglia, *The Absent City*, trans. Sergio Waisman (Durham, NC: Duke University Press, 2000), 62. Hereafter cited in the text as *AC*.

13. Ángel Rama, *La ciudad letrada* (Hanover, NH: Ediciones del Norte, 1984), 8.

14. Ángel Rama, *The Lettered City*, trans. John Charles Chasteen (Durham, NC: Duke University Press, 1996), 6.

15. Rama, *La ciudad letrada*, 8.

16. Rama, *The Lettered City*, 6.

17. Rama, *La ciudad letrada*, 9.

18. Ibid., 11, 12.

19. J. L. Austin, "Performative Utterances," in *Philosophical Papers*, ed. J. O. Urmson and G. J. Warnock (Oxford: Oxford University Press, 1979), 239–40. See note 16 in chapter 3.

20. Joanna Page notes that *The Absent City* situates itself precisely in what could be called a postmodern problematic. Although she does not refer to Rama's theory in her argument, Page notes that, in Piglia's novel, "There no longer seems to be any 'outside' from which one could mount opposition or present a critique. . . . Instead, resistance *from within*, embracing the system in order to infiltrate it, becomes the focus of Piglia's attempt to negotiate a (provisional, conflictual) role for the intellectual in contemporary society" (Joanna Page, "Writing as Resistance in Ricardo Piglia's *La ciudad ausente*," *Bulletin of Spanish Studies* 81.3 [2004]: 358). As I will show in what follows, conspiracy theory recontextualizes this problem of the "outside" by introducing the logic of the counterfeit.

21. Rama, *The Lettered City*, 118–19.

22. Rama, *La ciudad letrada*, 163.

23. Ricardo Piglia, *Artificial Respiration*, trans. Daniel Balderston (Durham, NC: Duke University Press, 1994), 132. For clarity's sake, it should be noted that Piglia began developing his reading of Arlt almost ten years before Rama's *La ciudad letrada* was published.

24. Ricardo Piglia, *Respiración artificial* (Barcelona: Editorial Anagrama, 2001), 134.

25. In this regard, the relationship between Piglia's translation machine and Poe's short story ends up doubling, as it were, the relationship between Borges's and Poe's detective fictions. John T. Irwin develops this point, along with the important concept of "antithetical doubling": "[Borges] set out to double Poe's three Dupin stories with three detective stories of his own—but with this difference: where Poe's detective solves the mystery and outwits the culprit, Borges's detectives, at least in the first two stories, are outwitted by the people they pursue, trapped in a labyrinth fashioned from the pursuer's ability to follow a trail until he arrives at the chosen spot at the expected moment" (John T. Irwin, *The Mystery to a Solution: Poe, Borges, and the Analytic Detective Story* [Baltimore and London: Johns Hopkins University Press, 1994], 37). Irwin goes

on to develop Borges's technique of doubling, focusing especially on specular images: "It is this notion of a mirror asymmetry, metaphorized as the self-constituting difference between polar opposites, that I mean to evoke by the term *antithetical doubling*" (Irwin, 97). While Piglia is equally interested in the way that Borges incorporates a previous author or genre in an antagonistic way (Piglia mentions this technique explicitly in "Tesis sobre el cuento"), nevertheless *The Absent City*'s emphasis on antithetical doubling (what I have called "counterfeiting" and what I will now call the "réplica") seems to be more radically asymmetrical.

26. Idelber Avelar and Joanna Page, among others, have noted the way Piglia's *The Absent City* often goes out of its way to respond to Benjamin's "The Storyteller," even if reference to Benjamin remains implicit throughout the novel. For instance, Page notes the way this allusion to the dying out of old storytellers "registers a crisis in the transmission of experience" (Joanna Page, "Ricardo Piglia: Towards a Re-socialized Literature," *Journal of Iberian and Latin American Studies* 10.2 [December 2004]: 182). She goes on to note that *The Absent City* seeks to keep this crisis at bay: "The stories told in *La ciudad ausente* are the fount of collective memory and culture. Their repetition, each time with variation, is essential to their grounding within the community" (Page, "Towards a Re-socialized Literature," 183).

27. In Walter Benjamin's "The Task of the Translator," this virtuality is called "pure language," a phrase that points to the relational nature of translation. Relation happens not so much as the relation between the original and the copy, but rather between languages. Furthermore, these relations are not the consequence of human intentions, but are rather an effect of the inner structure of language. Benjamin writes: "Translation thus ultimately serves the purpose of expressing the inner relationship between languages. It cannot possibly reveal or establish this hidden relationship itself; but it can present it by realizing it in embryonic or intensive form" (Walter Benjamin, "The Task of the Translator," in *Selected Writings: Volume 1, 1913–1926* [Cambridge: Harvard University Press, 1996], 255). The actualization of this hidden relationship is therefore not something a translator can plan on or account for. Rather, a translation can present this relationship—a relationship he calls "pure language"— through *Darstellung* or presentation. The presentation of this relationship is "hidden" in the sense that the relationship is never explicitly put forward. As Derrida remarks in "Des Tours de Babel": "in a mode that is solely anticipatory, annunciatory, almost prophetic, translation renders *present* an affinity that is never present in this presentation" (Jacques Derrida, "Des Tours de Babel," in *Acts of Religion*, ed. Gil Anidjar [New York: Routledge, 2002], 120). In Benjamin's "Epistemo-Critical Prologue" to *The Origin of German Tragic Drama*, written at the same time as "The Task of the Translator," he calls this presentation without presence "the idea," an image that does not rely on perception: an "objective, virtual arrangement" (Walter Benjamin, *The Origin of German Tragic Drama*, trans. John Osborne [London: Verso, 1977], 34).

28. As Joanna Page notes, "resistance cannot simply take the form of denouncing the state's versions as fictitious rather than real, as this complies with the very distinction imposed by the state. . . . Resistance must involve challenging the state's control of the code. Importantly, the narratives of the machine do not attempt to determine truth but to resist the control of the state by occupying a position that cannot be defined either as 'true' or as 'false'" (Page, "Writing as Resistance," 347, 348). While I agree that resistance in *The Absent City* must be thought in relation to performative utterances (those utterances that cannot be defined as true or false), nevertheless Piglia's emphasis on falsification or counterfeiting suggests that this resistance cannot remain a *pure* performative. In other words, the counterfeit responses of the machine—which take place according to the logic of the *réplica*—must hover between the performative and the constative (that which can be defined as true or false). As Derrida noted in relation to the American Declaration of Independence, "[t]his obscurity, this undecidability between, let us say, a performative structure and a constative structure, is *required* to produce the sought-after effect. It is essential to the very positing or position of a right as such" (Jacques Derrida, "Declarations of Independence," trans. Tom

Keenan and Tom Pepper, in *Negotiations: Interventions and Interviews, 1971–2001*, ed.
Elizabeth Rottenberg [Stanford, CA: Stanford University Press, 2002], 49). To be able to
respond to the State—that is, to be able to claim the *right* to respond to the State—
means that one cannot decide if that response is performative or constative, that is, if it
enacts what it says or if it discovers or refers back to a previous state of affairs. While
Page does not insist on this undecidability, she nevertheless does suggest that the
concept of resistance in *The Absent City* "is a shifting, provisional one and an appropriately tortuous response to the complex dynamics of power and language in Piglia's
fiction" (Page, "Writing as Resistance," 346).

29. Patrick Dove usefully relates this uncertainty to trauma theory. Dove finds a
persistent tone throughout *La ciudad ausente*, one that produces "a prevailing sense of
anxiety or unease whose origin remains difficult to identify. . . . The narrative warns
that something is afoot or amiss. It points to an impending conspiracy or disaster that
remains to be named or identified as such" (Patrick Dove, *The Catastrophe of Modernity:
Tragedy and the Nation in Latin American Literature* [Lewisburg, PA: Bucknell University
Press, 2004], 232, 233).

30. J. L. Austin notes that "infelicitous" performative utterances are very difficult to
classify, in part because these utterances are not *simply* without effect. Austin explains,
using the performative utterance "I bet" as an example: "To bet is not, as I pointed out
in passing, merely to utter the words 'I bet, &c.': someone might do that all right, and
yet we might still not agree that he had in fact, or at least entirely, succeeded in
betting. . . . Besides the uttering of the words of the so-called performative, a good
many other things have as a general rule to be right and to go right if we are to be said
to have happily brought off our action. What these are we may hope to discover by
looking at and classifying types of case in which something *goes wrong* and the act . . .
is therefore at least to some extent a failure: the utterance is then, we may say, not
indeed false but in general *unhappy*. And for this reason we call [this aspect of performative utterances] . . . the doctrine of the *Infelicities*" (J. L. Austin, *How to Do Things
with Words*, ed. J. O. Urmson and Marina Sbisà [Cambridge: Harvard University Press,
1975], 13–14). Austin admits here that the difference between happening and not
happening is not so clear, especially when he notes that we might not agree that an act
has *at least entirely* succeeded, or when he insists that an infelicitous performative is
one that is *to some extent* a failure. He later explains that a performative "without
effect" is not necessarily one that does not produce effects: "Two final words about
being void or without effect. This does not mean, of course, to say that we won't have
done anything: lots of things will have been done . . . but we shall *not* have done the
purported act, viz. marrying. Because despite the name, you do not when bigamous
marry twice. . . . Further, 'without effect' does not mean here 'without consequences,
results, effects'" (Austin, *How*, 17). Infelicitous performative utterances are therefore
strange because it can never be said that *nothing* happened, only that it is not quite
clear what exactly has happened. Infelicitous performative utterances both happen
and do not happen at the same time. This is what Derrida, following Austin's own
rhetoric, calls the "parasite": "*Never quite* taking place is thus part of [the parasite's]
performance, of its success as an event, of its taking-place" (Jacques Derrida, *Limited
Inc.*, trans. Samuel Weber [Evanston, IL: Northwestern University Press, 1988], 90).

31. Peter Brooks, *Reading for the Plot: Design and Intention in Narrative* (Cambridge:
Harvard University Press, 1984), 12.

32. I take this example from Jason Frank's *Constituent Moments*. He defines a "constituent moment" as any moment of "claims-making," rather than only those dramatic
moments when constitutional assemblies are convened: "In contrast to . . . the people's
higher lawmaking power, the narrative focus on constituent moments emphasizes
more than dramatic moments of constitutional lawmaking and constitutional realign-
ment. Constituent moments need not mark, to quote Ackerman, 'a radical break' from
the political past, a 'drastic change' and a new beginning. Instead a narrative focus on
constituent moments proliferates the dilemmas of authorization across an entire history of democratic claims-making—in such formal political contexts as constitutional

conventions and presidential politics, and also in the relatively informal contexts of crowd protest, political oratory, and poetry" (Jason Frank, *Constituent Moments: Enacting the People in Postrevolutionary America* [Durham, NC, and London: Duke University Press, 2010], 250). Frank then links this emphasis on constituent moments to Benjamin's figuration of the historiographer in "On the Concept of History": "To attend to the everyday possibility that constituent moments will reappear—rather than waiting for the coming of an epochal act of constitutional moments—is to be alert and open to the possibility of their reemergence, a disposition perhaps akin to what Walter Benjamin called the 'weak messianism' that infuses the political present" (Frank, 250–51). This "sensitivity to the unanticipated and the emergent" (Frank, 249) is similar to what I have called "reading for the complot," although I would want to emphasize the fact that the emergent must always remain illegitimate. To read for the complot describes not only a sensitivity to the unexpected (*lo inesperado*, in Piglia's terms), but also a way to read for that which does not fully emerge, that which *remains* irreducibly secret: "el arte de presentir lo inesperado; de saber esperar lo que viene, nítido, invisible" (Ricardo Piglia, *Formas breves* [Barcelona: Editorial Anagrama, 2000], 137). As I noted in chapter 1, it is not only the idea of waiting for the unexpected, but more precisely the paradoxical idea of waiting for that which you are *not* waiting for (or *esperar lo inesperado*).

33. It should be noted that quite a number of conspiracy theories about this protest movement have developed over the last few years. For instance, Lawrence Auster, writing for FrontPageMagazine.com (a publication of the David Horowitz Freedom Center), helped disseminate an invasion narrative about the movement: "The Mexican invasion of the United States began decades ago as a spontaneous migration of ordinary Mexicans into the U.S. seeking economic opportunities. It has morphed into a campaign to occupy and gain power over our country—a project encouraged, abetted, and organized by the Mexican state and supported by the leading elements of Mexican society" (Lawrence Auster, "The Second Mexican War," in *FrontPageMagazine.com*, February 17, 2006. Accessed July 23, 2011. http://archive.frontpagemag.com/readArticle.aspx?ARTID=5533). Of course, it could be argued that conspiracy theories about Latinos living in the United States are themselves an inevitable result of the Mexican-American War, which necessarily produced an "illegitimate" group within the borders of the United States. As Walter D. Mignolo puts it: "The Mexican-American war, during the first half of the nineteenth century, left vast numbers of Mexican people and areas of land (from Colorado to Texas and from Texas through Arizona and California) 'inside' the United States. Mexicans became immigrants in the territory of their own ancestors" (Walter D. Mignolo, *The Idea of Latin America* [Malden, MA: Blackwell Publishing, 2005], 134).

34. Frank, *Constituent Moments*, 253.

35. Ibid., 8.

36. Ibid., 10.

37. As Geoffrey Bennington has argued in his discussion of founding figures, "the duration of a political institution is not in fact indubitable proof of its quality (just as any sign of the genuineness of the legislator is necessarily open to the possibility of counterfeiting, so a durable state may always be a mere simulacrum of a good one). Legislator and charlatan thus remain undecidable" (Geoffrey Bennington, *Legislations: The Politics of Deconstruction* [London: Verso, 1994], 221–22). Bennington goes on to note, for example, that "Moses might still (have) turn(ed) out to be a charlatan after all" (Bennington, *Legislations*, 222). He then concludes: "Any event of thought, in so far as it is an event and not simply a programmed repetition, involves this undecidability and temporal *après-coup*" (Bennington, *Legislations*, 222).

Bibliography

Agamben, Giorgio. *State of Exception.* Trans. Kevin Attell. Chicago: University of Chicago Press, 2005.

Aguilar, Gonzalo. "Macedonio Fernández: Modos de aparición y ausencia." *Historia crítica de la literatura argentina: Macedonio* (Volumen VIII). Ed. Roberto Ferro. Buenos Aires: Emecé Editores, 2007.

Arendt, Hannah. *On Revolution.* London: Penguin Books, 1963.

Arias, Arturo. "Authoring Ethnicized Subjects: Rigoberta Menchú and the Performative Production of the Subaltern Self." *PMLA* 116 (January 2001): 75–88.

Auster, Lawrence. "The Second Mexican War." *FrontPageMagazine.com*, February 17, 2006. Accessed July 23, 2011. http://archive.frontpagemag.com/readArticle.aspx?ARTID=5533.

Austin, J. L. *How to Do Things with Words.* Ed. J. O. Urmson and Marina Sbisà. Cambridge: Harvard University Press, 1975.

———. "Performative Utterances." *Philosophical Papers.* Ed. J. O. Urmson and G. J. Warnock. Oxford: Oxford University Press, 1979.

Avelar, Idelber. "Cómo respiran los ausentes: La narrativa de Ricardo Piglia." *MLN* 110.2 (1995): 416–32.

———. *The Untimely Present: Postdictatorial Latin American Fiction and the Task of Mourning.* Durham, NC: Duke University Press, 1999.

Bahti, Timothy. *Allegories of History: Literary Historiography after Hegel.* Baltimore: Johns Hopkins University Press, 1992.

Benjamin, Walter. "Central Park." *Selected Writings, Volume 4: 1938–1940.* Trans. Edmund Jephcott et al. Cambridge: Harvard University Press, 2003.

———. *Gesammelte Schriften.* 7 vols. Ed. Rolf Tiedemann and Hermann Schweppenhäuser. Frankfurt : Suhrkamp, 1972–1989.

———. "On Some Motifs in Baudelaire." *Selected Writings, Volume 4: 1938–1940.* Trans. Edmund Jephcott and others. Cambridge: Harvard University Press, 2003.

———. *Origin of German Tragic Drama.* Trans. John Osborne. London: Verso, 1977.

———. "The Storyteller: Observations on the Works of Nikolai Leskov." *Selected Writings, Volume 3: 1935–1938.* Cambridge: Harvard University Press, 2002.

———. "The Task of the Translator." *Selected Writings, Volume 1: 1913–1926.* Cambridge: Harvard University Press, 1996.

———. *Ursprung des deutschen Trauerspiels.* Frankfurt: Suhrkamp Verlag, 1996.

Bennett, Drake. "The Amero Conspiracy." *New York Times*, November 25, 2007. Accessed August 19, 2009. http://www.nytimes.com/2007/11/25/world/americas/25iht-25Amero.8473833.html.

Bennington, Geoffrey. "Kant's Open Secret." *Theory, Culture & Society* 28.7–8 (2011): 26–40.

———. *Legislations: The Politics of Deconstruction.* London: Verso, 1994.

———. *Lyotard: Writing the Event.* New York: Columbia University Press, 1988.

———. "Political Animals." *Diacritics* 39.2 (Summer 2009): 21–35.

Berg, Edgardo H. "La conspiración literaria (sobre *La ciudad ausente* de Ricardo Piglia." *Hispamérica: Revista de literatura* 25 (December 1996): 37–47.

———. "Un mapa posible." *Ricardo Piglia: un narrador de historias clandestinas.* Ed. Edgardo H. Berg. Mar del Plata: Estanislao Balder, 2003.

———. "El relato ausente (Sobre la poética de Ricardo Piglia)." *Ricardo Piglia.* Ed. Jorge Fornet. Bogotá: Fondo Editorial Casa de las Américas, 2000.

Bersani, Leo. "Pynchon, Paranoia, and Literature." *Thomas Pynchon*. Ed. Harold Bloom. Philadelphia: Chelsea House Publishers, 2003.

Beverley, John. *Testimonio: On the Politics of Truth*. Minneapolis: University of Minnesota Press, 2004.

———. "Theses on Subalternity, Representation, and Politics." *Postcolonial Studies* 1.3 (November 1998): 305–19.

Borges, Jorge Luis. *Ficciones*. Ed. Anthony Kerrigan. New York: Grove Press, 1962.

———. *Obras completas I*. Barcelona: Emecé Editores, 1989.

———. *Prólogos con un prólogo de prólogos*. Madrid: Alianza Editorial, 1975.

Brescia, Pablo A. J. "Ricardo Piglia y el cuento ausente: El género en la posmodernidad." *Memorias: Primer congreso internacional: Medio siglo de literatura latinoamericana, 1945–1995*. Ed. Ana Rosa Domenella et al. México, D.F.: Universidad Autónoma Metropolitana, 1997.

Brooks, Peter. *Reading for the Plot: Design and Intention in Narrative*. Cambridge: Harvard University Press, 1984.

Butler, Judith. "Performative Acts and Gender Constitution: An Essay in Phenomenology and Feminist Theory." *Writing on the Body: Female Embodiment and Feminist Theory*. Ed. Katie Conboy, Nadia Medina, and Sarah Stanbury. New York: Columbia University Press, 1997.

Caruth, Cathy. *Unclaimed Experience: Trauma, Narrative, and History*. Baltimore: Johns Hopkins University Press, 1996.

Chávez Castañeda, Ricardo (ed). *Crack: Instrucciones de uso*. Mexico City: Mondadori, 2004.

Close, Glen S. *La imprenta enterrada: Baroja, Arlt y el imaginario anarquista*. Rosario, Argentina: Beatriz Viterbo Editora, 2000.

Coleridge, Samuel Taylor. *Biographia Literaria*. Ed. James Engell and W. Jackson Bate. Princeton, NJ: Princeton University Press, 1983.

Costigliola, Giuseppe. "Rubbish, Rubble, Ruins: The Allegorical in *Gravity's Rainbow*." *America Today: Highways and Labyrinths*. Ed. Gigliola Nocera. Siracusa, Italy: Grafia, 2003.

Davis, Mike Lee. *Reading the Text That Isn't There*. New York: Routledge, 2005.

Dean, Jodi. *Aliens in America: Conspiracy Cultures from Outerspace to Cyberspace*. Ithaca, NY: Cornell University Press, 1998.

DeLillo, Don. *Conversations with Don DeLillo*. Ed. Thomas DePietro. Jackson: University Press of Mississippi, 2005.

———. *Libra*. New York: Penguin Books, 1988.

———. *Libra*. New York: Viking, 1988.

———. *Running Dog*. New York: Vintage Books, 1978.

De Man, Paul. *Allegories of Reading: Figural Language in Rousseau, Nietzsche, Rilke, and Proust*. New Haven, CT, and London: Yale University Press, 1979.

———. "The Epistemology of Metaphor." *Aesthetic Ideology*. Ed. Andrzej Warminski. Minneapolis: University of Minnesota Press, 1996.

———. "A Modern Master: Jorge Luis Borges." *Critical Writings, 1953–1978*. Ed. Lindsay Waters. Minneapolis: University of Minnesota Press, 1989.

———. "Pascal's Allegory of Persuasion." *Aesthetic Ideology*. Ed. Andrzej Warminski. Minneapolis: University of Minnesota Press, 1996.

———. "The Rhetoric of Temporality." *Blindness and Insight: Essays in the Rhetoric of Contemporary Criticism*. Minneapolis: University of Minnesota Press, 1983.

———. "Shelley Disfigured." *The Rhetoric of Romanticism*. New York: Columbia University Press, 1984.

De Quincey, Thomas. "Secret Societies." *The Collected Writings of Thomas De Quincey*, Vol. 7. Ed. David Masson. Edinburgh: Adams and Charles Black, 1890.

Derrida, Jacques. "Autoimmunity: Real and Symbolic Suicides." *Philosophy in a Time of Terror: Dialogues with Jürgen Habermas and Jacques Derrida*. Ed. Giovanna Borradori. Chicago: University of Chicago Press, 2003.

———. "Declarations of Independence." Trans. Tom Keenan and Tom Pepper. *Negotiations: Interventions and Interviews, 1971–2001*. Ed. Elizabeth Rottenberg. Stanford, CA: Stanford University Press, 2002.

———. "History of the Lie: Prolegomena." *Without Alibi*. Ed. and trans. Peggy Kamuf. Stanford, CA: Stanford University Press, 2002.

———. *Limited Inc*. Trans. Samuel Weber. Evanston, IL: Northwestern University Press, 1988.

———. *Of Grammatology*. Trans. Gayatri Chakravorty Spivak. Baltimore: Johns Hopkins University Press, 1976.

———. *Rogues: Two Essays on Reason*. Trans. Pascale-Anne Brault and Michael Naas. Stanford, CA: Stanford University Press, 2005.

———. *Specters of Marx: The State of the Debt, the Work of Mourning, and the New International*. Trans. Peggy Kamuf. New York: Routledge, 1994.

———. "Des Tours de Babel." *Acts of Religion*. Ed. Gil Anidjar. New York: Routledge, 2002.

Dick, Philip K. *Do Androids Dream of Electric Sheep?* New York: Ballantine Books, 1968.

Dove, Patrick. *The Catastrophe of Modernity: Tragedy and the Nation in Latin American Literature*. Lewisburg, PA: Bucknell University Press, 2004.

Farrell, John. *Paranoia and Modernity: Cervantes to Rousseau*. Ithaca, NY: Cornell University Press, 2006.

Fenster, Mark. *Conspiracy Theories: Secrecy and Power in American Culture*. Minneapolis: University of Minnesota Press, 1999.

Foucault, Michel. *Discipline and Punish: The Birth of the Prison*. Trans. Alan Sheridan. New York: Vintage Books, 1977.

———. *History of Sexuality: Volume I, An Introduction*. Trans. Robert Hurley. New York: Vintage Books, 1978.

Fornet, Jorge. *El escritor y la tradición: En torno a la poética de Ricardo Piglia*. Havana: Letras Cubanas, 2005.

Frank, Jason. *Constituent Moments: Enacting the People in Postrevolutionary America*. Durham, NC, and London: Duke University Press, 2010.

Garth, Todd S. "Confused Oratory: Borges, Macedonio and the Creation of the Mythological Author." *MLN* 116 (March 2001): 350–70.

Gates, Henry Louis, Jr. "The 'Blackness of Blackness': A Critique of the Sign and the Signifying Monkey." *Critical Inquiry* 9.4 (June 1983): 685–723.

———. *The Signifying Monkey: A Theory of African-American Literary Criticism*. Oxford: Oxford University Press, 1988.

González, Horacio. *Filosofía de la conspiración: Marxistas, peronistas y carbonarios*. Buenos Aires: Ediciones Colihue, 2004.

González Echevarría, Roberto. *Myth and Archive: A Theory of Latin American Narrative*. Durham, NC: Duke University Press, 1998.

Grant, J. Kerry. *A Companion to* The Crying of Lot 49. Athens: University of Georgia Press, 1994.

Hayles, N. Katherine. "'A Metaphor of God Knew How Many Parts': The Engine That Drives *The Crying of Lot 49*." *New Essays on* The Crying of Lot 49. Ed. Patrick O'Donnell. Cambridge: Cambridge University Press, 1991.

Hemingway, Ernest. *In Our Time*. New York: Scribner, 1958.

Hofstadter, Richard. *The Paranoid Style in American Politics and Other Essays*. New York: Vintage Books, 1967.

Honig, Bonnie. *Political Theory and the Displacement of Politics*. Ithaca, NY, and London: Cornell University Press, 1993.

Horn, Eva. "Borges's Duels: Friends, Enemies, and the Fictions of History." *Thinking with Borges*. Ed. David E. Johnson and William Egginton. Aurora, CO: The Davies Group, Publishers, 2009.

Horn, Eva, and Anson Rabinbach. Introduction. *Dark Powers: Conspiracies and Conspiracy Theory in History and Literature*. Special issue of *New German Critique* 35 (Spring 2008): 1–8.

Irwin, John T. *The Mystery to a Solution: Poe, Borges, and the Analytic Detective Story*. Baltimore and London: Johns Hopkins University Press, 1994.

Jaén, Didier T. "The Esoteric Tradition in Borges' 'Tlön, Uqbar, Orbis Tertius.'" *Studies in Short Fiction* 21.1 (Winter 1984): 25–39.

Jameson, Fredric. "Cognitive Mapping." *Marxism and the Interpretation of Culture*. Ed. Cary Nelson and Lawrence Grossberg. Urbana: University of Illinois Press, 1988.

———. *The Geopolitical Aesthetic: Cinema and Space in the World System*. Bloomington: Indiana University Press, 1992.

———. *Postmodernism or, The Cultural Logic of Late Capitalism*. Durham, NC: Duke University Press, 1991.

Johnston, John. *Information Multiplicity: American Fiction in the Age of Media Saturation*. Baltimore: Johns Hopkins University Press, 1998.

Juan-Navarro, Santiago. *Archival Reflections: Postmodern Fiction of the Americas (Self-Reflexivity, Historical Revisionism, Utopia)*. Lewisburg, PA: Bucknell University Press, 2000.

Keenan, Thomas. *Fables of Responsibility: Aberrations and Predicaments in Ethics and Politics*. Stanford, CA: Stanford University Press, 1997.

———. "Re JD: Remembering Jacques Derrida (part 2)/Drift: Politics and the Simulation of Real Life." *Grey Room* 21 (Fall 2005): 94–111.

Kelman, David. "The Afterlife of Storytelling: Julio Cortázar's Reading of Walter Benjamin and Edgar Allan Poe." *Comparative Literature* 60.3 (Summer 2008): 244–60.

———. "The Inactuality of Aura: Figural Relations in Walter Benjamin's 'On Some Motifs in Baudelaire.'" *Actualities of Aura: Twelve Studies of Walter Benjamin*. Ed. Dag Petersson and Erik Steinskog. Svanesund, Sweden: NSU Press, 2005.

———. "The Theme of the Traitor: Disinheritance in Ricardo Piglia's *Artificial Respiration*." *CR: The New Centennial Review* 7.3 (Winter 2007): 239–62.

Knight, Peter. *Conspiracy Culture: From the Kennedy Assassination to* The X-Files. London: Routledge, 2000.

———. *The Kennedy Assassination*. Jackson: University Press of Mississippi, 2007.

Krauze, Enrique. *La presidencia imperial: Ascenso y caída del sistema político mexicano (1940–1996)*. Barcelona: Tusquets Editores, SA, 1997.

Kristal, Efraín. *Invisible Work: Borges and Translation*. Nashville, TN: Vanderbilt University Press, 2002.

Laclau, Ernesto. *On Populist Reason*. London: Verso, 2005.

———. "The Politics of Rhetoric." *Material Events: Paul de Man and the Afterlife of Theory*. Ed. Tom Cohen et al. Minneapolis: University of Minnesota Press, 2001.

———. "Populism: What's in a Name?" *Populism and the Mirror of Democracy*. Ed. F. Panizza. London: Verso, 2005.

———. "Why Do Empty Signifiers Matter to Politics?" *Emancipation(s)*. London: Verso, 1996.

Laclau, Ernesto, and Chantal Mouffe. *Hegemony and Socialist Strategy: Towards a Radical Democratic Politics*. London: Verso, 2001.

Lamb, Robert Paul. "Fishing for Stories: What 'Big Two-Hearted River' Is Really About." *MFS: Modern Fiction Studies* 37.2 (Summer 1991): 161–81.

Latin American Subaltern Studies Group. "Founding Statement." *Boundary 2* 20.3 (Autumn 1993): 110–21.

Lazcano, Pablo. "Historias de la argentina secreta: De escrituras del porvenir y ejercicios de la resistencia." *Ricardo Piglia: Un narrador de historias clandestinas*. Ed. Edgardo H. Berg. Mar del Plata: Estanislao Balder, 2003.

Lentricchia, Frank. "*Libra* as Postmodern Critique." *Introducing Don DeLillo*. Ed. Frank Lentricchia. Durham, NC: Duke University Press, 1991.

Levinas, Emmanuel. *Totality and Infinity: An Essay on Exteriority*. Trans. Alphonso Lingis. Pittsburgh: Duquesne University Press, 1969.

Levinson, Brett. *The Ends of Literature: The Latin American "Boom" in the Neoliberal Marketplace*. Stanford, CA: Stanford University Press, 2001.

———. *Market and Thought: Meditations on the Political and the Biopolitical.* New York: Fordham University Press, 2004.

Lipset, Seymour Martin, and Earl Raab. *The Politics of Unreason: Right-Wing Extremism in America, 1790–1977.* Chicago: University of Chicago Press, 1978.

Liste Noya, José. "Naming the Secret: Don DeLillo's *Libra.*" *Contemporary Literature* 45 (Summer 2004): 239–75.

Ludmer, Josefina. *The Corpus Delicti: A Manual of Argentine Fictions.* Trans. Glen S. Close. Pittsburgh: University of Pittsburgh Press, 2004.

Lyotard, Jean-François. *The Differend: Phrases in Dispute.* Trans. Georges van den Abbeele. Minneapolis: University of Minnesota Press, 1988.

———. *The Inhuman: Reflections on Time.* Trans. Geoffrey Bennington and Rachel Bowlby. Stanford, CA: Stanford University Press, 1991.

———. *Lectures d'enfance.* Paris: Éditions Galilée, 1991.

Madsen, Deborah L. *The Postmodernist Allegories of Thomas Pynchon.* New York: St. Martin's Press, 1991.

Marder, Elissa. *Dead Time: Temporal Disorders in the Wake of Modernity (Baudelaire and Flaubert).* Stanford, CA: Stanford University Press, 2001.

Mason, Fran. "A Poor Person's Cognitive Mapping." *Conspiracy Nation: The Politics of Paranoia in Postwar America.* Ed. Peter Knight. New York: New York University Press, 2002.

McClure, John A. "Postmodern Romance: Don DeLillo and the Age of Conspiracy." *Introducing Don DeLillo.* Ed. Frank Lentriccia. Durham, NC: Duke University Press, 1991.

Melley, Timothy. *Empire of Conspiracy: The Culture of Paranoia in Postwar America.* Ithaca, NY: Cornell University Press, 2000.

Menchú, Rigoberta. *I, Rigoberta Menchú: An Indian Woman in Guatemala.* Ed. Elisabeth Burgos-Debray. Trans. Ann Wright. London: Verso, 1984.

———. *Me llamo Rigoberta Menchú y así me nació la conciencia.* Ed. Elisabeth Burgos. Mexico City: Siglo Veintiuno Editores, S.A., 1985.

Merivale, Patricia, and Susan Elizabeth Sweeney. "The Game's Afoot: On the Trail of the Metaphysical Detective Story." *Detecting Texts: The Metaphysical Detective Story from Poe to Postmodernism.* Ed. Patricia Merivale and Susan Elizabeth Sweeney. Philadelphia: University of Pennsylvania Press, 1999.

Mesa Gancedo, Daniel. *Ricardo Piglia: La escritura y el arte nuevo de la sospecha.* Seville, Spain: Universidad de Sevilla, 2006.

Mignolo, Walter D. *The Idea of Latin America.* Malden, MA: Blackwell Publishing, 2005.

Miller, J. Hillis. *Speech Acts in Literature.* Stanford, CA: Stanford University Press, 2001.

Molloy, Sylvia. *Signs of Borges.* Trans. Oscar Montero. Durham, NC: Duke University Press, 1994.

Moreiras, Alberto. "The Aura of Testimonio." *The Real Thing: Testimonial Discourse and Latin America.* Ed. Georg M. Gugelberger. Durham, NC: Duke University Press, 1996.

———. *Tercer Espacio: Duelo y literatura en América Latina.* Santiago, Chile: Arcis-LOM, 1999.

Morrison, Toni. *Playing in the Dark: Whiteness and the Literary Imagination.* New York: Vintage Books, 1992.

Namaste, Viviane K. "The Use and Abuse of Queer Tropes: Metaphor and Catachresis in Queer Theory and Politics." *Social Semiotics* 9.2 (August 1999): 213–34.

Nouvet, Claire. "The Inarticulate Affect: Lyotard and Psychoanalytic Testimony." *Discourse: Journal for Theoretical Studies in Media and Culture* 25.1 and 2 (Winter and Spring 2003): 231–47.

O'Brien, Sarah Mary. "'I, Also, Am in Michigan': Pastoralism of Mind in 'Big Two-Hearted River.'" *Hemingway Review* 28.2 (Spring 2009): 66–86.

O'Donnell, Patrick. *Latent Destinies: Cultural Paranoia and Contemporary U.S. Narrative.* Durham, NC: Duke University Press, 2000.

Office of the Press Secretary. "President Bush Participates in Joint Press Availability with Prime Minister Harper of Canada, and President Calderón of Mexico." *The White House: President George W. Bush*. August 21, 2007. Accessed August 19, 2009. http://georgewbush-whitehouse.archives.gov/news/releases/2007/08/20070821-3.html.

Page, Joanna. "Ricardo Piglia: Towards a Re-socialized Literature." *Journal of Iberian and Latin American Studies* 10.2 (December 2004): 169–89.

———. "Writing as Resistance in Ricardo Piglia's *La ciudad ausente*." *Bulletin of Spanish Studies* 81.3 (2004): 343–60.

Parodi, Cristina. "El intrincado cronotopo de 'Tlön.'" *El fragmento infinito: Estudios sobre 'Tlön, Uqbar, Orbis Tertius' de J. L. Borges*. Ed. Iván Almeida and Cristina Parodi. Zaragoza, Spain: Prensas Universitarias de Zaragoza, 2006.

Pfau, Thomas. *Romantic Moods: Paranoia, Trauma, and Melancholy, 1790–1840*. Baltimore: Johns Hopkins University Press, 2005.

Piglia, Ricardo. *The Absent City*. Trans. Sergio Waisman. Durham, NC: Duke University Press, 2000.

———. "Afterword." *The Absent City*. Trans. Sergio Waisman. Durham, NC: Duke University Press, 2000.

———. *Artificial Respiration*. Trans. Daniel Balderston. Durham, NC: Duke University Press, 1994.

———. *La ciudad ausente*. Barcelona: Editorial Anagrama, 2003.

———. *Crítica y ficción*. Barcelona: Editorial Anagrama, 2001.

———. *Formas breves*. Barcelona: Editorial Anagrama, 2000.

———. "Ideología y ficción en Borges." *Ficciones argentinas: Antología de lecturas críticas*. Buenos Aires: Grupo Editorial Norma, 2004.

———. "Novela y complot." *Quimera* 280 (March 2007): 45–54.

———. *Respiración artificial*. Barcelona: Editorial Anagrama, 2001.

———. "Roberto Arlt: La ficción del dinero." *La Argentina en pedazos*. Buenos Aires: Ediciones de la Urraca, 1993.

———. "De la tragedia a la conspiración. Entrevista con Mauricio Montiel Figueiras." *La nación*, May 18, 2003. Accessed October 6, 2005. http://www.lanacion.com.ar/496728-de-la-tragedia-a-la-conspiracion.

———. *El último lector*. Barcelona: Editorial Anagrama, 2005.

Pionke, Albert D. *Plots of Opportunity: Representing Conspiracy in Victorian England*. Columbus: Ohio State University Press, 2004.

Pynchon, Thomas. *The Crying of Lot 49*. New York: Harper & Row, 1966.

———. *Gravity's Rainbow*. London: Penguin Books, 1973.

———. *Mason & Dixon*. New York: Picador, 1997.

Quilligan, Maureen. "Twentieth-Century American Allegory." *Thomas Pynchon*. Ed. Harold Bloom. Philadelphia: Chelsea House Publishers, 2003.

Rama, Ángel. *La ciudad letrada*. Hanover, NH: Ediciones del Norte, 1984.

———. *The Lettered City*. Trans. John Charles Chasteen. Durham, NC: Duke University Press, 1996.

Reed, Ishmael. *Mumbo Jumbo*. New York: Simon & Schuster, 1972.

Report of the Select Committee on Assassinations of the U.S. House of Representatives. H.R. Rept. No. 95-1828, Part 2, 95th Cong., 2nd Sess. (1979).

Richards, Thomas. *The Imperial Archive: Knowledge and the Fantasy of Empire*. London: Verso, 1993.

Roisman, Joseph. *The Rhetoric of Conspiracy in Ancient Athens*. Berkeley: University of California Press, 2006.

Sarlo, Beatriz. *Jorge Luis Borges: A Writer on the Edge*. London: Verso, 1993.

Sazbón, José. "La reflexión literaria." *Ricardo Piglia*. Ed. Jorge Fornet. Bogotá: Fondo Editorial Casa de las Américas, 2000.

Schaub, Thomas. "Open Letter in Response to Edward Mendelson's 'The Sacred, the Profane, and *The Crying of Lot 49*.'" *Boundary 2: An International Journal of Literature and Culture* 5 (Fall 1976): 93–102.

Simons, Jon. "Postmodern Paranoia? Pynchon and Jameson." *Paragraph: A Journal of Modern Critical Theory* 23.2 (July 2000): 207–21.

Solomianski, Alejandro. "El cuento de la patria: Una forma de su configuración en la cuentística de Ricardo Piglia." *Revista Iberoamericana* 63 (October–December 1997): 675–88.

Sommer, Doris. "No Secrets." *The Real Thing: Testimonial Discourse and Latin America.* Ed. Georg M. Gugelberger. Durham, NC: Duke University Press, 1996.

Spivak, Gayatri Chakravorty. "Can the Subaltern Speak?" *Marxism and the Interpretation of Culture.* Ed. Cary Nelson and Lawrence Grossberg. Urbana and Chicago: University of Illinois Press, 1988.

———. *In Other Worlds.* New York: Methuen, 1987.

Stoll, David. *Rigoberta Menchú and the Story of All Poor Guatemalans.* Philadelphia: Westview Press, 2008.

Swope, Richard. "Crossing Western Space, or the HooDoo Detective on the Boundary in Ishmael Reed's *Mumbo Jumbo.*" *African American Review* 36.4 (Winter 2002): 611–28.

Thomas, Samuel. *Pynchon and the Political.* New York: Routledge, 2007.

Todorov, Tzvetan. *The Poetics of Prose.* Trans. Richard Howard. Ithaca, NY: Cornell University Press, 1977.

Tomashevsky, Boris. "Thematics." *Russian Formalist Criticism: Four Essays.* Trans. Lee T. Lemon and Marion J. Reis. Lincoln: University of Nebraska Press, 1965.

Volpi, Jorge. *La paz de los sepulcros.* Mexico City: Editorial Planeta Mexicana, S.A., 2007.

———. "La segunda conspiración." *Letras libres* (March 1999): 44–51.

Willman, Skip. "Art after Dealey Plaza: DeLillo's *Libra.*" *MFS: Modern Fiction Studies* 45.3 (Fall 1999): 621–40.

———. "Spectres of Marx in Pynchon's *Vineland.*" *Critique: Studies in Contemporary Fiction* 51.3 (Spring 2010): 198–222.

———. "Traversing the Fantasies of the JFK Assassination: Conspiracy and Contingency in Don DeLillo's *Libra.*" *Contemporary Literature* 39.3 (Fall 1998): 405–33.

Wise, David, and Thomas B. Ross. *The Invisible Government.* New York: Bantam Books, 1964.

Wisnicki, Adrian S. *Conspiracy, Revolution, and Terrorism from Victorian Fiction to the Modern Novel.* London: Routledge, 2008.

Index

About the Author

David Kelman is assistant professor of English and comparative literature at California State University, Fullerton. He has published articles in *New Vico Studies, CR: The New Centennial Review, Comparative Literature, Pynchon Notes,* and *Discourse: Journal for Theoretical Studies in Media and Culture.*